Praise for Jennifer L. Wright

Historical fiction fans, get ready to fall in love with *Last Light over Galveston*! The early days of weather forecasting, the progression of photography, and a major weather event are the backdrop as Kathleen McDaniel's privileged life is upended and she's forced to come to terms with deep, personal betrayal. It is said tragedy oftentimes brings out the worst in some, yet the best in others. In this lyrical, uplifting novel, Wright showcases such human moments and excavates matters of the heart with the precision of a surgeon. A superb, compelling read.

DONNA EVERHART, *USA Today* bestselling author of *The Saints of Swallow Hill*

The seaside beauty of old Galveston shines in this beautifully written tale of a woman's quest to both lose herself and find herself. At land's end, a place of faith offers friendship, hope, and a fresh start, but with her past and a hurricane pressing in, Kathleen's newly reconstructed life will be threatened in ways she could never have imagined.

LISA WINGATE, #1 *New York Times* bestselling author of *Shelterwood*

Jennifer L. Wright's *Last Light over Galveston* is a gripping tale of endurance through storms beyond our control, both personal and natural. With historical accuracy, Wright crafts a captivating story that sweeps readers to the balmy beaches of Texas at the turn of the twentieth century.

MICHELLE SHOCKLEE, award-winning author of *All We Thought We Knew*

Jennifer Wright has expertly crafted an unforgettable tale of redemption, perseverance, and friendship in the midst of unspeakable tragedy. The characters gripped me from the first line and held me long after the story ended. Intense, empathetic, and vividly painted, this is a novel not to be missed.

JAMIE OGLE, Christy Award–winning author of *As Sure as the Sea*

A profoundly moving portrait of a historical tragedy, *Last Light over Galveston* explores both the ravages of disaster and the resilience of hope. Not only is this a novel steeped in rich historical detail, it is also a compelling exploration of a woman's journey toward faith and belonging. Poignant and powerful, this is a tale readers of Jocelyn Green and Cathy Gohlke will treasure.

AMANDA BARRATT, Christy Award–winning author of *The Warsaw Sisters*

In *Last Light over Galveston*, Jennifer L. Wright links arms with her readers to guide them through the fury of a hurricane, of both the literal and metaphorical variety. This page-turning historical tale probes deep and tender places where every heart and every foundation are tested. As earthly things crumble, the reader is left holding poignant reminders of what truly matters.

AMANDA COX, Christy Award–winning author of *Between the Sound and Sea*

A triumph of historical storytelling amid human conflicts, Jenn Wright's latest is a tense, taut, gripping, satisfying success.

PATRICIA RAYBON, Christy Award–winning author of the Annalee Spain series

Last Light over Galveston packs a powerful punch from the first page to the last. Wright doesn't hold back in depicting not only the horrors of the 1900 Galveston hurricane but also the storms that sometimes batter the human heart. Then she holds forth the light of hope and truth that shines all the brighter because of the darkness. If you love impactful historical fiction that you won't soon forget, I highly recommend *Last Light over Galveston*.

KATIE POWNER, Christy Award winner and author of *When the Road Comes Around*

Brimming with grit and beauty . . . A poignant study in human frailty and unending mercy. *The Girl from the Papers* will remain in your thoughts long after the last tearstained page is turned.

STEPHANIE LANDSEM, author of *Code Name Edelweiss*

This is historical fiction as it is meant to be told: a glimpse (based on true events) through the eyes of people caught up in the maelstrom of world events beyond their control.

LIBRARY JOURNAL on *Come Down Somewhere*

Intelligent and arresting. . . . In the moving historical novel *Come Down Somewhere*, a nuclear test has explosive consequences for a burgeoning friendship.

FOREWORD REVIEWS

[A] lovely debut. . . . Wright's adept depiction of the times capture the grit of the Dust Bowl. Fans of Tracie Peterson should check this out.

PUBLISHERS WEEKLY on *If It Rains*

Last Light over Galveston

LAST LIGHT OVER GALVESTON

JENNIFER L. WRIGHT

Tyndale House Publishers
Carol Stream, Illinois

Visit Tyndale online at tyndale.com.

Visit Jennifer L. Wright's website at jenniferlwright.com.

Tyndale and Tyndale's quill logo are registered trademarks of Tyndale House Ministries.

Last Light over Galveston

Copyright © 2025 by Jennifer L. Wright. All rights reserved.

Cover photograph of woman copyright © Mark Owen/Arcangel.com. All rights reserved.

Cover photograph of ocean copyright © Marek Piwnicki/Unsplash.com. All rights reserved.

Cover photograph of hairstyle copyright © Viktoriia Bielik/Depositphotos.com. All rights reserved.

Author photo taken by Jonathan Wright, copyright © 2022. All rights reserved.

Cover design by Libby Dykstra

Interior design by Cathy Miller

Edited by Sarah Mason Rische

Published in association with the literary agency of Martin Literary & Media Management, 914 164th Street SE, Suite B12, #307, Mill Creek, WA 98012.

2 Corinthians 13:11 is taken from The ESV® Bible (The Holy Bible, English Standard Version®), copyright © 2001 by Crossway, a publishing ministry of Good News Publishers. Used by permission. All rights reserved.

John 1:12-13 is taken from the Holy Bible, *New International Version*,® *NIV*.® Copyright © 1973, 1978, 1984, 2011 by Biblica, Inc.® Used by permission. All rights reserved worldwide.

Last Light over Galveston is a work of fiction. Where real people, events, establishments, organizations, or locales appear, they are used fictitiously. All other elements of the novel are drawn from the author's imagination.

For information about special discounts for bulk purchases, please contact Tyndale House Publishers at csresponse@tyndale.com, or call 1-855-277-9400.

Library of Congress Cataloging-in-Publication Data

A catalog record for this book is available from the Library of Congress.

ISBN 978-1-4964-7761-3 (HC)

ISBN 978-1-4964-7762-0 (SC)

Printed in the United States of America

31	30	29	28	27	26	25
7	6	5	4	3	2	1

This one is for Jan,
who never stopped believing in me even when I did

Prologue

MAY 1900

I walked until I could go no farther, until open water was all I could see.

It was the end of the road, for sure. Possibly the end of the world.

For me, they were one and the same.

Standing on the rocky sand, I watched angry waves roar ashore through flashes of lightning. The air was thick with salt and electricity as warm rivulets of rain streamed down my face. Or were those tears? It was impossible to tell. The thunder rolling across the Gulf of Mexico could just have easily been the sound of my bones rattling inside this lifeless cage.

Miles and miles of train tracks, chosen at random but always going south, going west, going *away*, had brought me here. It was as far as I could go.

And it still wasn't far enough.

He would find me.

White foam nudged the toe of my boot, soiling the edge of a dress already grimy from weeks of wear. When the wave retreated, it tugged the worn leather.

Beckoning me.

Exhaustion and despair pulled at me. The last few weeks were finally catching up to me, now that I was standing still, trapped on this small spit of land with nowhere to go. Too much traveling, too much fear, too much sorrow. I took a sluggish step forward, wet sand making a sucking sound as my boot rose.

I could do it. Just keep going. A few more steps, and it would all be over. The end of the road but in an entirely different way.

Another swell, stronger this time. The smell of damp assaulted my nostrils. In the distance, a fork of lightning kissed the top of the waves. My nerves tingled as electricity raced through the water toward shore, searching for me. Numb fingers found the strap of my bag, the one I'd bought from a street vendor outside the train station in Lexington, and I took a step back, out of the water.

This bag. What was in this bag was the reason I wouldn't. The reason I couldn't.

And the reason I wanted to.

Fresh streams of water coursed over my cheeks; this time, I knew it wasn't the rain. They were tears. Tears for the man I'd loved . . . and for the one who'd never truly loved me. Tears for myself and my own foolish naivete. Tears for the life about which I'd dreamed, the life I'd abandoned . . . and the one I'd never really had to begin with.

I closed my eyes, lifted my face to heaven, and let out a scream. Maybe God would hear me. Or maybe not. The wind swallowed my cries. But it didn't really matter anyway. All those Sunday mornings were a hazy memory, blurred in with the rest of it, relics of another life.

Another me.

That girl was a stranger now.

And, I was starting to believe, so was God.

I had never been so utterly alone.

I wept until my tears were spent. Wind whipped my hair as

I opened my eyes. Lightning crackled across the sky once again, casting shadows onto the sand.

And revealing, just beyond a row of salt cedars and tall grass, the vague shadow of a building.

I blinked against the downpour, sure I was imagining it. The town sat behind me, its crowds, lights, and bathhouses miles down the shore, ignored and left behind in my distress. The money was gone. There could be no more trains, no more wagons, no more nights spent in boardinghouses under a false name, moving on before the first light of dawn broke over the eastern sky. There weren't even any more roads left to travel. This island that was little more than a sandbar was as far as I could go. Here, where there was nothing but sand and wind and grief.

And also, suddenly, a building.

I don't know what possessed me to move toward it. Perhaps it was the reckless sense that I had nothing else to lose. All I knew was the ground became firmer the farther I got from the shoreline. Sharp tufts of grass snagged my skirt as I stumbled over weed-covered dunes. Rain continued to pelt my cheeks, my eyes, my hands, lashed about by a ferocious wind that did not abate until blocked by the building's massive brick facade. Even then, however, it howled around the corner, desperate to continue its assault.

I pounded on the thick door. Or, rather, I tried to. My muscles were weak, my fingers too raw and aching to register the hard wood beneath. "Help!" It came out frail, easily suffocated by the roar of the storm. I tried to remember the last time I'd spoken out loud. But I had only a moment to consider before the door fell away beneath my touch.

Light poured out onto the stoop, blinding me. I held an elbow to my face, a sound like a hiss escaping from my lips.

"Good heavens!"

A firm but gentle hand seized my upper arm and pulled me

over the threshold. The light grew brighter, the warmth more intense, and I slipped from the woman's grip, collapsing in a heap on the threadbare rug. There was a click and then a sudden change in pressure as the door was tugged shut, making my ears pop. With leaden hands, I wiped at my face, feeling days' worth of grime roll beneath my fingertips. It was only here, out of the wind, that I noticed my own smell, dirt and sweat and mildew. I rubbed the water remnants from my burning eyes, revealing the pale glow of a lantern and, in it, the shadow of a figure slowly taking shape before me.

A nun, I realized.

A very old, very concerned nun.

"Good gracious, child." The woman peered at me from behind large spectacles, wrinkles lining the skin above her pressed lips. "Are you all right?"

I wanted to laugh. I wanted to cry. I could not have answered her question even if I'd been able to speak. Staring at her, eyes bleary, my sodden dress suddenly felt as if it weighed a hundred pounds. I worried it would pull me right through the floorboards.

A part of me wished it would.

The corners of the nun's eyes crinkled. She placed a withered hand to my face. It was a gesture of kindness, of compassion, the touch as light as paper . . . yet as heavy as a slap.

I flinched.

The nun pulled back, mouth pinched in concern, clasping her hands together in front of her black habit. The beaded rosary hanging from her belt clinked with the sudden movement.

"Where . . . ," I managed to croak. "Where am I?"

"This is St. Mary's." There was a slight drawl in her voice. It was smooth and comforting, like honey over warm biscuits. "It's an orphanage here on Galveston Island."

I closed my eyes. *An orphanage.*

This time there was no stopping it. A laugh that may have actually been a sob welled up in my throat.

"Do you need help, dear?" The nun's fingers found the wooden cross near her hips. Her knobby fingers roamed over it as she watched me, eyebrows furrowed in worry. "Are you an orphan?"

My shoulders heaved under the weight of my weeping giggles. I knew I looked crazy. Sounded crazy. And yet I could not stop. Instead, I glanced down, trying to steady myself, my eyes landing on the small brown satchel in my lap. Instinctively, my arms wrapped around it, cradling it like a baby. At the touch, all trace of titters ceased. In their place, only broken, breathless whimpers.

"Yes." The word came out as a whisper, tasting of salt. "Yes, I am."

It might have been a lie. But it might also have been the truth. And I wasn't yet sure which one I wanted it to be.

Barometric Pressure: 29.974, steady

Temperature: 80 degrees

Winds: Calm

Conditions: Fair, clear

WEATHER OBSERVATIONS
Thursday, September 6, 1900, morning
US Weather Bureau office, Galveston, TX

ONE

FOUR MONTHS LATER
THURSDAY, SEPTEMBER 6, 1900

The birds woke me again.

It was one thing I still couldn't get used to, even after all these months. The birds in Galveston didn't chirp and coo like the ones on the East Coast, alerting you to the rising sun with a gentle nudge, a melodious murmur to transition you from sleep to wake. No, here, this close to the shore, the birds shrieked and screamed, a lingering echo from the nightmares I couldn't quite shake even after I'd emerged from my attempt at slumber.

I stared at the ceiling, made grayer by the early light of dawn, gripping the scratchy bedsheets. I'd kicked the top one off even before my usual nightly thrashing. The heat had been unbearable, the only air coming through the window more like a trickle of steam than a refreshing ocean breeze, and the night had done little to cool it. The humidity was already thick; I had to peel the thin, faded nightgown from my skin. And I didn't even want to think about what an untamable mess my hair would be.

Tiptoeing to the window, careful not to wake my still-sleeping roommate, I pushed back the wispy curtains. The first strands of pink were just beginning to thread the sky. Those cursed seagulls swooped through the salt cedars toward the beach, where they screeched at the waves thudding against the sand and crushed shells. I took in a deep breath. It had bothered me when I first arrived, that ever-present smell of fish and salt. But there was something comforting in it now.

Perhaps because it was so far removed from the earthy, woodsy smell of home.

Of what used to be my home.

"You're up."

I spun around. Though the light was dim, I could see my roommate stretching, her pale, delicate toes curling onto the wooden floor as she reached her arms toward the ceiling. Sleep creased her face, but she was smiling. Emily was always smiling.

"I'm sorry," I said. "Did I wake you? I didn't mean—"

She waved away my protestations, hiding a yawn behind her knuckles. "I couldn't really sleep anyway. It's too hot." She gathered her long dark hair in one hand and pulled it over her shoulder before wiping the sweat from her nose. "Like sleeping in human soup."

I giggled, mood instantly lifting. Emily had that way about her. "Well, since we're up," I said, returning her impish smile, "we might as well get a start on things. The first bell will be ringing soon."

We settled into our morning routine, Emily taking her turn at the washbasin while I changed into the same gray shapeless cotton frock I'd worn the day before. The navy-blue braided two-piece dress I'd worn on my arrival was long gone, the first concession I'd granted Mother Camillus. Not that there'd been much to salvage of the outfit. Still, I missed the feel of the silky-smooth fabric, the way it had accentuated my figure. This dress made me look frumpy, failed to compliment my red hair, and did nothing for my complexion. Even after all this time, I still felt naked and shapeless without my corset and petticoats. Worse, I felt ugly without all the colors and elaborate trims.

But I also felt invisible. And that was the whole point.

I smiled at Emily as we switched, me taking the basin while she changed into her habit. Well, it wasn't really a habit yet. No long robe or black-and-white wimple. Just a simple dark wool dress topped with a sleek cloth veil that started inches above her hairline. Although we were close in age, her twenty to my eighteen, vanity seemed to have no hold over Emily. She swore she liked her habit.

And, because it was Emily, I believed her.

Upon my arrival, Emily had seamlessly folded me into her space and her routine. Mother Camillus, though gracious in allowing me to stay, had been hesitant about my presence. As I was no longer a child, she believed it would be improper to allow me to board inside the children's dormitory, even more improper to allow a non-nun access to the private rooms of the Sisters of Charity. Emily, the orphanage's novice (or "nun-in-training" as she preferred to call it), was technically neither, so rooming with her seemed to be a suitable solution. Even though her lodging space was half the size of a full-fledged sister's, she never batted an eye at welcoming an additional body, and after the first few awkward dances of forced togetherness, I soon realized her cheerful generosity and loving spirit weren't a charade.

They were just . . . Emily.

I patted my face dry. There was no mirror in our room, of course, which had been quite an adjustment. But, by this point, I wouldn't have wanted to see what I looked like even if there had been. No makeup to cover my freckles, no hair products to tame the frizz. My heart panged for Stella. Not for the first time, I imagined her hands in my hair, smoothing my dress, powdering my nose. Pictured how she'd fuss if she could see me now.

Emily's voice startled me from my reverie, though her question was muted behind the sound of my toothbrush. I spat the chalky, soap-like paste into a cup. No Sheffield's tooth cream here. "I'm sorry?"

"I asked if you dreamed last night." She adjusted her rosary and glanced at me from beneath raised brows, her smile hopeful. "I didn't hear you."

I forced a smile back, pulling my lips across the gritty, bitter surface of my teeth. "No," I lied. "I guess I didn't."

She grinned. "I told you it would get better." With a wink, she sat on the edge of the bed and began rolling her stockings over her feet.

I turned back to the basin, sweaty fingers clenching the folds of my dress. That was the other thing about Emily—she never pried. Always took me at my word. Even on the nights when my screams were the loudest, when my tears refused to be quelled, she simply held me, never digging into wounds about which I knew she was curious, letting her prayers wash over me like the soothing balm they should have been. Though she offered her ear time and time again, she accepted my silence or one-word answers with a grace and gentleness that made me long to be honest, to lay it all bare before her.

But I couldn't. And because I couldn't, there would always be a wall, a certain level of deceit between us.

She could never know, would never truly understand. I was getting better at hiding them, yes. But the nightmares would never go away.

My throat burned as I attempted to swallow the lump rising inside it. There was a rustle of fabric behind me as Emily rose, the scuff of her flat leather shoes on wood. She was walking toward me. I blinked hard, trying to steady myself, and forced my trembling mouth back into a smile. "You ready?" I asked, spinning around.

Though the warmth in her face never faltered, I could see the moment she registered truth through my facade. The flicker of her eyes, the slight crease in her brow. Her fingertips brushed my elbow. "Annie?"

Clang! Clang! Clang!

My body jarred at the intrusion, then immediately slackened as it recognized the reprieve. "Call to morning prayers," I said quickly, slipping my arm out of her grasp. "We should hurry. You know how Mother Superior gets when we're late."

I didn't wait for her before opening the door and sliding into the hallway, where I was immediately swallowed by a mass of girls all dressed in white. Wood popped and creaked beneath dozens of shuffling feet making their way toward the large staircase leading to the ground floor, where daily chapel was held. The scents of morning breath and unwashed bodies were overwhelming; older girls were assigned a group of younger orphans to assist in their daily hygiene routines, but I'd been here long enough to know it was a lost cause for more than a few of them.

"Sister Annie! Sister Annie!"

I paused, allowing a familiar greasy-haired blonde to catch up to me. She grinned, that large hole where her front teeth should have been never failing to amuse me. Not only did it give her the look of perpetual playfulness, but it caused all her words to come out with a slight lisping whistle. I smiled. "Good morning, Margaret."

"Maggie," the girl said, face immediately hardening. Her dark-brown eyes narrowed. "It ain't Margaret. It's *Maggie*."

I tilted my head to my shoulder and raised my eyebrows. "I'll start calling you Maggie when you *stop* calling me Sister. I'm not a nun, Margaret. You know that."

She thrust a sticky hand into mine. "I know. I just like calling you that."

"And maybe I just like calling you Margaret."

She scowled but did not remove her hand. Instead, the two of us continued our journey in silence. Her hair was knotted, the smudge of dirt across her freckled nose revealing she had not properly washed last night or this morning, while the wrinkles in her dress told me she'd been storing it in a wadded ball rather than folded neatly in her assigned drawer like she was supposed to. My eyes flitted around the girls, trying to find Rebecca, the fifteen-year-old ward assigned as Maggie's helper, but it was no use. She was probably near the front of the pack with the rest of her charges. In the few short months I'd known her, Rebecca had proved herself to be mature, responsible, and good with children.

But she could not tame eight-year-old Maggie Sherwood, who, in a cruel twist of fate, had lost both her parents to yellow fever a full twenty years after the worst of the disease swept through the island. And who, for some reason I did not understand, listened only to me.

Yet another mark against me in Mother Camillus's already suspicious eyes.

Maggie was not allowed to sit with me during chapel; it was required she sit with the other children. Still, she made it a point to remain as close as possible, parking herself directly in front of me on one of the hard wooden benches lined up in rows on either side of a large ceramic crucifix near the front of the room. As the girls settled, a scuffling sound from the back signaled the arrival of the children from the boys' dormitory next door. They lumbered sleepily into their own section across the aisle. I took my usual spot next to Emily, behind the girls but segregated from the rest of the nuns proper, who sat on her other side.

A hush fell over restless bodies as Father Donovan appeared at the front of the room. He raised his hands. "Welcome, children. Sisters. This is the day the Lord has made . . ."

It was my cue to tune out.

Though I wasn't Catholic—another point against me in Mother Camillus's book—I *was* raised in the church. We never missed a Sunday in our reserved pew, right up front by the pulpit. It wasn't that I didn't believe in God. But it had been hard to face Him since that terrible night four months ago.

Especially since I could not untangle the memories of those long-ago sermons from the image of the man who'd sat beside me during them.

I did the motions, mouthed the words—after this long, it wasn't hard to figure out the routine—but I did not allow the clergyman's message to penetrate my heart. I kept my mind on the mess of Maggie's hair or the pilling wool of Emily's skirt or even the shrieks of those seagulls from the beach beyond. Just when I was starting to wonder if there was anything in this place I could use as a file—my nails looked absolutely ghastly—there came a quick jab under my rib cage. Emily stood up.

The service was over.

Finally.

Murmured voices immediately began to swell, along with the pops and creaks of benches. Through protestations, I attempted to run my fingers through Maggie's knots with little success before giving her shoulders a quick squeeze and following Emily out of the chapel. We ducked into the nearby kitchen, where both she and I draped aprons around our necks. There was no time to waste.

Ninety-three grumbling stomachs were making their way into the dining room.

Bread had been baked the night before by the dinner crew. I immediately began to slice it. Emily started the milk boiling and measured out oats. Sister Vincent was already at her station, cutting apples from a barrel. And Sister Bernice—the elderly nun who had greeted me upon my arrival—began piling trays on the counter, where they waited to be filled.

I didn't mind breakfast duty. Even though I'd never stepped foot in a kitchen before my arrival at St. Mary's, I soon found the routine soothing. I wondered why Miss Dover, our cook back home, had always been so grumpy; there was something very calming about preparing food. It occupied just enough of my mind to keep it from wandering but without the tedium of scrubbing toilets or ironing the laundry—chores to which Mother Camillus was more than happy to assign me. The nuns were cheerful but efficient, warm but rigorous. Theirs was a well-oiled system, and I felt a certain amount of pride at how well my particular cog fit into their wheel.

So long as I didn't think about how ashamed Father would be to see me with flour in my hair and milk on my clothes. Which was easier said than done.

Before I knew it, an hour had passed, breakfast was over, and the children were scattering to their respective classrooms, most of the nuns disappearing with them, including Emily. The empty trays seemed to echo when I gathered them, as if the room had expanded in the children's absence. Or maybe that was just the melancholy I felt, knowing the rest of the day would be spent alone, doing whatever additional chores Mother Camillus had dredged up from her never-ending list.

I completed the rest of my morning duties: scrubbing the dishes, wiping the tables, sweeping the floors, preparing for the lunch crew. When all was completed to the standards Mother Camillus demanded (and which, I suspected, not even Rosie or Joanne, our maids back home, could have achieved), I removed my apron and trudged from the kitchen to the small corner room that served as the head nun's office. I knocked.

No answer.

I knocked again, harder this time.

Still, from inside, only silence.

I scrunched up my face. Mother Camillus had never missed

an appointment with me. Or anyone, I would gather. I raised my hand to knock again.

"She isn't here."

I turned to find Sister Felicitus, an Austrian-born nun in her early fifties, whose thick accent made everything she said sound harsh, even when she was praying. Which was a shame because she was actually a lovely person, always kind to me, even in those early days when I was constantly stepping on toes and misremembering the dozens of Catholic rituals I was supposed to honor. She served as Mother Camillus's assistant, though I'm sure that wasn't the proper term for the position. All I knew was that wherever Mother Superior was, Sister Felicitus was surely two steps behind.

"Where is she?"

"She was called over to St. Patrick's this morning." She stopped in front of me, knuckles white as she clasped her hands together. "But she told me to tell you to wait here."

I squeezed the muscle connecting my neck to my shoulder. It already ached. The sooner I started with my work, the sooner I could finish. "Do you know what chores she wanted me to do? I might as well get started while I wait."

"No chores today." The nun's rosary made a gentle clinking sound as she shook her head. "She wants to talk."

"Talk?"

"Talk."

There was a heaviness to the word, one that had nothing to do with its European flavoring. I could sense it by the slight downturn of Sister Felicitus's mouth, the way her eyes refused to meet mine. The already stifling temperature seemed to rise a few degrees. Sweat broke out along my hairline at the back of my neck.

I'd been found out.

It was the only explanation. Somehow, Mother Camillus had learned the truth: who I was, where I'd come from, why I was here.

Saliva pooled in my mouth, and yet my throat was dry. Although I realized I should say something, I found that I couldn't. In front of me, Sister Felicitus shifted from one foot to the other, eyebrows raised.

"Of course," I finally managed. "I understand. I'll just . . . I'll finish up in the kitchen until she gets back. Would that be all right?"

Sister Felicitus pressed her lips together so hard they almost disappeared. Her voice, however, was soft. Almost apologetic. "Of course. I will let you know when she returns."

I lifted my chin as I turned from her, hoping my legs betrayed none of the tremble afflicting my insides. It was only when I heard the door click behind me, signaling that the nun had retired into Mother Superior's office, that I let out a breath I wasn't even aware I'd been holding. My eyes burned with unshed tears. The first hint of a sob had just escaped my mouth when it was jarred into silence by a door bursting open on my right.

Sister Catherine emerged, red-faced and sweaty, dragging an equally red-faced child.

Maggie Sherwood.

The girl howled. By the way she swung her fists, I knew it was less from the pain of Sister Catherine's grip and more from her own exasperation at not being able to free herself from it. The few knots I'd managed to untangle from her hair after chapel were back.

"What's going on?" I asked, though I wasn't sure Sister Catherine could even hear me over Maggie's shrieks.

Perspiration dripped down the nun's forehead. A few strands of hair had come loose from her wimple and lay matted against her skin. I'd never seen her hair before; I was surprised to discover it was red, like mine.

"This one," she spat from between gritted teeth, "has decided she'd rather spend the day in the company of Mother Superior than her peers."

"No I wouldn't!" Maggie shouted. Her blonde hair lashed her face as she swung her head wildly.

Sister Catherine let loose a short, bitter laugh. "That's where we disagree, Margaret. Because when a child decides to use her reader as a weapon rather than a tool for learning, it tells me that child has a need for higher companionship than her present company."

"I didn't hit her!" Maggie protested. "I only tapped her because she—"

"That's enough, Margaret!" Sister Catherine's voice echoed through the hallway. Even though I wasn't the one in trouble, I felt my own spine go a little straighter. "I don't want to hear another word. Mother Camillus will deal with you and your excuses from now on."

"I didn't—"

But Sister Catherine was done listening. Shoring up her grip on Maggie's arm, she began to pull the girl in the direction of Mother Superior's office.

"Wait!" I called. "Mother Camillus isn't here!"

Sister Catherine paused, her posture stiffening. She turned back to me slowly.

"She—she's at St. Patrick's," I stuttered. "I'm not sure when she'll be back."

Maggie had stilled. Her muscles were like noodles under the nun's clutch, heavy with defeat and dread. She raised her head at the sound of my voice, and I noticed the tears leaving dirt trails down her face. Inside my chest, my heart cleaved.

"Gone?" Sister Catherine sputtered. "Then what am I supposed to—"

"I'll take her." The words came out before I truly understood what I was saying.

"You?"

"I . . . I . . ." I fished for an explanation, a reason, anything that would allow me to get to Maggie. "I'm waiting for Mother Camillus too. She . . . has me scrubbing dishes until she returns. Margaret could do that as well. So you can get back to your class."

I could see the turmoil on Sister Catherine's face. She didn't like me. Oh, she was always polite, but I'd grown up in New York society; I could spot false civility a mile away. And Sister Catherine was as civil as they came. Leaving Maggie in my care would go against every prejudice she not-so-secretly harbored about me.

But being forced to return the child to the classroom would be even worse.

It was with a huff and no small amount of chagrin that Sister Catherine thrust Maggie toward me and stomped back into her classroom, slamming the door behind her for good measure.

I knelt in front of Maggie, sweeping the hair from her face. "Are you all right?"

She sniffed in response.

"Oh, Maggie." I wrapped her in a tight hug.

"Do I really have to scrub dishes?"

I pulled away, and her dark eyes met mine. They were red-rimmed and watery. Her face was splotchy, the lines of dirt from her tears having dried into streaks that looked like wrinkles. It gave her the appearance of a very tiny, very wild, old person.

I bit down on a smile.

"The dishes are done," I said, rising and pulling her hand into mine. Somehow, it was even stickier than before. "I need some fresh air."

Maggie broke into a wide, gap-toothed grin.

"Those waves have been calling to me all morning. Let's take a walk."

TWO

I hadn't been dreaming that first night, when St. Mary's seemed to rise out of the dunes like a mirage. Though the building was actually two structures rather than just one as I'd first thought—the boys' and girls' dormitories were separate—it really was a ghost of an edifice. An isolated mass of bricks and stone nestled among a thicket of salt cedars right on the beach, segregated from the rest of Galveston proper. Out here, there were no trolley cars, no streetlamps, no pleasure bathers. There was only the sun, the sand, and the sea.

And, this morning, me and Maggie Sherwood.

The girl had barely made it past the scraggly clumps of grass collecting behind the fence posts before her shoes were off. Her bare feet made a loud slapping sound as she raced into the tide, tears long since forgotten. She shrieked when the waves chased her up the shore, then spun around to continue the game as they retreated once more.

I shielded my eyes, watching her. The bright sun reflected off the water, and my mind flitted longingly back to the hats lining the top shelf of my closet in New York. I wished I'd thought to bring one. Not just to the beach but to Texas in general. Then again, I hadn't known I was going to Texas when I'd stepped foot on that first train, and it wasn't exactly as if I could have gone back to the house to pack.

I shook the memory away, propelling myself farther down the beach. Splintered shells and strands of dried seaweed crunched under my boots. I took them off when I reached the tide line, where the sand had been beaten smooth by the constant waves, and hiked up my gray dress. It wasn't proper, showing my ankles like this, but no one was around besides Maggie. And, anyway, the crust of salt that formed on my hemline after getting soaked by seawater was impossible to remove. The dress was ugly enough without adding a stain.

The wet sand was cool and slick. It curled between my toes deliciously. Using one hand to carry my boots and the other to keep a firm grip on my skirt, I hurried to catch up with Maggie.

By the time I reached her, she had given up her game of tag and was instead squatting in the surf. I leaned down beside her, careful to keep my skirt out of the water. "What are you looking at?"

Her hair draped over her face as she ran her hands through the shallow waves. She had no qualms about allowing her dress to get damp; it was soaked up to her midsection. "Just looking for critters."

"Critters?"

"Worms, bugs, starfish. Sometimes you can even find a crab or two, but you have to be careful." She glanced at me. "You ever been pinched by a crab?"

"Can't say that I have."

"You ain't missing anything."

I paused, allowing a pair of seagulls to scream at each other over our heads. "Maggie," I said, tentatively. "Was Sister Catherine telling the truth? Did you . . . hit someone?"

She slapped the top of the water with her fingertips, not looking at me. "Yes."

"Who? Why?"

"Angela," she replied, supplying the name of a ten-year-old brunette with whom she'd tangled in the past. I knew I shouldn't harbor feelings of dislike for Angela—she was only a child, after all—but, based on the things Maggie had told me in the past, I was willing to admit she was not among my favorites at the orphanage.

"What did Angela do?"

She pulled a rock from beneath the water, examined it, then tossed it back in.

"Maggie?"

"She said no one would ever adopt me."

The words were soft, yet piercing. I closed my eyes. Memories swirled, a grief so sudden and so intense, it stole my breath. Cold rain on my face, smooth leather beneath my fingertips, a voice in the night, as sharp and cruel as a blade.

Oh, come on, Kitty Kat. Are you really telling me you didn't suspect anything?

The touch of Maggie's hand pulled me from my nightmare. I forced a breath from my lungs, training my gaze on the fearful brown eyes before me. Her pain radiated through my own, just as cutting, just as agonizing. Doubling it. But, also, redirecting it.

I squeezed her cold, wet fingers. "Well," I said slowly, "what does she know? She hasn't been adopted either."

"Her new mom and dad come next week." Her lisp made the words all the more heartbreaking, making her seem younger and more vulnerable than she already was.

More wounded.

The tang of fish soured my mouth when I was finally able to

swallow. I forced the corners of my mouth upward. "Well, bully for her! That just means someone else will have to look at her ugly face every day now instead of us."

It was mean, I know. But it got Maggie to smile, and that was all that mattered.

Fat blue dragonflies danced around us as we made our way down the beach. The sky was cloudless, the Gulf calm. It wasn't long before I was sweating, despite the ever-present sea breeze. Salt rubbed on my exposed skin; even the parts that were hidden beneath thick fabric felt as if they were beginning to burn. But I barely registered any of it. I kept one eye on Maggie, galloping up ahead of me, as my mind turned once more to the problem at hand.

It didn't matter how far I walked from St. Mary's. Mother Camillus would be waiting for me when I returned.

And so, I imagined, would my past.

It wasn't unexpected, of course. Mother Camillus had let me know in no uncertain terms that this arrangement was temporary when she'd agreed to let me stay. I knew it wouldn't last forever; I didn't *want* it to last forever. What would a person like me possibly do at a Catholic orphanage for the rest of her life? And yet with every day that passed, I allowed myself to get a little bit more comfortable, a little bit more attached, a little bit more unhurried. I had no money, no place to go, and I was still being pursued; I knew he would never give up that easily. But I had started to believe I was safe here, out on this remote end of a glorified sandbar in the Gulf of Mexico, living with a bunch of unwanted children and pious nuns. I was hidden.

More important, *it* was hidden. The brown satchel. Stored safely under my bed. It was the one thing I hadn't allowed the nuns to take from me when I arrived. Apparently, I'd screamed like a banshee when they'd tried, though I didn't remember doing so. The memory of that night came only in snippets, like from one of those moving-picture machines. I'd been so dehydrated, so exhausted, so emotionally depleted, I'd spent two weeks in bed before even bothering to rouse.

No, I knew this arrangement wouldn't last forever. But if Mother Camillus had learned the truth about who I was . . .

I needed a plan. I would not go back. I *wouldn't*. Mother Camillus could force me out of the orphanage—had every right to, honestly—but she could not force me to return to New York. I would run. I didn't know how, and I didn't know where, but I would run. My time in Galveston was coming to an end. And that scared me.

But I was also surprised by just how much it *hurt*.

"Maggie! Maggie, wait up!"

The pier was a lively, crowded place, even on a weekday, a world away from the lonely beachfront near St. Mary's. Maggie was already past the skeletons of buildings being erected for the new Army fort—there were rumors it was going to be named after Davy Crockett, that legendary hero of the Alamo whose name was never far from any Texan's lips—and was close to being swallowed by the mass of colorful bathers blotting out the brown sand of the beach beneath them. The only reason I was able to catch up to her was because she stopped to stare at the trolley as it rumbled past, clicking and clacking beneath buzzing electrical wires, the ocean gently lapping at its elevated tracks.

Her lips parted slightly. "Can we ride it?"

She asked me the same thing every time. And my response was always the same: "Do you have any money?"

She scrunched up her nose. But her displeasure was short-lived. She grasped my hand and began pulling me deeper into the crowd.

It had taken weeks for me to be comfortable enough to venture into the city. Every sideways glance, every turned head, I was sure came from someone sent by *him*. But as time passed and no bogeymen emerged, I began to relax. Not completely—I wasn't so naive as to think I was safe. I would probably never be completely safe again. But there was a kind of peaceful anonymity to be found within Galveston's masses. Its multitude of tourists and ever-revolving port made its population highly in flux. What was one more nameless face?

Especially one dressed as shabbily as myself, with no rouge on my cheeks or pins to hold back the mass of frizz that my hair had become. I certainly drew no eyes.

Maggie and I strolled past the Beach Hotel, a four-and-a-half-story behemoth built directly on top of the crushed-shell sand. With its large red and white stripes and green eaves, it looked like a circus tent, albeit a fancier, more permanent one. In front of it lay hundreds of patrons in their bathing costumes. The pale, naked legs of the men made me blush. The women, of course, were fully covered. From the top, their outfits looked like any other proper female attire, with long sleeves and buttoned-to-the-neck bodices. Only the bottoms were different . . . and not in a good way. The puffed trousers reminded me of pantaloons, and I couldn't help but see a throng of court jesters lounging on the beach, splashing in the surf, or else traversing the boardwalk that headed straight out into the Gulf, where the familiar octagonal pavilion of the Pagoda Bathhouse stood waiting.

It wasn't the only bathhouse on this stretch of beach. Far from it. In fact, from this spot, I could see Murdoch's (which was bigger) and the Electric Pavilion (which was grander). But, for Maggie, there was no place better than the Pagoda. I had to admit its whimsical design, so different from its boxy counterparts, drew me in as well. There was something magical about sitting right on top of the water and hearing the waves beat against the pilings holding it aloft.

The atmosphere under the two covered piers stretching out on either side only added to the allure.

Every manner of treat and goody was offered under its wooden roof, from cinnamon roasted pecans to fairy floss to orange and raspberry sorbet, kept inside special portable cooling boxes. The competing spicy and sweet smells made my mouth water. My poverty stung; it wasn't so very long ago when I could have bought one of each of the offerings on that pier.

Maggie Sherwood, on the other hand, was able to ignore the myriad of temptations. Because she only had eyes for one thing: the popcorn machine at the far end of the jetty.

And the dark-haired, strong-jawed man working it.

Matthew Richter's face broke into a grin when he saw her. "Maggie! I was wondering if I would see you today! It's been a while."

Maggie's hand left mine, swinging forward to give his a firm shake. He didn't flinch at its sweatiness. A shy smile played across her lips.

He crouched down so that he was eye level with her and creased his brow. "I was starting to worry you'd found another person whose popcorn you like better than mine."

She shook her head violently, eyes wide with concern.

Matthew's lips twitched. He was struggling to maintain his seriousness. "Do you promise?"

Maggie nodded.

"Well, in that case . . ." He rose, scooped a load of freshly popped kernels into a bag, then leaned back down and pressed it into her hand. "We need to make sure it stays that way."

Maggie cradled the bag, staring at the mound of overflowing popcorn. When she finally tore her eyes away, she was beaming. "Thank you," she whispered in awed reverence.

"You're welcome. As long as you promise to come back. And sooner this time."

"I promise."

He stood, facing me for the first time. I tried not to notice the dimples in his cheeks as he grinned. "And you, Miss Not Nun. It's good to see you again as well."

I pressed my lips together. It was a running joke between us, one that had been born from my initial refusal to give him my name, no matter how many times he asked. He gathered only, from my outfit and Maggie's, that we were from St. Mary's. When I insisted he not call me Sister because I was not, in fact, a nun, he took to calling me "Not Nun," and the nickname still stuck even after I'd let him call me Annie.

I had to work very hard to convince myself I did not find it charming.

"No Emily today?"

I shook my head. "She's working."

He gave me a wink that brought color to my cheeks. "And you two are playing hooky?"

I sputtered, "No. We're—"

"We sure are!" Maggie interrupted with a mouth full of popcorn. "I'm supposed to be in class and Annie should be in the kitchen."

Matthew let out an explosive laugh. "Well, I'd say you two made the right choice." He winked at me again.

I looked away, feeling a fresh round of sweat dampen my armpits. "Mr. Richter," I began.

"Matthew," he corrected. "How many times do I have to tell you? It's Matthew." His hazel eyes danced mischievously.

I let out a long breath through my nose and clasped my hands in front of me. "Matthew," I said pointedly, "you don't have to give her popcorn every time we come here. It's really not necessary."

"I know it's not. I want to."

"But it can't be—"

"It's my popcorn. I can do what I want with it."

His tone was firm but kind, and I knew there was no use arguing. It wasn't the first time we'd had this conversation.

"And what I also want to do"—he grabbed another bag from the stack and, in one swift motion, scooped in a mound of popcorn and held it out to me—"is give some to you."

Saliva pooled in my mouth, the scent of warm butter mingling with the ocean breeze. The food at the orphanage was filling but bland; what I wouldn't give to taste actual flavors once again upon my tongue. But there was something else besides hunger driving my desire for that bag. It was the sudden, unbidden thought that I might brush Matthew's fingertips as I reached for it.

And that realization was enough to douse any inkling of hunger I might have been feeling.

I dug my nails into my palms. "No thank you. It's . . . it's too hot."

I might have been imagining it, but I swore I saw Matthew's face fall slightly. If it did, however, he quickly recovered, the usual, laid-back smile remaining on his face as he dropped the popcorn back into the machine. "Yes," he said, wiping his hands on his dark trousers. "It is. But it's hot everywhere. At least here we have a bit of a breeze today." He gestured out the open-air windows toward the sparkling Gulf.

I didn't respond. Instead, I glanced down at Maggie, suddenly self-conscious, but she was munching away happily, too absorbed in her treat to notice any awkward tension.

Matthew fiddled with a knob on the side of his machine. "It's worse elsewhere. Chicago lost three people to the heat, if you can believe it. And, for the first time in recorded history, the Bering Glacier is beginning to shrink. *Calving* is what they call it. Breaking off lots of little icebergs." He wiggled his fingers, demonstrating.

"The Bering what?"

He pulled his hands back to his sides, grinning sheepishly,

revealing those two small dimples in his cheeks. "Sorry. I get carried away sometimes."

I couldn't help it. I smiled back. "What were you even talking about?"

He shook his head. "Nothing. Just . . . weather."

"Weather?"

Leaning an elbow against his machine, he placed one hand on his hip. The redness in his face was gone, the usual easy charm back. "I ain't just an expert popcorn maker, Miss Not Nun. I also recently entered into the employ of one Mr. Isaac Cline."

He let the name hang in the air. All around us, other beachgoers shuffled about, laughing and chatting, enjoying their sweets under the shade of the pier. The smell of sun-kissed flesh and wet fabric ebbed and flowed as they passed, planks creaking beneath their feet. In the midst of this, Matthew stood expectant, waiting for me to react to his statement.

"Who?"

His jaw dropped. "Isaac Cline! You don't know who Isaac Cline is?"

I gave a tiny shake of my head.

"He's only one of the top scientists of our age. He's the one who predicted that Colorado River dam break in Austin. Saved hundreds of lives. He's a genius. Chief at the Weather Bureau here in town. Knows everything there is to know about weather. And now . . . he's teaching me." He puffed out his chest, causing the silver buttons on his vest to strain.

"Oh." I knew I was supposed to be impressed. But his words meant absolutely nothing to me.

His shoulders drooped slightly.

I instantly felt guilty. "That's . . . nice." I forced enthusiasm into my tone.

There it was again. That smile. I both craved and dreaded it.

"Would you like . . ." He paused, chewing his bottom lip. "Would you like to come down to the Bureau sometime? See how it all works? He has these fancy instruments and . . ."

Matthew was still talking. But I was no longer listening.

Would you like to see how it works?

His words, the pier, the Gulf—it all melted away. Suddenly, I was back in the forest. I could feel the moss squish beneath my shoes, smell the damp earth. See a stray blond lock falling across vibrant green eyes. So wide. So cautious. So vulnerable.

Would you like to see how it works?

My chest constricted. I couldn't breathe.

"Annie? Annie, are you all right?"

Annie? Who's Annie?

The image faded. In its place, the thump of waves against wood, the distant horn of a ship, the smell of brine and mildew and fish.

And Matthew. His face. His voice.

Saying that name.

Annie.

Me. He meant me. Only I wasn't Annie.

I came back to myself then, blinking away the last of my stupor and grabbing Maggie's hand. She glanced up at me, startled. "We have to go," I croaked.

"Wha—" she started.

"We have to get back." I nodded once to Matthew, not meeting his eye. "Mr. Richter. Thank you again for the popcorn. Have a lovely day."

"Annie, wait. I didn't mean . . . Well, I just wondered . . . Since you said you weren't a nun, I thought . . . I'm sorry. Annie!" He stretched his arm out as if to touch me.

But I was already gone, fleeing in vain from the ghosts I knew would never leave me.

No matter what name I used.

THREE

**SIX MONTHS EARLIER
MARCH 1900
CROTON-ON-HUDSON, NEW YORK**

I had to fight every urge not to jump out of the carriage and run. The problem was I wasn't sure which direction to go.

To... or from?

My driver had slowed to a crawl for the last half mile. I knew the lingering ice had something to do with it, but it felt intentional. Like a sign.

An omen?

I squeezed my gloved hands inside their muff. *Stop it, Kathleen.*

The carriage bumped over frozen ruts in the long, winding road, jostling me and making my already tender stomach sour. Shifting in my seat, I craned my neck to look out the steam-covered window into the world beyond. The yellow hills of the countryside stretched out beneath a canopy of bare trees, their spindly branches stretching up toward the weak sunlight barely breaking through the clouds.

I sighed. I had hoped my homecoming would correspond with the spring thaw. In Switzerland, I'd had enough of winter to last me a lifetime. But it was not to be. Still, there was a certain sense of—

My breath caught in my throat. There it was.

Its familiar gleaming white columns and opulent porticos burst through the dreary gray of the surrounding forest. The tiled gables and brick turrets, tall chimneys and row after row of warm, lighted windows, all surrounded by a massive expanse of lawn.

The McDaniel Manor.

Home.

It was just as I remembered it.

And the ache that had been percolating in my chest from the moment I'd stepped foot back on American soil began to deepen.

The crunch of gravel beneath the carriage's wheels grew louder as the driver directed the horses into the large oval that buttressed the front of the house. As he swung around, I caught sight of the barn in the distance. It looked bigger. Newer. Definitely had a fresh coat of paint. My heart panged, fear and yearning wrestling within my chest. How I wished I could go see the animals first. The cows, the horses, the pigs, even the cranky old barn cat.

The animals would be easier. Safer.

Stop it, Kathleen.

The carriage swung around, blocking the barn from my view and revealing a row of shivering servants, all lined up along the front steps, waiting to welcome me home in the exact same location and manner in which they had bid me farewell two years earlier. I caught sight of Archie, the old butler, standing beside two footmen I didn't recognize, as well as Rosie and Joanne, two chambermaids I did. And there was Rupert, the groundskeeper, and Miss Dover, the cook. And Stella. Good old, reliable Stella.

And . . . *him.*

All trepidation vanished. I didn't let the coachman open my

door or help me from my seat; I barely let the wheels stop turning. Before the last creak had echoed across the frozen landscape, I was out of the warm confines of the interior, out into the blistering cold . . . and straight into my father's arms. He let out a bark of delighted surprise as I nuzzled myself under the arms for which I'd yearned for so long, breathing in the tangy, comforting scent of his tobacco and aftershave.

"Kitty Kat."

I didn't even bristle at the nickname I had long since outgrown. It didn't matter. I was here. He was here. And all my doubts were smothered by the feel of his strong arms around me. "Father." I swallowed back a lump of emotion rising in my throat. "I missed you."

"Did you now?" Gently, he removed my arms from around his waist, pushing me back slightly so he could get a good look at me. His dark mustache twitched as he took in my dress, my hair, my physique. "You've grown, Kitty Kat. Has it really been two years?"

With his question, the removal of his touch, I instantly felt cold again. Pain broke through my elation, refusing to be ignored. Yes, it had been two years.

Two years during which my father—the man who'd hung the moon—never once ventured overseas to see me.

Two years in which questions began to loom larger than his presence in my life.

Two years during which he'd become a stranger.

Or perhaps I had.

He tilted my chin, pinching it between two fingers, still studying me. His gray hair shone silver beneath a thick layer of pomade. "Well, I'd say that time at Brillantmont was well spent. Look at you. A regular Gibson girl now, aren't you?"

Heat bloomed in my cheeks. It wasn't true, of course; I wasn't tall enough, slender enough, delicate enough to fit Charles Gibson's ideals of feminine beauty. My hair was too red, my skin too freckled. In fact, there were times I believed my two years of finishing school in Switzerland wasted. I would never compete with the other girls and their charms.

But it felt good to hear him say it, nonetheless.

"Come on. Let's get you inside before you catch your death of cold."

The servants bowed their heads as we passed, murmuring quiet hellos. My father paid them no mind, keeping his pace brisk, but the marked change in their countenances caused my feet to stumble. None of them would look at me. Archie, whose coattails I used to pull on and whose grin I used to covet, glanced over the top of my head rather than look me in the eyes. Even Miss Dover—the same Miss Dover who used to chase me from the kitchen with a playful smack on the bottom when she caught me swiping tarts from their cooling rack—kept her eyes on my shoes as she curtsied before me.

Curtsied.

"Stella." The maid who'd been my constant companion for as long as I could remember was last in line, her gray hair pulled from her face in a tight bun at the back of her head. "You're looking well."

"Welcome home, Miss McDaniel." Though she smiled, there was a tightness in her tone I'd never heard before. And "Miss McDaniel"? That was new. I'd always been Kathleen or Kathleen Anne (if I was in trouble) or, on more formal occasions, Miss Kathleen. But never, ever Miss McDaniel.

I tightened my grip on my father's elbow, frowning slightly. It was a chilly welcome, and not just because of the frigid air. But as I directed my attention to my father—his raised chin, erect posture, purposeful stride—it hit me: the servants weren't being aloof. They were being respectful. Just as they were with my father.

I *was* Miss McDaniel now. No longer a child but lady of the house. And deserving of the same airs and esteem as Mr. McDaniel himself.

It was a peculiar sensation. But not a completely unpleasant one.

Inside, the grand staircase still gleamed, the high ceilings still echoed, the furnishings still sat in their usual places. It even smelled the same: cleaning oil and cigars tinged with the scent of baking bread from the downstairs kitchen. It took a few moments for me to realize some things *had*, in fact, changed. There were new paintings on the wall—including a Prendergast, I recognized with a gasp—a plush new rug down the hallway, and . . .

"Lights!" My mouth fell open as the soft yellow glow finally registered.

My father beamed. "We're entirely electric now, Kitty Kat. No more gas, no more coal. Completely, one hundred percent modern."

A silhouette moved in behind him, catching my eye. I craned my neck, thinking perhaps it was Stella.

It wasn't.

Father cleared his throat. "Ah, yes. Kitty, this is Otto Zimmerman. I hired him a few months ago to serve as my . . . Let's just call him my man, shall we?"

I wasn't quite sure what "my man" meant, but I figured now was not the time to ask. Especially when I directed my attention to Mr. Zimmerman and found him scowling at me from beneath heavy brows. Even his dark, bushy beard and the shadows from which he refused to move could not conceal it: he was most definitely scowling. His crossed arms and balding, beefy frame didn't help matters.

Still, I gave him a slight curtsy that would have made Mademoiselle Dubois proud. "How do you do, Mr. Zimmerman?"

He did not answer. In fact, he did not even blink.

Perhaps Mr. Zimmerman could have used a finishing school of his own.

Luckily, at that moment, Archie appeared behind me, subtly directing a footman to take my coat. "Miss McDaniel, if you please."

"Of course." I removed my thick coat and gloves, trying to catch the servant's eye and share a smile as I handed them over, but his gaze remained focused on my outerwear. Feeling chastised, I cleared my throat, hoping my voice held more confidence than I felt. "See to my trunks, please."

"Yes, ma'am."

My father winked at me, clearly pleased with my poise, and I grinned. Brushing past Archie, he placed his own coat on top of mine in the footman's arms. Both servants disappeared with a slight bow. "How was the trip home?"

My smile fell. I had an urge to pull at my collar, but two years under the tutelage of Mademoiselle Dubois would not allow me to indulge it. Instead, I thrust my shoulders back, straightening a spine already stiff from travel. "It was . . . fine."

"Fine? Just fine?" My father glanced up from his pocket watch. "I paid for a first-class berth on the *Oceanic*. Surely, it must have been better than *fine*. Did your chaperone—"

"The ship was beautiful, Father, and the chaperone more than adequate. She saw me all the way into my carriage in New York, just as you instructed."

But Father wasn't listening. "I knew we should have sent Stella with you. You can't trust those European—"

I placed a hand on his arm, stilling him. "All was well, Father. I apologize for being less than loquacious. I'm tired is all."

He raised an eyebrow, and I looked away, hoping it passed for demure rather than guilty. The *Oceanic* had been magnificent, the largest and most luxurious liner on which I'd ever sailed. The grand dome that capped the first-class dining room on the saloon deck alone was more ornate than many homes I'd visited. And the chaperone Father had paid to accompany me had been sufficient. Boring and practically mute, but sufficient.

My displeasure had nothing to do with the manner in which I'd been brought here. Instead, it had everything to do with being here at all. And the longing I felt for the faces—the life—I had left behind in Switzerland.

Louisa, Margarite, Hazel. My friends. These European women had been so different from anyone I'd met in the States; in fact, they had been different from all the other women at Brillantmont too. They'd been determined to make a mark on the world with more than just their beauty or their pedigrees. And they weren't afraid to get their hands—or their dresses—dirty, no matter the looks from high society. They had substance. Grit. Purpose.

And they made me feel like perhaps I did too.

It was a sentiment I'd started to believe . . . until the *Oceanic* had pulled me away from them. Back into the world where I was no longer Kathleen but Kitty Kat—*Miss McDaniel*—once again.

The snap of Father's pocket watch pulled me from my thoughts. "Goodness. You best go get dressed."

"Dressed?"

"For dinner!" My father laughed. "Teddy is making a special trip all the way from Sagamore Hill! The *governor*," he added for emphasis, as if I didn't know how the Roosevelts' position—and name—had grown during my time away. "Edith can't come, unfortunately. One of the little ones is ill, as I understand it. But still, Teddy will be here, and I want everything to be perfect for him. Including you, Kitty Kat."

I frowned. "But, Father, I've only just arrived. I'd hoped to—"

He gave me a kiss on the forehead, a gesture that felt oddly dismissive. "Nonsense. This dinner with Teddy has been planned for weeks. Besides, it will also be a celebration of your homecoming. Two birds, one stone, as they say."

"I—"

But Father was already walking away, Mr. Zimmerman on his heels. "I'll send Stella upstairs to help you dress. I've bought you a new gown for the occasion!" He paused. Turning to look at me, he pressed one finger to his lips. "Hair up, I would say. If Stella can manage to do something with those curls."

"Father . . ."

"Dinner begins at eight!"

I sucked in my cheeks. Two years. I hadn't seen my father in two years. And our reunion had lasted less than ten minutes. I'd had no chance to talk to him about anything, let alone the things—the questions, the insecurities—that lay on my chest like bricks.

Don't be stupid, I scolded myself. *He's planned a grand dinner for you. Your first one as lady of McDaniel Manor. Isn't that enough?*

It was only as I began my weary trudge up the stairs that I realized my homecoming had been second on my father's list of things to celebrate.

My head started to throb less than thirty minutes into our meal.

It could have been the champagne. There were several toasts, some to me but far more to Mr. Roosevelt, and no matter how low my drink became, the glass never seemed to empty. But, despite my rising headache, I had to keep partaking; it would be rude not to. And, if finishing school had taught me anything, it was that a lady should be well-mannered above everything else.

But my discomfort came less from the drink and more from the incessant, droning conversations. I'd been excited at first, answering questions about my time in Switzerland. Before I'd left, I'd received nothing more than a passing glance from these people. Even though my official coming out wouldn't take place until early summer, for all intents and purposes, I was lady of the house now.

But it was a title that meant very little to this crowd, apparently.

Conversation shifted rapidly beyond my time overseas to news from the New York Stock Exchange and the latest meeting of the Aqueduct Commission. Vanderbilt and Morgan, du Pont and Ludwig, even the "new money" Rockefeller and Carnegie—none of these men present for *my* homecoming dinner even let me get past describing my first encounter with raclette and the world-famous Swiss chocolate.

Instead, it was Roosevelt who held the dinner table rapt.

"Come now, Teddy, I'd thought you were coming tonight to let us all in on a little secret." My father winked mischievously over the top of his glass. "We all know you're going to do it. Why not make it official?"

Even sitting down, Mr. Roosevelt was an intimidating presence, thick and broad-shouldered, the physique from his Rough Riders days still well-established despite his switch to politics. His long mustache twitched as he held up large hands. "I've said it before, and I will say it again, Lawrence: I have no interest in running."

"Bah!"

Roosevelt laughed at my father's dismissal. "It's true! There's much more important work I can do here in New York as governor than I can in Washington as vice president. Like help promote projects that will continue to make New York City the most important and prosperous metropolis in this country. Projects like your dam, Lawrence." He raised his glass in my father's direction.

A chorus of "Hear! Hear!" broke out across the table. My father's cheeks reddened slightly, but I noticed he did not pooh-pooh their admiration.

"McKinley's going to need you, though," Mr. Rockefeller broke in. "The longer this war in the Philippines drags on, the lower his popularity sinks, and the greater the chance his reelection bid fails."

"He must stand strong, though," Mr. du Pont chimed in. "We cannot back down. We must break the Filipinos' spirits, detach them from their old, savage ways, and bring them into the twentieth century. That land is our right as victors under the Treaty of Paris."

"You're right," my father concurred. "The Philippine people will learn soon enough. And those who don't? Well . . . that's what our troops are for."

"I heard the number of civilian casualties is unprecedented," I said. "The newspapers were estimating tens of thousands dead already."

The clink of silverware halted, filling the room with stifling silence. The other women at the table immediately looked down at their laps, as if proving that they understood the rules of womanly decorum—and the rules when someone broke them. All other eyes turned to me. Andrew Carnegie held a fork to his open mouth, eyebrows raised in surprise. Mr. Vanderbilt's napkin remained pressed to his lips, shielding his expression but not his bewildered stare. Even Otto Zimmerman, standing in the corner with his arms crossed, blinked. Only Mr. Roosevelt seemed impressed, the tiniest hint of a smile poking out from beneath his mustache.

"Kathleen." My father's tone was both horrified and amused, as if waiting for a cue from his companions about which emotion was more appropriate.

"You're talking about the Philippine War, right? I just . . ." My lips suddenly felt numb. Louisa, Hazel, Margarite, and I had followed the war in the Philippines closely. Hazel managed to get ahold of American newspapers—how, I never found out—and we discussed them late at night in our bunks, when we were supposed to be getting our beauty rest. Before meeting them, I'd never considered the debate over Philippine independence versus the American need for a solid trade route to the Asian market, much less the ensuing humanitarian crisis there. It was a topic about which I was now more than qualified to contribute intellectually. But, I was realizing, not socially. At least, not among this crowd.

"I just heard there were a lot of deaths," I finished lamely.

"Not undeserved," Mr. Morgan sniffed after a few moments. "That's what happens when you attack American soldiers, unprovoked."

"I'm not sure they were unprovoked, Mr. Morgan."

The words slipped out before I could stop them. My father's eyes bulged.

"Hogwash!" Mr. Morgan flipped his wrist. "That land is rightfully ours. Any changes or policies we enact are . . . What were McKinley's words? 'For the greatest good of the governed.'"

I needed to stop. A crimson flush crept over my father's cheeks, rapid blinking changing his inspection of me from one of stupefaction to daggers and back again. Yet I still found myself saying, "Perhaps the Filipinos don't want to *be* governed."

A noise erupted from my father's throat, something between a laugh and a cry, echoing through the still air, bouncing off the crystal glasses and fine china. "Forgive my daughter," he said with a voice that could have cut glass. "As you know, she's just returned from a long trip overseas. From my understanding, there was little to read on the ship besides newspapers." He gave another curt guffaw. "And to those who claim newspapers more suitable than novels, I can now say definitively: you are wrong."

The table erupted in laughter. I creased my brow, twisting the napkin in my lap as indignation rose. I couldn't tell if they were laughing at my father's joke . . . or at me.

With one peek at my father's icy gaze, the fire in my breast withered, my soul retreating behind the mask of propriety and proper breeding. "You're right, Father," I said, mouth once again beyond my control but in a very different way. "Forgive me, gentlemen. Ladies. It was such a long voyage, and I'm afraid fatigue has affected my manners. I spoke out of turn. Men's affairs are no business of mine. I only wish for peace."

Louisa, Margarite, and Hazel would have been so ashamed.

My father, on the other hand, looked relieved. Proud even.

I shouldn't have been surprised. Or hurt. And yet, I was very much both. Still, for the rest of the dinner, no matter the topic, I kept my back straight, my smile wide, and my mouth shut, just as I'd been taught. *Ladyhood is pain*, Mademoiselle Dubois always said.

This was the first time I understood she hadn't just been talking about corsets.

After what seemed like hours, once the courses had been served and the wine drunk, the men pushed up from their chairs and thanked the women for the pleasure of our company, intent on retiring to the drawing room for cigars and brandy. This left the ladies to retreat to the parlor, where we would entertain ourselves as we waited for them to finish.

My apprehension soared, but so did my hope. I wasn't prepared for this; I'd been preparing my whole life. My first time being included in a proper ladies' circle. My first time to be counted as an equal with the women I'd only viewed from afar as a child. These were to be my people. My friends. Perhaps I'd find a Louisa, a Hazel, a Margarite in the bunch. Unlikely, as those girls were truly one of a kind. But perhaps I'd find a close substitute to fill the void. At the very least, this group held the promise of more stimulating conversation.

Or, at least, conversation in which I was allowed to participate.

I followed the ladies into the parlor, hand pressed to my abdomen to calm the fluttering inside it. This room, too, had been subtly improved, I realized. The furniture was new, as was the large blue and gray damask rug covering much of the polished wooden floor. The paintings remained the same, however. One of Central Park, the top of the Park Row building just visible in the distance, and one of the Hudson, its waters sparkling beneath a setting sun. It was the biggest painting that drew me, though.

The one of my mother.

Oil shone in the glow of the new electric lights, as if it had been painted yesterday rather than ten years earlier, right before her sudden death. Wearing an olive-green dress, long blonde hair pulled up at the sides, she stared out at me from in front of a black background. Though her back was straight, hands folded neatly in her lap, she looked as if she had been caught at the beginning of a laugh; those demure lips were parted slightly, corners turned up in a way that made you question whether they were turned up at all.

"She was beautiful." Carolyn Gardner, the wife of Croton-on-Hudson's newly elected sheriff, stepped up beside me, nodding to the painting. "You look just like her, you know?"

It was a lie. I looked nothing like my mother. Nothing like either of my parents. But manners—and a desire for the sentiment to be true—caused me to smile anyway. "Thank you."

"She'd be so proud of you."

That ever-present ache panged again. "I hope so."

Mrs. Gardner gave my arm a tight squeeze. I tried not to flinch under her touch; two years ago, before I'd left, I could have counted the number of words Carolyn Gardner had spoken to me on one hand. Now she was admiring my mother's portrait and touching me? Things in the world of ladyhood were truly bizarre.

She pulled her hand away, grinning. "Really, Kathleen, you must tell us all about Switzerland."

The other women in the room, perched on the settee or conversing by the gramophone, which was quietly playing the mournful tune of "Hearts and Flowers," murmured their agreement.

A tight smile spread over my lips as I fiddled with the velvet piping along the collar of my dress. It was sky blue, rhinestone accented, and perfectly complemented my fire-red hair—not an easy feat.

"Switzerland was beautiful," I said. "My school was nestled right in the Alps and had views of Lake Geneva, which was always clear, no matter the season. And we were only a few minutes' walk from the city center. It was no New York, of course, but I would spend hours exploring the cobbled streets, smelling food from the street vendors, and listening to the church bells ring." I sighed, remembering. "It was lovely."

"Sounds . . . quaint."

There was an air of something I couldn't place in the words, spoken by a yellow-haired lady seated on a wingback chair in the corner. Though I recalled her cream dress from across the table at dinner—it clashed horribly with her skin—her name escaped me now.

"It was," I said slowly, feeling suddenly defensive. "But it was also spectacularly modern."

"Modern?" Carolyn let out a tinkling laugh. "Europe? Oh come, Kitty, that entire continent is ages behind the United States. I hear they are just now getting motorcars over there!"

The other women giggled. Never mind I knew for a fact that only two of the gentlemen had shown up in motorcars that evening—it was impossible not to hear the clanking, sputtering engines from inside—and neither of those gentlemen had been accompanied by any of the women inside this room.

My mouth drooped into an involuntary frown which I immediately tried to stifle. I squared my shoulders just as Mademoiselle

Dubois had taught me and forced a smile. "It's true they still rely mainly on carriages and trains. I saw more motorcars when I made port in New York than I did my entire stay on the Continent." I released a laugh I did not recognize. "What I meant was it was very modern in terms of thinking."

An older woman, her dark hair peppered with streaks of gray, lowered her monocle. Mrs. O'Donnell, I remembered. Her husband was president of the O'Donnell Bank and Trust. "How do you mean?"

Her gaze was as sharp and demeaning as an old schoolmarm's. Or so I imagined. I'd only ever had private tutors. "Nothing improper," I said hurriedly. "And nothing disgraceful. We were there to become ladies, after all. But some of the women there also had . . . other interests."

"Such as?" The yellow-haired woman again. Was she a Vanderbilt? I couldn't remember.

I swallowed. It was now or never. "Well . . . some of the girls were looking to volunteer to help refugees of the Boer War—"

"You mean travel to Africa?"

The words might have come from Mrs. Porter, the mayor's wife, but horror was etched across the face of every woman in that room. The scratching of the long-finished gramophone recording echoed their condemnation.

"Yes, or, um . . ." My mouth suddenly felt dry. "To other parts of the Continent. Paris, London. There's terrible poverty, I've been told, and some of the girls wanted to use their positions to help, however they could. Journalists, nurses, teachers. Some even mentioned going to work for relief—"

A dramatic moan startled me silent.

"Oh, Kathleen." Carolyn placed a hand on my shoulder, the corners of her dark eyes crinkling. "How *awful*. I am so glad you came home when you did. I mean, *really*. What kind of riffraff are they admitting to Brillantmont these days? Filling your head with such nonsense. Imagine, a woman like you working in the streets or fields like some kind of peasant. It's so uncouth, not to mention dangerous."

"I've been saying for years we need more finishing schools here in the United States!" Mrs. O'Donnell said, one pudgy finger raised in the air. "Sending our daughters to Europe used to be a mark of prestige, but things on the Continent are rapidly declining. It's bad enough our cities are filling up with immigrants and their backward ideas. We don't need our ladies subjected to the same type of corruption in the very institutions for which we pay a hefty sum!"

A hearty ripple of agreement flowed through the parlor.

My cheeks reddened. So it wasn't just the men. Images of my school friends flashed in front of me. Of the debates we'd had, the dreams we'd shared, of the person they'd made me believe I was, the person I could be.

A person who was more than just a name. A face. A pedigree. A person who could make a difference.

I suddenly felt desperately, painfully lonely. What a fool I'd been to believe I could still be that person, back in the high society of New York. I'd left Brillantmont . . . but not its binds. In fact, I had been back on American soil less than twenty-four hours, and already I felt more shackled than I'd been my entire time abroad. Without my friends—and the space they'd given me to breathe—I was once again bound by my emotions, my mind, and my position, confined to the rules and regulations of a world that now seemed so small, considering all I'd seen and done and learned.

A world which was now *my* world once again. And forevermore.

I managed a weak, defeated smile that I hoped passed for the same relief my companions were feeling.

The yellow-haired woman tittered. "Well, I for one am concerned with only one aspect of modernity from Europe."

The rest of the women leaned forward in anticipation.

She smoothed back a stray curl and licked her lips. "Tell us, Kathleen. What news have you of the latest fashions?"

I glanced at the portrait of my mother on the wall. She still looked as if she was laughing.

"Knock, knock." My father's voice came in time with the raps on my bedchamber door. He entered without waiting for a response.

I quickly shoved the novel I was reading under my blanket. *The War of the Worlds,* by H. G. Wells. I'd picked it up in Manhattan while waiting for my carriage. Although nothing scandalous, I knew my father disapproved of novels and of science fiction in particular, the new genre sweeping through popular literature. And, after the near-disastrous dinner, I didn't need anything else to upset him, especially since I was pretty sure that was what he had come to discuss.

"You're still awake?" he said, sitting on the edge of my bed. "I thought you said you were exhausted, even before the party."

"I was. I *am*. So exhausted, in fact, that I'm too tired to sleep."

He smiled and patted my hand, his skin dry but soft. There was a glassy redness in his eyes, and I wondered how many snifters of brandy he'd imbibed after the standard two with our guests. "Ah, Kitty. It's good to have you home."

Is it? The question arose unbidden and bitter. I thought of the dismissive way our reunion had been cut short for Teddy Roosevelt. The excuses, the embarrassed looks Father had given me at dinner—practically the only looks I had received from him all evening.

I blinked rapidly, biting the inside of a lip that threatened to quiver.

"Kitty Kat." My father tilted his head. "That display at dinner tonight..."

"I'm sorry." The words came out automatically. But I wasn't sorry. I *wasn't*. I hated lying to him, but the moment felt too delicate, too thin, not to.

"It's so unlike you to break decorum. We're lucky Teddy is a good sport; his wife was quite the spitfire back in the day, from what I understand. But I can't have another outburst like that from you. Do you understand me?"

I picked at a string on my quilt. "Yes, Father."

He sighed. "Kitty, what's wrong? You've been acting strange since you arrived home, and I know it can't only be because you're tired."

I glanced up. His eyes were familiar. Kind. So kind, they caused my heart to break. The incident at dinner, the conversation with those women... They had defeated me, made me feel silly. Childish.

And desperately isolated.

But this was my *father*. The man who loved me, treasured me, indulged me, even if sometimes, like tonight, his position required him to set aside everything else, including me. I had no reason to be afraid of him, to hide from him. I could be honest with him. He would have answers. He would understand. Or, at the very least, try to.

He was all I had. And I couldn't keep hiding from him forever.

"Father, I had a wonderful time at school. I truly did. And I appreciate you spending all that money to send me there."

He beamed. "Only the very best for my daughter."

I clasped my hands in my lap, running one thumb over the other. "But... while I was there... I started feeling... different."

"Different?"

"Well, I . . . I began having these . . . dreams. Or, rather, I think they were dreams. They were so vivid. And they all felt connected. Disjointed, but connected."

He placed a finger to his lips. "How do you mean?"

"It was like a scene here and a scene there. Not a coherent story but chapters from the same book. I'd see a flash of a man, hazy and unrecognizable, on a farm somewhere. And then, later, a barn. Or me, nursing a calf from a bottle with a woman whose face I couldn't see."

My father squeezed my hand, shoulders relaxing. "Oh, Kitty Kat. I'm sure you were just missing *our* barn. You always did love the animals. I could barely keep you out of the pen during birthing season, remember?" He chuckled. "All those baby animals. You wanted to hold each and every one. Even the foals."

I gave a weak laugh. It was true; I *had* missed our animals. I had plans to go out to see them first thing tomorrow morning. But the barn in my dreams had been smaller, the animals less grand, donkeys and goats rather than thoroughbred horses. For some reason, though, I couldn't bring myself to admit this to my father. "You're probably right. But I wasn't always asleep when it happened. These flashes, these visions . . . They came even when I was awake."

Something subtle flickered across my father's face. A twitch of his mustache, a slight pressing of his lips. And then he was smiling again, his warm hands enveloping mine. "Kitty. You were away from home. In a foreign country. All alone. It makes sense that your mind would play tricks on you. That it would conjure up images where you might feel safe." He patted my cheek. "It was simply a way for your delicate heart to cope."

"Yes, but—"

"Kitty." Although he was still smiling, his tone was lower now.

Less gentle. "They were a figment of your imagination, fueled by female sensitivity. That's all."

I was aware he was waiting for me to agree. So I did, despite how readily, and painfully, he'd dismissed my discomfiture. His explanation made sense, after all. Those first few months at Brillantmont *had* been quite frightening. But then I'd met Louisa and Hazel and Margarite, and things had gotten better. More than better, in fact. Good. Wonderful.

But the dreams hadn't stopped.

Still, I decided to let it drop. I had more weighing me down than just those confusing visions.

"Kitty? Is there something else?"

No use hiding it. My father was a master at reading me.

I licked my lips. "At times . . . it felt like the only goal of the teachers at Brillantmont was to make us fit wives for well-positioned men."

My father blinked. "And?"

My heart began to thud. Heavy, loud, and sluggish. My tongue felt heavy. "And . . . I guess I was wondering . . . Is that all there is for me in this life? I mean, is that all I am? All I'm worth?"

My father pressed the tips of his fingers together, bloodshot eyes studying me. His voice was quiet, controlled, when he spoke. "Am I to understand you aspire to more?"

I gave a shaky nod. "Ye-yes." I cursed myself for my stutter. "I do."

"Such as?"

Though nothing in the room had changed, I suddenly felt as if I were under a spotlight, as if my father's steady gaze were made up of thousands of Edison's bulbs, looking right through my skin to the soul beneath.

I'd never felt so exposed.

So . . . fragile.

Because, the truth was, I didn't know. For all my words, all my longing, I couldn't name exactly what it was I wanted. My friends had laid out grand plans for their futures—writing and teaching and caring for those in need—and, while I recognized a yearning in me to do something similar, the exact path that pining should take remained a mystery. I only knew I wanted to do *something*.

To matter. To be seen.

"I . . ." I licked my lips, pulling the covers up near my chin. "I don't know. I just . . . I want to do something that makes others' lives better. To have a life of meaning, Father. Of importance. That's all."

For several moments, my father didn't speak. Didn't move. When he finally did, the rustle of my quilt beneath his body seemed to echo in the taut stillness. He took a long, deep breath, exhaling the scent of pipe tobacco. "Kathleen Anne. Let me explain something to you. We are building a kingdom here. You and I." He leaned closer to me. "The governor of New York—the future president of the United States, mark my words—sat and dined with us tonight. At our table. In our home. And he complimented us. That is no small thing. *We* are no small thing."

He stared at me with raised eyebrows, clearly expecting assent. So I nodded, though I wasn't sure what I was agreeing to.

"Of course I desire a good marriage for you; what father doesn't? Of course I insist on proper etiquette, respectability, and all the mores that come along with being a lady in our society. But you already *are* important, Kitty. You are a McDaniel. What we're doing, what we're building, *is* making others' lives better. And you," he continued, raising his chin, "are a part of it. Your future is more than most girls your age could ever dream of. Isn't that meaning enough?"

His words, though kind, chided me, and I lay awake for hours after he left, after he had kissed my cheek and shut off my light, turning them over in my mind. He was right, of course. I was privileged. I had no reason to feel such discontent, especially not compared to others. So what if I had to play by a certain set of rules? Every class did. I was selfish to think I could run off, chasing ideals like the tail of the wind, especially when I had no clear-set plan. My place was *here*. With my father. I needed nothing else. Those visions—the ones that had haunted me during my time abroad—had been nothing more than a product of homesickness. But I was home now. Louisa, Hazel, and Margarite were wonderful, and Switzerland a dream. But this was reality. This was my life.

And it was a good one.

So why, under my thick quilt, head resting on a down pillow, while a legion of servants rose early to prepare a breakfast larger than what most of the inhabitants of Croton-on-Hudson ate in a full day, was I still unable to sleep?

Barometric Pressure: 29.818, steady

Temperature: 90.5 degrees

Winds: N 13-15 mph

Conditions: Scattered clouds

WEATHER OBSERVATIONS
Thursday, September 6, 1900, afternoon
US Weather Bureau office, Galveston, TX

FOUR

THURSDAY, SEPTEMBER 6, 1900
GALVESTON, TEXAS

The children were at lunch when Maggie and I arrived back at St. Mary's.

Though it wasn't the first time I'd snuck away, it was my first with an orphan in tow; my adventures with Maggie usually took place on the weekend, on those rare Saturday mornings when the list of service work happened to run short or else on Sunday afternoons when outside play was encouraged so many of the nuns could take advantage of their Sabbath rest. The sight of me with Maggie or any number of other children was not unusual.

Unless it was eleven thirty on a Thursday morning, when I should have been working and Maggie should have been with her peers.

Rather than walk up the front steps, I led Maggie through a thick clump of salt cedars toward the rear of the building. To her credit, she didn't complain when the slender red branches tripped her feet or the scaly leaves snagged her hair. And she didn't ask questions. She simply slithered through, lithe as a cat, and crouched beside the gray picket fence that marked the boundary of the makeshift yard.

The sound of clanking silverware drifted through an open window, carrying with it the scent of boiled potatoes, which tinged my nostrils despite the overwhelmingly salty, soap-like smell of the brush around us. Even with the constant thudding of the waves behind us, I heard Maggie's stomach growl.

She grinned at me sheepishly.

"Really?" I asked, stifling a laugh despite myself. "Even after all that . . . popcorn?" The word tasted bad in my mouth. It conjured images of Matthew, his bewildered expression as I'd abruptly fled his presence. But there was no time to dwell on that now. I pushed it—and him—out of my mind.

She raised and lowered one shoulder. "I'm always hungry."

I gave her a half smile. "Then we best get you to lunch."

After a few scouting glances across the yard, I nodded to Maggie, who squirreled through a section of loose planking and darted over the sandy lawn until she was safe under the first-story awning. I joined her a few seconds later.

"Do you think anyone saw us?"

Here on the porch, sheltered from the ocean breeze, the air was stifling. A drop of sweat ran down my spine. I pulled at the gray fabric of my dress, which was sticking to my chest as if pasted, and fanned myself with my other hand. "No, I think we're fine." I placed a hand to my cheek, feeling its warmth. "You get on inside. Just tell them I had you out here sweeping and you lost track of time."

"But I don't have a broom."

"Say you left it with me."

"But you don't have a broom either!"

I smiled and gestured toward the side of the building, where a weathered broom stood propped in the corner. "Yes, I do."

Maggie glanced between it and me, chewing her lip. Her fingers fluttered at her sides, and with an internal groan, I noticed there were streaks of butter down her white dress. I could only hope no one would notice. "Sister Annie," she said finally, eyebrows meeting in the middle.

I didn't correct her this time. "Yes?"

"Ain't that lying?"

My chest went tight. Though the smile remained on my face, it was merely paint. Frozen. On the inside, I was suddenly churning with guilt. "Yes," I managed tightly. "Yes, it is a lie. But it's just a little one."

Maggie's brown eyes narrowed. The tiniest sliver of tongue was visible out the side of her mouth. Then, with one quick motion, she snatched the broom from its corner, holding it in her outstretched hand. Her lips were set in a determined line. "Give it to me," she lisped.

"What?"

"Give me the broom."

"But you already—"

"Take it, and then give it back."

My fingers hovered over the broom handle for a moment before wrapping themselves around it. Maggie let out a long breath, took a step backward, then held out her hand again. I placed the broom in her small palm. Hunching her back, she gave four big sweeps across the porch, raising dust which then settled immediately back on the wooden planks. Satisfied, she shoved the broom into my hand.

"There," she said. "Now it ain't a lie. You had me sweep." She grinned, revealing that precious teeth-size hole.

The tightness from my chest crept to my throat as I remembered the inescapable confrontation waiting for me inside these walls, the inevitable conclusion.

How on earth was I supposed to say goodbye to that smile?

I gave her a strained smile back and nodded, shooing her away. Gripping the broom in sweaty hands, I watched the last of her blonde hair disappear through the side door before taking a few half-hearted passes at the porch, willing tears from my eyes. When it became obvious no one was coming to check up on her story and I'd finally forced my heart back into its rightful spot, I returned the broom to the corner and slipped inside. The smell of freshly baked bread enveloped me. Blinking against the dim light, I tried to ignore the rumble in my stomach and crept toward the back staircase.

I'd gone to the beach to clear my mind. I'd only made it more muddled. I couldn't face Mother Camillus. Couldn't bear the exposure of my lies, the devastation it would cause to those about whom I cared deeply. It didn't matter that I had nowhere to go. I needed to run. Now. Before things got even more painful.

But I was only four steps up when it came:

"Miss Odell."

My stomach dropped to my knees. I took a deep breath before turning, trying to steel myself for what I knew was coming next.

Mother Camillus stood at the foot of the stairs. Shadows danced across her face, but I didn't need to see it to know its severity. She was barely over thirty by the look of it, but her countenance carried a sternness that made nuns twice her age approach her with reverence. That wasn't to say she was harsh; I'd witnessed her gentleness with the children, her warm hugs and soft-spoken care. I'd even seen her laughing during a performance of Noah's Ark put on by the youngest of the orphans. Though a strict disciplinarian, she delighted in her charges.

She just never seemed to take delight in *me*.

"M-M-Mother Camillus," I stammered. "I—"

"I've been looking for you." Her Irish accent was thick. But, rather than jolly, it made her voice sound terrifying.

"I know. Sister Felicitus informed me. I was—"

"And yet you did not wait outside my office like she instructed you to do."

I bit the inside of my cheek. Though darkness covered her eyes, I could feel them boring into me. "I . . . I decided to do some chores. I did not want to waste any time." The lie sounded weak, even to me.

Mother Camillus raised her chin, as if smelling the dishonesty on me. And maybe she did. After all, Maggie and I had been next to the popcorn machine long enough for its aroma to seep into our clothes.

I held my breath.

"Well, I'm here now," she said in a clipped voice. "If you'll follow me to my office, please." Then she turned, black shoes clicking against the scuffed wood, and disappeared down the dim hallway, not bothering to see if I would follow. She knew I would.

And I did.

Her office was as hot and stuffy as the rest of building, yet I still somehow found a chill traveling over my arms as I entered. I hadn't been inside since the night I arrived; Mother Camillus preferred to give me my daily assignments in the hallway just outside. In a place like St. Mary's, which offered very little in the way of privacy, Mother Superior guarded hers fiercely. Not that I blamed her; there wasn't a day gone by that I didn't miss the solitude I'd taken for granted—along with so many other things—in my bedroom back in New York. Even though I'd been invited—no, *ordered*—inside this room, I couldn't help but feel I wasn't welcome.

The office was small but tidy, with not even a whiff of the mildew that invaded every other part of the orphanage. A wide, solitary window offered the only light, leaving the corners darkened but illuminating a plain wooden desk covered in papers and books. There were no trinkets, no photographs, no personal touches. Only a desk, a shelf full of green bound volumes, and a painting of

Jesus, which hung from the wall directly behind Mother Camillus's head. His kind gaze seemed directed at her rather than me.

Mother Camillus rested her hands on her desk and interlocked her fingers, staring at me beneath raised brows. "Miss Odell."

"Yes, Mother Superior?"

She let out a heavy breath. "Miss Odell, St. Mary's Orphan Asylum has been an integral part of the Galveston community since 1874, when Bishop Dubuis bought the land between Green's Bayou and the oceanfront, far from the hustle and bustle of the city proper. He was determined to make it a safe, healing home for all those children left behind by the yellow fever outbreak that decimated this island. When it opened, it was the first of its kind in all of Texas. We, the Sisters of Charity of the Incarnate Word, have been tasked ever since with keeping the bishop's vision alive. And it is a heavy responsibility, one we do not take lightly. We are answerable to God for the heart and soul of every single lost child who walks through that door." She paused. "And that includes you."

I opened my mouth, but she held up a hand.

"When you arrived that night, during the storm, I simply . . ." She coughed. Wetted her lips. "Well, I could not turn you away. You were not technically a child, but you were a soul in need; that much was obvious."

I was struck by the surprising note of emotion in her voice. But as quickly as it had arisen, it was gone, her tone once again steady.

"Because of this, we have allowed you to stay with us these past months. To your credit, though your attitude and work ethic expose a heart unused to manual labor, you have contributed to the work of the mission—as I've asked you to do—and for that, I pass along my gratitude."

My fingers tightened around the folds of my dress, dampening the fabric with sweat. Here it came.

"But . . . as we discussed upon your arrival, this arrangement was to be temporary. As you know, you're past the age at which we usually release unadopted children into the community. By this point in their lives, most of our charges have secured steady employment and housing. They've made a commitment to follow God and contribute to society."

And I haven't. She didn't need to say it. Her pressed lips said more than enough.

"So, I'm sorry to say, Miss Odell, our time together has come to an end."

I knew it was coming. Had known for a long time. And still her words cut as sharply as glass. It didn't matter that they were spoken gently or that another twinge of surprising sympathy flickered through Mother Camillus's eyes. All that mattered was I had been set adrift once again.

"Mother Superior, please." A sob rose in my throat, choking me. "I beg of you, give me a little more time. I'll do whatever you need me to do around here. I'll take breakfast, lunch, and dinner duty. I'll scrub the soiled linens four times a week instead of three. I'll—"

"Miss Odell—"

"I'll even take night shift! I'll prepare bottles, prep lesson plans, clean the chapel. Whatever you need. And I won't complain anymore, I swear. I'll—"

"Miss Odell—"

"—do my chores without a word. I'll even start reading the Bible like you told me I should. Every night. I can—"

"Miss Odell!"

Her raised voice cut through my panic, rendering me speechless but doing little to still my inner trembling. I looked down to discover I'd been digging my nails into my palms. Crescent-shaped lines of blood now fringed my skin. From outside the window came the ever-present shriek of the gulls. Had it really only been a few hours since I'd awoken irritated by their cries? Now I'd give anything for the promise of being able to rise to their calls for a few more days. Unshed tears stung my eyes. "Please," I managed, "don't throw me out."

Mother Camillus's shoulders slumped. She leaned back in her chair, seeming to melt into her thick black robes. Clutching at the silver cross hanging from her neck, she sucked in her cheeks, considering me. "I had a meeting yesterday," she said finally, "with the bishop."

My lower lip quivered, but I kept my watery eyes on her face, trying to discern her meaning.

"Just a normal meeting. He likes to keep apprised of how things are going down here, to see if we need anything. Nothing out of the ordinary. Except for one tiny thing. A newspaper. On the bishop's desk." She chewed at a small piece of skin on her lip for a moment before continuing. "I tried not to read it. But I couldn't help myself. Because there, staring up at me, from a picture right below the fold, was you, Miss Odell. In a great fancy hat and pretty frilled dress. But you all the same."

She paused, allowing the words to land.

"Kathleen Anne McDaniel from Croton-on-Hudson, New York. Apparently, she's been missing for several months. Seems there was rather messy business surrounding her disappearance. Her father is desperate to find her. He's taken out ads in nearly every newspaper across the country, begging folks to keep an eye out for her. Offering a hefty reward for her safe return."

Bile rose in the back of my throat. Though I gripped the sides of my chair, trying to clench my muscles, every one of them began to shudder uncontrollably.

It did not go unnoticed. The nun leaned forward. "Out of compassion, I have not pried into your past. The night you arrived here, it was obvious you had experienced something traumatic. But this story . . . It concerns me greatly. You are running from something, and one can only imagine why a daughter would put her father through such heartbreak. I can only surmise it's something . . . untoward. And I will not risk anything happening to these children or the women who have dedicated their lives to caring for them. So, I will give you this one chance to come clean, Miss McDaniel: Why are you here?"

The sound of my real name physically pained me. I hated the sound of it, the weight it carried, the memories.

The betrayal.

I wanted to tell her the truth. As the tears finally broke free and began to stream down my face, I desperately wanted to come clean. I was so tired. Tired of hiding. Tired of lying.

But, with lips salty from tears, I said the only thing I could: "I can't be found."

Mother Camillus remained still; the only sign of life was the long stream of air I heard passing through her nostrils. But she did not move. Did not blink. Did not speak. For several long, agonizing moments, we simply stared at one another, a thousand unspoken questions filling the unbearable silence. Even the seagulls had flown away to voice their displeasure elsewhere.

Finally, after what seemed like an eternity, she leaned back in her chair again. It squeaked rudely. "Very well. If you refuse to tell me the truth—"

"It's not that I don't want to. I—"

She held up a hand, silencing me once again. So much power she held in those five bony fingers. "Without the truth, I cannot help you."

I closed my eyes, dropping my chin to my chest.

"But . . ."

My eyes flew open.

". . . that does not mean I am hardening my heart toward you. God is merciful, and He calls us to be as well."

I raised my head to find her dark eyes peering at me above steepled fingers.

"You may have aged out of our purview, but if you truly wish to start anew, as it seems you do, we can still help you. The Sisters of Charity welcome any woman, regardless of her past, to a better future. One lived in service to the Almighty."

I blinked. Though the tears had lessened, my eyes still burned, and my head felt heavy, throbbing from the exertion. My mind struggled to make sense of her words beyond the fog.

"You could begin the process of taking the vows."

"Vows? What vows?"

Mother Camillus raised her eyebrows and, as she did so, the haze cleared.

"You mean I could become a nun?"

She gave a small, curt nod.

"But I'm not even Catholic."

"The first of many imperfections that will need correcting. You would be sent away to begin your conversion courses, wherever the bishop decides, followed by lessons and charity work, as you begin molding your heart into the image of a servant. After that, you would—"

"I would still have to leave St. Mary's?"

Mother Camillus's face softened. "This is not a punishment. I know you're fond of the place. And of the children." She smiled sadly, and I knew she was thinking about Maggie. I certainly was. "But this is how the process works. It is just one of the many ways you will learn to set aside your own wants and desires and go where the good Lord is calling you."

I swallowed hard, my brain racing to catch up with the emotions coursing through my body. I *had* been found out, but rather than forcing me home or back on the streets, Mother Camillus was offering me a future.

A chance to live a life that mattered.

It was an answer to prayers I'd long since stopped praying. Only a few short months ago, I'd wanted a chance to follow my whims, to go out into the world and discover who I was, who I could be. Now, after everything that had happened, those desires were still there, but they had been overshadowed, replaced by something deeper. More urgent.

I wanted a home.

I wanted family.

I wanted every single thing that had been stolen from me that night.

I couldn't have that. I understood. But Mother Camillus was offering me a way to have everything else. As a nun I'd have shelter, companionship, purpose. And I'd be safe; it was the one place I'd be almost guaranteed not to be found. Ever.

But it would also mean living a life in service to a God who had let me down.

Who had allowed the very foundation of my world to crumble, brick by brick.

Who I no longer trusted.

Mother Camillus seemed to see the battle waging inside my heart. To my great surprise, she reached across the desk and wrapped one of my hands in hers. It was soft, nothing like the clamminess in my own.

"I know it's a big decision, and certainly not one to take lightly. Ours is a life of hardship, but it is also one of great reward. I beg you to at least consider my offer. I will give you until Saturday morning to think it over."

Saturday. It was already after noon on Thursday.

Less than forty-eight hours to decide my entire future.

I rose to leave on wobbly legs. I could barely feel the doorknob beneath my hands. When Mother Camillus called to me one last time, it was as if she were speaking underwater.

"Jesus offers us a new life, Miss McDaniel. A new identity. This is something we nuns take to heart." She paused. "Your days don't have to be spent running away from whatever it is that's haunting you. You can choose to run *toward* something instead."

"The tropical storm is central this morning slightly north of Key West. It has increased somewhat in energy and caused severe northeast gales over portions of southern Florida. It will probably continue slowly northward and its effects will be felt as far as the lower portion of the middle Atlantic coast by Friday night."

US WEATHER BUREAU IN WASHINGTON, DC, TO ALL WEATHER STATIONS
Thursday, September 6, 1900

FIVE

FRIDAY, SEPTEMBER 7, 1900
GALVESTON, TEXAS

The visions and dreams that haunted me back in New York had stopped upon my arrival in Galveston. I had spent so long wishing away those dreams, fearful of what they meant. Now I would have given anything to slip into them again, even knowing their tragic truth.

Anything was better than the nightmares.

The blood, the guns, the wails.

The fear.

But, on what could well be one of my last mornings in Galveston, a different anxiety woke me, even before the gulls.

In the pale-gray twilight, I slipped from my nightgown and into my dress, careful to keep an eye on Emily as she slumbered, peaceful as a newborn, in the bed beside mine.

I hadn't told her about Mother Camillus's offer. My roommate was kind, but even she wouldn't be able to avoid the inevitable questions telling her would bring. Questions I couldn't bring myself to answer. Instead, I had feigned a headache—what was one more lie?—and curled up in bed, facing away from her so she would be unable to see the tears I was powerless to stop.

If she heard them, she didn't say anything.

Which only made me cry harder.

Now, in the morning light, my tears were gone, leaving salty tracks down my face. Trying to splash as little as possible so as not to awaken my friend, I scrubbed my face over the washbasin and did a cursory once-over with my toothbrush before grabbing my shoes, tiptoeing to the door, and stealing out into the still-darkened hallway.

The orphanage was quiet; not even the breakfast-duty nuns had taken up their posts. It would still be another hour before the time I usually joined them. But Mother Camillus had given me the day off, a small mercy considering the monumental decision that lay ahead. And I didn't intend to waste it.

Venturing out would be dangerous; if the newspaper article Mother Camillus had seen was any indication, there were sure to be eyes and ears roaming the streets of Galveston, searching for me—and their hefty reward. But, with my bleeding heart so very near the surface, staying in—facing Maggie, Emily, or any of the others—felt even riskier. And anyway, I no longer looked much like the girl in the grainy photograph in the paper, a ghost of a similarity that would vanish upon second glance. Only my flaming red hair would stand out from the physical description. So I made sure to grab one of the bonnets the nuns kept on hand for the older girls' chaperoned strolls into town. Tying its satin ribbons under my chin, I took a deep breath and, wincing as the thick wooden door popped and creaked, stepped out onto the front porch.

The sun was only an inkling on the horizon, and yet it was already hot. Unlike yesterday, however, there was no breeze. No clouds. Instead, the air hung thick and heavy like saturated curtains;

I was sweating even before I reached the shoreline. The Gulf was calm as I made my way eastward, the crunch of broken shells beneath my feet punctuating the dull thumps of waves knocking lazily against the sand, too sluggish to even bring the usual smell of fish.

The trolley wasn't running yet. The gurgle of the Pavilion's fountain was the only sound as I bypassed the still-sleeping pier and headed north, away from the shore and into the city proper. Rows of modest, two-story houses and lime-washed bungalows lined the numbered streets running north and south. Small, fenced yards surrounded them, many with whisps of cardinal flowers, hearty rosebushes, and charming patches of black-eyed Susans. A few even held chickens and goats, already noisily announcing the morning's arrival. I smiled at them as I passed, memories of lazy afternoons spent inside our barn in New York swelling inside me. Instantly, an ache spread through my chest, and I averted my eyes, desperate to see them no more.

Making my way farther northward, the houses gave way to shops and businesses, mighty in their brick and stone. The city's slumber was giving way too. Already the air was filled with the scent of fresh-cut lumber from the Hildebrandt Mill and coffee from the bulk roasters set up in the alleys between Mechanic and Market streets. And, of course, all around was the inescapable smell of horses, of industry, of the sea.

Not for the first time, I longed to put pen to paper. To share this island with Hazel, Margarite, and Louisa, all of the sights, scents, and sounds. How giddy they'd be, thrilled by the endless possibilities this port city offered. Not that I would write. No, not that I *could*. The risk of discovery was small but still far too great.

My European friends—these women who were as dear to me as sisters—were yet another part of my old life I had to leave behind.

I walked as far north as I could before the sea, once again, hemmed me in. Galveston Bay lay between me and the Texas mainland, miles of stone-capped piers stretching out like fingers toward it. Despite the early hour, each one was already filled with crates and boxes being loaded or unloaded with ropes and pulleys from the plethora of ships waiting in the harbor. The shouts of dockworkers arose in a dozen different languages as bales of cotton, bushels of corn, barrels of flour, and bundles of lumber all awaited the next leg of their journey. On the horizon, I could just make out the train and wagon bridges connecting the island to Texas City across the bay.

The ache in my chest returned. But, this time, for a very different reason. I'd crossed one of the bridges not so very long ago. And soon, I would have to cross it again, no matter what decision I made.

I'd begun my stroll with the intent to think. To plan. To choose. But I wasn't ready to do that just yet.

I turned south again, away from the rest of the world and back toward the cocoon to which I was desperate to cling. I ventured west on the Strand, the heart of downtown Galveston, just waking up as the first rays of golden sunlight began washing over the tiled roofs. The low heels of my boots clicked against the hammered wooden blocks of the pavement, echoing against the knee-high curbs. Soon, this street would be filled with carriages and sulkies, bicyclists and pedestrians. Men with handlebar mustaches and three-piece suits and straw hats, women with petticoats and parasols, toddlers begging for ice cream or cherry phosphate soda. Bathers with hair still damp from their swim. The electric streetcars would hum, the saloons would fill with cigar smoke, and hooves would pound on the pavement like mallets, carrying lawyers, bankers, and businessmen into the promise of progress.

I'd heard Galveston called "the New York of the Southwest." It wasn't hard to see why. Perhaps that's why I'd felt so at home here: a little taste of the familiar when everything else in my life—in my heart—had become foreign.

But all that busyness would come later. At this hour, there was only a trickle of customers, the lone drunk sleeping off his vice in the alleyway, and the shopkeepers sweeping their stoops.

I paused in front of one, using my hand as a visor to peer through the window into the darkened interior. MacDoogal always had new animals on display at the front of his pet shop. One day there were turtles, heads poking in and out of their shells as they munched on hearts of romaine; another time, it was hermit crabs, their tiny shells painted in all manner of purples, oranges, and blues. There was even a litter of dachshund puppies once; I'd stood there for nearly thirty minutes giggling as their squat sausage bodies tumbled over one another in a clumsy attempt at play. I wondered what I'd see today.

My eyes searched until they found a few fuzzy masses, huddled in the corner, as far from the window as possible. I narrowed my gaze. Floppy, clover ears. Pink noses. Delicate paws and thick, rounded bottoms.

Guinea pigs.

It should have been a familiar sensation by now, this simultaneous swelling and breaking of my heart. And yet it wasn't. I clutched at my throat, willing myself to keep breathing. Memories twisted in me as sharp as a knife. I knew well the feel of their soft little bodies, the adorable sound of their wheeks. And yet the sight of these creatures brought about a pain different from the one I felt about the other animals I'd left behind. This pain was one born of guilt and regret, of broken promises I'd never wanted to make in the first place.

A sudden thud behind me caused me to jump. I spun around, finding a small cloud of dust rising from a recently dropped stack of newspapers. A boy, no older than twelve, stood beside them, his back turned, pulling another load from the cart. I leaned over, half expecting to see my own face smiling up at me from the front page. Instead, the large headline proclaimed *American Forces Occupy Peking.*

I frowned, relief short-lived. My interest in the affairs of the world had been starved over the past few months; the sisters strictly forbade newspapers within the orphanage. But it appeared nothing had changed—we had simply exchanged one war in Asia with another. I wondered if the Filipinos had ever acquiesced to our rule.

I turned my head, taking in another headline. *Wild to See Roosevelt*, it said, with a picture of Mr. Roosevelt himself waving to supporters from the back of a moving train. Despite my unease, I felt a slight ripple of nostalgia wash over me as I skimmed what was visible of the article. *The recently announced vice presidential candidate made a stop in Houston yesterday, where he was greeted by riotous applause and unprecedented crowds. Mr. Roosevelt gave a short speech . . .*

I smiled. So he had decided to run after all. Just as everyone knew he would.

"You wanna keep reading, it'll cost two cents, miss."

The towheaded newsie dropped another load of papers onto the stack, then stuck out an ink-stained palm. He was trying to look tough, all square shoulders and twisted lips, but his face still held the rounded cherubic glow of boyhood.

"No thank you."

He scowled.

I turned from him quickly, ducking back under the galleries shading the sidewalks, past a display of gleaming red apples stacked high beneath an awning outside Thomas Gonzales and Sons Grocery. My stomach grumbled, and I paused, admiring them.

"Can I help you?"

A man with skin the color of toffee poked his head out from the doorway. The tips of his dark mustache were greased to points.

"No," I said, dipping my chin to hide my face. "I was just . . . admiring your produce."

He grinned. "We aren't quite open for the day yet, but I'll sell you an apple if you'd like."

Color bloomed in my cheeks. *Sell.* As if I had money to spend. For a newspaper or an apple.

"No thank you," I stuttered, taking a step back. "I'm fine."

"Are you sure? I—"

But I simply spun around, cutting off his words as cleanly as scissors, and hurried off down the street. More and more people were crowding into the space, and I kept my bonnet pulled low, red hair tucked beneath the white brim.

Enough nonsense. I needed to think. If I didn't accept Mother Camillus's offer, this would be my life. I had no employable skills. No way to earn money besides . . . No, I would not let my mind wander to those professions of ill repute. But how would I eat? Where would I live? I didn't even have the money to get myself out of Galveston, to another charity house that might not recognize my face and possibly take me in. I'd be constantly pursued by hunger, by the elements . . . and by the men who would never give up the hunt.

The air seemed to sour at this realization. I pulled my bonnet tighter, skin prickling. Every eye appeared to be looking at me now. Shadowy men lurked around corners, disappearing when I reached them, and shopkeepers whispered behind their newspapers. Up ahead, two men smoked cigarettes in front of their drays, ignoring the donkeys pawing anxiously at the ground, their glares narrowed in my direction.

This was a bad idea. I never should have come here. I was stupid to think a bonnet would hide me, that a convent dress would be enough to fool my pursuers.

I wasn't safe here. I wasn't safe anywhere.

Sudden movement flickered in the corner of my vision. To my left, a man emerged from the alleyway, bowler hat tugged low. He walked briskly toward me, hands in his pockets, steps thudding on the wooden sidewalk.

My breath caught in my throat.

Those shoulders, that beard. I hadn't known the man long, but it had been enough to burn his physique into my brain.

Otto Zimmerman.

I should have known he would be the one sent. That he would be the one to finally find me.

I forced my sluggish body to move. Measured, deliberate steps. Swift but not panicked, nothing to betray any recognition. Just an ordinary girl out on a stroll. Perhaps a nanny out on errands for her impatient mistress. I counted my breaths, long, painful, and shaking, making it to ten before allowing myself to glance over my shoulder.

He was still there. Closer this time.

And no longer bothering to hide his face.

I broke into a run. My boots wobbled on the uneven pavement. The coarse fabric of my dress acted like adhesive, binding my legs; my muscles quickly grew weary. But still I ran. The crowd was thicker now, and I had to dodge landaus and victorias, their calash tops lifted against the rising sun. Pedestrians cried out in alarm as I pushed past, finely dressed ladies throwing up their hands as if I were a common, thieving street rat. I bumped the end of one monocled man's cane, causing him to stumble. I didn't stop to apologize, and I didn't dare attempt to look over my shoulder at my pursuer.

He was gaining. I could *feel* it.

Just past Sheldon's Commissary, where the smell of yesterday's beef mingled with today's fresh fish, I darted in front of a passing sulky, causing its driver to let loose a string of curse words, then immediately turned to dash back to the other side of the street, hoping to lose my pursuer in the confusion. Because I was still watching the sulky, however, I failed to see another shape materialize directly in front of me. I crashed into it with a force that knocked the air from my lungs.

"Excuse me!" came a startled voice. "I didn't . . ."

Black spots swam in my vision. I couldn't see. Couldn't breathe. Couldn't *stop*.

A pair of strong arms gripped mine. "Not Nun? Is that you?"

I blinked. Matthew Richter's face floated in front of me, his brows furrowed.

"Annie?"

Although I recognized him, it did not put my mind at ease. Still it spun, urging me onward. Away. I wrestled under his grasp, straining my neck to look over my shoulder. Behind me, the Strand moved on, oblivious to my terror, aside from a few grumbling glances from the patrons I'd accosted. Carriages squeaked. Horses neighed. Pedestrians ambled.

But my pursuer was nowhere to be seen.

"Annie, are you okay?"

I swung my head around. Up and down the street, shops were opening, restaurants were serving, businesses were booming. There were people everywhere. But not him. He was gone. Somehow, he was just . . . gone.

I struggled to catch my breath. Sweat dripped down my back, mooring my undergarments to my skin.

"Annie?"

Trying to swallow my heart, which felt as if it were attempting to escape through my throat, I forced my attention back to Matthew. He was dressed in a white button-down, slightly yellowed with age, with a brown-and-black checkered vest and black trousers. His dark hair was slicked back from his forehead, shining almost violet in the sun.

He pressed his lips together, revealing those dimples I pretended not to notice. "Are you all right?" he asked again.

It took every ounce of energy I had left to turn the corners of my mouth up into a smile. "Yes, I . . ." Suddenly remembering myself, I took a step backward, out of his grip. "Forgive me, Mr. Richter. I did not mean to run into you like that."

He tilted his head to his shoulder. "No need to apologize. I should have been paying more attention. But what's got you in such a tizzy this morning?"

"I . . ." I licked my dry lips, tasting salt. "Silly me, I . . . I thought I saw a rat."

"A rat?"

I tittered. "Such ugly, vicious things, don't you think? It gave me quite a startle."

He put his hands in his pockets, considering. "Yes, I suppose they are. But they're just trying to survive. Kind of like the rest of us, right?"

I gave a nervous, high-pitched chuckle. "Right."

"What are you doing out here? On the Strand, I mean. You're a long way from St. Mary's."

"Just . . . out for a stroll."

"Alone?"

I gave a small, noncommittal shrug. "I needed some air."

"All right." He wasn't buying it. I could tell by the way he rolled himself up on the balls of his feet and curled his shoulders. But, still, his next words were kind. Nonchalant. "Care for some company?"

Yes. The thought was immediate and unbidden, sending tingles from my gut right down to the tips of my toes. Matthew Richter was the last person I needed to spend time with right now; my mind was muddled enough as it was. And yet, despite it all, I *wanted* to spend time with him.

After all, this was, perhaps, my last chance, a sudden realization that pained me more than I cared to admit.

Not to mention I had seen that man. I *had*. He had chased me. I didn't imagine it.

And, though he had disappeared like a vapor in the mist, that didn't mean he was gone. He was still out there somewhere. Watching. Waiting.

I suppressed a shiver, plastering a smile I did not feel onto my face. "I'd love some."

Matthew offered his elbow, which I accepted hesitantly. There was nothing improper about it. All around us, the city grumbled about its business, my earlier incivility forgotten, the merchants and customers oblivious to a couple of nobodies in their midst. There was too much work to be done. And yet still I was filled with unease. Part of it was lingering paranoia, that feeling of being watched by unknown eyes from the shadows. But another part came from watching myself. From seeing my hand wrapped around Matthew's arm, being close enough to see the nick on his jawbone where he'd cut himself shaving, smelling the musky scent of his pomade.

Despite everything, it stirred something in me. A feeling, a longing that immediately ignited a flame of guilt.

This was right. This was wrong.

How was I supposed to know which was true anymore? Absolutely nothing had made sense since that night when everything I'd known for certain had crumbled. I could no longer trust my instincts.

I could no longer trust *anything*.

This, coupled with the heat and the last dregs of adrenaline draining from my limbs, suddenly made me feel faint. My fingers clenched involuntarily, and I could feel Matthew's sinewy muscles tense under my grip.

"You sure you're all right?"

"I'm fine."

He sucked in his cheeks but didn't argue, instead placing one hand over mine and navigating me gently down a side street. I tried not to flinch at the feel of his skin. We bypassed Mechanic Street, with its blacksmiths and greasers, and Market Street, filled with shoppers already loaded down with parcels, not slowing until the din of activity had faded to a hum. The browns and grays of the cityscape were replaced with the greens of lawns and shrubbery, and the sudden appearance of towering oaks gave us a much-needed break from the overpowering sun. Matthew took a sudden turn left, easing his pace and removing his hand from atop mine. My flesh burned at its absence.

I recognized our location. A wide boulevard with a well-landscaped median, beautiful despite the tracks and the electric wires hanging overhead for the trolley. In addition to the lofty oaks, bushes of oleander and blue sage added further splashes of color, broken up by the wide yellow green of palm leaves. It felt a world away from the Strand, and yet not very far at all.

Because lining either side of the street were the palaces of the Strand's elite.

Broadway Avenue. Where Galveston's wealth came home.

Each house along this stretch had its own personality; nevertheless, every single one looked as if it belonged on an estate in Europe rather than on a sandbar at the edge of the Gulf. Rambling gables. Ornate Gothic details coupled with touches of Spanish flair. Brick and iron, stone and tile. They screamed money. Power. Privilege.

The type of house I once called home.

I dropped my hand from Matthew's elbow. A slight shuffle in his step was the only reaction, though I could feel his eyes on me, voicing questions his mouth thankfully did not ask. Instead, he put his hands in his pockets and craned his neck, taking in the scenery.

"You know, I've walked this street a hundred times, and I never get tired of it. Kind of makes you forget you're in Texas, doesn't it?"

I did not respond.

"They're all great, I suppose. But this one . . . This one is my favorite." He stopped abruptly and moved his arm in a wide arc, gesturing.

I glanced up from under my bonnet. The building before us was more chateau than house, with two rounded towers flanking a wide, central stairway. Black iron railings lined porticos on both the first and second stories, disappearing behind the structure in a curtain of wide palms. The large stones making up its edifice were more brown than gray, giving it the appearance of sandstone, though I was sure the actual construction was made of something much more solid. I could only imagine the airy light inside, let in by the rows and rows of long, rectangular windows.

"The Gresham House." Matthew used his hand as a visor as he peered up at it. "Solicitor, I believe. Dabbles in the railroad too. Swimming in money, obviously."

"Obviously," I said quietly.

I pressed onward. After a few moments, Matthew followed. He knew the names of all the houses, pointing them out as we passed. Trueheart, Blum, Kenison. He was enthusiastic. Giddy, almost. So much so I don't believe he realized I wasn't looking. Wasn't even listening. I was too lost inside myself to let any of his words in.

I'd tried to push it down. Tried to will it away. But the truth was I missed it. So help me, I missed it. These houses, this life. The way people looked at me. Never having to worry about food or clothing, never giving thought to the day-to-day struggle that had been my world for the past few months. Everything had been so *easy*. It had been *safe*.

Why hadn't I been content to just leave well enough alone?

As Matthew's excited commentary continued, I glanced at the

house to my left, rising out of the ground like a fortress. Accepting Mother Camillus's offer would essentially be putting a padlock on the door to that kind of house—that kind of life—forever. And yet, despite everything that had happened, I wasn't sure I was ready to throw away the key.

Nunnery or destitution weren't the only options; I could go back. Swallow my pride, paint a smile on my lips. Face the consequences. It wouldn't be pretty. It would be downright scary, in fact, taking up those shackles once again. He was furious, for sure. But he wouldn't harm me.

Or, at least, that's what I used to believe.

But nothing could shake the memory of the look in his eyes the night I'd left. The rage. The—there was no other word for it—*viciousness*. No matter how the newspapers portrayed him, I found it hard to believe he was a grieving father. He was an angry one. I had betrayed him. Never mind that he had been the one to first break that trust; I was the guilty party here.

But if I apologized? Groveled? Came running home with my tail tucked like the scared Kitty Kat I truly was and took the punishment I knew I had coming? Would he forgive me then? Did he still even want me? He *had* sent Mr. Zimmerman for me, after all.

But to retrieve me . . . or to hurt me?

I wasn't sure what frightened me more: that I didn't know the answer . . . or that I was asking the question in the first place.

And yet, they were moot queries. Back inside that life, I knew I would be miserable. I was culpable for my sins, yes, but it did not change the fact that he had his own. I wasn't sure I'd ever be able to forgive; I would most certainly never forget.

If I went home, said I was sorry, perhaps my father and I could find a way to move forward.

Except . . . it wasn't my home anymore.

And I *wasn't* sorry.

Not after everything I'd seen, after hearing all the things I wished he'd never said.

Therein lay my true problem: I wasn't sure I was strong enough to go back. But I wasn't sure I was strong enough to walk away completely either.

"Hey," came a quiet voice beside me.

I blinked. Matthew had stopped, and I'd been too wrapped up in myself to even notice. I felt my cheeks go hot as I backtracked to where he stood. "Sorry." My lips were numb and heavy. "Must still be a little overheated from all the excitement. What were you saying?"

Matthew studied me, hands still in his pockets. After a moment, he rolled his shoulders. "Nothing. It's not important."

"No," I protested, shame burning my throat. "I'm sure it was. Forgive me. I've just . . . I've had a busy morning. I'm not myself."

"Want me to walk you home?"

Home. He had no idea how loaded that word was.

I shook my head. For as twisted as my heart was here with Matthew, I knew it would be even worse back at St. Mary's.

"Okay." He tilted his head from side to side. "The beach then? No popcorn today—I'm off-duty—but I could get you a lemonade. Or some flavored ice."

I shook my head again. As tempting as it was, I knew there was no way my anxious stomach could handle anything at the moment.

He crossed his arms over his chest, causing the fabric of his vest to ride up slightly. He scrutinized me, drumming his fingers on his biceps. Suddenly, he jumped, snapping his fingers. "I got it!"

I started. "What?"

He pointed a finger at my nose playfully. "I'm not giving you a chance to say no to this one." With a wide grin, he grabbed my hand and wrapped it once again around his elbow.

"Matthew! What—"

But now it was his turn not to listen. His eyes searched out the nearest street sign. Then, satisfied, he gave a gentle tug and began leading me north. I struggled to keep up with the pep in his step.

"Matthew!"

"Never fear, Miss Not Nun. You're safe with me." He gave me a sideways wink that made my insides flutter. "I'm taking you to see the future."

SIX

MARCH 1900
CROTON-ON-HUDSON, NEW YORK

"Shall we spend the morning together?"

I looked up from my poached egg and croissant. I'd barely made a dent in either, even though it was my favorite breakfast. I'd been touched that Father had remembered (although perhaps it had actually been Miss Dover, our cook), yet I struggled to bring fork to lips. I was exhausted from lack of sleep, a condition only exacerbated by a still-sour stomach, brought about by last night's champagne.

And my own disquieted heart.

Stella had helped me dress smartly that morning in a navy side-plaited skirt with seven gores and three rows of satin piping around the hem. It was topped by an ornate shirtwaist with princess tucks below the elbow and a tucked Gibson collar, its chest and neckline silhouetted with lace. After piling my unruly red curls into a tight bun at my neck and pinching my cheeks for some color, I'd hoped no one would be the wiser about my restless night.

Father stared at me over the rim of his coffee cup, the smoke from his morning pipe rendering the air between us hazy. The newspaper he'd been reading now lay folded over his own plate. The last vestiges of sausage grease made the edges translucent.

"I'm sorry?" I asked meekly.

"I said, let's spend the morning together. To make up for our lack of time yesterday."

Secretly, I was thrilled, but I tried my best to maintain ladylike humility. "Oh, that's not necessary. I know you're a busy man—"

"Nonsense." He let out another puff of smoke from between his teeth. "I'm never too busy for my daughter. Besides, wouldn't you like to see the progress we've made since you've been gone? I meant what I said last night—you are a part of what we're building here. Wouldn't you like to see it?"

Despite my lingering unease, I couldn't help a smile from pulling up the corners of my mouth. "If you're sure, Father."

"Of course I'm sure!" He rose, taking one final swig of his coffee. "You finish up and put on some suitable walking clothes. Something warm—it's quite chilly, I'm afraid. Have Archie come get me from the study when you're ready."

"Yes, Father."

He kissed the top of my head, then tilted my chin upward, his gray eyes roaming over my cheeks. "And ask Stella to run some powder over your nose. That Swiss air seems to have multiplied your freckles."

An hour later, I stood on the front portico, resting a hand on one of the stone columns, staring out across the pastures and forests that made up our estate. I had an urge to run to the barn and see the animals, one I would have given in to if I hadn't been so anxious to start this time with Father. The frosty air burned my lungs and, despite being clothed in a beautiful modified Robespierre coat that perfectly matched my skirt, I could still feel the chill through every layer of fabric. I wondered if the nip would at least color my cheeks enough for Father's taste; even with all her tutting, Stella's powder did little for my freckles.

"There she is!"

My father's jovial voice cut through the late-morning air, instantly warming me. He exited the house, shadowed by two men. There was no mistaking the distinct shape of Otto Zimmerman, lumbering a pace or two behind, but I did not recognize the second gentleman, whose gait was much more refined than his heavy-footed companion's.

"My daughter, Kathleen, will be joining us on our tour today. She's just returned from Switzerland and is desperate for a bit of American ingenuity after all that time on the Continent."

The two men laughed. I smiled, Brillantmont's training kicking in on instinct, even though I failed to see the humor.

"Kathleen, may I present to you, Mr. Theodore Walsh?"

I gave a slight bend of my knees. "How do you do, Mr. Walsh?"

Mr. Walsh was around my father's age, early fifties perhaps, with a full dark beard just starting to whiten below the chin. Sharp blue eyes shone out from beneath a heavy brow, and his streaked-gray hair was slicked back from his high forehead. Not a strand moved when he leaned over, raised one of my gloved hands to his lips, and kissed it through the thick wool. "The pleasure is all mine, Miss McDaniel."

My father grinned. "Mr. Walsh is interested in a tour of the damsite, so I suggested he accompany us today."

I felt a momentary stab of disappointment. Apparently, our morning together wasn't really to be ours. Mr. Zimmerman was bad enough, although I was starting to learn that the term *my man* was synonymous with *puppy*. But this? Had Mr. Walsh's arrival been a last-minute addition? Or had his presence been planned all along? Judging by the man's attire—heavy brown coat and tall boats—I suspected the latter; he was clearly a man who'd come prepared for a walk in the cold.

Still, I supposed I should be grateful to be included, extraneous company or not. It was better than being left to my own thoughts all day. Or, even worse, to Stella's suggestion of needlepoint.

We set out across the drive and made for the woods at the edge of the property. The frosty grass crunched beneath our feet. I shivered under my layers. Despite two winters in the mountains, I still hated the cold. Yet I couldn't deny the beauty of it, the landscape aglow with crystalized tips of white. Even the bare trees, which to so many resembled skeletons or spooks, seemed almost magical in the sun, shimmering fingertips stretched skyward. Here and there, tiny birds flitted about, filling the air with their questions, wondering aloud if perhaps they had returned north too early. There was a crisp cleanness to the air, earthy and new, a smell that couldn't be matched even in the pristine atmosphere of the Alps.

The smell of rural New York. The smell of home.

But still I found my disappointment growing. My father and Mr. Walsh had fallen into step beside one another, leaving me to the rear with Mr. Zimmerman. Water droplets collected in his beard where his warm breath met the frozen air, and he'd forgone a hat, a choice I thought most unwise considering his bald head. He was scowling again, though I wasn't sure if, this time, it was on account of the cold or me. Perhaps it was both.

Still, I was a lady, schooled in the art of conversation and manners. Surly disposition or not, it would be a mark against myself and my father if I did not at least try to make conversation.

"So, Mr. Zimmerman." I clenched fingers that had begun to stiffen inside my gloves. "My father tells me you're from Germany. What part?"

He did not respond.

"I went to Munich on holiday with a friend from school," I continued after a moment, undeterred. "It was lovely. I went—"

"Bonn," he grunted. His tone was so gruff, it took me a moment to realize he was naming a town.

"Oh," I responded lightly, trying not to be put off by his rudeness in interrupting. "Is it nice?"

He nodded.

"Do you still have family there?"

Another nod.

"When did you arrive in America?"

"One year."

"One year ago?"

A nod.

"Do you like it here so far?"

A slight raise and lower of one shoulder.

I sighed loudly. It was impolite, of course; Mademoiselle Dubois would be horrified. But if Mr. Zimmerman didn't care about manners—his answers left open no doors to the further discussion dictated by etiquette—then why should I?

Instead, I turned my attention to the conversation between my father and Mr. Walsh. Though they were only a few steps ahead, I strained to make out the topic. Casting a sideways glance at Mr. Zimmerman, whose eyes remained steadfastly on the ground, I hurried my pace just slightly—*Ladies do not run, Miss McDaniel*—to close the distance.

"McKinley is committing more troops," I heard my father say. "I have to wonder if it's worth it."

"Of course it's worth it," Mr. Walsh replied. "American goods—goods that can be produced at an exponential rate thanks to this dam you're building—have already saturated the European market. If we want our economy to continue to grow, we must turn our attention to the East. The Philippines are the gateway to that."

The war. They were talking about the war again.

I bit down on my lip. I hadn't forgotten about my father's displeasure during last night's dinner, but it still felt as if words would burst from my mouth, no matter how hard I tried to hold them in. *But what about the cost to human lives? The sovereignty of a people with their own culture and traditions?*

Just then my father glanced back at me, and one look at the pinched expression on his face withered the questions in my throat. He obviously hadn't forgotten about last night either. "Perhaps we should change the subject," he said quickly. "Kathleen . . . The war, it upsets her. Delicate heart and all. Isn't that right, Kitty?"

No. Not at all. But I found myself responding automatically, just as I'd been taught. A shy smile, a nod, even an unsolicited blush.

An invisible string seemed to tie the two men together; when Mr. Walsh's posture softened, so did my father's.

"Forgive me, Miss McDaniel." Mr. Walsh gave a slight bob of his head. "I should be more cognizant of our company."

"It's quite all right, Mr. Walsh. I—"

"No, it's not. My manners have been atrocious. I haven't even yet apologized for missing your homecoming dinner last night. I had business in the city that could not be deferred, but I was sorry to miss it all the same."

"Roosevelt was the star of the evening," my father interjected. "Regaling us all with tales of his time in Cuba. Though I dare say he remained coy about the possibility of joining McKinley's ticket."

Mr. Walsh waved a hand. "I've heard enough of Teddy's stories. I see the man weekly. We share a name and a love for Old Overholt. Mind you, he's not a big drinker, Teddy, and nor am I. But whiskey is a gentleman's vice, and so we imbibe on occasion." He gave me a wink. "I, on the other hand, would like to hear some of Miss McDaniel's stories."

He offered his arm, which I accepted.

As he escorted me, he listened, rapt, while I told him of Switzerland, being careful to leave out the questionable exploits with my friends or any mention of my dreams. Though the conversation felt shackled, it was nice to hold someone's attention, to be spoken to rather than at, even if the topics were censored. We kept our conversation light—things like the weather ("unusually cold for this time of year"), family ("my dear Gladys has been gone these two years now, sadly leaving me no children"), and the latest Broadway offerings ("you must make it a point to get to the city for *The Chimes of Normandy*. It really is quite magnificent"). I was just finishing up a story about a particularly lovely afternoon I'd spent at the Louvre in Paris when the goal of our journey finally came into view.

"There it is," my father said, unnecessarily.

In the valley below, where a picturesque waterway used to flow over an equally picturesque stone dam and into the fertile green lands of the countryside beyond, lay nothing but a dark stain of mud and stone. I had to stop myself from gasping at the sight of it.

My father placed a gentle hand on my shoulder. "We've made a lot of progress since you've been gone, Kathleen. I know it doesn't look like much now, but soon it will. In fact, it will be everything."

Still holding Mr. Walsh's arm, I let myself be led closer to the empty waterfront, trying to mask any signs of horror over the decimated, once-beautiful countryside.

"The new dam will be there," he said, gesturing to a spot farther east. "As you can see, the old dam wall extends six hundred feet along the south bank, holding back the current river waters as we excavate for the newer, larger reservoir. We've had to put a halt on that for the past months, the ground being as frozen as it is, but we expect to be able to pick back up in a few weeks. The rest of the water has been pumped dry by steam engines."

Mr. Walsh helped me navigate a particularly large muddy puddle, the ice across its surface starting to crack in the rapidly intensifying late-morning sun.

"Marvelous," he said, returning his attention to my father. "Truly extraordinary."

"Ah, you think that now," Father said, directing his words at his companion but his wink at me. "Just wait until it's complete. New York City will have a limitless supply of fresh water thanks to this project. The new reservoir will be three times larger than the old one, fifty-seven square miles to be exact, and directed right into the Croton aqueduct, which will then take it straight into New York City."

Mr. Walsh paused, raising his hand to his brow as he looked out over the mess of mud, timber, and stone. "And how does that translate to profits?"

"Well, the Aqueduct Commission will hold the rights to the water," my father said. "But I own the company in charge of building and maintaining the dam, along with a substantial piece of land on which both it and the new reservoir will lie. I would say the McDaniel Corporation will stand to gain more than its fair share . . . with interest, over the coming years."

"Very good," Mr. Walsh said, a faint smile tracing his lips. "Very good."

"More than good," my father responded. He did not try to hide his grin. "Take a look around, Mr. Walsh. This is the future. And water is the key to it. Soon, there will be nothing we can't do."

The two men shared a look I couldn't read but one in which

I had little interest in at the moment. I was too busy still trying to process the devastation in front of me. I'd known my father's company had been hired to replace the old dam with this newer, larger one. It was a slow, painstakingly complex project they'd been working on for years. I knew it meant good things for New York and for my family. But it was still hard to see it like this, land torn up and laid bare, the natural beauty of the Croton River mangled by human hands.

My father kept walking, Mr. Zimmerman moving up to become his shadow once again. Mr. Walsh and I followed him along the edge of the pit. "As you can see, we've already started laying masonry for the new wall. Salt keeps the mortar from freezing, so the men can keep working, even in these frigid conditions."

"Better for everyone," Mr. Walsh said. "Keeping the men busy."

"Precisely," my father agreed.

Along the wall stood a row of blackened, mud-stained men, their breath visible, boots covered in muck. They paused in their work as we passed, tools in hand. Remembering my manners, I tried to avert my gaze, but it was impossible not to look. Their faces were gray, though I wasn't sure if it was dirt or the natural pallor of their skin. From the look of it, there was a wide range of ages represented—from mine to my father's—yet each man held an exhaustion in his eyes, a hollowing of flesh over his cheeks. But despite this, there was a hardness in their sinewy frames.

A hardness that bordered on menacing.

I shivered as a brisk wind cut through my coat. The men, however, did not flinch in their tattered flannels and holey shoes.

"Don't they get cold?" I tried to keep my tone light. Innocently inquisitive. But that old sense of unease was back, and it would not be silent.

Mr. Walsh merely laughed. "You're right, McDaniel. Your daughter *is* sensitive to plight. It's quite charming." He looked at me, the dark hair above his lip twitching in a bemused smile. "I can assure you, Miss McDaniel, that these workers are perfectly fine. They don't have the delicacies of the upper class. They are healthier and better cared for here than they would be elsewhere."

"Too true," my father broke in. "Recent immigrants, the lot of them. No homes, no prospects. Here they have a job. They have purpose. They also have food, a bed, shelter, and a warm fire." He gestured toward a distant spot where I could just make out a row of white tents. "Don't you worry about them. They are perfectly happy." He patted my cheek.

I forced a weak smile.

Just then, one of the men separated himself from the group, taking hulking steps toward my father with obvious determination. As he walked, his fingers twitched. Even from here, I could see his full lips, chapped from the cold, itching with unspoken words.

Quicker than I could blink, Otto Zimmerman intervened, placing himself squarely between my father and the worker, causing the man to come to a sudden halt.

Mr. Walsh tensed, taking a step backward and dropping my arm. Mr. Zimmerman's massive arms flexed, his shoulders squared, but the man did not back away. Instead, his nostrils flared as his eyes flicked back and forth between Mr. Zimmerman and my father. The air grew thick as the moments leeched by, the surprise of the sudden standoff morphing into discomfort. No one moved; no one spoke. The only sounds were the distant shouts of the workers and the hammering of mallets upon stone.

Suddenly, from the masses, another man broke free, slipping on a patch of ice as he rushed toward the worker. He was smaller than the other man but no less muscular, a fact obvious even beneath his baggy, ratty clothes. He placed a hand on the first man's arm, knuckles turning white with the force of his grip, causing the man to finally break his stare. Over the next several moments, the two of them seemed to hold an entire conversation without moving their mouths. Finally, the first man's shoulders loosened, and he retreated to the anonymity of the group, leaving the second man behind.

Mr. Zimmerman, however, did not budge.

My father let out an unnatural titter. "Come now, Otto. It's fine. I'm sure this gentleman means us no harm. Perhaps he just needed a word. Isn't that so, Mr. . . . ."

The remaining man's eyes drifted from my father to Mr. Zimmerman to Mr. Walsh. When they met mine, unexpected heat rushed through my body. They were green, striking and deep as the Hudson itself, as though one could fall headfirst into them. He was close to my age, I realized with a start, with dark blond hair, high cheekbones, full lips.

And those *eyes*.

I averted my gaze as a flush of embarrassment warmed my cheeks. He was . . . *handsome*. Even with the dirt crisscrossing his brow, the tattered collar around his neck, he was attractive. I clasped my hands together, trying to will the inappropriate thought from my mind.

"Odell," he said eventually. "Wesley Odell. *Sir*."

His voice held the faint trace of an accent—Irish, perhaps?—but there was no mistaking his tone. He had spoken the last word as if it were a curse.

My father, either oblivious or unconcerned, merely smiled. "Mr. Odell. Is there something you or your friend wish to speak to me about?"

Again, a taut silence began to stretch. My father cleared his throat. Behind me, Mr. Walsh shifted. Otto remained as he was, a dog with its hackles raised. Inside my gloves, my hands began to sweat.

"No . . . sir."

Wesley's words, polite but spoken through clenched teeth, released the air, though they did little to negate the chill that had intensified as we'd stood.

"Very well," my father replied, clapping his hands. "Moving on." He strode forward, back erect, hands outstretched to the west. "Now, if you'll look over here . . ."

After a few moments, Otto followed him. Mr. Walsh, finally coming to his senses, took my arm and led me forward, my knees wobbly, every nerve tingling.

I tried not to look over my shoulder. I really did. It wasn't proper, especially with a gentleman holding my arm, nor would it do any good. There was a heaviness here at the dam, an ominousness I didn't quite understand. I did, however, believe I finally understood why my father had needed Mr. Zimmerman to be "his man."

Something was happening here.

Something dangerous.

Something that got my blood pumping and heart racing in a way I hadn't felt since I'd left Switzerland.

And so, despite all my training, all my self-scolding, I found myself chancing one last glance over my shoulder. Wesley Odell remained where he'd stood, green eyes unblinking, watching me walk away.

It was a good thing Mr. Walsh was deep in conversation with my father. Otherwise, he might have noticed the way my step faltered.

Or the hitch in my breathing that didn't quite return to normal until long after the dam disappeared from my sight.

SEVEN

FRIDAY, SEPTEMBER 7, 1900
GALVESTON, TEXAS

"I don't feel like going shopping today."

There was no way Matthew Richter was going to get me through the doors of the E.S. Levy and Company department store. When he'd promised to take me "to the future," window displays full of Modjeska jackets, ladies' kimonos, and colorful turbans bedecked with ostrich feathers weren't exactly what I'd had in mind.

Those items were not my future; they were my past. And I'd had quite enough reminiscing for one day.

Besides, after our stroll through the affluent houses along Broadway, I certainly didn't need another reminder of my newfound—and possibly long-lasting—poverty. We'd stopped at a hot dog cart along the way, my first such experience with these mobile concessionaires, and the only force stronger than my pride was my hunger. It was bad enough I had allowed Matthew to buy me a frankfurter; I would not allow myself to fall further into his debt.

Matthew laughed. "Well, that's a good thing. Because we're not going shopping."

Swallowing the last of my lunch, I followed his finger as he moved it slowly up the edifice of the four-story brick building before us. Rows of windows glinted in the sunlight, and I had to use my hand to shield my eyes from the glare. He stopped at the uppermost floor.

"We're going up there."

The inner stairwell was blessedly dark but somehow even more stifling than the oppressive heat outside. I was sweating before we started to climb. After the first flight of stairs, I removed my bonnet, feeling more secure away from prying eyes but also desperately needing to get my hair off my neck. After the second, I began to pluck at the fabric on my chest, trying to coax a nonexistent breeze onto the drenched skin underneath. Midway up the third flight, I was ready to tell Matthew to forget the whole thing—if only I could catch a breath. Thankfully, however, at just that moment, he stopped and pulled open a door, releasing a breeze that smelled of salt and cigarettes.

He held the door, allowing me to go first, and I found myself inside a cluttered office. Two desks sat facing each other, lit by small electric lamps and covered with books and papers, which ruffled in the meager wind flowing through the open windows on either side of the room. Several bookshelves, filled with green volumes, lined the walls. And, in the middle of it all, hunched over another table, leaned a man, brow furrowed in concentration, charcoal pencil moving rapidly. A cigarette dangled from his lips. His dark eyes flickered to me momentarily when I entered, returned to his work, then, as if on a double take, widened as he straightened his back and cleared his throat.

"I'm sorry, miss, are you lost? This is—"

"Joseph!" Matthew appeared from behind me, striding toward

the man with an outstretched hand. "What are you doing? You know you're not supposed to be smoking in here."

The man smashed his cigarette into a nearby ashtray with a sheepish grin. "I know, I know, I know. You caught me."

"What was it Moore said again? Cigarettes are a moral blight which"—Matthew paused, closing one eye—"brings discredit upon the weather service. Not to mention they make you stupid."

The man laughed. "Well, I guess it's a good thing he's in DC and not here. Wouldn't want my immorality *or* my stupidity upsetting the old boss man." He strode forward and shook Matthew's hand with a grin. "I didn't know you'd be in today."

"I wasn't supposed to be. But I ran into my friend here, and I figured I'd show her around. If that's all right with you?"

"Of course!" The man directed his smile at me. He looked to be about thirty, with dark hair swept neatly to the side and a clean-shaven face that offered a full view of the slight cleft in his chin. His brown eyes sparkled as he removed his hand from Matthew's and extended it toward me. "I'm Joseph Cline. It's nice to meet you, Miss . . ."

I offered my fingers delicately. "Annie. Just Annie."

He blinked, smile twitching slightly at the corners. It was a breach of manners for a gentleman to address an unmarried lady by her Christian name upon first meeting. But I was no longer a lady. Hadn't been for several months and might not ever be again. And, silly or not, it felt wrong to give him my fake last name now that someone here had discovered its fraudulence. But it was still too risky to give him my real one, considering the newspaper article and disappearing henchman I knew I hadn't imagined. Annie—just Annie—at least had a grain of truth within it.

"Annie." He said it slowly, as if tasting it, then allowed warmth to flow back into his smile. "It's lovely to meet you. Welcome to the Galveston office of the US Weather Bureau."

Matthew grinned, first at me then at Joseph. "What are you working on, Joe?"

Joseph stepped back and gestured to the table with a wide sweep of his arm. "The weather map. I'm running a little behind. I've got to get it finished and down to the Cotton Exchange. You know how those traders get." He rolled his eyes good-naturedly. "They think they can control the stock market with science."

"Because they can!" Matthew interjected.

Joseph shook his head and chuckled. He motioned for me to come closer. "Our boss in Washington collects weather reports from stations just like this one all across the country. Then, every morning, he sends out a telegraph, and we create maps of the day's weather based on the information he gives us."

Beneath his fingers lay an outline of the United States marked over in colored chalk. Small numbers were written beneath cities such as New York and Chicago. Large letters *R* and *S* lay scattered from east to west, intermixed with swirling lines and tiny circles with arrows and crosses. It was pretty in its own way, vibrant and elaborate, like a child's irreverent painting.

And also completely dumbfounding.

"You can predict the weather from those squiggly lines?"

Joseph let out a laugh. "Yes, actually. If you know how to read them. Those numbers represent temperature and wind speed. And the letters? *R* is for rain, *S* is for snow. An open circle like here means clear skies, while one with a cross in it means cloudy."

"What are all these lines?"

"Oh, these here"—he pointed to a group of solid looping lines—"are called isobars. They link together areas of equal atmospheric pressure. And these"—he pointed to similarly looping lines, dotted instead of solid—"are called isotherms. It's the same kind of thing, but in regard to temperature."

I pressed my lips together. "You've lost me again."

This time, it was Matthew's turn to laugh. "Don't worry about it too much. I'm not going to quiz you." His eyes roamed over the map, wide smile falling as it reached the Atlantic coast. "Hey, Joe, what's this? These barometer readings and wind speeds . . . They look like it could be a cyclone."

Joseph groaned. "You sound just like the Cubans. You know we don't use that word."

I tilted my head questioningly.

"*Cyclone,*" Joseph said, seeing my face. "Or *hurricane.* The Cubans call every storm a hurricane. And all it does is cause panic along the shoreline. That's why we try not to use it unless absolutely necessary. This here"—he gestured back toward the map—"is a storm that passed over the island a few days ago. And, sure enough, those so-called weather forecasters down there say it was a hurricane." He sighed. "More than likely, it was nothing but a cloudburst and stiff breeze. Doesn't really matter, though. Our estimates put it about one hundred and fifty miles northeast of the Keys now."

"How can you know?" I asked. "If it's out in the middle of the ocean, I mean. How can you know where it is when there are no weather stations to send you reports?"

Joseph nodded his head approvingly. "Very shrewd, Annie. Very shrewd. To put it simply, all hurricanes are subject to the laws of nature, just like everything else. And, because of a law known as 'recurve,' storms exiting the Caribbean on a northerly track cannot go northwest. It's impossible."

"It's *science*. The Coriolis effect." Matthew winked at me again.

I felt an unexpected rush of attraction. Flustered, I turned my attention back to the map, not even bothering to ask him what a Coriolis was, hoping to hide the flush I knew was coloring my cheeks. "What about this here?" I asked quickly instead, pointing to a red-and-black dot near New Orleans. "What's that mean?"

Joseph squinted. "That just means they've posted storm

warnings. Ships out in the Gulf have reported some moderately disturbed waters. Probably an off-spur from that Cuba storm." He shrugged, smiling at me. "But you have nothing to worry about. I promise. If anything, we might get a refreshing summer shower to take the edge off this heat. Nothing more. You can take that to the bank. And I," he said, glancing at the clock on the wall, "can take this over to the wharf." He moved to the end of the table and began rolling the map. "I apologize for cutting things short. Annie, it was a pleasure to meet you. Matthew, Isaac's on the roof taking readings."

"So that's how you were getting away with smoking!"

Joseph Cline waved away Matthew's jest with a wiggle of his eyebrows and, tipping his hat, disappeared out the door, tightly rolled map tucked under his arm. Matthew stared after him for a moment before turning to me.

"Think you can make it up one more flight of stairs?"

When Matthew opened the door to the Levy building's roof, I stepped tentatively into the bright sunlight. The heat was stronger up here, but so was the breeze, yet I paid little attention to either of them. Instead, my breath caught at the sight of Galveston spreading out below me. Miles of brick and stone and wood. I'd never seen it from this vantage point. From here, I could see the looming spires of St. Patrick's Church, the rounded cupola of the Galveston Opera House, and the lone tower of the Tremont House hotel. Lush green vegetation was crisscrossed by gray angular streets, and to the north and the south lay the sea, a vast carpet of blue, its surface sparkling like diamonds under a cloudless sky.

It made me realize, for all its spectacle and grandeur, just how small Galveston really was, pinched between these two mighty ocean fingers.

Made me realize just how small I was too.

"Matthew?"

Consumed by the view, I hadn't noticed a man emerge from

behind a pole. He was tall but not gangly, dressed in a crisp gray suit that spoke of money, a sentiment only enhanced by the gold chain of a pocket watch dangling from his vest pocket. His face was angular, with pronounced cheekbones, a well-defined nose, and a slight dimple in his chin that echoed Joseph's. In fact, all in all, he looked remarkably like Joseph, albeit older and with a mustache. He smiled warmly as he approached.

"Mr. Cline, hello!" The two men shook hands, and Matthew turned to me. "Annie, this is Mr. Isaac Cline. Mr. Cline, this is Annie."

Unlike Joseph, Mr. Cline didn't balk at my sudden appearance or the use of my first name. Or, if he did, he gave no outward hint of his discomfort. Instead, from the way he took my hand and pressed it to his lips, I got the distinct impression he wasn't a man easily rattled.

"Annie," he said. "It's lovely to meet you." There was a slight drawl to his words, a dragging out of the last syllable. *Yeeeeew.*

"Cline? So are you any relation to—"

Mr. Cline waved away my question, smiling. "I take it you've met my brother."

"He was just finishing up the map to take to the Cotton Exchange," Matthew said.

Mr. Cline nodded. "Good. I'm almost finished up here myself."

"Mr. Cline—"

"Matthew, how many times do I have to tell you? You can call me Isaac."

Color bloomed in Matthew's cheeks. He dropped his chin to his chest like a schoolboy. "With all due respect, Mr. Cline. I can't. Not a man in your position." Then, to me: "Mr. Cline is chief meteorologist of Galveston, but he's also in charge of all of Texas for the Weather Bureau."

The name struck me suddenly. Isaac Cline. The man Matthew had spoken about yesterday at the Pagoda. The man he'd bragged about with such pomp and circumstance that I'd half expected him to be made of solid gold. No wonder Matthew was in such an obvious tizzy.

"So, you're the boss?" I asked.

Mr. Cline—Isaac—laughed. "*Here* I am, yes. But I'm not nearly as high on the totem pole as Mr. Richter would have you believe. There's a whole wide world out there that doesn't even know my name."

"That's going to change soon!"

Matthew was staring at Isaac with such unadulterated admiration that it was Isaac's turn to blush. I noticed he didn't, however, correct him. Instead, he merely smiled and gestured behind him. "I assume you're here to show your friend the instruments."

"If that's all right with you, Mr. Cline?"

"Of course. In fact, let's use this as another training opportunity. I've just finished with my readings." He patted his front pocket, where the top of a notebook was visible above the gray fabric. "How about you take yours, and we'll compare?"

Matthew's face lit up in a way I pretended not to find adorable. With one hand lightly touching the small of my back, he guided me to a collection of metal gadgets that looked like something out of a Jules Verne novel. He approached the first one, a small metal box containing a round dial. On top of it, a short, metal cylinder with four cups branched out from posts that met in the center, forming a cross. "This is an anemometer," he said, crouching in front of it. "It measures wind speed."

He scribbled a few things in his notebook before moving on to the next instrument, this one comprised of two glass bulbs hanging from opposing ends of a glass tube that passed through the top of a wooden post. "And this is a hygrometer. Measures relative humidity."

There were more after that. Barometer, thermometer, and a handful of other *ometers* that recorded everything from wind direction to the number of hours of sunshine. Matthew explained each in detail, and while I can't say I matched his level of enthusiasm, I couldn't help but be amused by his total, unabashed glee. It caused me to grin, which, in turn, caused Matthew, mistaking my smile for interest, to go deeper into the science behind his readings.

"Well, Mr. Cline," he said, after writing the last of his observations in his notebook. "The temperature is approaching ninety, wind is out of the north, barometer slowly falling, and there's cirrostratus clouds on the horizon. I'd say we have some rain—possibly a thunderstorm—approaching later this evening or tomorrow."

Isaac crossed his arms over his chest and nodded, a smile breaking out beneath his dark mustache. "Well done, Mr. Richter. That's my exact forecast as well."

Matthew's chest puffed out a little bit at Isaac's words.

His obvious satisfaction made me swell with pride for him, but it was a feeling that morphed quickly into piercing grief.

Images came to my mind of the last time I'd delighted in a man and his gadgets. The exuberance I'd felt when he'd shared his passion with me.

The smile we were sharing fell from Matthew's face as he saw it leave mine.

I cleared my throat and looked away. "A storm?"

Isaac tutted. "Nothing to be concerned about." His words echoed his brother's from earlier. "Though I may have to warn some beachgoers that the tide's about to get rough. Might ruin a few people's vacations." He chuckled.

"But how can you know?"

Isaac's laughter bit off cleanly. "I'm sorry?"

"How can you know what's coming based solely on these devices? Forgive me if I'm wrong, Mr. Cline, but it seems these readings are only giving you the here and now. How can you know there's a storm coming, let alone how strong it is, based just on these gadgets?" My voice rose. And, even though I was very aware

I was using my own haughty skepticism as a means to push away my sadness, it wasn't enough to change my tone. "I mean, you can't see the future. No one can. Isn't it a bit arrogant to assume so?"

"Annie." There was a note of shocked embarrassment in Matthew's tone.

Isaac held up his hand. "It's quite all right, Mr. Richter. She's just asking questions." Then, turning to me: "Gone are the days of telling weather through aches in our bones. With these devices, we are starting to understand the mechanics of weather—how it happens and why. No, we can't see the future. But, through these devices, we're getting awfully close. It won't be long before we won't just be predicting the weather. We'll be changing it."

"Some vineyard owners in Italy were able to divert a hailstorm and save their crops by firing cannons at developing cloud formations," Matthew interjected. "And in France, where they've been suffering from drought, they've had success at producing rain through bombardment."

"Initial success," Isaac corrected gently. "But, still, a promising start." He turned to me. "The world is changing. And science is leading the way. We're cracking the code to the universe, Annie. Soon, there will be nothing we cannot do."

Somehow, no one else in the room realized I was falling. Realized I was no longer standing atop the Levy building, staring at the face of Isaac Cline.

Soon, there will be nothing we cannot do.

Despite the smell of the Gulf and the warm Texas sunshine on my face, I was back in New York, looking out at the Croton Dam. Hearing my father's words.

Remembering the chain of events I hadn't even realized was already set in motion by the time he'd spoken them.

And staring, once again, at the pained face of Wesley Odell, watching me walk away.

EIGHT

"What was that about in there?"

Back on ground level, the full intensity of the day's heat returned. The strands of clouds that had begun threading themselves across the sky offered no relief. I tucked my hair into my bonnet and tied the ribbons under my chin before ducking beneath the shade of a nearby awning. Matthew followed.

"What was what about?" I echoed. It was a stupid question. As if I couldn't feel the displeasure radiating from his body as he fell into step beside me.

"You. In there. Challenging Mr. Cline. Insulting him."

"I wasn't insulting him. I was just trying to understand." *And trying to distract everyone from the misery of a memory I was sure was etched across my face.* "Besides," I added, pausing to let a passing carriage rumble by before crossing the street, "I don't think he minded. In fact, I rather think he enjoyed getting a chance to defend himself."

"What does that mean?"

"I don't know. He's nice and all, but he came across as a little"—I glanced at Matthew sideways—"pompous."

"Pompous?"

"All that 'building the future' stuff. You really buy into that?"

"Of course I do! Annie, you don't understand. Mr. Cline, he . . ." He stopped, as if there were too many words, all vying for a chance to escape. "There's no one else like him. He is, far and away, the smartest person I have ever met. And he's challenging everything we thought we knew about the science of weather. Remember that flood on the Brazos I was telling you about?"

I didn't, but I nodded anyway.

"Well, it used to be forbidden for a local weather office to issue any kind of warning. The DC bigwigs thought there were too many instances of amateurs crying wolf. But Mr. Cline . . . Well, he knew the Brazos was going to flood. Knew it from the *science* he himself was pioneering. Weather Bureau be doggoned, he went ahead and issued a flood warning anyway, without permission. And guess what? When the Brazos reached record flood level a few days later, not a single life was lost. All because of Mr. Cline." He shook his head. "He changed the whole system, Annie. Changed how the entire field of meteorology approaches their work."

My heart throbbed inside my chest. Matthew's words, his eyes . . . I remembered when I had felt that way about someone. When I had once believed in heroes. "You certainly think a lot of him, don't you?" I asked quietly.

For the first time since we'd left the Levy building, Matthew's shoulders relaxed. When he hopped up on the wooden sidewalk lining 23rd Street, he offered his hand to assist me, then moved my fingers to his elbow.

All was forgiven on his end. But not forgotten on my own. At his touch, the memory that had swum in front of my face up there on the rooftop once again began to creep in from the sides. Another hand.

Another face. I tried to push it away, concentrating on Matthew's words rather than the feel of his body heat beneath my palm.

"It's not just me, Annie. Everyone in Galveston wants to know what he thinks. After the Indianola storm back in eighty-six, there was talk of building a seawall along the Gulf. You know, just in case a big storm ever came our way. And you know whose opinion the committee asked for first?" He raised his chin at me.

"Mr. Cline's?"

"Mr. Cline's. He wrote an article in the paper saying that, if a storm ever were to push onto the island, water would simply flow *over* the island and into the bay. The city would barely feel it. The Gulf coastline is too shallow, see, and it would fragment any effects from incoming surf. And besides—hurricanes don't strike Texas."

"The Coriolis effect," I said, glad I remembered at least one thing from the barrage of terms thrown at me that day.

"The Coriolis effect," he parroted, grinning. "And because Mr. Cline said it wasn't necessary, the seawall wasn't built." He took a deep breath. "He knows, Annie. He just knows." And then, quieter: "Not like my old man."

My hand stiffened around Matthew's elbow. He'd never spoken about his family before. And I'd never asked. Not because I didn't want to know, but because I knew he'd reciprocate, asking questions I'd never acquiesce to answer.

We'd crossed a line today. The touching, the smiling, the laughter. An entire day spent together without Maggie or Emily as a buffer had removed one too many bricks in the wall I'd erected between us.

And he felt it too. Enough to broach a subject that ought not have ever been broached.

The past.

"My father was a cowboy over by Corpus Christi," he continued hesitantly. "Rode with the Rangers for a while. I can remember

Jack Helms and Sergeant Rudds both coming to dinner at my house."

I didn't recognize either of the names, but it felt wrong to ask. Matthew's eyes pointed straight ahead, yet I was pretty sure he wasn't seeing the yellow-and-red streetcar ambling down its tracks.

"But those days faded. The Old West became tamed. Momma died, and we sold the ranch. Moved to Houston. But Pa never could get over it. I think losing his spurs was worse than losing Ma. Then, the day after I turned twelve, he up and left me. Just so he could go ride again, this time with Buffalo Bill's Wild West show. I've been on my own ever since."

Compassion pinged in my chest, just one of a thousand different emotions swelling inside me. I wanted to tell him to stop talking, that I couldn't handle it; my heart was too tender, too broken, and I didn't need any more threads ensnaring it to him or to this place. I also wanted to tell him I was sorry. That I understood. That families would always let you down.

Instead, I said nothing.

Not that it mattered. Matthew seemed to have forgotten me. When he spoke again, it was as if he were speaking to himself. "That man left me nothing—no money, no skills, no way forward. He was so consumed by the past that he didn't give a single thought to my future. Me. His own *son*." He stopped suddenly, turning to look at me. We were under a canopy of oak, the filtered sunlight casting shadows across his face. "That's why Mr. Cline means so much to me, Annie. He's not looking back. He's looking ahead. And not just for himself but for all of us."

His hazel eyes searched mine. I tried to look away, but the intensity of his gaze bound me.

"We all have a choice to make, Annie: the past . . . or the future. We have to decide which way we're going to lean. Which side we're going to build our lives on. As for me, I'm going to center mine on science. On the mind and the words of Mr. Isaac Cline."

The orphanage was quiet when I returned.

I had allowed Matthew to accompany me to the pier, though I begged off permitting him to walk me the rest of the way back to St. Mary's. And it wasn't just because I didn't believe it would bode well for Mother Camillus to see me in the company of a young man.

An awkwardness had hung between us after his revelation. He had exposed a little bit of his soul to me, far more than what was proper between an unmarried man and woman, and it was a gesture I could not reciprocate. It was as if Matthew had tried building a bridge, fully expecting me to lay my own supports and meet him in the middle. Instead, I'd left him hanging over a crevasse while remaining steadfastly on the opposite ridge. When we said our goodbyes near the trolley stop, I did not look at his face. Instead, I made some silly comment about the waves, how large and unusual they were, tinged dullish brown with sand, before mumbling my thanks for the day, turning, and walking away.

I thought I could feel his eyes boring into my back. But, when I dared glance over my shoulder, he wasn't looking at me. Instead, he was staring out across the Gulf, eyes fixed on the clouds gathering above the horizon.

I knew then I had finally succeeded in pushing him away, in resolutely ending this thing—whatever it may have been—with Matthew. My head had finally prevailed over my heart.

So why did it feel like a loss?

The children's lessons had finished, the orphans filing into the dining room for supper as I slipped back inside. Maggie's face lit up when she saw me, causing my heart to further splinter. Thankfully, I had only enough time to give her a quick hug before Sister Catherine ushered her away with a scowl in my direction. I made a face when her back was turned, making Maggie giggle.

The sound caused my eyes to burn. I turned away before she could see the tears I refused to let fall.

In the kitchen, Sister Bernice offered me some bread and an apple—I passed on the watery, pea-green soup—and did not even tsk when she noticed I wasn't taking it into the dining room to eat like I was supposed to. I wondered if she knew about Mother Camillus's ultimatum. Or if my troubles were written all too plainly on my face.

Emily wasn't in our room, a small gift I felt guilty about appreciating. Early evening sunlight filtered through the open window, light turned gray by the approaching blanket of clouds. It stretched across the floor as if searching for the item I myself had come up here to see. With the gentle thump of waves matching the thudding in my chest, I tugged the brown satchel out from under my bed. My hands shook as I pulled an object from its depths.

Instant tears sprung to my eyes. I hadn't looked at it since that night. I'd wanted to, but I just . . . couldn't.

It was the reason I was hunted.

It was the reason I had fled.

It was . . . all I had left.

I clutched the square object to my chest. Memories leached from it, soaking into my clothes, my skin, my blood. His face, his eyes, his lips. The first time I'd ever seen that smile was when he'd been holding this thing.

And the last words I'd heard him speak were to tell me to take it.

To keep it safe.

I ran my fingers over the leather covering, the glass-plated hole, the brass clasp. I still carried the pain of his absence with me; it was a heaviness, a gray-tinged film that would forever color my world.

I did not regret our time together. But I did regret how it had ended.

I regretted a lot of things.

Inexplicably, my mind flitted to Matthew again. But, rather than guilt, a sudden, fresh sense of loss filled me. In this moment, I realized I struggled so much around Matthew not only because of my past but because he reminded me so much of *him*.

Not my father.

But Wesley.

The way Matthew talked to me, looked at me. It was as if he *saw* me. Not the me I presented to the world, which was even more false now than it had been back in New York, but the me inside. Somehow, just like Wesley, it seemed as if he was able to see through me. See *to* me.

And, whether or not I accepted Mother Camillus's offer, it was something I'd have to leave behind. I either had to put on the habit, forgoing all relationships with the opposite sex . . . or else run. It didn't matter where. So long as I was away from here, away from Matthew.

Because, if nothing else, I *was* certain of one thing: being around me was dangerous. That henchman today had made it crystal clear. And I would not chance any risk to Matthew's life. Or Emily's or Maggie's. I could not bear the thought of seeing anyone I cared about hurt because of my own selfishness.

I'd already made that mistake once.

The doorknob rattled, startling me out of my stupor.

"Annie? Are you in there?"

I shoved the object back into its bag, then stuffed both underneath my bed. Rising to my feet, I quickly slapped at my cheeks, trying to hide the evidence of my tears before unlocking the door and swinging it open with a frozen smile. "Emily!"

Her hand hovered in midair, key balanced between her fingers. "There you are! Why was the door locked?"

"I was, uh, washing up. I spent most of the day at the beach, and my skin feels raw. Needed to get the salt and sun off of it."

She raised her chin, eyes taking in my tearstained face. Once again, there it was: that look. She knew I was lying. But, also once again, she was too kind to say anything. Instead, she merely smiled, tight and slightly wounded, but smiled all the same. "Well," she said hesitantly, "can I come in?"

I hadn't realized I'd been blocking the doorway. "Of course!" My voice was squeaky; it cracked on the second word.

Closing the door behind us, Emily washed and changed in silence. I nibbled my bread. I wasn't hungry, but it gave me something to do. Emily had always respected my distance. Her silence and expertly practiced neutrality made our room one of the few places I felt truly safe. But there was a difference in the quiet between us now. A tautness.

And after the day I'd had, it was something I simply couldn't abide.

Her bed squeaked as I sat down on the corner of it. "Emily?" I ventured. "Do you like being a nun?"

She paused at the washbasin. The sudden absence of her toothbrushing made the already deafening stillness seem even louder. "What?"

"Do you like being a nun?"

She turned to me, wiping her mouth with a faded white towel. "Why are you asking?"

"Just . . . curious."

"Well, I'm not a nun. Not yet. But yes, I like it."

I let out a long breath. "Why?"

She raised one eyebrow. "Are you thinking of becoming a nun?"

I dipped my chin, staring at my hands in my lap. They were callused, my nails short and broken. I would have found them abhorrent not so long ago. Common. Now, the sight of them just made me sad. "How did you know?" I asked after a few moments. "I mean, how did you know it was the right path for you?"

There was a rustle of fabric as Emily sat down next to me. "I knew I wanted to be a nun from a young age. I loved people. Loved God. And somehow, I just always knew I wanted to dedicate my life to serving Him and others."

"It was that easy, huh?"

She let out a small, disbelieving laugh. "Easy? I wouldn't go that far. Yes, I always knew I wanted to be a nun, but when I found out the church was assigning me here to Galveston?" She snorted. "I grew up in the mountains. The snow and the trees . . . That's home to me. I didn't understand why God was bringing me here, of all places. I'd been prepared to move, of course, but I assumed it would be someplace . . . I don't know . . . a bit more rugged? A bit more needful? A place where my skills could actually be put to use. Galveston felt so . . . ritzy. It was so far removed from everything I knew and loved, everything I had expected for my life. And it shook me. I began to doubt myself. Began to doubt God."

She paused. Cleared her throat. "But slowly, I started to realize His reasoning was twofold. On the surface, Galveston may seem shiny, but the need here *is* great. These poor children. So many of them, left alone after the fever. They needed someone to love them. To care for them. They needed . . . *me*. But, more than that, I needed them. I needed them to show me how to truly trust God. I had to get away from everything comfortable, from my expectations, to see Him more clearly. To understand."

Her hand slipped into mine. It, too, was callused. But there was a softness to her touch that caused me to look up. The corner of her mouth curved into a half smile. "When we suffer, it reminds us that this life is short, and this world is not our home. You see, I wanted to live my life in service *to* Him; He wanted to teach me to live it *in* Him. I loved God, but I'd been believing so many wrong things. About myself, about others." She shook her head. "Sometimes God has to tear down all the distractions, all the lies in our lives, in order for us to see the truth. To see that after everything else is gone, He's still there."

I hugged her then, as much to leech the warmth of her heart into the frigid depths of my soul as to keep her from seeing my tears. Her body tensed at my unusual display of affection, before softening and leaning into my embrace. I clung to her. I wanted to remember this moment. The kindness of this woman, this self-assured peace I'd never witnessed in another living soul. I wanted so desperately to have what she had, to take it with me.

To take *her* with me.

"Annie, what's going on? Are you unwell?" Emily's voice was little more than a murmur in my hair.

I managed a small shake of the head, fighting with everything in me to hold back sobs.

"You can tell me, you know. Whatever it is."

And, oh, how I wanted that to be true. In that moment, I wanted to tell her everything. Confess all my sins. Tell her that at one time I, too, knew exactly what I would grow up to be. I had known my destiny. Known my calling. The road to my future had been paved, choice by choice, dress by dress, dollar by dollar.

But all of that was gone. No matter which way I turned, it felt as if I was reaching a dead end. I knew nothing now. Not even God.

Emily's story was like mine in one way: He *had* torn down my life.

But, unlike her, I'd never felt further from the truth.

In the quiet darkness after lights out, I lay listening to the pounding of waves in the distance. Isaac's science had been right: there did seem to be a storm coming. The Gulf was in a foul mood tonight. The thump of water against land was louder than I'd ever heard it. Mixing with the whistle of the north wind, it created a melody that reminded me once again of Matthew. I wondered if he was hearing it too, wherever he was.

My mind floated to his words. The past . . . or the future. We need only pick which way to lean. He had said he was looking ahead, building his life on science. Emily, very obviously, was centering hers on God.

Building a foundation. Stone by stone, layer by layer. Apparently, that's what it all came down to.

But how was I supposed to do the same when both my past *and* my future seemed completely devoid of bricks?

NINE

MARCH 1900
CROTON-ON-HUDSON, NEW YORK

The spring freeze broke suddenly, bright green-yellow buds erupting along the gray, otherwise lifeless, limbs of the sycamores, maples, and beech trees that dotted our property. Two weeks after our frost-covered trek down to the dam site, the McDaniel estate was a frenzy of new life and new growth.

Gardeners crisscrossed the soggy lawn, pruning and planting, preparing the magnificent grounds for both beauty (my late mother's beloved rosebushes) and bounty (our prizewinning vegetable garden). Maintenance workers washed windows, cleared sidewalks and porches, and dusted off the wicker furniture that would soon host dinner guests on the backyard patio from which one could see the sparkling waters of the Croton River in the distance, swollen with melted snow.

My favorite part of spring, however, could be found farther down our winding lane, in the two-story barn, where new babies were being born each day. Already we'd been blessed with piglets and calves, chicklets and ducklings, and even a small litter of kittens, courtesy of one of the many barn cats who had made their way onto our property and decided to stay.

Today, however, was extra special. Because last night as I slept, a brand-new foal had been born.

Once Stella had told me the news, I'd barely even given her time to tighten my corset. I'd allowed her to pin my hair up however she wished and dress me in any outfit that could be quickly put together—a pale-green linen dress with pearl buttons down the front and wide insertions of torchon lace on both sides—before hurrying from the room, her protestations of my lack of facial powder ringing in my ears.

The soft ground squished beneath my boots as I made my way across the lawn. Breaching the threshold of the barn, I blinked against the dim light, the smells of hay and manure welcoming me with warm familiarity.

"Miss McDaniel." The groundskeeper was shoveling the pig stall, but he paused when I entered, removing his hat and nodding at me.

"Good morning, Rupert."

"Here to check on the kittens?"

"In a moment." I removed my hat and pushed some loose hair from my forehead. "I heard there was a new foal."

"Aye. Just down there." He gestured to the far end of the barn. "We didn't even know Beauty was in labor. She was fine last night. Normal. Then we come out this morning and boom—there's a wee one, right there in the stall with her."

"May I see it?"

Something flickered over Rupert's face. "Of course, ma'am. It's your barn."

I pulled my elbows in to my sides. He was right. It *was* my barn; I wasn't sure why it still felt odd to hear someone mention it.

Wasn't sure why, two weeks after I'd returned home, I continued to feel like a stranger in my own house, no matter how much I tried to own the position.

Why the strange dreams that had plagued me for the past two years had intensified since my arrival back at McDaniel Manor, despite my father's assurances that they'd merely been a result of homesickness. The hazy man again. The mystery woman. The gently waving fields.

And, last night, a dinner: small table, meager portions, faceless companions.

Shaking off both the memory and my own consternation, I strode down the wide middle aisle, past the snorting cows and lowing sheep, until I came to the last stall. Sure enough, inside, my father's horse Beauty lay in a pile of hay, newborn baby nuzzled against her side. The foal was dark, just like her, but with a spot of brown on its forehead, as if God's paintbrush had dripped. Beauty stared at me, and I saw pride in her liquid eyes. She looked away only when her baby began to stir, the faintest of movements, imperceptible to anyone but its mother.

"It's incredible, isn't it? The miracle of life."

I jumped at the sound of a voice behind me, letting out a surprised cry. Beauty gave an irritated snort as I spun, coming face-to-face with Theodore Walsh.

"Mr. Walsh! You startled me!"

He was dressed impeccably once again, a crisp gray three-piece suit bringing out both the white in his beard and the blue of his eyes, which were crinkled at the corners, clearly amused. "Forgive me, Miss McDaniel. That was not my intention." He raised one of my gloved hands to his lips and kissed it. "It's lovely to see you again."

"And you." I gave a slight curtsy. "You slept well, I presume?"

He gave a smile and an assenting nod. "I always do here."

Since his initial appearance at my home two weeks ago, Mr. Walsh had been in and out of the estate, present at more dinners than he was absent. Though I didn't mind the intrusion—I understood he and my father were in the process of working out some business deal—I did wonder what was taking so long; my father's other business associates were rarely here more than a day or two. "There is so much to take in on this beautiful estate. By the end of the day, my body is absolutely exhausted by the sheer amount of delight. Good food, breathtaking scenery . . . and, of course, lovely company."

I looked at the ground and swallowed. It wasn't the first time Mr. Walsh had made such comments. They were meant to be flattering, I knew.

But I only found them uncomfortable.

"The new foal is marvelous," I said quickly, taking a step backward and raising a hand to the stall. "That marking on his head. It's so unusual."

Mr. Walsh stepped up beside me, placing his own hands on the wooden gate. "You like animals, don't you? I've seen you down here several times."

I nodded. "I do. There's something so pure about a relationship between people and animals. No pretension, no rules. Just primal understanding. Respect."

Mr. Walsh tugged at the tip of his beard. "Do you know Mr. Roosevelt feels the same way?"

"He does?"

"I've visited his house in Albany many times. A veritable zoo, it is. The entire cellar is filled with animals: rabbits, squirrels, raccoons, opossums. He even has twenty-one guinea pigs, including one Teddy calls 'Father O'Grady.'"

I laughed. "Father O'Grady! What kind of name is that for a rodent?"

Mr. Walsh's stiff suit barely moved beneath his chuckle. "Who knows? They're quite cute, though."

"Yes," I agreed. I'd seen the funny animals with their short legs and floppy ears at a shop in the city. They were all the rage among the elite. "They are."

Mr. Walsh turned to me, face suddenly serious. "Would you like something like that? A home zoo?"

Heat rushed up my collar despite the sudden iciness invading my core. Why was he asking me such a question?

More important, why was he looking at me like that?

"I, um . . ." My lips stumbled to find words. "I—"

"There you are!"

My father's crisp voice cut through the stillness of the barn, rescuing me. He was shadowed, as always, by Mr. Zimmerman. My tongue suddenly loose, I broke into a wide smile. "Father!"

His brow raised momentarily, then furrowed. "Kitty? What are you doing out here?"

My face fell. Apparently the *you* he'd been speaking about had not been me.

"Your daughter was showing me the latest addition," Mr. Walsh said. "There's a new foal."

"Was she now?" My father reached us and gave me a rough peck on the cheek, winking. "How charming." He gave only a fleeting glance over the gate to the newborn before turning his attention to our companion. "Are you ready, Mr. Walsh?"

"Quite."

"Where are you going?"

Both men turned to look at me, surprised. As if my father's presence had somehow, in the last ten seconds, negated mine.

Father gave me a tight smile. "We have business to attend to, my dear."

"Down at the dam? May I come?"

"Not today, Kitty." There was annoyance beneath my father's attempt at a light tone. "We're far too busy, and it's far too muddy for your expensive boots. Besides, Stella mentioned a painting you'd been working on? Perhaps you could get it done and have it ready to show us at dinner this evening."

I pressed my nails into my palms, piercing the skin through the thin fabric of my gloves. Painting? Though I would never dare utter it out loud, the truth was I was *sick* of painting. And novels and music and scrapbooking. Even writing letters to Louisa, Hazel, and Margarite was beginning to lose its luster. Not because I didn't miss them. But because life had somehow become so unbearably dull, I found I had nothing to say. Or, rather, nothing *worth* saying. Not when compared to their current exploits: Hazel serving in the International Red Cross, Margarite attending college in Munich, and Louisa volunteering on a missionary team to Egypt.

"But I—"

"Another time, Kathleen." Father was already walking away, his hand raised in a dismissive wave, Mr. Zimmerman trailing closely behind.

Mr. Walsh gave my rigid hand another kiss before following my father out of the barn, leaving me staring at the dust particles, dancing in the filtered sunlight, in their wake.

I did not attend to my painting after they left.

In fact, I did not go back up to the main house at all.

This was *our* kingdom, my father had said. His and mine. I was *part* of this family, part of its future. And my role would not be relegated to watercolors. I had every right to know what was happening down at the dam.

So, I followed.

At a distance and at a much more leisurely pace, but follow I did. Or, at least, that's how it started. But soon, I found myself distracted by the forest around me. The flora and fauna were slowly awakening from their long winter slumber. Though I adored the house and grounds of our manor, a large portion of the McDaniel land was undeveloped wilderness, and it was these wild, overgrown, unmanicured lands I loved best. I'd spent hours as a child exploring under the dark canopy of trees, simultaneously calmed and excited by the scent of damp earth, pine, and wildflowers. The smell of possibility and adventure. Of freedom. Back then, I'd become quite adept at finding mushrooms and spotting deer camouflaged amidst the branches. I felt a momentary twinge of sadness when, after an hour of walking through the forest, I'd discovered neither.

I guess some skills had to give way inside my brain to make room for rules about silverware placement and proper sleeve length.

The sun was high in the sky by the time I finally decided to take a rest. I wasn't tired necessarily, but sweat was beginning to drip down my neck. And ladies, I remembered, were *never* to sweat. Best to take a breather before it began to dampen my already wild hair. I didn't need another mark against me when I arrived at the site; both my boots and the bottoms of my dress and petticoats were indeed covered in mud.

I leaned against a birch tree, removing my gloves and running my fingers over the rough bark. Turning my face to the sun, I closed my eyes, taking in the crisp, clean air. Out here, I could breathe. Away from the house, the rules, the dreams, the disquiet. Among the trees, everything else melted away. There were no servants, no Otto Zimmerman, no Theodore Walsh.

No Father.

With the intrusive thought, a needle of alarm pierced my moment of bliss. I loved my father; he was everything to me. What an ugly, impossible notion that being without him was preferable to being with him. It simply wasn't true.

Except, a small voice whispered, *sometimes it is.*

I thought back to the barn, to the dismissive way he had acted around me. His words said one thing—*you are important, you are a part of this*—and yet his actions often made me feel the opposite. Small, insignificant.

Invisible.

I shook away the thought, scolding myself. No. I would not allow insecurities to creep back in. Not today. Not when the air was crisp and the sun was shining. When, out here in God's creation, there was peace, the sound of my breathing interweaving with the melody of the forest—chirping birds, rubbing branches, whispering grass.

And . . . a breaking twig.

My eyes snapped open. I gripped the tree, muscles stiff. The birds had stopped singing; in their absence the silence grew taut. A sudden breeze whistled through the branches above me, cooling my sweat, causing my skin to prickle. How quickly my solitude had changed from tranquil to ominous.

No one knew I was out here.

A lady. In the woods. By herself.

Another crack of a twig, closer this time.

I could run. Should run. Surely Mademoiselle Dubois's instructions on poise didn't include moments of imminent danger. But with the thick mud and my jumble of petticoats, I knew I wouldn't get too far. I had absolutely no choice but to stand and face it, whatever it was. Perhaps it was just a deer. Or a squirrel even. With a courage I did not feel, I spun around, eyes fluttering about wildly for the source of the disturbance. Thankfully, my childhood skills chose this moment to return; through the thick mess of brambles, I could just make out a shape, peering out at me from behind the thicket.

A man.

A man with eyes that still haunted me, even two weeks later. Eyes that made my heart pound and my mouth go dry at their memory.

"Wesley," I blurted. "Wesley Odell."

If I'd had any doubts about the man's identity, they vanished when he stepped into the light. His walk was bold. Brazen. Not at all ashamed or self-conscious about encountering a lone woman on private property.

He stopped several feet in front of me, studying me suspiciously. He was cleaner today, no dirt on his face or trousers, though I was pretty sure his yellow button-down had, at one time, been white. His blond hair was tucked inside a newsboy cap. "How do you know my name?"

"I'm Kathleen McDaniel," I stuttered through disappointment. I obviously hadn't made as much of an impression on him as he had on me. "I was there. That day at the dam. With my father."

Those strikingly deep eyes hardened, and I recognized the moment he recognized me. "You."

Sudden fright trembled my limbs. The earlier fear I'd held about encountering a strange man alone in the woods paled in comparison to the new dread I held. Judging by the look on Wesley Odell's face, perhaps stumbling across a stranger would have been better.

I lifted my chin, hoping he did not see it quiver. "I was just making my way to the worksite. My father is expecting me."

Lying wasn't proper for ladies, but I figured this was another exception that could be made in matters of life and death.

"I bet he is." His accent was thicker than I'd first thought. Definitely Irish.

"So, if you'll excuse me, I best be on my way."

Wesley hesitated, hands behind his back. His face twitched with thoughts I was pretty sure I didn't want to know. But still, I held my ground, and eventually, he took a step back, spreading his arms out wide. "Of course."

I took a step, preparing to move past him, only to freeze when he pulled something out from behind his back. Something large. Brown.

A rock? A club?

Was he going to bash me over the head when I tried to pass?

Seeing my hesitation, Wesley followed my eyes to his palm. He released an amused breath through his nostrils. "Relax. It's just a camera. And it's worth more to me than anything I could ever do to you."

"A camera?" My eyes widened in spite of myself. The only cameras I'd ever encountered were the large, bulky ones inside portrait studios. Though I'd seen the advertisements in magazines for these new smaller models—nicknamed Brownies—I hadn't yet met anyone who actually owned one. Though less expensive than their bulkier counterparts, my father considered them too much of a passing fad to waste even the meagerest of funds on one. Still, I was fascinated by them. Fascinated even more by the pictures now being taken by "laymen," such as Edward S. Curtis and Samuel Bourne, who captured images of things like the plight of Native Americans and the slums of India. Things the upper class—*my* class—thought shouldn't be photographed.

"How did you get a camera?" The words came out before I could stop them, to my instant regret.

"I didn't steal it, if that's what you're implying," Wesley said, scowling.

A flush crept across my cheeks and down my neck. "No, not at all. I—"

"I bought it," he interrupted. "Well, my *da* did. He saved up for it."

"That was kind of him. To give it to you, I mean." Why did everything that came out of my mouth suddenly sound wrong?

"Yeah, well, he wasn't going to use it. Typhus makes everything worthless."

I choked on a hard swallow. Death was not a topic usually broached in a polite conversation, especially one between two people who'd only known each other for five minutes. I shifted from one foot to the other. "So, um, is that what you're doing? Taking pictures?"

Wesley turned the camera over in his hand. "It's my one day off. Figured I might as well make good use of it." He gestured vaguely through the trees. "Ain't like I'll have many more opportunities to capture scenes like this."

I squinted. Across the valley, through the forest, I could just make out a smattering of buildings, white against dark. I recognized them as the small farms situated just on the other side of our property line. I turned to find Wesley staring at me, irritation once again clouding his face. "What do you mean?" I asked slowly.

"Well, most of it will be gone soon," he said with a scowl. "Flooded for the new reservoir. For your *da*."

I frowned. "The new reservoir is on our land—"

A short bark of laughter cut me short. "Yeah, the part your *da* owns but doesn't really need. He's got that much to go around. The rest of it will be right where those houses are sitting now. They've all been condemned, the owners forced to move. Taken right out from under their feet. They even dug up some graves, just over that hill. Bones that have lain there for a hundred years. Gone."

Saliva collected in my mouth. My father hadn't told me about that. But still . . .

"I'm sure the people have been more than compensated for their losses."

"Compensated." Wesley spat the word. "For pennies on the dollar of what their property was worth."

I squared my shoulders, hearing my father's words flow from

my mouth. "The new reservoir is needed for the water supply and for economic growth—"

"Economic growth." He snorted. "It's needed to make your *da* money, you mean."

Any fear or trepidation I felt toward Wesley Odell melted, replaced by indignation. And, even though I knew it wasn't ladylike, flat-out anger. "That's a pretty high and mighty thing to say when your pockets are also getting filled by this same project."

Wesley's laugh echoed off the trees, causing me to cringe. "You think my pockets are getting filled?" With his free hand, he pulled at the fabric of his trousers. Sure enough, nothing but a few pieces of lint floated to the dead leaves below. "I bet your *afternoon tea*"—these words he spoke with a sneer—"cost more than an entire week of my wages."

I let out a huff, lips sputtering. The *audacity*. The *gall*.

The niggling sensation that he was probably right.

I'd seen the worksite. Seen the men. More than that, I was seeing Wesley now. Yes, he was cleaner, but his hair was still greasy, and not with pomade. His skin was dry, fingernails tinged with dirt. The shirt he wore was threadbare in places, pants sagging around his skinny frame. He was a working man, obviously, but not a man of means.

He was a man of *survival*.

My hands ran down the sides of my skirt, catching on the delicate lace trim. I was suddenly self-conscious in a way I'd never felt before.

Still, I resented the implications his words laid on my father. Lawrence McDaniel was a good man. A successful, kind man who'd pulled himself up by his bootstraps and earned every cent he'd ever made. Cents he now used to create something the citizens of New York desperately needed. Cents used to employ men who might not otherwise eat. His workers might not have been getting rich, but they were certainly better off than they'd be if he hadn't given them jobs. It was an outrage.

I should storm away in protest.

No, I thought, suddenly remembering my place. This was my land. *He* should leave.

I told him as much.

"I'm not done taking pictures."

"Well, I say you are."

"You're very rude for a *lady*, you know that?"

My mouth dropped open. "*I'm* rude? You're the one—"

"Look, I'll leave in a little bit. I'm waiting for the right light on the river, and then I'll go. I ain't hurting anything. And, anyways, ain't there somewhere you need to be? Some new pair of shoes you need to buy?" The last question was spoken under his breath.

A hundred rebuttals came to my lips, but it was a question that passed through them instead. "What do you mean, the right light?"

He rolled his eyes. "Photography is all about the right light. It determines the shadow, sets the mood. It takes persistence. Patience. There's more to it than just clicking a button. There's . . . an art to it."

I tilted my head. There was no spite in Wesley's tone. Instead, there was a hint of reverence, of something sensitive beneath his surly, ill-mannered exterior. Something to which only those bright-green eyes—the ones that I couldn't look away from, the ones that made me feel every drop of anger, umbrage, and something else deeper that I couldn't quite place—gave whisper.

Something that pulled me back to Switzerland. To Hazel, Louisa, Margarite.

And to a dream. Rolling green fields. The thud of a plow, pulling up rich brown earth. That man again. Hazy in features but strong in presence, pointing out the delicacy of the seeds being laid in soil. *There's an art to it. The beauty of God's hands, working through ours.*

Stop it, Kitty. It was my father's voice now, inside my head but as real as if he were standing beside me. *You're being ridiculous.*

The scene vanished. I coughed into my palms and, suddenly remembering the impropriety of my bare hands, retrieved my gloves, shoving my fingers into them with more force than was necessary. "You're right," I said, not looking at him. "I do have somewhere to be."

But Wesley had already forgotten me. He was turning a knob on the side of the camera, looking through the viewfinder.

With a huff made of equal parts hurt and chagrin, I turned and began walking through the woods. I was ten minutes in before I realized I was making my way back toward the main house rather than the damsite, like I'd originally intended.

I tried to believe it was a mistake, a result of becoming so incensed by Wesley's rudeness and indifference. That had to be it. I hadn't turned around on purpose, hadn't meant to go back to the main house to avoid my father and Mr. Walsh. It was absurd.

Even more absurd was the notion that I was afraid they'd have been able to see my encounter with Wesley written all over my face.

> "For eastern Texas: Rain Saturday, with high northerly winds; Sunday, rain, followed by clearing."

GALVESTON DAILY NEWS WEATHER FORECAST
Saturday, September 8, 1900

TEN

SATURDAY, SEPTEMBER 8, 1900
GALVESTON, TEXAS

Sleep had not come easily. The conversation with Emily replayed in my head, interspersed with snippets of Matthew's sure-footed assertions. I dozed in fits, small naps beleaguered by unsettling dreams. Scenes filled with blood and water, shadows and sunlight. Dreams of Wesley, my father, Matthew, Emily—the past, the present, and the future, all spiraling inside my head. I finally awoke for good, thin nightgown sticky with sweat, at the first pale light.

Anxiety thrummed in my veins. I rubbed my throat, willing myself to breathe. The room felt stuffy and hot, the air thick, and it took me several moments to pinpoint the source of my unease. It wasn't just the lingering shadows from my nightmares, which still refused to fade even after I'd opened my eyes. No, it was the silence.

There were no gulls.

For the first time ever, their impatient, incessant screams were not floating through our open window. Instead, there was only the steady, unvarying thud of waves crashing onto shore. Louder than I'd ever heard it before.

Thump . . . thump . . . thump.

Like an ominous clock, ticking for all to hear, counting down my remaining moments at St. Mary's.

It was Saturday morning. Deadline day. Decision day.

And I had made my choice.

Because it had never really been a choice at all.

I had been foolish to even consider Mother Camillus's offer. And it wasn't just because I knew I would eventually be found, even in a convent. My gaze traveled across the room, landing on Emily.

Her chest rose and fell gently. Unencumbered. Peaceful.

I longed for what she had, her peace and her purpose. Although they seemed opposite in nearly every way, she reminded me of Hazel. Of Louisa and Margarite. She'd found a life where she could make a difference. Where she mattered. I rolled her words over again in my head: *Sometimes God has to tear down all the distractions, all the lies in our lives, in order for us to see the truth. To see that after everything else is gone, He's still there.*

Since that awful night, my faith had felt like one more thread in a knot of deception I was too heartbroken to untangle. I wasn't strong enough to truly consider devoting my life to God, no matter how much I craved what Emily was offering. Unlike her, I would be living a lie while pretending to serve Truth. And that would not do. My conscience was burdened enough.

And so, I would do the only thing I could—I would run.

Again.

For the second morning in a row, I found myself dressing, washing, and slipping from the room before sunrise, only this time, the brown satchel hung over my shoulder. My heart panged as I glanced at my roommate one last time. It was better this way,

I told myself. Better not to get bogged down with goodbyes. Safer. Safer for her. For Maggie.

Sweet Maggie.

Tears burned my eyes as I passed the closed door to her room. She would think I had abandoned her.

And I had. I had my reasons, of course, but they would do little to soothe her broken heart when she awoke.

I could only hope she would forgive me. And that, someday, she would understand.

It was that rare kind of morning when the sky glows iridescent, the fingerlike clouds awash in shades of pink and pearl as the sun began its slow, sleepy ascent into the eastern sky. Beautiful, otherworldly, and completely at odds with my mood. The salty wind whistled between the dormitories, and the crash of the ocean grew even louder as I bypassed the last row of salt cedars, leaving nothing between myself and the Gulf but a thin strip of crushed-shell beach.

Farther up the shore, a man stood beside a two-wheeled wagon, one hand on the muzzle of his horse, the other held in front of his face, fingers curled around a small metal object.

I almost turned back. Not only was it not safe or proper for a woman to be alone with a man in a place as deserted as this stretch of beach, but there was the added danger that this person could be another henchman sent to search for me. Best to stay out of sight until he was gone. But there was something familiar in the man's posture, the overly straight position of his spine and squareness of his shoulders. I took a few tentative steps, the wind at my back pushing me forward.

I was only a few yards away when I finally recognized him.

"Mr. Cline," I said, raising a hand to my head in an attempt to keep my hair from blowing into my face.

Isaac Cline turned, eyes widening. "Annie! What are you doing down here at this hour?"

"I could ask you the same thing." I hoped I came off as more coy than elusive. I tucked my satchel behind my back. It wasn't that I didn't trust Isaac, but I didn't know him well either.

"I'm timing the waves." He waved his right hand, revealing a pocket watch. Another swell thudded before us, as if to emphasize his statement. Like yesterday evening's waves, the crest was darkened by sand. Foam-like strands of white lace crisscrossed its surface as it retreated.

"Timing the waves?"

But he'd already turned back to the ocean, a deep crease lining his forehead. His eyes flickered between his watch and the sea, lips moving silently.

Unease prickled the back of my neck. His posture may have been the same as yesterday, but his countenance was not. And as another wave thumped ashore, I felt my fingers grow cold. "Mr. Cline?"

"It doesn't make any sense." The words were spoken out loud, but they weren't directed at me. Instead, he stared at the watch in his hand. "With a wind this strong coming from the north, the swells should not be so fast or so strong. The tide is already four and a half feet above where it should be. It simply doesn't calculate. It's . . . it's scientifically impossible." He glanced up at the sky.

I followed his gaze. The magic of sunrise had vanished. The mother-of-pearl sky was gone, threads of clouds now interlocking to form a solid mass, painted in shades of orange and gray, like fire behind a wall of smoke.

Under my long sleeves, goose bumps sprouted over my arms. "It appears you were right about the rain." I forced a hint of cheerfulness into my tone to which Isaac did not respond.

To our left, we heard a shout and a squeal. Using my hand as a shield, I squinted, surprised to see a group of bathers farther up the beach, already laughing and splashing in the large surf. It was a joyful scene, lighthearted and blissful.

Perhaps that's what made Isaac's expression seem all the more dark. "They need to get out of the water."

He made a move to jump into his wagon, but I grabbed his arm. His body jerked beneath my touch, shocked at either my continued presence or my impropriety. He spun around to face me. When his eyes met mine, I wished they hadn't.

I didn't take much stock in arrogant men; I'd had enough of those to last a lifetime. But, in that moment, I wished desperately to see hubris in Isaac Cline's face once more. Anything would have been better than what I was seeing right now.

Because the only thing I saw . . . was fear.

"Mr. Cline . . ." The wind stole my words, but he finally seemed to hear me. He pulled out of my grasp and gripped both of my shoulders.

"Annie, there's a storm coming."

"Yes, you said it would rain."

He shook his head, a few strands of dark hair falling loose across his forehead. "No. Not just rain. It's . . . different than what we thought. Farther up the shore, water is already creeping into the streets."

"But that happens all the time. It's—"

"Not like this."

Despite the wind whipping our backs, Isaac's words lingered between us, heavy and stagnant. Another wave slammed onto the shore, louder and more insistent. Closer. As I stared at his furrowed brow and bloodshot eyes, dread dripped down my spine.

"People must get away from the beach. Move to higher ground. Now."

"Mr. Cline—"

"I have to go." He released me, swinging his long frame over the side of the wagon and into the driver's seat. Gathering the reins in his hands, he began to tug on them, then paused. He looked down at me. Frowned. "I'm sorry."

I didn't quite understand his words. He was sorry? Sorry for what? But a sense of foreboding evaporated those questions before I even had time to consider them. Instead, I seized the side of his wagon with numb fingers. "Are we in danger?"

Something bleak and unreadable passed over Isaac's face. Something that answered my question without his needing to say a word.

"Stay safe, Annie."

And then he was gone.

Apprehension needled me as I clutched the strap of my satchel. I needed to go. To run. I'd made my decision.

And yet . . .

Isaac's tone. His face, his words.

Something was wrong. Seriously wrong.

He'd said everyone needed to get off the beach. But he'd headed east, toward the bathhouses and the city proper, presumably to notify people there. St. Mary's sat in the opposite direction. Alone, away from the city, directly on the beach.

No one would be warning them.

But I could.

Faces flashed before me. And not just those from the orphanage. I saw the faces from New York, Wesley there with them.

With all those I could have helped—should have helped—and didn't.

I trudged back to the orphanage, second-guessing myself with every step. The wind pressed against me, stronger now, roaring in my ears, the only sound loud enough to drown out the crashing of the waves—and the pounding of my own heart. I was overreacting; weathermen were wrong all the time. The beachfront flooded constantly. Storms were common.

They'll be fine, Kathleen. Go. Just go.

Nevertheless, I could not shake the memory of Isaac's eyes. Of the look on his face as he'd driven away, the unanswered question still hanging in the air between us.

Are we in danger?

When I arrived, the children were filing into the dining room, cheeks freshly scrubbed and hair combed. Even though I was hungry, the smell of fresh-baked bread and hard-boiled eggs rolled my stomach. I'd been hoping to avoid Mother Camillus—to avoid everyone—today. But here I was, heading straight for her office.

"Sister Annie!"

I closed my eyes as a sweet, familiar voice rang through the entryway. Full of self-loathing, I continued striding forward, pretending I didn't hear.

"Sister Annie?"

It took every ounce of willpower I possessed to turn at the feel of Maggie's small hand on my arm. I wondered if she could sense the falseness of my smile. She was only a child, yes, but an astute one.

Sure enough, her grin immediately turned southward. "What are you doing?" Her gaze darted to my satchel, which I immediately tried to hide behind my back. "Are you going somewhere?"

"I was just . . . taking a walk." This was why I had wanted to leave. To make a clean break. I hated lying to Maggie. But the sight of her rounded cheeks and deep, soulful eyes made it impossible to tell the truth.

She pressed her lips together. She didn't believe me; I could see it on her face. And yet she wrestled with the *need* to believe, to not allow doubt to creep into the one relationship in which she put her faith.

I felt my soul crack. "I . . ." My mouth was dry. I swallowed and pretended to busy myself untangling the knots in my hair. "I'm sorry, Maggie. I have to go. I need to see Mother Camillus."

"Why?"

From across the entryway, I spotted Sister Felicitus. I met her eye over the heads of the children. She raised one thin eyebrow at me.

Giving Maggie's shoulders a quick squeeze, I forced a smile down at her. She did not return it. "You should go eat. Before Angela takes yours."

Maggie scowled but eventually obeyed, watching me out of the corner of her eye until she disappeared inside the dining hall.

I hurried over to Sister Felicitus. "I need to speak with Mother Camillus."

She raised her chin. "Yes, I would say you do. She's been looking for you. You weren't at your assigned duty station this morning."

Shame burned my cheeks. "I know. I—"

"She's in her office." Sister Felicitus gave me a pointed look before spinning on her heel and stalking away, rosary beads clicking as she followed the children into the dining room.

With a measured sigh, I wrapped my sweaty hands around the strap of my satchel and made my way toward the imposing wooden door of Mother Camillus's office. I rapped twice before I could stop myself and entered without being commanded. "Mother Camillus?"

She was standing at her window, staring out at the rolling hills of sand. Rain had begun to dot the glass, wind moaning through a crack in the sash.

"Mother Camillus, I need to—"

My words bit off as she turned around. Her face was drawn,

lips tight and bloodless, and her eyes immediately drifted to the bag on my shoulder. "I see you've made your decision."

I licked my lips, tightening my grip on the bag. "I have, yes. But that's not why—"

"And you have chosen not to take me up on my offer."

I nodded once. Slowly.

"I see." She clasped her hands in front of her. They disappeared under the black fabric of her habit. "Well, I can't say I'm not disappointed. But God gives us all free will. So . . ." She straightened her spine. "Best of luck to you, Miss McDaniel. And Godspeed."

There was no malice in her tone. Just the customary detached, no-nonsense timbre she used with the orphans. But still her words slammed into me like a punch to the gut.

Leaving was the right thing to do, the only realistic option. So why now, here in her presence, did it feel so *wrong*?

I swallowed my hurt, forcing it down along with the lump in my throat. "That's not why I've come to see you."

Mother Camillus leaned back slightly. "Oh?"

"There's . . . a storm coming." The words came out so weak, so very small, especially considering the weight of trepidation that accompanied them.

She let out a dismissive laugh. "It may surprise you to learn, Miss McDaniel, that I'm well aware there's a storm coming. I do have eyes, you know." She gestured to the window. "And Mr. Cline put a weather report in the paper yesterday, saying we should expect some rain this morning."

I shook my head. "No, you don't understand."

"Understand what?"

"I . . . I saw Mr. Cline on the beach this morning." I glanced at her quickly before directing my eyes to my boots.

Mother Camillus's mouth opened and closed twice, lips twitching. I saw her question, the inquiry about my acquaintance with

Mr. Cline. More than that, however, I saw her realization of the truth. She understood all the things I left unsaid in my statement. My bag, the beach.

I'd been running away. Hiding from this very conversation.

And yet here I stood.

I believe that alone was what caused her to allow me to continue.

"He was timing the waves," I stammered. "They were . . . well, they were huge. Bigger than I'd ever seen. And, I think, bigger than any *he'd* ever seen." I glanced up. "He told me that everyone needed to get off the beach. Away from the sea."

"Away from the sea?"

I nodded. "We need to move to higher ground."

Mother Camillus let out a short, barking laugh. "I'm not sure if you've noticed, Miss McDaniel, but there's no such thing as 'higher ground' on Galveston. I don't believe there is any flatter place on God's green earth."

Another gust of wind, stronger this time, caused us both to jump. Glancing out the window, I noticed the rain had begun to come down in sheets.

"Then, just, away then." I struggled to contain the anxiety in my tone. "Away from the beach."

"Mr. Cline said that?"

I nodded.

She exhaled a long, steady sigh. "And where did he propose we go? In the driving rain? Nearly a hundred children and a dozen nuns with no wagons, no carts, and certainly no automobiles?"

"He didn't . . ." My voice trailed off. I closed my eyes, letting out a deep breath through my nose. She was right. Evacuating was impractical. There was nowhere to go . . . and no way to get there.

When I opened my eyes, Mother Camillus was staring at me. Or rather, I realized, staring *through* me. Though she remained still, her eyes swam with rapid thoughts. "We'll gather the children together," she said finally. "Everyone in this building. It's newer. Stronger. And farther from the ocean than the boys' dormitory. It's survived many a storm. We'll be safe here."

I wondered if she truly believed what she was saying or if she was merely trying to convince herself of the suitability of her only option. There was no way to be sure. In true Mother Camillus fashion, her expression relayed nothing but firm resolution.

"We'll need to make a list," she continued, starting to pace. "Account for every soul under our care. Gather supplies: candles, food, blankets. We'll take everything up to the second story." She was speaking fast, her Irish lilt causing her words to melt together. "Medicine. Some of the children require daily medication. We'll need to make sure—"

"I can help."

But Mother Camillus talked right over me, counting off needs on her fingers. "And books. Drawing paper. Pencils. The children will need something to do, something to keep them calm. We'll—"

"I can help," I repeated, louder this time. The words surprised even me. I had intended to warn the sisters and then continue on my way; I wasn't sure when or why I had suddenly changed my mind. Perhaps it was the reality of the situation; the danger, although always genuine, had somehow been made more tangible by Mother Camillus's acknowledgment of it. The fear I felt for the orphans and sisters who had become like my family was suddenly overwhelming. And yet I knew that my motivations lay deeper.

As deep as the reservoir created by my father's new dam.

I needed to stay and prove that I wasn't a bad person.

To the nuns, to God.

To myself.

A sudden crack of thunder punctuated my thoughts. Mother Camillus froze in her pacing. From outside came a low, rumbling roar, though whether from the wind or the waves, it was impossible to tell. It rose and then fell, leaving an eerie, unsettling silence in its wake, broken only by the sound of rain lashing the window.

"I can help." It felt insane to say it again. I barely recognized the sound of my own voice. Spoken barely above a whisper, my words were still loud enough to echo through the anxious quiet.

Mother Camillus turned her eyes to me. It was as if she'd only just remembered who I was, why I was there. I could see a thousand words collecting on her tongue.

But it wasn't the time or the place for any of them.

With a curt nod from her, we got to work. Thankfully, all the children were already inside the building, having gathered for breakfast. They buzzed with excitement inside the dining room, sensing an unexpected and not wholly unwelcome disruption to their normal routine. Many of them pressed their faces to the windows, straining to see past the sheets of rain, willing to risk the rod of correction for a chance to be one of the select few with firsthand knowledge of the storm. Upon Mother Camillus's instruction, Sister Catherine and Sister Elizabeth quickly took charge, herding the children out of the room and up the stairs, though it did not lessen the excited tittering. Sister Raphael and Sister Vincent oversaw the gathering of blankets and candles; Sister Bernice, food. Sister Sarah enlisted a few of the older children to help her load up on books, while Sister Felicitus collected supplies from the infirmary.

I was given a list of names from Mother Camillus's office. The chaos made it nearly impossible to take roll; the children refused to sit still or remain with their peer groups. Not that I blamed them. I, too, felt as if I would jump out of my skin if I didn't move around. The entire building seemed to vibrate, from within and without, a sensation that traveled up through my toes and into every nerve. With all of us gathered in one large room, the heat quickly became unbearable, the smell of body odor and morning breath overpowering. The wind was louder up here, moaning like the spooks of old campfire stories. It was second only to the hammering of rain on the roof right over our heads.

I had just finished checking off the names of all the boys when there was a tug on my skirt. Maggie stared up at me, brown eyes wide with a mixture of awe and fear. "What's going on?" she whispered.

"It's just a storm," I said lamely.

"I'm scared."

"There's nothing to be scared of."

She stuck the tip of her tongue out from between her lips. "You promise?"

There it was again. That face. That look. And that ache it caused inside of me, making me desperate not to lie but incapable of telling the truth.

"Why don't you go sit down with Rebecca?" I said thickly. "She'll look out for you. I bet she might even read you a story if you ask nicely."

"I want to stay with you."

I crouched down next to her, blinking rapidly. "I want you to stay with me too. But I need to finish taking roll. I have to make sure everyone is here. That everyone is safe."

Maggie's lips trembled, but she retreated stoically, breaking my heart all over again in the process.

I moved from the boys to the girls, checking names as I matched faces. After that, it was the sisters. Sister Raphael, check. Sister Sarah, check. Sister Hannah, check. And on and on down the list, until only one name remained.

Emily.

My pulse went sluggish, fingers cold. Whipping my head around wildly, I scanned the faces in the room again, praying a prayer I somehow already knew wouldn't be answered. Emily wasn't here. I could feel it in my bones. Hers wasn't a face I would miss, nor would my presence have gone unremarked upon had she seen me. Not after I'd slipped out again this morning without waking her. I allowed my eyes to rest on each soul in the room, a sour taste collecting in the back of my mouth.

No Emily.

"Mother Camillus," I said, crossing the room in a brisk stride. "Emily's not here."

She frowned. "What?"

I waved the paper in her face. "I took roll. Every single person is accounted for except Emily."

"That doesn't make any sense. Where else would she possibly be?"

"I don't know, but she's not here. We have to—"

"She left."

Mother Camillus and I turned. Sister Bernice stood behind us, peering at us through her large spectacles, a towheaded baby on her hip.

"What do you mean she left?" Mother Camillus took a step toward her.

The baby on her hip babbled and reached for her rosary. Sister Bernice gently wrapped the child's fingers in her own wrinkled ones. "I saw her leave this morning. During breakfast. I tried to ask her where she was going, but she waved me off." A deep groove formed between her brows. "It was very unlike her."

"She didn't talk to anybody? Say anything?"

Sister Bernice shook her head. "She went into the kitchen, but she didn't eat. It was like she was looking for something. She seemed agitated. Upset. And then she just . . . left."

A weight slid over my chest. I pressed a shaking hand to my lips, breath coming out in shallow gasps.

Emily hadn't been looking for something. She'd been looking for some*one*. Me. She'd awoken to find me gone and set out to find me. And when she hadn't found me in the kitchen, where I was supposed to be . . .

We must have missed each other. Perhaps she'd slipped out when I was in Mother Camillus's office.

It didn't matter when. It didn't matter how. All that mattered was that Emily was out in this storm.

Because of me.

I suddenly felt dizzy. I grabbed Mother Camillus's arm, causing her to start.

A gust of wind rattled the nearest window accusingly. From outside came another rumble, lower this time. More ominous.

"I'll find her." My voice was high-pitched and unrecognizable. I released my grip on Mother Camillus. "I'll go and find her."

"You can't. You yourself said it wasn't safe."

"I don't care. I have to—"

"Annie . . ."

It didn't escape my notice that Mother Camillus had used my false name, nor did I miss the tenderness in her tone when she said it. But it was kindness I did not deserve and would not have heeded even if I'd stopped to listen. Despite her gentle pleading, I was already gone, flying down the stairs, panic and guilt rising with each step forward.

She couldn't have gotten far. There was no way. Not in the short amount of time, not in this storm.

I would find her. Somehow, somewhere, I would find her.

I reached the bottom landing, putting a hand out to steady the still-bouncing satchel on my hip.

The satchel.

My fingers curled around the strap. The sound of the driving rain echoed through the eerie stillness of the cavernous downstairs, stiffening my muscles. I pulled the bag to my chest, cradling it like a baby. I couldn't leave it. Wouldn't even think of leaving it.

And yet that rain. Like curtains of water, hanging from the sky. No umbrella in the world could protect the satchel and its contents from this rain, not that amount, not with this wind. It would get drenched. Damaged.

Destroyed.

The thought strangled the breath in my throat, a physical ache rising up from beneath my ribcage. I pawed at the flap, removing the sacred object from the depths.

Wesley's camera.

Holding the lone reminder of that awful night, I felt suddenly, completely, heartbreakingly alone, although I knew the children were just upstairs. No longer could I smell the lingering scent of the orphans' breakfast; instead, all around me were the scents of thick mud, flowing water, and freshly applied mortar. I squeezed its side, both hating and cherishing this camera for the memories it held. For the lies—and the truth—it had exposed.

I could not take a chance of anything happening to it.

Tucking the camera back inside the satchel, I removed the strap from around my neck. Without allowing myself a moment to second-guess my decision, I flew up the stairs, tucked the bag back in its hiding spot beneath my bed, and retreated quickly to the foyer. The camera would be safer here. Safe from the wind, from the rain, until I returned.

Until I could find Emily. Then I would bring her back, wait out the storm, grab the camera, and disappear, once and for all.

Steeling myself, I stepped outside, gasping as a sudden torrent of brown foamy water wrapped itself around my ankles. My skirt grew heavy as it became instantly sodden. Sloshing forward a few paces, I gagged on the stench of fish. Wind whipped around me, pushing my hair into my eyes. I yanked it back in frustration and squinted toward the Gulf.

Dread washed over me, in waves as real as those licking at my feet. Just beyond the moaning salt cedars, where once there had been a strip of sand, lay nothing but the great gray expanse of ocean.

I could only hope that Emily had not started her search for me on the beach.

Because the beach was no more.

ELEVEN

APRIL 1900
CROTON-ON-HUDSON, NEW YORK

"I can't believe they gave John his own dish." My father sniffed as one of the footmen set a plate in front of him. "Oysters Rockefeller, indeed."

"Now, now, Lawrence," Mr. Walsh laughed. "It doesn't matter what they're called. What matters is how they taste." He used a fork to pull the baked oyster topped with shredded greens from its shell and devoured it with a slurp. "Absolutely delicious. Don't you agree, Miss McDaniel?"

I smiled, hoping he couldn't read the tightness in my lips. Truth be told, I didn't care much for seafood, especially oysters, no matter how they were cooked. But Mr. Walsh did. And Father had acquiesced to serving them tonight—despite his misgivings over the name—because they were our guest's favorite.

And one of the most expensive things on Miss Dover's menu.

"They're . . . wonderful," I finished with fake enthusiasm, though I could not bring myself to raise the slimy concoction to my lips. "It's a shame I'm not hungry."

"Too much cake with the ladies this afternoon?" my father teased.

My mouth grew even tauter. "Something like that."

At my father's insistence, I had spent the afternoon with my "friends." Or, rather, the friends he *wanted* me to have, Mrs. Carolyn Gardner and Mrs. O'Donnell chief among them. Wanting to avoid a repeat of my homecoming dinner, I did not bring up politics, world events, or anything outside the realm of fashion or gossip. *Suitable* topics of conversation. This meant the afternoon had passed swimmingly, as pleasant as a get-together among such well-brought-up ladies should have been.

It also meant it had been mind-numbingly dull.

"Yes," I managed. "What can I say? We are all very excited about the latest fashions coming from Paris."

"Paris! Bah!" My father finished his last oyster and laid his fork down with a clang. "Is anything good coming out of Paris these days?"

"Oh, come now," Mr. Walsh said, laughing. "I think that's a little unfair. The dress you're wearing tonight, Miss McDaniel—it's French, is it not?"

I glanced down at my gown. It was lilac satin with white-and-gold lace trim up the bodice and around the collar line. A scarf of gold-dotted black gauze nuzzled my throat, matching my long black gloves. "It is, actually."

He winked. "Well, there you go."

"Dresses are one thing." Though his tone was serious, my father gave me a subtle wink. "But this whole nonsense about the Universal Exposition. I heard the construction crews aren't even finished, and the opening is only a few weeks away. It wouldn't surprise me if the Parisians were doing it on purpose."

"On purpose?" I asked.

"The United States will have more exhibits than any other nation. I imagine it will be an embarrassment to the French, being shown up like that in their own country. I bet they are trying to sabotage it for that very reason."

Mr. Walsh tipped his wineglass to his lips thoughtfully. "Well, still, we can't fault the French for being . . . French, I suppose. Their talents lie elsewhere. Like in Miss McDaniel's dress here." He tilted his head in my direction, sly smile barely visible under his facial hair.

I forced the corners of my mouth upward, pulling my hands into my lap.

"Besides," he continued, "it's not as if they really stood a chance. There is no other nation in the world that can compete with American ingenuity and industrialization."

"Hear! Hear!" my father said, raising his glass. "And this new dam will be a testament to that!"

Mr. Walsh raised his own in earnest agreement.

I lifted my goblet, though I did not parrot their cheer. As the men drained their wine, I kept mine in front of my face, pretending to partake but, in reality, doing my best to disguise my racing heart, which I was sure would be obvious to a single glance.

Because at the mention of the dam, there he was.

As if he'd ever actually left.

Wesley.

Those green eyes. That crooked, arrogant smirk. The perception that he was a man of both less and more than any other person I'd ever met.

There's an art to it.

At the memory of his words, Wesley faded away, and the vision from that day swam in front of me instead. The farm, the fields, the mysterious man. Truth was, this daydream had haunted me just as much over the past few days as Wesley had. It was the first time the man inside one of my visions had spoken. And the sound of his voice, so familiar and yet so uncertain, seemed to tug me both closer and further away from some revelation just outside my grasp. It was there, floating at the periphery of my perception. If only I could reach it. If only I could see.

If only I could stop being distracted by the memory of Wesley's rough hands. How delicately they'd maneuvered the camera.

There's an art to it.

"Kathleen, are you ill?"

I sputtered into my glass, wrenching my thoughts back to the present. "I'm sorry?"

My father was staring at me, brow furrowed. "Your face . . . It's red."

I coughed and replaced my wine on the tabletop. "I apologize. I . . ." I stammered, trying to find an excuse for my flushed countenance. Instead, Wesley's face floated before me once again. "Just a little warm," I squeaked out. "Would you find me terribly rude if I excused myself for a breath of air?"

"Not at all," Mr. Walsh interjected, rising suddenly. "Do you need me to accompany you?"

"No, please, I don't mean to be a bother. You two enjoy your oysters. I'll be back in a moment." I gestured to one of the footmen near the back of the room. "Please don't hold the next course. You may go ahead and serve without me." Taking a step toward the door, I paused at the feel of a hand on my back. When I turned up, Mr. Walsh's sharp blue eyes met mine.

"Are you sure you're quite well?"

"I'm fine. Just need a little air."

His eyes crinkled in the corners. After several moments, he let out a long breath through his nostrils, causing the dark hair above his lip to quiver. "If you insist. But please hurry back." He lowered his voice. "Dinners are not nearly so engaging without your presence."

Mr. Zimmerman, ever stone-faced, held the door open as I exited the room, chest tight. I waited until it closed behind me before breaking into a run.

Because now it was no longer just Wesley muddling my mind.

I couldn't believe I hadn't seen it. It was all suddenly so clear and, somehow, also completely unfathomable. Was Mr. Walsh trying to *court* me? Was that why he was here? His compliments and interest in me had gone past anything I'd experienced with any of my father's other business associates. But, rather than concern, I'd seen nothing but a look of deep satisfaction on my father's face tonight.

Another thought struck me, its verity once again as obvious yet disconcerting as those that had come before: had such a courtship been my father's plan all along?

The idea rolled my stomach as I pushed open the balcony door and sucked in a large breath of crisp, dewy air. I crossed the patio at a brisk pace, not stopping until the cool concrete of the banister pressed against my torso. Staring out across the wide expanse of open lawn, glistening from an earlier rain shower, I swallowed several times, trying to still my reeling.

"Kitty?"

I spun around, letting out a small, startled cry.

My father emerged from the shadows. "Are you all right?"

"Is Mr. Walsh pursuing me?" The question arose unbidden, but I wouldn't have been able to stop it if I'd tried.

There was a flash of orange and then the familiar tangy scent of my father's tobacco. He took a long puff from his pipe before answering. "Would it be such a terrible thing if he was? You do want to get married someday, I presume?"

"Yes, *someday*. Eventually. But . . ."

But what? My father did not speak the words, but I heard them all the same.

But he's old? But I do not love him? But I'm not ready? None of these excuses would matter to my father; I knew how our world worked. Instead, I found myself saying, "But you said I was a part of all this." I gestured across the darkened landscape.

"You are." *This is your part.*

As before, he did not say those last words. But, also as before, I heard them loud and clear.

My posture deflated. "I—"

"Kathleen Anne, it's time to stop acting like a child." His tone, suddenly sharp, sliced through the evening. "I understand your time at Brillantmont has put some . . . ideas . . . in your head." He raised his chin as he said this, as if appraising me. And not in a positive way. "But you must understand that Europe is an entirely different world than the one we live in. This is America, and in America, our world is not built on titles. It is built on money. Money . . . and partnerships."

I stepped back as he moved toward me, feeling the cold concrete through the thin fabric of my dress.

"I told you before, your name and position in this family can offer you a big future. But how you achieve that is through a marriage to someone like Theodore Walsh."

"But why? Why can't I—"

"Don't you understand?" he hissed angrily, his face leaning so close to mine that white flecks of spittle landed on my cheek. "Because we need his money!"

His sudden fury startled me. But though his words and bearing left me wobbly, I didn't dare move.

After a few moments, he took a step back, as if remembering himself. He smoothed his suit. Placed his pipe back in his mouth. "This dam . . . It's taking more money and more time than we originally had planned. And it's absolutely bleeding us. Once it's complete, it will be a gold mine but, in the meantime . . ." He began to pace, puffing irritably. "The only way to finish without going completely bankrupt is to take on a partner. A partner whose money will take us over the finish line, where the greenbacks will finally start flowing again. And the only way to get a partner you can trust . . ."

". . . is by marriage," I finished for him. "My marriage."

Father stopped his pacing. He turned and walked toward me, enveloping both of my hands in his. "You know I wouldn't do this if I didn't know Theodore to be a kind, upstanding gentleman who would love and care for you, all your days." His eyes searched mine. "He's a good man. A rich man. And a marriage between the two of you would be a win for all of us."

My throat burned as he kissed my forehead and turned to make his way back inside. He paused at the threshold, his silhouette a dark shadow against the lights within. "Think it over, Kitty Kat. You said you wanted to feel important. To help people. And this will do both. This dam—our family—they won't survive without you. Without this. And neither will the thousands of people whose livelihoods depend on the dam's completion."

I'm not sure how long I stood on the porch after he left. Long enough for the lingering moisture in the air to saturate my hair and my gown, for trembles to move from my insides to my limbs. Long enough for me to realize two things.

First off, Father was right. This was the way of our world. Women my age got married, plain and simple, and often those marriages were arranged. Besides, Mr. Walsh *was* kind. He was polite, attentive, inquisitive. Regardless of the age difference, marrying him wouldn't be the worst thing in the world. In all actuality, as my father had said, it would be beneficial, not just to my father, but to me and countless others as well.

But perhaps the trouble with Mr. Walsh lay not so much in him as with me. With whatever it was that had been discomposing me since I'd stepped foot off that boat and arrived back home to a world as unchanged as I was altered. For as thoughtful and obliging as he was, sitting next to him, much as with Carolyn Gardner and all the other bodies orbiting our world, I felt nothing like what I'd felt with Hazel, Louisa, and Margarite. What I'd felt when I'd been out on my own, away from my father and this life. What I'd felt in the woods the other day, when that man had spoken to me inside my vision.

When I'd been with Wesley Odell.

And that was the second thing I realized: It wasn't marriage itself that scared me. It was the thought of spending the rest of my days feeling the way I did right now in this place, with these people.

Completely and utterly empty.

The next day, I only meant to go for a walk in the woods. To clear my head, get away from it all. To think.

It was purely a coincidence that it put me back in Wesley's path.

I found him, once again, hunched over his camera, taking pictures of the swollen river. He showed no reaction when he saw me, only raising his brow for a moment before refocusing his gaze on the box in front of him. "You again?"

Instantly, fire began to burn in my belly. "Yes, *me* again. It is *my* land, or have you forgotten?"

"Like you'd ever let me."

I took a deep breath. He was baiting me, I knew. Trying to get me to storm off again and leave him in peace.

But that wasn't going to happen.

"What are you taking pictures of today?" I raised my chin, trying not to let my voice betray my nerves.

He looked at me then, green eyes raising goosebumps across arms hidden beneath the Gibson sleeves of my floral embroidered shirt. There was a smudge of dirt across his nose. "What do you care?"

"I don't."

"Then why are you asking?"

"I'm just being polite."

"Why?"

"Because I have manners," I snapped.

For the first time, a wide grin spread across his face. "Ah, yes. I see now. There they are. Lucky me."

I pressed my lips into a straight line. This had been a mistake, coming out here like this.

I turned, prepared to leave, when he spoke up once again. "I was taking pictures of these." I spun around to find him gesturing to a patch of bright yellow flowers, partially hidden beneath the felled leaves of a tall oak.

I tilted my head, taking in the green leaves and cup-like petals. "What are those?"

"Aconite. They're beautiful, aye, but they only grow in winter. So, as the rest of these plants are coming to life in the spring, these aconites are starting to die. Bit melancholy for this time of year, I suppose."

"I can barely conceive of a type of beauty in which there is no melancholy." The words fell from my lips like a melody.

Wesley's head snapped in my direction. "You know Baudelaire?"

It was my turn to gape. "*You* know Baudelaire?"

The French's poet's work was nothing new, but it was hardly considered appropriate reading for a society lady, especially *Les Fleurs du mal*, with its scandalous focus on the corruption of city life, loss of innocence, and the oppressiveness of living—all things antithesis to the values instilled in American girls of my age and standing. Still, Louisa had slipped me a copy during my second month abroad, and I'd immediately fallen in love with the poet's cadence and language. Not that I'd ever tell anyone from my world that.

Or that I'd ever suspect Wesley Odell of feeling the same way.

His grin slowly went lopsided. "Of course I know Baudelaire. I'm not as dumb as I look. I can read. But I wouldn't figure the man to be a part of your daddy's library."

"Well, maybe I'm not as innocent as *I* look."

It was a wicked thing to say. Yet, rather than embarrassed, I felt strangely liberated. I had not self-censored. The rules of etiquette had not once crossed my mind. Much like with the line of Baudelaire, I'd simply said what I had been thinking.

And, for the first time since arriving back on American soil, I did not feel bad about it. Probably because rather than the horror or consternation I knew would be etched across the faces of my father, Mr. Walsh, or any of the ladies at tea if they had heard those words, I saw a look of only bemused surprise on Wesley's.

"If you say so."

A sudden rush of delight brought warmth to my cheeks. I quickly stifled it with a clearing of my throat. "So, um, is this what you always take pictures of? Landscapes?"

He shifted the camera from one hand to the other. "Aye. I believe there's something to be said for capturing nature just as she is. No staging or manipulating the negatives to retouch flaws. Just the world as God created it. He is the master artist, after all. I don't believe you can improve on that."

I raised a gloved hand to my lips, surprised once again. I would never have pegged Wesley as a believer, and I immediately chastised myself for the thought. Even though the Bible made it clear

God wasn't just for the rich, it would have been easy to assume so looking at the congregation of our particular church. "No. I suppose you can't."

"Would you like to see how it works?"

"Me?" I couldn't keep the shock out of my voice. Not since Switzerland had I been asked to engage in this manner. To take part. To be involved rather than just seen.

"Sure. Unless you don't think a guy like me could teach you?"

Heat crept up my neck. "Not at all. I just assumed you believed a girl like me couldn't be taught."

The fabric of his coat rustled as he shrugged. "Eh. We'll see about that one."

He grinned, smothering my irritation before it had a chance to spark again, and pulled the camera to his chest. "It's really pretty simple. This here's the lens." He pointed to a round hole at the front of the rectangular, leatherette-covered box. "And this is the viewfinder." A rectangular window on the top. "You look through it to frame your subject." He held it out to me. "Try it."

I pulled my hands to my chest. "Are you sure? What if I break it?"

"Then you can buy me another one." Snideness tinged his Irish brogue, but this time it didn't bother me so much. Perhaps because he was smiling when he said it.

With a huff only partly authentic, I took the box from his hands, fingertips brushing against his. Even through my gloves, I could feel their roughness, his calluses snagging on the thin fabric. As they did, the world around me melted away, a new vision springing up in its stead. Another hand. Large, scarred, worn. Holding mine. It was the man from before, the shadow who haunted all these daydreams. My heart lunged, trying desperately to move closer, to see him, but his face remained frustratingly vague, blocked by the glow of a summer sunset.

It made no sense. I'd held no man's hand except my father's. Who was this person? Why was I still seeing things like this?

What was wrong with me?

"You all right?"

I blinked. Wesley. It was Wesley again. Forehead creased, eyes crinkled at the corners. Around us, the smells and sounds of the forest—dirt and leaves, birds and breeze—and, in my hands, the camera.

He tilted his head. "You all right?" he repeated.

I ran my hands over the soft, worn casing, attempting to reorient myself. "Yes," I managed. "Yes, I'm fine. Go on."

Wesley raised one eyebrow but did as he was told. "Okay, well, this is the shutter lever." He leaned over me. He smelled different than Mr. Walsh, of oil and old cigarettes rather than clove and mint. But he betrayed no self-consciousness at all as he pointed to a small metal piece on the side of the box. "Pushing on it is what exposes the film inside and captures the image. It's as simple as that."

"But there's an art to it."

He glanced up at me, lips parting slowly, one blond lock falling across his forehead.

Once again, I felt myself flush. "That's . . . what you said," I stuttered. "Last time."

I felt instantly exposed, as if repeating his words back to him somehow laid bare every thought I'd had about him since our last meeting. He could see it; I knew he could. I braced myself for a mocking remark or, worse, a humiliating jab.

But neither came. Instead, he simply replied, "Aye. There is. It ain't like the slogans on Mr. Eastman's advertisements."

"You press the button. We do the rest." I parroted the ad, relief outweighing my fear of appearing foolish.

He smiled. "In a sense, yes, you do just press the button. But getting the right light, finding the right angle, choosing the right subject . . ." He held his fingers up in front of his face like a window, moving them around the forest until they landed on me. My ears grew hot as he winked. "Yes, there it is."

I flung my head around, as much searching as trying to break eye contact. "There what is?"

"My subject."

"Where?" Try as I may, I saw nothing but bare limbs behind me, the yellow buds of new leaves not yet sprouted, and clumps of dead grass. There weren't even any aconite blooms.

He gave a hearty laugh, the first I'd ever heard pass his lips. It was deep and joyous, from the gut, a sound that instantly warmed me. "You! Let me take a picture of you."

A tingling sensation swept over my body. I instinctively took a step back and held up my free hand. "Oh no. No, no. Not me."

"Why not? Haven't you ever had your picture taken before?"

"Of course I have. We had a traveling cameraman come to our house once. And I've had my portrait painted. Both experiences were dreadful."

"Dreadful?"

"I didn't like how I looked in either. And they took forever."

Wesley withdrew the camera from my hands. "This time will be different, I promise. It's not the eighteen hundreds anymore. And I'm not a traveling cameraman or a painter."

I chewed the inside of my cheek, considering. "I don't know . . ."

"Look, I ain't gonna force you. But I promise it won't hurt any more than that blasted corset you ladies insist on wearing. In fact, probably a whole lot less."

Every instinct I possessed told me to refuse.

And that was precisely why I agreed to do it.

Wesley walked around for several minutes, looking through the viewfinder at different areas, testing angles and lights before finally deciding on a large rock just in front of a thicket of trees. The bare branches created a shimmering effect, filtering the sunlight overhead, and the moss on the stone glistened with collected rain. He motioned me over. "Here," he said. "Let's do it here."

I joined him, standing in front of the rock and straightening my back in a posture even Mademoiselle Dubois could not have criticized. While Wesley fiddled with the camera, I placed my hands on the rock, then by my sides, then clasped them in front of my waist, trying to figure out their best location. I looked up to find him staring at me.

"What are you doing?"

"Trying to find the right pose."

"But I don't want you to pose."

I frowned. "Don't want me to pose? But what else am I supposed to do for pictures?"

He looked through the viewfinder at me. "I don't know. Relax? Just be . . . normal."

"This *is* me being normal."

Now it was his turn to frown. "That? All stiff-necked and rigid? That's normal?"

I scowled. "Yes."

"All right." He raised his eyebrows. "If you say so. But just so you know, what passes for normal in your world . . . Well, to the rest of us, it looks like you haven't gone to the privy in over a week."

My mouth fell open. This time, his words were beyond offensive. They were crass. Indelicate. Vulgar.

And . . . funny.

Really, really funny.

My indignant glower morphed into an unexpected grin, and I threw my head back as a large, unladylike guffaw escaped from between my lips.

And that was the moment Wesley Odell decided to pull the

shutter lever. "There," he said, as my laughter finally quieted. "Now *that* was a real picture. The real you."

His words both buoyed and deflated me, the kindness in them flavoring a sudden moroseness deep within. *The real me.* It was a nice thought. And I certainly felt more like me, here and now, than I had in a very long time.

But this wasn't real. None of this was real, could ever be real. Soon, Wesley would go back to camp, and I would go back to McDaniel Manor, to my father. To Mr. Walsh.

To my future.

I pushed the thought out of my head by snatching the camera from Wesley's hands. "Come on," I said, pretending not to delight in the amused surprise etched across his visage. "Let me try."

Over the next few hours, Wesley and I walked through the woods, taking pictures of various objects and wildlife, though I did not venture in front of the lens again. Instead, we found some newly hatched robins in a nest, the first greening leaves in a patch of wild strawberries, and even a monarch butterfly who paused long enough on a twig for Wesley to get in a snap. The morning was alive with the scents of fresh rain and new blossoms, and for a few blissful hours, I felt a million miles away from myself. From my own life. The ghosts were always there, always hovering—the dam, Mr. Walsh, the daydreams, my father—but none were strong enough to penetrate the beautiful cocoon created by the warm sunshine, Wesley Odell, and his camera.

"So, when will I get to see the pictures?" I asked, trying to hide the disappointment in my voice after Wesley had announced he had to be getting back to the work camp for his shift. My question had as much to do with a genuine desire to see the pictures as it did with avoiding the topic of the dam.

He grimaced. "Um . . . it might . . . be a while."

"Why?"

When he glanced at me from below furrowed brows, I saw the first hint of hardness return to his eyes. He sucked on his bottom lip for a moment before responding, tone unexpectedly harsh. "Because it costs money. Money I won't have for another couple of weeks."

I instantly reddened. Money. Of course it cost money. It felt as if the past few magical hours had vanished with my one small misstep.

Except it wasn't a small misstep. Not in Wesley's eyes.

"Oh." I sputtered around, wracking my brain desperately for an olive branch. "What if . . . what if I paid for it?"

I knew instantly it was the wrong thing to say.

The old Wesley Odell was back. In place of the smiling, laid-back, roguishly charming man I'd spent the morning with, there was the surly, scowling brute I'd first encountered down at the dam. "Oh, please." He nearly spat the words. "I don't need your charity. I am perfectly capable of processing my own film. I just need a few weeks to save up—"

"It's not charity," I interrupted.

He narrowed his gaze.

"You took a picture of me," I said, crossing my arms over my chest. "Paying for the cost of processing is a fair price to have one's portrait done by a professional photographer."

Wesley scoffed. "I ain't no professional photographer."

"You will be once I pay you. That's what *professional* means."

For several tense moments, I thought he would storm away. Thought he might mistake my impetuousness for patronizing. But finally, with a hitch in his movements that might have been actual, physical pain, he held the camera out to me. "The mailing address is on the bottom. You send the whole camera in, and they process the film and put in a new roll before sending it back."

"All right." I made to grab for it.

He did not let go. The tips of our fingers overlapped slightly on the edge of the box. This time, however, no vision sprang up in my mind. Instead, even through my gloves, I was very aware that it was Wesley I was touching.

His green eyes penetrated mine with a stare that both liquified my muscles and turned my veins to ice. "Besides a handful of clothes, this is the only thing in the world I own. And I'm trusting you with it."

I nodded shakily.

And then, for all the hardness in his expression and his soul, when he released his next words, they came out as a whisper. Tormented, almost pleading.

"Don't make me regret it."

> "Unusually heavy swells from the southeast, intervals of one to five minutes, overflowing low places south portion of city three to four blocks from beach. Such high water with opposing winds never observed previously."

TELEGRAPH FROM US WEATHER BUREAU OFFICE, GALVESTON
To Willis Moore, chief, US Weather Bureau, Washington, DC
Saturday, September 8, 1900, morning

TWELVE

SATURDAY, SEPTEMBER 8, 1900
GALVESTON, TEXAS

Even though I headed east, keeping to the beachfront road and away from the angry ocean, the waves seemed determined to find me. They were no longer content to merely consume the sand; now they were eating away at Galveston's city streets as well. The water was constantly at my heels, adding pounds to the already-heavy fabric as dampness spread from my hem to my knees. My muscles ached with the exertion of each step, as if stuck in thick mud, adding insult to the injury of eyes stung by rainwater and tears.

"Oh, God, please let her be safe." The first prayer in months passed through my lips. Where could she *be*? Where could Emily have possibly gone?

If she thought I'd run, where would be the first place she'd look? The train station? The dock? Those would be the most logical places. But the thought of Emily trying to make her way to the far north side of the island in this weather because of me...

Suddenly the weight of my dress didn't seem so heavy after all. Not compared to my guilt.

The clouds overhead remained heavy and pregnant with rain, but the downpour had reduced to a mere shower by the time I reached the bathhouses at the end of 25th, where I planned to turn northward into Galveston proper. The lights of the Beach Hotel glowed eerily in the gloom. Lamps swung from their perches along the boardwalk, their electric wires oscillating in the wind like a strange, violent version of jump rope no one was playing.

People were too busy with the waves.

Wiping at my gritty eyes, I stared in astonishment as brightly costumed bathers splashed about in the aggressive surf, squealing with delight when rough, sandy waves knocked many to their knees. As the water retreated, they scrambled upright, only to paste silly grins back on their faces and brace themselves for another assault, dots of color against an angry gray. Either Mr. Cline hadn't warned these merrymakers yet or else his cautions had gone unheeded. Judging by the ruckus, I was inclined to believe the latter.

"Hey!" I tried to shout. "Get out of the—" But my protestations were carried off by another large gust, which slammed into me from behind.

At just that moment, out of the corner of my eye, I saw something else emerge from the drizzle. Though I couldn't hear its familiar bell until it got closer to my spot on the beach, there was no mistaking it.

The trolley was still running.

Although the tracks normally skirted the edge of the beach, they now lay in the surf, frothy water licking the bottom of the ties. The trolley pole that connected the car to the wires overhead bowed under the weight of the wind.

And yet still the trolley ran.

Packed full of gawkers, smiling, waving, and staring in awe at the unprecedented fury of the Gulf. With the bathers near the boardwalk smiling and waving right back.

It was absurd. Dangerous.

But it was also a way inland. A way that wouldn't involve the exhausting and time-consuming process of dragging my sodden skirt through the increasingly flooded streets.

Trying to ignore the ache in my legs, I began pushing forward once more, chin to my chest. I didn't have any money for the trolley, but perhaps the conductor would take pity on me. I imagined I looked just as dreadful as I felt. If I could just make it to the trolley stop . . .

"Get out of the water!"

The sudden command caused me to jerk my head upward. Through the rain, I could just make out the shape of a man, arms flailing, trudging through the water toward the crowd of revelers on the beach. Rather than steal his voice, the wind seemed to amplify it, carrying it back to where I stood, muscles burning, on the edge of the flooded street.

A few of the bathers stopped to stare at him. Most, however, ignored him, shrieking with delight as another large wave dragged them to their knees.

Thud. Thud. Thud.

The pounding of the Gulf against the shores created a dull rumble that echoed off the boardwalk, causing me to flinch. It wasn't the time nor the place for ghosts, yet despite the very real danger all around me, one chose this moment to haunt me all the same. The sound transported me back to New York, to relaxing on the back patio, listening to the distant booms and bangs radiating from the work at the dam.

The dam.

The camera.

My fingers reached for the strap no longer across my chest. The camera was safe. It was secure, well-hidden. And yet I couldn't shake the feeling of nakedness its absence created, like the stories of phantom limbs I'd heard from Civil War veterans. It had been right to leave it behind, temporarily. Wesley would understand.

Wesley.

"Get out of the water!"

That voice again. Loud and insistent.

Familiar.

"Matthew?"

The man on the beach paused, arms still raised. He turned his head in my direction, using one hand as a visor against the rain. "Not Nun?" His face swung between me and the bathers, as if debating whether to come to me or continue his fruitless appeals. When another chorus of giggles punctuated the latest swell, his shoulders drooped. Shaking his head, he splashed his way off the beach to where I stood. His dark locks hung in strands over his forehead, dripping water between eyes that bored into mine, both incredulous and accusatory. "What are you doing here? It's not safe."

I tried to ignore his scolding tone. I didn't have time for that now. Or, worse, the care and concern I sensed behind it. Not now.

Not, I remembered with a pang, ever.

"It's Emily," I said thickly, trying to mask the emotion in my voice. "She's"—*looking for me*—"missing," I finished instead.

His features immediately softened, melting into worry. "How long?"

"I don't know. An hour? Maybe more?" Quickly, I filled him in on what was happening at the orphanage, how we'd only discovered that Emily was gone when we'd attempted to gather everyone onto the second floor.

"Where would she have gone? I mean, what reason could she possibly have to be out in this?" He gestured vaguely to the waves, the wind, the rain.

I averted my gaze. "I . . . I don't know." Goodness, would I ever be able to stop lying? "But I have to find her."

Matthew's hazel eyes drifted to the beach. A few of the bathers seemed to have finally heeded his warning, their colorful costumes stark against the gray sky as they trudged away from the sea. Others, unbelievably, remained. His jaw hardened. "Yes, *we* do." He turned back to me, his face communicating that the change in pronoun was nonnegotiable. "Mr. Cline stopped by the Bureau this morning while Joseph and I were taking readings. He believes this storm, it's . . . it's going to be a bad one."

"How bad?"

I watched his Adam's apple bob up and down as he swallowed. "I don't know. Nothing makes sense. None of the readings, none of the measurements. But Mr. Cline is worried. He's never seen anything like this."

I didn't tell him that I already knew. That I'd seen Isaac that very morning, witnessed the fear in the man's eyes as he'd timed the waves. Not only because I couldn't convey my knowledge without betraying my secret, but also because, in that moment, the alarm in Matthew's voice caused panic to wash over me anew.

"Do you have any idea where she may have gone?"

I bit my lip, nodding slightly. "The train depot. Or the dock."

He tilted his head. I could see the question forming on his lips. But before it could pass, a loud crash erupted behind us.

Startled, I grabbed Matthew's arm, spinning around just as a second boom splintered the air. My eyes combed the beach, the sky, the waves, searching for the cause. It wasn't until Matthew's whispered words found my ear—"Lord, help us"—that I finally realized.

I couldn't find the source of the commotion . . . because it was no longer there.

What we'd heard was the sound of the trolley bridge collapsing, its timbers and ties already disappearing into the sea.

Several screams pierced the wind. The last of the bathers began to flee from the beach, stumbling and tripping. There was no more amusement on their faces now. The waves that had, just moments ago, been an object of mirth now suddenly appeared a monster, foreboding and ravenous.

My nails dug into the damp fabric on Matthew's arm.

"We need to go. Now." Matthew slipped his hand into mine and began to pull. "We can head inland on 25th," he shouted over his shoulder. "Go north. Get away from the water."

I struggled to keep up. My skirt was now soaked to the knees; each leg felt as if it were encased in concrete. The burning spread to my arm as Matthew tugged, his own legs moving frantically through water that never seemed to abate, no matter how far we got from the shore. "Annie, come on. We have to—" He bit off his words. I could see his eyes travel down my skirt, taking in the wet fabric. He stopped, pressing his lips together in clearly etched frustration.

For a moment, I almost thought he'd go on without me. It was what he *should* do, what would have been smart. I was not his girl.

I wasn't even Annie Odell.

And yet Matthew Richter did not let go of my hand.

"Come on," he said, squeezing my fingers. He gave me a somber half smile, nodding to my skirt. "We're going to have to do something about that."

Even with the waters of the Gulf licking our heels, my conscience screamed at the impropriety of entering Matthew Richter's home alone and unchaperoned.

It was silly, really. No one was watching us. Away from the beach, more sensible heads were prevailing; the storm was keeping most of Galveston inside their homes. The ones that did venture out—children, mostly—were way too fascinated by the sudden rivers flowing in front of their yards to pay any attention to the man and woman slipping quickly into one of the limewashed bungalows along Avenue S.

I, however, was *very* aware. The momentary relief I felt to be away from the wind, the rain, and the waves vanished as the door closed behind us, enveloping Matthew's small living room in a silence somehow louder than the roar of the gusts just outside.

I knew what Mother Camillus would think. I knew what my *father* would think.

And it was enough to send a shiver down my spine, despite the almost unbearable stuffiness. I drew my elbows into my sides and tried to suppress a tremble.

Matthew, on the other hand, seemed to have no such qualms. He brushed past me to look out one of the narrow windows that faced the street. Nose pressed against the glass, his fingers gripped the curtains. I could hear him muttering to himself, though I couldn't make out the words.

Instead, I took in my surroundings, trying to focus my mind on something—anything—other than the storm outside or my own niggling guilt. The room was shabby but clean, a small couch and lounge chair obviously well-used but free from rips or stains. There was a stack of books on the chipped wooden coffee table—*The Adventures of Huckleberry Finn* and *Treasure Island* were the only two spines facing me—with a few loose sheets of paper tucked underneath. Weather charts, from the looks of them. A braided rug covered the wooden floor, which, along with the rest of the furniture, was free from dust. From my spot, I could see a few feet down a darkened hallway to my right where, presumably, the rest of the rooms lay.

For all the mystery of the opposite sex, there was nothing remotely scandalous about a bachelor's home. Nothing unusual or even particularly memorable. I felt a small twinge of disappointment, despite myself.

A drop of water dripped from my hair onto the floor. I glanced down only to realize my skirt had been doing more than just dripping this whole time; there was a veritable puddle on Matthew's rug.

"Matthew . . . ," I said softly.

He turned, startled. It was as if he had forgotten I was there.

And I suddenly felt like a bigger imposition in his small home than I already was. Why was he helping me? I was a liar, practically a fugitive, and by all accounts a mess, emotionally and now physically. I did not deserve his kindness. The burden of finding Emily was mine to bear alone.

And yet I made no move to leave.

He tugged the curtains shut and rushed toward me. "I can't believe how fast the water is rising. It's like all the laws of weather have just . . . broken." He ran a hand over his face. "We have to hurry."

"But what do I—" My question was clipped clean as Matthew disappeared down the hallway. He returned moments later with a wad of brown fabric, which he stuffed into my hands. "Here," he said. "Put these on."

I unrolled them, revealing a shirt and a pair of men's trousers. My mouth fell agape.

"They'll probably be too big, but you can use this." He pressed a thin rope into my other hand.

"Are you serious?" I sputtered. "I can't wear these! It's . . . immoral. It's—"

"A whole heck of a lot faster than trudging through water with a dress on."

I pressed my lips together, blowing a long breath through my nostrils. He was right, of course. The pants would weigh me down a lot less than this skirt. But what was left of Kathleen McDaniel still struggled with the thought.

"Here," Matthew said, reading my silence for the quiet acceptance it was. He put a hand on my elbow, guiding me toward the hallway. "My bedroom is back there. End of the hall. You can change in there."

My body stiffened. "Absolutely not."

Matthew dropped his hand.

"I'm not going into your bedroom."

"Annie, it's not like that . . ."

"I don't care whether it's like that or not. I won't allow myself—"

"Do you want to find Emily or not?"

The sharpness in his words instantly shamed me. I was being ridiculous. Matthew was a gentleman; there was nothing untoward in his offer. He was only trying to give me privacy. To be considerate. To help me find my friend.

The one I myself had put in danger.

I tightened my hands around the clothes, feeling properly chastised. "Of course," I whispered. "Thank you."

Matthew's shoulders dropped. He gave me a rueful half smile. "You can change in the washroom if it makes you feel more comfortable. It's right through here."

My dress revealed its true weight the moment I released the last button and let it fall to the washroom floor in a sodden heap. I instantly felt ten pounds lighter, my tight muscles expanding like a down pillow at the reprieve. Though my underthings were damp, I kept them on; no reason to throw all propriety out the window, storm or not. Instead, I grabbed a towel—trying not to think of what the fabric had last touched—and patted both them and my hair until no more water dripped onto the tiles beneath my feet.

The wind caused the house to pop and creak as I pulled on Matthew's pants. They made me feel exposed, even with the baggy fabric; it felt strange to look down and see two distinct lines revealing the exact location of my legs. I had to loop the rope around me twice to secure them. The shirt was more comfortable. Unlike the pants, I felt hidden beneath its volume, my curves even more of a mystery than they'd been in my dress, like a blanket with buttons and sleeves. I left the last three buttons undone, tying the shirt's tails into a knot, which I then wrapped around the mass of rope. Finally I looped the rope over my shoulder, turning it into a makeshift suspender.

I made it a point not to look in the mirror before I exited the room.

"Matthew," I called, moving down the hallway. "I'm ready. I just need to put my boots back—"

"Annie?"

The sound of my name caused me to feel faint. Not only because it hadn't come from Matthew. But because I recognized it.

I rounded the corner to the living area, praying I was mistaken.

Just as I'd feared, there on the sofa, blonde hair turned dark by the rain, sat a red-eyed and thoroughly drenched Maggie Sherwood.

THIRTEEN

"Maggie!"

The child's name came out as both a reprimand and a relief. I rushed over to where she sat on the couch, the self-consciousness I'd felt about my appearance in Matthew's clothes momentarily forgotten. The rope belt pressed roughly into my stomach as I crouched before her and wiped a strand of wet hair from her forehead. I glanced at Matthew. He stood near the window, hands in his pockets, the worried expression on his face belying his attempt at a shrug.

I returned my attention to Maggie. "What are you doing here? How did you—? Where did you—?" A thousand questions fought for space on my tongue, yet all of them dissolved when her big brown eyes finally met mine. They were snaked with veins, lids swollen.

"I'm scared, Annie."

I pulled her into a fervent embrace. She felt so small in my arms, her breath coming in minute hiccups, muscles trembling. I inhaled the smell of the sea as I tried to calm her. In the ensuing silence, rain continued to lash the windows. The house creaked and popped, straining in the ever-increasing wind, the storm unwilling to be ignored, no matter what was going on inside these four walls.

"Annie . . . ," Matthew said softly.

I refused to look at him. Refused to acknowledge his tone. The fear and the desperation.

Maggie was staring at me, frantic for reassurance. I could not give space to one more person's fear. Not when my own was already battling so ferociously inside me.

"How did you get here?" I asked gently.

"I followed you." Maggie's voice was a whisper, her lisp making her seem even more heartbreakingly young. "When the nuns weren't looking, I . . . I slipped away. I didn't want to stay there. Not without you. The wind was so . . . and the waves . . ." She shook her head, another tremble coursing through her body. "The whole building was shaking. And I knew . . . I just knew . . ." Fresh tears formed in her eyes. "There were too many kids, and not enough grown-ups. No one was going to look out for me. Care about me. Not really."

My chest burned even as my shoulders deflated. "That's not true."

Maggie's lips turned downward. We both knew I was lying. The Sisters of Charity did their very best, but there simply weren't enough arms and eyes to go around even in the most ideal of circumstances.

And these were certainly not those.

Still, Maggie would be safer there than here with me. Scared, yes, but safe.

"I'm sorry, sweetie, but you have to go back. Matthew and I are trying to find Sister Emily. It would be too dangerous for us to drag you around in this storm. You'll be better protected at the orphanage and when"—*not if,* I reiterated to myself—"I find

Emily, we'll come back and all ride out the storm together." I didn't allow myself to think of what would come afterward, when the wind ceased and the rains abated.

When my absence would become permanent.

"I need you to be brave, just until then. Can you do that?"

At that moment, another gale rattled the windowpane as if seeking to expose my dishonesty. Maggie's bottom lip quivered. I stood quickly, unable to bear the sight of her broken heart, and made to move toward Matthew, but the child refused to let go of my hand.

I lowered my voice, leaning as far away from her as possible. "I need to get her back to the orphanage," I whispered. "If we go—"

"No!" Maggie scrambled to her feet, pulling on my fingers in despair. "You can't! The waves . . ." Her words grew muffled as she buried her face in my stomach. "They were so big. So loud. I tried to yell to you, and you couldn't hear me. I didn't think I was going to make it here." Sobs overtook her. "Please don't leave me, Annie. Don't take me back."

I looked to Matthew. He grimaced. "She's right, you know. You saw what happened at the beach. The trestle collapsing. How quickly things went south." The floorboard creaked as he shifted his weight, leaning over to part curtains covering the window. "The water on the street has risen in the short time we've been in here. That means it's even worse on the shore." When he turned back to me, his face was pale. "I don't think we could get to the orphanage even if we tried."

"But we can't just leave her here."

"No. We can't." Matthew held my gaze. There was so much unspoken in his look, in those simple words. He was trying to convey the seriousness of the situation without scaring Maggie. But it didn't stop him from scaring me.

Even here, blocks from the beach, the sea had found us. We needed to get farther inland.

And no longer just because of Emily.

I looked down at Maggie, taking in her matted hair and saturated dress. Air rattled in my chest as I attempted a shaky breath. "You wouldn't happen to have any child-size clothes, would you?"

Less than twenty minutes later, the three of us stood huddled by Matthew's front door, listening to the wind just on the other side. From here, it sounded like an old man snoring, alternately whooshing and whistling through the cracks. A part of me wanted to confide in Maggie about this, break the tension, lighten the mood. But I hadn't the heart.

"Are you ready?" Matthew paused, one hand on the doorframe. His shoulders were squared, his jaw set. I hoped—for all our sakes—he felt as brave as he looked.

I gave him a small nod, then turned. "Are you?"

Maggie stood behind me, though I wouldn't have believed it was her if I hadn't witnessed the transformation firsthand. She hadn't balked as I had at the clothes Matthew offered, brown knee pants and a checkered button-down scrounged from a neighbor. In fact, despite the worry lines etching her forehead, I'd have almost described her as delighted when she'd slipped them on, stretching her bony legs this way and that, marveling over the range of motion. I'd pulled her blonde hair into a wet, messy braid, which she'd promptly tucked down the back of her shirt. Even now, as we stood on the precipice, though her face was pale and her thin lips had all but disappeared beneath the weight of her worry, there was a marked change in her demeanor from earlier. She was frightened but determined, anxious but undaunted.

She trusted me. Completely.

And that was a weight heavier than any saturated skirt.

"You keep your head down and just keep walking. Whatever you do, do not let go of my hand. Do you understand me?"

Maggie squeezed my fingers until they hurt. She nodded.

I felt something warm slip into my other palm. Glancing up, I found Matthew's strong hand enveloping mine. One corner of his mouth turned upward. "The same goes for you too."

There was a beat. A pause as I seemed to look at the three of us from outside my own body. A human chain. Strong. Unbreakable.

Or were we dominoes, just waiting for the first one to fall?

"The worst of the waves should subside by the time we reach Broadway. It's the highest point on the island, and water has never breached that street in any storm Galveston has ever weathered. That means everything on the north side of the island should be dry. Emily's a smart girl. If she truly went to the train station, it would make sense that she's either still there or is at least staying above Broadway, where it's safe." He ran a thumb over the heel of my palm.

I knew he was trying to be comforting. Logically, what he was saying made sense. But what if Emily *had* turned around? What if, not seeing me, she'd given up and was out in these waterlogged streets this very moment, trudging against the ever-increasing waves, trying to make it back to the very place Matthew had just said was impossible to reach?

I suddenly felt as if I was going to cry. The task was too big, too hopeless, like finding a needle in a haystack.

In a storm.

As the haystack was being swept out to sea.

Matthew let out a slow breath. Nodded once. "Let's go."

I turned to give Maggie one last reassuring look, but I was too late. Before I could catch her eye, the door that Matthew had begun to ease open was wrenched from his grasp. It slammed into the side of the house with a bang, leaving a gaping hole through which the wind, with its greedy, invisible fingers, tugged at our bodies, sucking us from the relative calm of the house and into the swirling, chaotic mess of the street below.

The stream that had, not an hour earlier, merely meandered down Avenue S was now a river. It spread away from the beach like tentacles, reclaiming every nook and cranny of dry land for the sea, oblivious to the losing fight the roaring wind seemed to be raging, trying to push it back. My eyes immediately slammed shut, burning from the rain; I struggled to open them. Stumbling blindly into the water, my other senses went into overtime—the whoosh of air in my ears, the constant patter of raindrops on waves, the surprising warmth of the water. I gagged on the intensity of the smell of fish, of salt, of wet animals. But mostly I tried to concentrate on the feel of both Matthew's and Maggie's hands in mine, straining, growing slick, but never letting go.

It wasn't just the landscape that had been rapidly altered during our short time inside Matthew's small home. The storm itself was no longer an amusing oddity. Neighbors that once stood dumbstruck on their front porches, watching their children frolic, had now sprung into action. We were not alone in our slog northward. Brown seawater frothed at my knees, churned not only by the steady push of the Gulf, but also by the hordes of likeminded people who, though perhaps not fully understanding the situation at hand, still began to answer the urge to get inward, away from the shore. Many of them were loaded with whatever possessions they could carry: suitcases, trunks, boxes. I even saw a few carrying lamps and, in one case, a gramophone.

"Watch it!" came a sharp yell from somewhere in front of me.

I tore my eyes from their latest fascination—a middle-aged woman with a baby strapped to her back, sewing basket full of china clutched to her chest—just in time to see something large and dark come barreling down the street, carried rapidly on the current. Matthew yanked me roughly to the left. Thankfully, I had enough wherewithal to tighten my grip on Maggie and pull her closer to me before the object—which I soon discovered was a telephone pole—could strike her.

Matthew blinked at me through the rain, his eyes widening. I turned. We watched in impotent horror as the pole slammed into a family of four, the smallest of the two children disappearing under the water from the force. Miraculously, the child emerged moments later, pulled to the surface by his father's firm grip. The boy's face was pale, his breath sputtering, but he appeared otherwise unharmed.

Maggie looked up at me. The panic in her gaze quickly dashed any hopes I might have harbored that she hadn't witnessed the incident. I tightened my hold on her, though the wind—and my own powerlessness—stole any words of reassurance I could have offered.

"Stay close to me!" Matthew's lips brushed against my ear as he shouted to be heard above the roar, though I barely registered the touch.

There was no impropriety at this moment. No excitement.

There was only fear. And the realization that escaping was no longer about comfort. It was about our very lives.

Matthew pulled my hand to his side, pressing my arm beneath his elbow. I did the same to Maggie. The debris came faster now—clothes, planks of wood, even, chillingly, a child's tricycle—but we were able to dodge them for the most part, having learned quickly that keeping our heads down was not a viable, or smart, option. A few riderless horses galloped through the surf, sending even more water spraying into our eyes as they, too, fled northward. Dogs, cats, chickens, goats. Even toads joined the caravan, every creature that drew breath now fleeing on instinct, some primal need to be away from the very water that had drawn most of us here in the first place. The wind continued to howl and the rain beat down on our exposed skin like needles, but, no matter how far we trudged, the waves at our feet never abated. Traveling in reverse through the alphabet, we crossed Avenues N, M, and L before the street signs disappeared, early victims of the storm. Though I knew, logically, the next street had to be K, I suddenly felt disoriented. There was too much water, too much air, too much motion all around me. I swayed, struggling to keep my eyes on Matthew's back, nerves focused on Maggie's small palm in mine.

Matthew must have felt my unsteadiness because, unexpectedly, he pulled me to the right. The three of us took shelter beneath a cluster of palm trees, a small break from the wind and the rain that, while not complete, at least allowed us to take a non-soggy breath. I squeezed my eyes shut, willing the dizzy spell to pass. But when I finally opened them again, I wished I hadn't.

There, just visible beyond the palm branches and sheets of rain, I saw a bronze statue, nearly as dark as the sky, the flowers at the base completely engulfed in cloudy water. As I watched, lightning—the first I'd seen all day—flickered in the sky above it, stretching toward the crown of laurels in the statue's outstretched hand, as if wanting to snatch it.

The Texas Heroes Monument.

Broadway. We'd made it to Broadway Avenue. The highest point on the island.

And we were still completely surrounded by water.

For the first time since we'd left his house, Matthew dropped my hand. He ran it through his dark locks, squeezing out the water before wiping the droplets from his face.

"Matthew?"

He could hear me, this much I knew, the palms creating an eerie bubble, safe from the worst of the wind's constant shout. But still he did not answer. Instead, he started to pace, hands on his hips, eyes flickering from the ground to the sky, from the stately mansions lining the streets to the submerged trolley tracks beside us.

"Matthew," I repeated, louder this time.

Maggie buried her face in my side. I wrapped an arm around her, using my other to try to press the water out of her braid. I did not, however, take my eyes off the man in front of us.

"Matthew."

He finally turned, acknowledging me. His eyes were veiny and waterlogged, his face ashen. The tendons in his neck strained, and there were red spots on his bottom lip where he had chewed it raw. "This isn't right," he murmured. "There shouldn't be any water here. Mr. Cline said the water would never—could never—reach here."

The sound of a dry swallow was loud in my ears. Despite the ever-present water, my mouth felt parched. "All right," I managed. "So . . . we just keep going inland. We're trying to get up to the wharf anyway, right? The train station? North side of the island?"

Water flecks flew from his hair as he shook his head. "You don't understand. Broadway is the highest point on the island. The land slopes to the sea on either side of it. Even if we went farther north, we'd be no better off because we'd actually be going down in elevation. The water would just flow over the top and then continue on toward us."

"Yes, but we'd still be farther away from the Gulf. Isn't that the most important thing?"

"In normal circumstances, yes. But this . . . this is not normal." He grimaced and waved his hand.

I looked to where he was pointing. Sure enough, there was no end to the muddy river that Galveston's streets had become. Water pooled as far as my eye could see. The sea hadn't just reached Broadway; it had surpassed it.

"I think . . . I think it's going to sweep across the entire island. The only question is . . ." He paused. Glanced down at Maggie. When he spoke again, his voice was lower. "The only question is how deep it's going to get when it does."

Over the top of Maggie's head, I watched the waves press against my feet. Though smaller, even this far inland they were still strong, still pressing northward.

Still hungry.

I didn't want Matthew to be right. But that didn't mean he wasn't.

"But what about Emily? The train station—"

"Annie, we can't. I'm sorry. We need to find shelter somewhere. And soon."

"But we can't just stop looking! She's out there somewhere!" *Because of me,* I wanted to say. *Because of who I really am.* "She—"

"I'm sure she's found shelter somewhere too. Most of the buildings on the Strand are made of stone. They're sturdy. She'll be safe there. Emily's too smart to be out in this. She's waiting out the storm somewhere. And we should be too."

A lump welled up in my throat. What he was saying was all wrong. We couldn't stop. We had to find her. Make sure she was all right. Make sure that I hadn't—once again—put someone I cared about in danger. If the situation was as dire as Matthew said it was, and I had no reason other than my own willful doubt to believe that it wasn't, then it was even more imperative that I locate her.

No. I couldn't quit, no matter what Matthew said.

"You take Maggie," I said, hoping he couldn't hear the quiver in my voice. "Get her to shelter."

"No!" Maggie's desperate plea pierced my heart. She seized the baggy fabric around my waist, scraping the delicate skin underneath.

Matthew's brow furrowed. "Annie, no—"

"I trust you. She trusts you. Get her to safety. I have to find Emily."

"Annie, this is madness. I can't let you—"

But his protest was cut off by an ear-piercing shriek. It took me a moment to realize the enormous sound was coming from the small girl clinging to my hips. Maggie was pointing at something just downriver—down the street—from where we stood. Something puffy and light-colored. Someone's bedding or a wad of laundry ripped from a line, perhaps.

Only it wasn't. I pressed Maggie's face into my stomach roughly as the object pushed toward us, hoping that stifling her scream would somehow suppress my own.

It was a body. A man, lifeless eyes open to the sky, the white fabric of his shirt almost obscene against the dirty water. His arms were splayed limply at his sides, bobbing in a macabre dance to the sway of the waves.

Bile rose in my throat. Instinctively, I lifted Maggie, wrapping her around my body like a child half her age, oblivious to the way my muscles screamed at the effort. Matthew's strong arms caught me as I attempted to stumble away. He moved in between me and the corpse, and I slammed my eyes shut. I don't know what he did with it. Don't know if he nudged it away or pressed it beneath the waves, out of our view. I didn't want to know. Didn't want to *see*.

When I finally opened my eyes again, the body was gone and Matthew's face, his entire countenance, had changed.

"We need to find shelter."

This time I agreed with him.

FOURTEEN

APRIL 1900
CROTON-ON-HUDSON, NEW YORK

For all my initial apprehension about getting caught, it was surprisingly easy to mail Wesley's camera without raising any suspicions. Mr. Walsh had been called back to the city for business. In his absence, my father, aside from breakfast and dinner, became too consumed by things at the dam to pay me much mind. Perhaps that should have hurt my feelings.

But honestly, I felt nothing but relief.

Ten days and less than three dollars after I'd slipped into Croton-on-Hudson's post office unnoticed, Wesley's camera was returned to me, along with a stack of prints in a shiny yellow envelope marked *Kodak*. Though the footman who delivered it to my bedroom door did so with raised eyebrows, he remained wordless, as befitted his position, and I offered no explanation, as befitted mine.

Locking my bedroom door, I placed the camera on my bedspread and opened the envelope with shaking hands, fear of damaging the prints the only thing tempering my excitement. The pictures were small, barely larger than the palm of my hand, and a bit grainy, but also utterly transportive. Despite the cushioned settee at my back and the rug beneath my feet, I felt as if I were back in the woods with Wesley. Flipping through the photographs, I could smell the earth, feel the sun, hear the chirp of the birds, each small detail as vivid as the moment we'd snapped the picture. And Wesley had been right—the angle of light made all the difference. The contrasting tones of gray and black created a dance of hues across each still image that made the subject seem to come to life in my hands. The baby robin, the aconites, the monarch butterfly—Wesley hadn't just captured their likenesses. He'd somehow managed to capture their *souls*.

I smiled as I studied the picture of the wild strawberry blooms. It was obvious I had taken this one; it wasn't nearly as good as the others. Still, there was promise there, a distinct touch of Wesley upon my own work that felt oddly yet not unpleasantly intimate.

I slid it to the back of the stack and moved on to the next, immediately wishing I hadn't. It was the photograph Wesley had taken of me. In it, my head was thrown back, my mouth wide open in a laugh that made me look very much like a braying donkey. Several curls had escaped from their pins, and they flew out to the sides in frizzy, frozen motion. The black-and-white coloring made my freckles more pronounced, my nose more prominent, and had my lips always had that flat, duckbillish quality to them? Cringing, I closed my eyes and pushed the photograph away, fighting the urge to crumple it.

It was unseemly. Unladylike, uncivilized, unpolished.

It was . . . me.

My eyes fluttered open, my gaze inching across my bedspread until it landed on the photograph once more. The *real* me. Not the stiff, proper puppet from the portrait downstairs. No, this was me slipping out of all my manners, all my rules, all my training. I studied the picture, fighting the urge to focus once again on my flaws. I was no great beauty. But, on closer inspection, I realized I didn't look as hideous in this photograph as I had first thought. I looked . . . happy.

I looked *alive*.

Somehow, a man I barely knew was able to capture *me*.

Smiling, and feeling slightly dizzy, I placed the photograph back with the others and moved on to the next.

Instantly, that intoxicated feeling vanished.

The next photograph—the next several photographs—were not ones Wesley and I had taken together. And they certainly were not taken in the woods. Gone were the delicate flowers, burgeoning wildlife, and picturesque landscape. In their place, I found an image of an overflowing bucket of what appeared to be human waste. A photograph of a man curled under a thin blanket, fabric laced with a layer of frost. An overturned work boot with a family of cockroaches nesting inside, a blistered pair of hands clearly visible in between the shredded remains of a man's gloves, and a spoonful of watery gruel that looked less edible than what Rupert fed our pigs.

My stomach rolled as I flipped through the pictures. But no matter how disturbing, how horrifying, I could not look away, even as I came toward the end of the stack with a weight in my chest, as if my body knew what I was about to see before my mind did.

A final shot, framed in Wesley's signature style, of row after row of white tents, bowed with snow, the new construction of the dam just visible in the background.

These were pictures of the work camp.

I tore my eyes from the photographs, trying to blink away the images, landing instead on the fire in the hearth, the soft carpet at my feet, the tray of tea and scones Stella had left on my table. My hands fell to the plush blanket by my side. The material felt like needles. The men who were constructing this new wonder of ingenuity, who were building both my father's fortune and my own future—this was how they were living. This was how they were eating, sleeping, surviving, all while, less than a handful of miles away, their boss and his daughter were living like *this*.

"No." I said the word aloud in my empty room. My father was a good man. An honest, hardworking man. Yes, we had wealth, but he had *earned* that wealth, every penny, and certainly not in any unscrupulous way that would endanger others. He was providing jobs, shelter, and meals when there was a distressing lack of all three going around. Certainly, he required his men to work, but that was because there was a job to do. An *important* job to do. He was not unfair or exploitative. There was no way he would allow conditions like these to persist in his work camp.

My initial horror began to melt into outrage. This was some kind of trickery. Wesley must have staged these images. It was the only explanation. He'd mentioned the possibility of such photographic deceit the first time I'd met him. I had heard my father and Mr. Walsh railing about the labor issues recently, the workers who were creating more trouble than products. Many of my father's friends, also good men, were facing ruin because of these rabble-rousers who refused to play by the rules and work for their bread. Wesley's pictures must be a part of that. Skullduggery meant to punish the rich for simply being rich.

Another thought flashed into my mind, causing my pulse to quicken. This was why Wesley had agreed to allow me to get the film developed. Why he'd suddenly started being so nice to me. He *wanted* me to see these pictures. But why? To shame me? Make me feel bad?

Or to try to win me to his cause? What a hoot that would be, involving the boss's daughter in his downfall. He probably assumed my delicate femininity would sway me to his side. Or his own irresistible charms.

And I'd played right into his hands.

A frustrated growl escaped my lips. I grabbed my gloves and hat from where Stella had left them on the dresser, not bothering to call out to her, to tell her I was leaving. She'd ask where I was going, fuss with my hair, insist on retouching my powder, second-guess the appropriateness of my lemon-yellow day dress. And I didn't have time for any of that.

I needed to speak to Wesley Odell.

Now.

But it wasn't Stella who slipped between me and the front door just before I reached it.

"Where do you think you're going?"

Otto Zimmerman's rough German accent slid over me like sandpaper as he crossed his beefy arms over his chest and scowled.

Rage gurgled at the base of my throat. Though Mr. Zimmerman wasn't its source, his unexpected interference was doing him no favors. I'd gotten used to his sullen, lumbering haunting of our home. It was constant, ever-present, but more a shadow than a thorn. He rarely spoke, let alone interfered.

And yet now, of all times, was when he chose to break form.

"I am going out," I managed from between clenched teeth. "I shall return later."

"Where?"

"That is no concern of yours."

"It is actually."

I drew a deep breath in through my nostrils. *Manners, Kathleen. Manners. You let your guard down around one man and look how that turned out.* Still, my next words came out clipped: "You are my father's toady, not mine, and I'll thank you to remember your place, Mr. Zimmerman." I made to move past him.

He held up a hand. "Your father wants the entire household kept inside today. The rumblings are getting too loud."

"Rumblings? What rumblings?"

"Zimmerman! Get in here!" From down the hallway came my father's voice, echoing off the rich mahogany of his study.

I recognized his tone instantly. And, from the look of distress in Mr. Zimmerman's eyes, so did he.

Lawrence McDaniel was angry.

Frustration crossed Mr. Zimmerman's heavy features as his dark, liquid eyes flitted from me to the study and back again. "You stay," he growled.

I raised my chin.

"Zimmerman!" My father was losing his patience.

With a dagger-like glare cast in my direction and what I assumed were a few muttered German swear words, Otto Zimmerman moved his massive frame from the doorway and disappeared down the hall.

I was outside before the last of his shadow vanished from sight.

The sky was heavy with the threat of rain, casting a pall over the blooming countryside that perfectly complemented my mood. The foal born just a few weeks ago was galloping around the pasture with its mother. Nearby, the cows and sheep lounged, eating the sprouts of new grass bursting up through the mud. And, from inside the barn as I passed, I heard a chorus of mewls as the kittens cried out for their lunch.

But today I did not stop to visit. I was a woman on a mission. And neither mud nor muck nor baby animals nor—as I finally approached the dam site—overactive nerves would stop me.

Construction had progressed quickly since the last time I'd been by. The bypass had been completed, and almost all the bricks for the new wall had been laid. A steady thrum of scrapes and bangs could be heard from over a mile away as workers set, leveled, and mortared cement blocks around poles of iron driven over a hundred feet into the earth below. From here on the overlook, the workers gave the impression of ants.

Or roaches.

Clenching my fists, I maneuvered down the hill, toward the site. The first place I'd look was the work camp. Not only because I assumed that was where I'd find Wesley, but also because I needed to see it for myself. Needed to see the camp now, as it was, without any of Wesley's intervention or trickery. *There's an art to it*, he'd said of his photography, and I was going to expose the artist behind those crafted images.

"Kathleen!"

The sound of my name cut through the damp air just as the white peaks of the work-camp tents came into view. I squinted my eyes. Wesley Odell was hurrying toward me. He was dressed again—or still—in the same tattered button-down I'd seen him in over a week ago, though his pants were brown now, not black. When he finally reached me, his smile was tight, eyes flitting wildly between myself and the workers mixing mortar behind him.

"What are you doing here?"

"I need to see the camp."

"What? Why are you—"

I thrust both the camera and the envelope of prints in his direction. "Here are your stupid pictures. Now let me through. I need to see the camp."

"No, Kathleen, you don't."

"I said let me through!" I tried to brush past him, wincing as his hand wrapped around my upper arm painfully.

"Kathleen."

"Let me go!" I didn't realize the power of my own shout until silence rushed in to take its place. Though the hammers of the construction site continued unabated in the distance, an ominous stillness rose up from the camp, the tension made even more taut by the appearance of dirty, weary bodies emerging from the tents.

These were men. My father's workers. And yet they were little more than muscle and bones, dirt and rags. Had they been like this the last time I'd been here? Or was I only seeing them clearly now? My eyes washed slowly over the holes in their boots, the scabs on their knuckles, all the hollow places in their cheeks, at the base of their throats. Though a few appeared freshly scrubbed, most were filthy, the true tone of their skin barely perceptible under a layer of thick grime. Even from this distance, I could smell the scent of body odor, of human waste, of the stale tobacco that seemed to be their primary source of sustenance. The only part that seemed alive on the men was their eyes.

They absolutely blazed with hatred.

At *me*.

And in that moment, I knew. I knew without knowing, without seeing a single thing more.

The pictures were real. The conditions inside the work camp were real. Wesley was not trying to dupe me. He hadn't even wanted me to pose when he'd snapped that picture. It was as he had said: he was determined to capture things as they really were.

And this was how things really were for him. For the men working for my father.

For the men working . . . for me. For my house, my clothes, my food. For my ridiculous needlepoint and fancy schooling and countless trips to the city. They had paid for it all, with their labor and their starvation, their sweltering days and freezing nights.

Our kingdom built on their emaciated, broken backs.

Sudden hot tears blurred faces I no longer wished to see.

"You need to go," Wesley said quietly. "Now. Meet me at our spot in an hour. We'll talk then."

I shook my head. I couldn't move. Couldn't speak.

"Kathleen, please." His whisper was pleading now. "You have to go." His hand released my arm, replaced by a gentle push on my shoulder blades that somehow loosened my muscles from their paralysis.

"Wesley..."

"We'll talk later," he whispered. "Trust me. This is for your own protection." And, as I finally turned away, tripping over my own feet, I heard him add under his breath, "And mine."

My tears still hadn't stopped flowing by the time Wesley arrived at our spot in the woods, late and breathless, the smell of woodsmoke heavy on his clothes. The snap of twigs and crunch of leaves signaled his arrival long before he reached me, but I still couldn't bring myself to look at him, even when I felt the fallen log I was sitting on shudder with his weight as he sat down next to me.

"You saw the pictures," he said after a few moments.

I sniffed.

There was a pop of the wood as he sighed heavily. "I knew I shouldn't have given them to you to process. I've been torn up about it since I did. It's not the type of thing any lady should have to see." From the corner of my eye, I watched one of his thumbs rub over the other. They were callused, the cracks on them ingrained with dirt. "But then I thought..."

I looked up. I could feel the splotchiness of my face, the dried tears. But, rather than less, it seemed to give me more boldness in looking Wesley square in the eye. Perhaps because allowing him to see my ugliness felt like atonement for the ugliness of which I'd secretly accused him.

The ugliness he'd been forced to live these past few months.

"Then I thought, maybe if you saw them..." His words trailed off, but he did not break his stare.

"If I saw them what?"

Silence stretched between us. Overhead, goldfinches and sparrows chirruped happily, oblivious.

Finally, Wesley drew in a deep breath. Slowly. As if it pained him. He directed his words at the forest beyond. "My *mam* and *da* had a farm not far from here, you know? They scraped and saved every penny after immigrating, finally buying a small plot of land that my *da* believed was our destiny. He even named the farm 'Providence.'" He laughed, but there was no humor in it. Only sadness. "And things were good . . . for a while. But no matter how hard he worked, *Da* couldn't keep up with all the changes. On a good day, it would take us two and a half hours to reap, bind, and thresh a bushel of wheat. Meanwhile, the farmer down the road? The one with the fancy tractor? He could do all that in four minutes." He closed his eyes, remembering. "We had to buy equipment we couldn't afford, only to find any profit we could make slashed by rising rail rates and falling prices." He frowned. "The doctors can call it whatever they want, but I know it was the stress of that—of trying to survive, trying to compete—that killed him. And took my *mam* not long after." He paused, and I pretended not to notice the emotion in his voice, the noisy way he tried to swallow it back down. "I had to sell the land to pay off *Da*'s debts. There was nothing left for me afterward. Nothing . . . but this."

He tilted the camera in his palm, running his fingers over it gently. "Farming was *Da*'s dream. But he knew it wasn't mine. This was the last thing he ever gave me. For my future, he said. *My Providence.*" He looked at me then, sad eyes boring into my own. "I hoped I'd be able to make a living with my camera someday. To help people with it. To make a difference."

I looked away, hoping he didn't hear the breath catch in my throat. *To help people. Make a difference.* The exact same words I'd spoken to my father all those weeks ago. I understood his longing.

And yet, as I lifted a palm to comfort Wesley, I hesitated. My white gloves hovered above his dirty hands, suddenly more obscene than they'd ever been.

We may have been united in this desire, but we were certainly not the same.

"Not that that will ever happen." His voice was heavy with defeat. "No matter how much I work, no matter how much I save, I can't ever get ahead. Can't ever save enough. Not if I want food in my belly or clothes on my back."

His fingers brushed my chin slightly, forcing me to look at him. Any thrill at his boldness withered when I saw the heartbreak in his eyes.

"I know what's being said about the labor movement. But we're not asking to live in your mansion or even have one of our own, you know? We just want to be treated like human beings. Proper food, sanitation, living wages." He bit his bottom lip. "We want to be allowed to hope. To dream."

I pulled away from his touch, skin tingling where his fingers had been. At his words, something else had begun to rise inside me, something that caused my teeth to set themselves on edge. Wesley's story was heartbreaking, yes. But underlying his sentiments were accusations.

Accusations against my father. Against my family.

And, by default, against *me*.

Despite all I'd seen, all I'd learned, the sudden, unexpected defensiveness I'd felt earlier flared once again in my chest. "And you thought if I saw these pictures, what? That I'd somehow be able to fix things?"

He raised and lowered one shoulder, somehow undisturbed by my vicious tone. "I don't know. Maybe you'd see and understand. Maybe you'd be on our side."

"So you were using me?"

"No!" Wesley's calm demeanor finally broke. He stood, throwing his hands in the air. Grabbing the sides of his head, he pulled on his blond locks in frustration. "I never set out to . . . You came looking for me, remember? It's not like I had this master plan to seduce the boss's daughter." He sucked in a large breath, cheeks instantly reddening as he slammed his lips together.

"Seduce?" I stood and took a step back, feeling my own face go hot.

"That's not what I meant," he stammered. "Not seduce. There was no seducing. Not that I think you're the type of woman who can be seduced. Or would be. Or . . ." He bared his teeth in exasperation. "Look. I was just out here taking pictures. And then you were here. And you were . . . not what I thought you were going to be." The last words were spoken quietly.

I shifted from one foot to the other, feeling embarrassed. Feeling pleased. Feeling frustrated that curiosity was overtaking my anger. "Oh?"

"You spoke to me like a person. A real person. Even if you were rude to me—"

"You were rude to me first!" I objected.

He let out a small laugh. "Aye. We were *both* rude. But still you . . . you asked questions. Looked at me like I had something to say. And then you actually listened when I did." He rubbed the back of his neck. "I've never had a lady treat me that way, especially not one from the upper class."

I toed the ground, releasing a few fake coughs to cover my stammer. "Well . . . it's only because you knew Baudelaire. I would never have spoken to you otherwise."

"Then I'll forever be grateful I found his book in the gutter."

I looked up to find Wesley grinning. But when his eyes met mine, he looked away, unexpected shyness creeping into his voice. "I don't know. It felt . . . like providence. *Real* providence. Like maybe we—the workers, I mean—might have a chance now." He cleared his throat. "Because of you."

I pulled back my shoulders. Folded my arms over my chest and tried to keep my tone steady. "A chance for what?"

"Things are bad in camp. The workers are getting restless. Agitated. Dangerous." He glanced at me beneath raised brows. "I thought maybe, if you saw these pictures, you could help. Before things get violent."

Though I did not allow his words to affect my posture, beneath my dress, my skin chilled. *The rumblings.* That had to be what Mr. Zimmerman was talking about. I remembered the angry man that first day at the damsite, the murderous glares of the workers earlier today. The violence Wesley spoke of . . . It didn't take much imagination to understand who would be at the receiving end of it.

"I thought maybe . . . you could give us a voice."

Wesley's pleading tone snapped me back to the present. A new, different kind of ice crept down my spine. "A voice?" I sputtered. "You mean you want me to say something to my father?"

Wesley gave a slow, tentative nod.

"Are you crazy? He won't listen to me!"

"Why not? You're his daughter!"

"Yes, his *daughter*. I'm not his son. Not his partner. A lady has no place in a man's business." Even as I said them, the words rankled me. They were what I'd been taught my entire life. But speaking them aloud, in Wesley's presence, they felt burdensome.

Cowardly.

The next thing I knew, Wesley wrapped his hands around mine. And when he did, for all my initial trepidation, the difference in their appearance was the last thing on my mind. He was close, too close to be proper, but not close enough to satisfy. I could see the stubble poking through his chin, the chapped skin on his lips, the flecks of brown in the green of his irises.

"Kathleen..."

That something was in his eyes again. In his touch. In the air. I couldn't name it. Couldn't place it. But I could feel it. With every nerve in my body, I could feel it.

It was the exact opposite of what I experienced when I was with Mr. Walsh.

I didn't understand what was happening between Wesley and me. There was attraction, yes. An intensity. But I still wasn't sure I could trust him. Still wasn't sure this was more than a ruse to trick me, to bring my family down. And, anyway, it was too fast. Courtship should be slow, Mademoiselle Dubois had taught me. Anything else was wicked and common. Unbecoming. Whatever this was was unlike anything I'd ever felt before, but it was also complicated. Messy.

Scary.

I pulled my hands from his and looked away.

Though nothing stirred but the leaves in the trees above our heads, there was a sudden deflating of air, as if something had fled at our separation, leaving disappointment in its wake.

Twigs cracked under Wesley's feet as he took a step backward, running his hands over his upper arms. "Can we meet again? My next day off is a week from today. I could be here by noon."

When I nodded, it felt as if someone else were controlling my movements.

He pressed his lips together in a line, a smile that wasn't quite a smile.

A smile that broke my heart.

"Wesley?"

He had turned to leave but paused, head tilted. "Yeah?"

"About my father..." My throat burned as I tried to swallow. "I... I'll see what I can do."

He smiled for real this time, chin dipping in the smallest of nods. "Thank you, Kathleen."

I liked the way he said my name. Not Miss McDaniel. *Kathleen*. The Irish lilt that made it sound more exotic and melodious than it really was. But I couldn't enjoy it then. Not when another heaviness weighed on my mind.

"And Wesley?"

He turned once again.

"I know you can't control the other men. But . . ." I chewed the inside of my cheek, unsure what I was asking. "Just, please don't do anything rash. In the meantime."

Though his smile remained, something flickered deep in the pools of his eyes. "I'll see what I can do."

I didn't breathe again until he was out of sight. But, even then, his presence lingered, as real and tangible as the small smudge of dirt he had left on my pristine white gloves.

"Where were you?"

I had barely gotten the door latched behind me when my father's voice boomed out from the hallway. I spun around. "Father?" I asked meekly.

He strode toward me, hands on his hips, looking disturbingly disheveled. His tie was loose, top button undone, pocket square rumpled and poking at an odd angle from his vest pocket. Even his hair was mussed, the gray locks falling haphazardly over his forehead rather than slicked back in the normal fashion.

Mr. Zimmerman shadowed him.

I lowered my brow in concern, apprehension over my discovery momentarily forgotten. "Father, are you unwell? What—"

"Where were you?" He talked over me. "I sent for you two hours ago, and you were nowhere to be found. Even Stella didn't know where you were."

"I, um, I . . ." This was my chance. To be brave, tell the truth. I could help Wesley, make Hazel, Louisa, Margarite—myself—proud. But the anger in his eyes rendered my voice mute. Even if I had known what to say or how to say it, now was not the time.

"Mr. Walsh came calling for you! He drove all the way in from the city. For *you*." He pointed a finger accusingly in my direction. "And you weren't here to receive him."

"I . . . I'm sorry. I didn't know he was coming. I went for a walk in the woods, and I—"

"A *walk* in the *woods*?" His words exploded between a laugh and a shout. The muscles in his neck strained. "Now is not the time to go walking through the woods, Kitty!"

I glanced at Mr. Zimmerman, half-concealed by shadows, but he was not looking at me.

"You are to be here, in this house, at Mr. Walsh's beck and call, at all times. Do you understand me? A proposal could come any day now, and you *will* be ready for it. Poised and perfect, you hear?"

I pulled my arms into my sides, stomach lurching as if I'd just missed a step. A proposal? Already? What happened to *think it over, Kitty Kat*? When had we decided this? When had—

"Look at you." My father waved his hand, disgusted. "It's probably best Mr. Walsh didn't see you today anyway. You're an absolute mess."

Instinctively, I hid my dirt-covered gloves behind my back. But, glancing down, I realized it didn't matter. Mud splattered the hem of my dress, the edges of my petticoat. I could only guess what my face looked like; I was sure the torrent of emotions that had washed over it during the last few hours had left it a cracked mask, haggard and worn.

"Go get yourself cleaned up. And here." He took a small box from Mr. Zimmerman and thrust it in my direction. "Mr. Walsh left this for you. A long, flowing thank-you note better be posted before dinnertime."

My hands trembled as I watched him disappear back down the hallway. With a shaky breath, I lifted one of the flaps to reveal a brown bundle of fur, huddled in the corner.

A guinea pig. Its dark eyes stared at me with a fear I was just starting to understand.

> "Gulf rising rapidly,
> half of city now underwater."

TELEGRAPH FROM US WEATHER BUREAU OFFICE, GALVESTON
To Willis Moore, chief, US Weather Bureau, Washington, DC
Saturday, September 8, 1900, afternoon

FIFTEEN

SATURDAY, SEPTEMBER 8, 1900
GALVESTON, TEXAS

This was still Galveston.

That was the Sealy residence, barely visible through the driving rain, its red brick and iron porches still intact. The oleander in front of the Blum house still harbored a few bright pink petals. And there, underneath the muck and the mud, the metal of the trolley line running the length of the median still held firm.

I knew these things. I could see and feel these things. And yet none brought me any comfort as Matthew, Maggie, and I made our way down Broadway Avenue in search of shelter. Conditions were rapidly deteriorating. A fresh gale tugged at my clothes while water simultaneously pushed at me from above and pulled at me from below, making me feel as if I were drowning even with lungs full of air. How could this possibly be the same road I had walked along the day before, basking in the sunshine, breathing in the smell of the cardinal flowers and penstemons? It couldn't be. Galveston was beautiful. Familiar. The landscape through which we slogged now was foreign, dark, and dangerous, covered in frothing, angry seawater that stank of fish. I found myself disoriented, beleaguered by a world that would no longer sit still.

I wanted to ask Matthew if he knew where we were. If he knew where we were going. But, even if I'd had the courage to ask, doing so would have been impossible. I hadn't thought it conceivable for the wind to intensify past its current strength and yet, somehow, it had; its howl stole every sound besides the thudding of my heart inside my ears. Every step forward, already made difficult by the pull of waves, felt as if it were being done through wet sheets; the wind clung to me, pushed at me, snared me. Even though I knew my body was in motion, the storm made it seem as if we remained stagnant. The scenery never changed. No matter how long we walked, there was only water, churning beneath an ominous sky.

My eyes and muscles burned. Despite this, when I felt Maggie go slack behind me, I tightened my grip on her. I did not have the energy to turn, to speak to her, to offer gestures of comfort. But I hoped she could read it in the squeeze of my hand. No matter how tired, how weary, I would not let go of her. I could at least, I prayed, give her that much.

Though I wasn't sure for how much longer.

The storm muddled all sense of time and place. There was no telling how long we walked—minutes? hours?—nor how far we trudged. All I knew was that when Matthew finally stopped, the building before us looked so much like a mirage, I believed I was dreaming. Three stories of brick and stone, as wide as a city block, its chateau-like spires stretching bravely into the wrathful sky. Though water splashed against its foundation, it did not breach its doors set at the top of a wide concrete staircase.

Doors that, miraculously, swung open, flanked by men waving us inside.

Stepping over the threshold, the sudden cessation of wind caused my ears to ring and my muscles to go limp, as if it alone had been holding me aloft. I leaned on Matthew to steady myself, pulling Maggie close to my sagging body as my eyes struggled to adjust to the light. Flames flickered inside gas fixtures along the walls, revealing a cavernous foyer flanked by two broad staircases leading to upper floors. Dozens of people huddled in groups, some with trunks and suitcases piled around them like makeshift forts, others with seemingly nothing but the clothes on their backs, their hands clinging only to one another.

I glanced at Matthew. He, too, was taking in the scene, expressionless. There was a small cut above his eyebrow that hadn't been there earlier. When had he gotten it? And how? I didn't remember him making any kind of motion to indicate he'd been injured. Or had I simply been so consumed by my own survival that I'd missed it?

"Where are we?" I managed to whisper.

"It's the Rosenberg Free School. It's strong. Sturdy. We'll be safe here. It's been used as a shelter before. In other storms."

He didn't look at me when he spoke those last words. I wondered if it was because he knew I'd see what lay unsaid beneath them, worried he'd see the recognition of my own thoughts in his eyes.

But this storm isn't like the others.

Instead, he looked down at Maggie. I followed his gaze. Her eyes were red from the wind, the rain, fatigue, but they were alert, wide, and searching. Water dripped from her hair, her nose, her brow, yet she seemed oblivious; I hoped it was because she was too saturated to notice and not because shock had taken hold of her senses.

I crouched down in front of her. "Maggie? Are you all right?"

She blinked. Licked her lips. Then, slowly, hesitantly, she nodded.

And started to cry.

The sight of those tears sprang both of us into action. While Matthew went off in search of supplies, I led Maggie to an unoccupied corner. Pulling her into my lap, I wrapped my arms around her and pressed her head under my chin. Despite the overwhelming warmth of the room, she was shivering. Though he hadn't been able to find food, Matthew soon returned with a blanket he'd located in an upstairs classroom. I wrapped it around her. The fabric was thin and scratchy, but it seemed to act as a shield of sorts to Maggie, a barrier, no matter how weak, between her and the storm beyond. To my surprise and relief, she drifted off to sleep almost instantaneously, her small thumb tucked into the corner of her mouth.

Matthew settled in beside me, lips contorted into a sad smile. "Exhaustion defeats fear every time. I think it might be the most powerful force in nature."

I let out a small burst of air through my nostrils. "I'm not so sure about that."

Though the building did, indeed, remain firm against the raging storm just beyond its walls, a steady if slightly muted roar, like the sound of a thousand freight trains, vibrated the stones at my back. Rain pelted the windows, obscuring our vision of anything except the black sky. The group of men standing sentry at the front door took turns holding it shut; three times it blew open before one of them produced what appeared to be a metal pipe, which they lodged through the handles. Even then, the men still sat in front of it, prepared for its failure, while the rest of us pretended we couldn't hear the rattle of the hinges, straining against the beast outside that would, we all feared, eventually force its way in.

"There was a mob at Union Station." The words came from one of the newcomers, a man who had arrived just after Matthew and me, stumbling in on a gust of wind that sucked the derby hat right from his head. Even now, he still patted at his dark hair, as if he couldn't quite fathom its absence. He murmured the news, keeping it barely audible, but the name of the train depot snagged my attention away from the storm.

Union Station. One of the places I believed Emily might be.

"Seemed like half the island was trying to get to the mainland. It was pure chaos."

My fingers clenched instinctively. It was only a small whimper from Maggie that reminded me her arm was at the receiving end. I relented, but it did not quiet the dread rising in my chest.

Emily. In the midst of all those pushing, shoving, panicked bodies. I didn't know what was worse: the thought of her there, her delicate frame being jostled and squeezed, or the image of her going back out into the storm alone to escape the pandemonium.

"The trains are still running?" another man asked. There was incredulity in his voice, tinged with obvious hope.

The dark-haired man shook his head. "The trains could run just fine. The problem is there ain't no more tracks." He paused for a moment, letting his words land. "The bridges to the mainland are gone. We're trapped."

The shrieks of the storm outside did not abate, and yet silence rushed in behind his words. They seemed to linger, to echo, though I knew it wasn't true; the noise and his hushed tone probably meant only the closest few had heard them.

I wished I wasn't one of them.

My entire body tensed, acid rising in the back of my throat. I leaned forward, muscles working on instinct rather than logic. Trapped? I couldn't be trapped. I needed to run. Needed to flee. Needed to get away from this place, this water, this wind.

From the danger that would not go away once the one rampaging just outside the schoolhouse door stopped.

There was a gentle but firm touch on my arm, and I blinked. Matthew's eyes met mine. Searching. Reading. Questions swam inside his gaze but also somehow, impossibly, understanding. As if he could read my fear.

It's okay, he said without saying. *Just stay. Please, stay.*

I stared at him for several agonizing moments, wondering if he could see the war raging inside me. And then, against my chest, Maggie let out a small sigh, nuzzling her head farther under my chin. I let out a long breath, body deflating.

I wouldn't run. Couldn't run.

Yet.

I settled back against the wall. Matthew did the same. But he did not remove his hand from my arm.

And I did not make him.

The storm still seethed outside, but an odd sort of calm settled over the room, a stillness that wasn't quite still. People spoke in desperate whispers, frightened babies cried, uneasy adults coughed and shuffled. Even here, out of the rain, the air was damp, heavy with the smell of sweat and the sea, wet clothes and exhausted bodies. It was crowded. Hot. Stifling.

I soon found my eyelids growing heavy. I wondered if Matthew had, indeed, been right. Because even though every nerve prickled with danger, I was powerless to fight the strength of my exhaustion. Without even realizing I was doing it, I collapsed into a deep, dreamless sleep.

I didn't know how long I slept. All I knew was, when I was finally jolted awake, I realized two things very quickly:

Night was falling.

And the storm had still not abated.

My wet clothes had dried stiff and scratchy, pungent with the smell of mildew, which quelled my rumbling stomach; they scratched against my tender skin as I shifted, trying to look out one of the windows. I could see nothing but fast-moving rivulets streaming down the glass. Beyond them, only darkness.

The floor beneath me was damp, almost slimy, and I desperately wanted to stand. But, in my lap, Maggie still snoozed. I didn't dare wake her. I knew it would only lead to questions I hadn't any answers for.

"Matthew," I whispered. "Do you—"

My question bit off as cleanly as if snipped by scissors. Because a third realization had just hit me.

Matthew was gone.

After begging me to stay, he'd left me. Left Maggie.

Here. In the storm.

Trapped.

Fighting against rising panic, I eased Maggie off my lap, curling the top of the blanket into a makeshift pillow before sliding her gently onto the floor. Her face scrunched, lips releasing an irritated sigh before her thumb found her mouth again, and she stilled. I kept one eye on her, swallowing my guilt at leaving her exposed, albeit momentarily, and made my way toward the group of gentlemen at the front of the building. The metal pipe had held, thankfully, and the door remained shut, although I noticed with no small sense of unease that part of the wooden frame near the middle hinge had begun to crack. Tongues of water lapped in at its base.

"Excuse me?" The wind was louder here, less of a groan and more of a growl, interspersed with whistles and shrieks as tendrils of it found its way through various crevices. The men looked at me. "Have you seen the man I came in here with? Tall, dark hair?"

One of them, a mustachioed man with flecks of silver near his temples, shook his head. It spoke to the direness of our circumstances that he did not even seem to register my masculine clothes. "Sorry, miss."

"But you didn't see anyone leave?"

He let out a disbelieving laugh. "Ain't no one left. I guarantee you that."

I released a shaky breath. So he was here. Matthew was still here. Somewhere. "Thank you."

After another quick check on Maggie, I wove my way through the mass of bodies. The lights from the lamps cast long shadows over their faces, some awake, some sleeping, all of them disheveled. There were women in corsets and lace beside men with holey shoes and worn-out trousers. It no longer mattered. Upper class, lower class. How silly it all seemed now, when we were, every one of us, at the mercy of the wind and the waves.

My mind flitted to Wesley. To my father. How they would have looked, side by side, here in this place. It was an image that stirred up feelings of love and sadness, grief and rage, all of which I quickly swallowed.

There was no time for that now.

The sound of raised voices led me to a hallway at the rear of the building. Peering around the corner, I saw the door to one of the classrooms propped open, about half a dozen souls huddled in the center, talking animatedly.

One of them, I noticed with relief, was Matthew.

Another, impossibly, was Emily.

I rushed into the room without thinking, without planning, without any regard at all to the conversation I was interrupting, and wrapped my friend in a tight embrace, instant tears streaming down my face. I felt her body relax as realization sank in, squeezing me with a strength I hadn't known she possessed. My cries turned to laughter when she pulled away, blue eyes wide with joy.

"Annie! Is it really you?"

I nodded, too choked up to speak.

Across the circle, Matthew grinned. "I found her not five

minutes ago. I was looking for food, and lo and behold . . ." He gestured to Emily.

She grasped my hands. "He told me you were here. He swore it, but I didn't believe him. He was just getting ready to—" Her words collapsed under a relieved sob, and she wrapped her arms around me once again.

"I was just getting ready to take her to you," Matthew finished for her. "And then . . . here you are."

"Here I am." My words came out muffled, as my mouth was pressed into Emily's shoulder.

After a few moments, she pulled back. "But how did you—? Where did you—?" Her questions rushed out in a jumble. "I woke up, and you were gone. I went to the train—"

"It doesn't matter," I said quickly, seeing Matthew's eyebrows furrow. "I'm here now. And you're here now. We're safe. All is well."

Elation began to slowly leach from Emily's face. Her small hands, which had gripped me so tightly, slackened. "All is not well."

A small cough from behind me caused me to jump. Overcome with emotion, I had forgotten we weren't the only ones in the room. I took a step backward, out of the center of the circle, and took in the other faces. All five of them were men. Three were dressed in priestly garments, black, though the oldest of the trio had a scarlet sash around his waist. The other two were in street clothes, dark trousers and white button-downs, one with a gray vest, the other with patches sewn on the elbows. Workmen, from the look of it.

An interesting group, with nothing similar aside from the matching frowns and creased foreheads, every brow knotted with worry.

"When I couldn't find you," Emily began. She paused. There was a question in her words, directed only at me, though, in her kindness, she did not allow it to linger. It did not stop me from dropping my gaze to the ground, all the same. "I decided to go back to the orphanage," she continued. "But I thought maybe I should head to Moody's first. You know how kind Mr. Moody is. I knew he'd give me some provisions on credit. I could tell the storm was going to be a bad one, and I wasn't sure we'd have enough resources to last, should we get stranded for a few days." She gestured to several bags on the floor I hadn't noticed before, overflowing with food and medical supplies. "But, while I was there, the storm seemed to keep getting worse. There were rumors the Gulf was overflowing the beach."

"They weren't rumors," Matthew said quietly.

Emily's lips pressed into a line. "It all deteriorated so quickly. Mr. Moody was closing his shop, as were so many others, and I knew, if things were as bad at the shore as they were saying, I'd never make it back to St. Mary's. Mr. Moody offered me shelter at his home above the store, but I decided to wait out the storm at Sacred Heart instead." She nodded at the priests.

The eldest, the one with the scarlet sash, steepled his fingers in front of his chest. "And we were happy to take you in. I only wish we could have greeted your arrival with better news."

My stomach sank. "What do you mean?"

The priest looked at me. His hooded eyes drooped at the corners. "We, too, had been hearing stories about the situation on the beach, and we were worried. We tried several times to reach Mother Camillus before we left the church, seeking shelter here, but all our attempts at communication with the orphanage went unanswered."

"Telephone lines are down all over the island," Matthew interjected, seeing my face. "It doesn't mean anything bad has happened."

"But our messenger has also not returned. We sent him to—"

Matthew held up his hand. "He's probably holed up somewhere, just like we are, waiting out the storm. Again, it doesn't mean anything bad has happened."

I wondered if his words sounded as empty to him as they did to me. As they did, judging by the faces around me, to all of us.

In the ensuing silence, the wind echoed. Except now, in light of the priest's story, it no longer sounded like a roar. It sounded like laughter, wicked and forbidding, mocking our concern. It caused a shiver to creep up my spine. From the other side of the blackboard, something large thumped against the window, as if punctuating the storm's glee.

"We're attempting to put together a rescue party," one of the other priests said finally.

"And I say again, absolutely not," Matthew said. "It's too dangerous."

"And what's the other option?" Emily said, her fierceness startling me. "To leave them all out there alone? Women and children?"

"We have no proof they're in any danger," Matthew responded testily. "Those buildings are made of thick stone. They're sturdy. Secure. I'm sure they are all perfectly fine."

"But this hurricane. It's—"

"It's not a hurricane!" Matthew's voice came out at a near shout, a fact he only seemed to recognize when he saw Emily wince. When he continued, it was with measured control. "It's just a storm. And that means it will be over soon."

"How do you know?"

"Because hurricanes do not strike the Texas coast. Mr. Cline said it was impossible." That old arrogance had crept back into Matthew's tone. It should have relieved me; he was the one with all the weather knowledge, after all. But he'd been wrong about everything regarding this storm. I no longer trusted Mr. Cline or his science. And Matthew's steadfast clinging to it no longer seemed charming. It seemed delusional.

More than that, it seemed downright dangerous.

"We just need to wait a little longer. It will be over soon," he said. "And then we can go get them."

Emily's gaze narrowed. "If you're not willing to help us, Mr. Richter, we will find others who are." With that, she turned and strode from the room, the three priests scurrying after her.

Matthew sputtered and fumed, throwing his hands in the air. "They're crazy," he murmured. "Absolutely crazy. It's suicide, going down to the Gulf right now. Give it an hour, maybe two, and this will all be over. It *has to be* almost over."

I watched him beneath raised brows, chewing the inside of my cheek, but I wasn't really seeing him. I was seeing little Lucas, with his cowlick and adorable snaggletooth. Quiet Agnes and boisterous Mildred, the most unlikely—and sweetest—pair of friends I'd ever seen. Baby Pierce and just-learning-to-walk Laura. I was seeing Sister Bernice. Sister Elizabeth. Sister Sarah.

And Mother Camillus. Strict, hard, big-hearted Mother Camillus. Who had taken me in, given me a home, even when she didn't want to. Even when I caused her trouble.

Who had offered me a future that I had so readily cast aside.

All these faces and so many more, who had nurtured and cared for me at my lowest point, each in their own way. Who had taken pity, shown love, to an undeserving soul like mine.

Now they were alone and in peril. Abandoned. As the storm—I couldn't bring myself to use the word Emily had, the term Matthew steadfastly denied—devoured Galveston.

My chest tightened. And then, just as suddenly, it seemed to fold in on itself.

Because it wasn't only the sisters and the children at St. Mary's.

My hand reached for the phantom strap on my shoulder. The *camera*.

I'd left it there, thinking it would be safe. Thinking I'd be back to protect it, like I'd sworn to Wesley I would.

But now I was here. And it was there.

And there was a literal ocean between us.

Tears sprang to my eyes. Wesley. I'd promised him. I'd *promised*. At first, I had done it out of necessity, out of panic. But, as the days went by, and true grief and understanding had taken hold, the vow had become more than words. It became a quest to prove he hadn't been mistaken; to prove that, for all my flaws and weaknesses, I could still be the girl he believed I was. I had failed him—failed everyone—so many times.

I could not bear to do it again.

I spoke without thinking, without allowing myself to second-guess what I knew guilt, inflamed by no small amount of brash stupidity, was forcing me to do. I knew deep down that this was me continuing my desperate attempt to outrun my past. To right wrongs that could not be undone. But I couldn't allow space for any of that. Instead, all I registered was Matthew's eyes widening, his jaw going slack, as I left him standing in the middle of the room with these words:

"I'm going with them."

SIXTEEN

In the end, Matthew, surprisingly, had been easier to convince than Emily.

After my sudden outburst, he'd regained composure quickly enough to chase after me, cornering me in the darkened hallway and forbidding me from attempting something so reckless. So foolish. So stupid. He would go, he said, if only I would stay. Emily, conversing with the priests and a new group of men just feet down the hallway, had heard his protestations and, learning what it was I wanted to do, joined him in his tirade, their annoyance with one another forgotten at my expense.

But there was no talking me out of it. There was no going back. All their objections fell on deaf ears. I was set on my course, determined.

Only the sight of Maggie was strong enough to give me pause.

In all my bravado, I'm ashamed to admit I'd forgotten about her. Guilt needled my stomach instantly, however, as I retreated from an irritated Matthew and an incensed Emily to the main foyer, where I spotted Maggie curled under the blanket, still sleeping. Her blonde hair had dried stiff, crusted to her cheek with salt. Her eyelids fluttered as I crouched down and tried to gently peel it away.

"Annie?"

I gave her a tempered smile. "Hi, Mags."

"Is it still raining?"

"It is."

She sat up, rubbing her eyes with the back of her hand. Sleep lines creased her face. "What time is it?"

"I don't know. Listen . . ." My mouth tasted sour when I swallowed. "Mags, I—"

"Sister Emily!"

In a flash of brown fabric, Maggie was on her feet, launching herself without preamble at Emily, who had just appeared from the side hallway. My friend gasped in delight, hugging the child back ferociously, running her hands through her tangles. "What are you doing here?" Emily tried to sound stern, but it was impossible with the grin stretching across her face.

"I came with Annie."

Feeling awkward, I rose, scratching the back of my leg with one foot. "She followed me. When I went looking for you."

Surprise flickered over Emily's features. "*You* came looking for *me*? But I thought . . ."

Her words trailed off at the sound of raised voices by the door. The priests were gathering volunteers, much to the chagrin of the temporary sentries. Even from here, I could hear their protestations, see their disbelieving headshakes. I recognized the exasperated defeat in their sagging shoulders.

I gave a sideways glance at Emily. Her face was still drawn, the inquisitiveness upon her lips dying as her mind returned to the problem at hand. For the first time since I'd known her, a battle raged inside her eyes.

Someone needed to go to St. Mary's. She knew that. She wanted that.

She just didn't want it to be me.

I placed a hand on her arm. From over the top of Maggie's head, her eyes tore away from the men, meeting mine. *Why are you doing this?* The question was there, as clear as if she'd spoken it aloud. *What is going on?* And then, painfully, pleading, *Why are you hiding from me?*

All of it faded away then, the wind, the rain, the fear. The storm was nothing compared to the self-condemnation I felt in that moment. I had shared a room with Emily for months. Shared tears, laughter, work. But, really, I hadn't shared anything at all with her. I'd told myself I was protecting her with my dishonesty and evasiveness. But all I was really doing was hurting her.

I had thought I was just hiding from the man who pursued me. But I had also hidden myself away from the love she was so desperately trying to extend.

And trying to receive in return.

I understood then that I would carry that regret—along with so many others—with me for the rest of my life.

I pulled my eyes away from hers before grief threatened to overpower my nerves.

"Maggie," I said, swallowing my misery and crouching before her. "I have to go out for a little while."

Her dark eyes widened, her bottom lip trembling. "No . . ."

"Our friends at the orphanage need my help."

"I'll go with you."

"No, Maggie. You can't. It's not safe."

Tears began to form in the corners of her eyes. "If it's not safe, then why are you going?"

My throat thickened. If only she knew. If only I could explain. Yet another victim of my lies. Instead, I found myself repeating,

"Because our friends at the orphanage need my help. Think of Sister Hannah. Sister Raphael. Rebecca. And what about Billy?" I tossed in the name of the only child I ever saw her play with on a regular basis. "I bet he's scared to death right now."

Maggie's face crumpled. "Do you think he's all right?"

"He will be soon." Taking one of her hands, I enveloped it between both of mine, pulling her until her nose was nearly touching my own. "I will come back to you. I promise."

Maggie Sherwood stared at me, the ache in her heart as tangible as the salt on her skin. But she nodded. Shakily. Once, twice. As stoically as a woman five times her age.

Blinking back tears of my own, I wrapped her in a tight hug, praying the storm would not make a bigger liar out of me than I already was.

"Emily will stay with you," I choked out, voicing a question that, with one look at my former roommate, I knew had never been a question at all. "She'll keep you safe."

Emily wrapped her arm around Maggie's shoulders, gently transferring the girl's embrace to herself. "Of course I will," she said. Her voice was confident, though I noticed a few tears of her own glistening on her cheeks. "We will wait here for our friends."

Friends. I didn't think Emily knew the effect that word had on me; there was no possible way she could have perceived my inward spiral. And yet as I looked away, tears clouding my vision, she reached up and touched my hand. Her fingers were cold as they squeezed mine. There was melancholy in her weak smile. But also, acceptance.

She didn't understand why I had to go. Didn't like it. But she was going to love me through it all the same.

Just as she had always done.

"Thank you" was all I could manage. It was insufficient. Too few words for too much need, too much remorse. And yet I hoped she could read everything underneath that inadequate sentiment. Hoped it would convey my apologies for the heartbreak I never meant to give and that she didn't deserve.

She nodded—small, subtle, and sad—and released my hand.

Maggie's expression remained steady until I took a step back, away from them, at which point fresh tears began to fall. Emily, however, moved quickly, kneeling in front of her with exaggerated excitement. "Are you hungry, Mags? I have some food in a bag in the next room. Maybe we could have a little bit, and then you can help me pass some out to the others? Would you like that?"

Maggie gave her a look that spoke plainly to her awareness of being manipulated, cajoled like a toddler. But still, she nodded, placating Emily—placating *me*—with a grim smile. Before allowing herself to be led to the adjoining hallway, she paused. "Annie?"

"Yes?"

"You can save Angela, too. If you have time."

I gave her a small nod, my heart melting at her concern even for her nemesis at the orphanage. I managed to stay upright until the two of them rounded the corner. Only then did I allow myself to sink to my knees, my entire body quaking with deep, quiet sobs. Was I doing the right thing? Leaving Maggie, this place, safety . . . and for what?

If we did somehow manage, against all odds, to get there, there was no guarantee we'd be able to get the nuns and children to safety. No guarantee I'd be able to secure Wesley's camera against the waves.

Even if we did succeed, it still would not change the past.

Or my future.

Yet I did not feel I'd be able to face myself—whoever I was or ended up being—if I didn't at least try.

And so, summoning the last of my strength, I gathered myself up off the floor, adjusted the rope around my sagging pants, and made my way over to where the rescue party stood. In addition to the three priests and two workmen from before, they had added two additional men to their number—all seven of whom stared at me as I asserted myself into their circle.

"I'm joining you."

To their credit, not a single man laughed. But none of them welcomed me either. Instead, the wind merely howled beneath the door crack, a shrill, eerie whistling noise that echoed through the antechamber.

Amidst the astonished stares and gaping mouths, it was the head priest—the one with the sash—that spoke first. "No, miss, I'm sorry. I can't allow you to—"

"She's with me," came a voice.

I turned to find Matthew, arms crossed over his chest. His face still held the irritated scowl I'd left him with earlier, only this time it was directed not at me, but to the group of men.

"Mr. Richter," began one of the priests. "I must insist. This is not an appropriate task for a la—"

"She's with me," Matthew repeated, speaking over him. "If I go, she goes." There was a challenge in his words, one I could very quickly see the others had no energy to counter. All eyes turned to the priest who, after several moments, gave a roll of his shoulders, admitting defeat but also, perhaps, washing his hands of our petulant nonsense.

I joined the group as they began tucking the legs of their trousers into their boots, silently cursing my high laces. "I didn't ask you to come with me," I hissed at Matthew, who had settled down beside me. "Why did you do that?"

Matthew didn't look at me. Instead, his hands wrapped around his ankle, squashing the fabric against his sock, trying to make it fit snugly beneath the leather. He let out a long breath of air. "Why did I do that?" He turned to face me then. The hardness was gone from his visage, replaced with something I didn't recognize.

Couldn't read. "If you don't know the answer to that question by now, Miss Not Nun, then I don't think you ever will."

And then he rose, leaving me there, mouth open and stomach in knots, and went to assist the other men with their preparations.

We hadn't been inside the Rosenberg Free School for very long, a few hours at most. My body hadn't yet forgotten the push of the wind, the sting of the rain, the smell of the sea. It tingled with dread as our group of nine prepared to exit through the back door, where a small fleet of skiffs and dinghies, brought by various families seeking shelter, had been assembled for our journey.

But the memory did little to prepare me for what actually awaited me outside the walls of the school.

I hadn't even made it into the boat before the first rush of wind knocked my feet out from underneath me. It was only Matthew's strong grip that kept me from plummeting down the stone staircase into the swirling water below. The gale pushed his weight against me, buckling my knees, toppling me unceremoniously into the waiting boat. I struggled to pull myself into a sitting position. Not only was the wind insistent in knocking me back down, but the choppiness of the waves also caused the boat to lurch dangerously from side to side.

The noise was deafening. Though I could still liken it to the roar of a freight train, it was no longer like a passing one. Rather, it was as if I were lying on the tracks, the never-ending, screaming locomotive passing directly overhead. The men's mouths moved in silent shouts, falling on ears too full to heed their instructions. Frustrated, I clapped my hands to the sides of my head, trying to create a windbreak.

It didn't work.

Matthew climbed in behind me, pulling my body close to his to allow our other passenger—one of the workmen—to move up to the bow of the small craft. The nine of us separated into three boats, which another man struggled to tie together with rope. I felt stupid sitting there watching him, helpless and overwhelmed.

This was madness. Sheer madness. I needed to get back inside. Out of the wind. Out of the rain. Out of the—

But then we were off.

Night had fallen. Or perhaps it was just the clouds and the rain that made it seem that way. There were no streetlights, no illuminated windows, nothing but sporadic flashes of lightning to reveal the path of our oars.

If I'd thought the wind was bad there in the shelter of the backdoor alcove, it was nothing compared to what awaited us when we rounded the corner. Like a raging bull, it barreled right into my chest, stealing my breath and knocking me into Matthew with a force that caused my head to snap back painfully. I let out a cry no one could hear. Matthew gripped my shoulders and forced me upright. Through flashes, I could just make out his lips.

Are you all right?

I assumed that's what he was asking. I couldn't hear. Couldn't see. But I nodded all the same. At least in the chaos, it would be harder for him to see my tears.

Shapes rose out of the darkness on either side of us. Buildings. Homes, offices. I wondered how many people were huddled inside of them. Some of the bricks had started to tumble, walls melting into the sea below. In others, glass had been blown out of windows, the jagged shards reflecting the lightning, like razor-sharp teeth in gaping mouths. The effect was beastly, terrifying, an illusion further heightened by the relentless roar of the wind and sheets of blinding rain.

But, as fearsome as the buildings were, their regularity served to give our party some semblance of direction. Thanks to a shifting wind, we were moving steadily west, toward the orphanage. Our boat was the last in the train, and it was no small feat to keep the group together. Mounds of wreckage rushed along with us, slamming into the boats like a ravenous sea creature. Several times, I thought I heard the wood splinter. But how could I be sure with all the noise? The boats became jammed, the ropes binding us tangled, but somehow we remained tethered, bumping along through foaming ocean water even darker than the night sky.

The situation only worsened as we made our way out of the city proper. The buildings became fewer and farther between, landmarks nonexistent. The wind grew even more intense, no longer buffered by man-made blockades. Salt stung my eyes, the rain my skin. Every inch of me felt on fire, a peculiar sensation considering the amount of water saturating my clothes and pooling at the bottom of our boat. Out here, debris was no longer confined to the waves; it soared through the air, flung about like children's toys. Every flash of lightning revealed new danger: lumber, roof tiles, tree branches, road signs. All innocuous objects turned deadly.

It was as I had feared. Even if we made it to St. Mary's, we would not be able to bring the sisters and orphans out in these conditions. It was too dangerous. Our only hope now was to reach them, to hunker down beside them, and wait out the storm.

As Matthew had insisted we do in the first place.

I had only time to feel a quick, momentary prick of guilt before something big and black—it was too dark to see what—smashed into the man in front of me. I'd been deaf before, too overwhelmed to hear anything over the roar of the storm, but somehow I heard that smack. Heard the sound of metal on bone. As the man fell backward, collapsing into my lap, I had the sudden thought that I didn't even know his name. There had been no time for introductions. Blood poured from a wound on his dented forehead. *Dented?* It was an absurd word. Obscene. But there was no other term.

The man's dark eyes met mine before rolling into the back of his head. I screamed. There may have been no sound, but I screamed all the same.

Then something lashed against my brow, slicing off my shriek and causing white hot pain to erupt behind my eyes. I blinked, blinded. Where once there had been darkness now there were only spots. Spots . . . and warmth. I reached my hand up, still unable to see, feeling sticky wetness on my lid.

I was bleeding.

I was . . . *blind*.

In a panic, I shoved the man from my lap. Feeling my way to the side of the boat, I leaned over the hull and splashed water on my face, trying to rinse away the blood, remembering too late that it was seawater. Fresh pain seared across my brow. Even over the roar of the wind, I could hear the thudding of my pulse in my ears. I blinked several times, trying to clear the throb, the blood, relief washing over me despite my agony when my eyesight began to clear.

I wasn't blind.

Yet the respite was short-lived. Because as the tears and blood cleared from my eyes, they came to rest not on the waves, but on the mound of debris knocking against the hull.

Pieces of wood, nailed into the shape of a cross. The name *Benjamin Jones* carved into one, a jumble of numbers beneath it. Another flash of lightning revealed *Alice Williams, 1812-1878*. Darkness. Then light. And another cross: *Charlotte Johnson, 1888-1890*.

Grave markers. They were grave markers.

Horrified, I scrambled away from the side, pushing against the wind, stumbling over the still-unmoving body of . . . who? I didn't know. Didn't know the workman's name, if he was alive. I didn't know where we were, if we were still in Galveston or if we'd been washed out to sea. All I knew was I was in a boat, bleeding, surrounded by grave markers and possibly the corpses to which they belonged.

My chest constricted. The storm was strangling me. The wind. The rain. The waves. It came from every direction.

I couldn't breathe. I couldn't see. I couldn't—

Suddenly Matthew's face was before me, his saturated handkerchief pressed to my forehead. He did not speak—not that I would have been able to hear him anyway—but pressed my hand to my temple, holding the cloth in place while he bent and began untying my shoes. I should have been curious, but I felt too numb. Instead, I watched as if outside of myself as he removed my boots, tied the laces together, and then draped them over my head, securing them under my chin. He made a motion in front of his face, forming his hands into barriers.

A helmet, I realized. He had made me a helmet.

I squeezed his hand in a pathetic thank-you. The shoes rattled around my ears. I wasn't sure how much they could possibly shield me, but I was thankful for the sense of protection, no matter how small.

Matthew bent over beside me. When he arose, he had his own shoes wrapped around his head. It would have been comical, in different circumstances. Now, however, coupled with the look of dread slowly washing over his face, it was anything but.

I turned, the rain whipping my face in a fresh burst, bile rising in my throat. I didn't want to see. But not seeing would not change our circumstances.

Through flashes of lightning, I came to understand the source of his terror.

Our trio of boats had become untethered in the chaos. The other two skiffs were nowhere to be seen.

We were alone in the swirling, angry, wreckage-filled water.

Before panic and grief could seize me completely, however, another sight took hold. Buildings rose ahead of us, their silhouettes jutting out of the ocean like pillars, somehow even blacker than the darkened sky.

No, not just buildings.

Dormitories.

We had made it to St. Mary's.

My initial relief soon morphed into confusion. Something was wrong, off. It was only when another piece of debris slammed into our boat, knocking us to the side, that I finally understood.

It was St. Mary's, yes. That much was certain. Even from here, I could make out the familiar shapes of the windows, the decorative awnings, the timber-lined porticos.

But where once there had been two buildings, now there stood only one.

One of the dormitories was gone.

Was it the boys'? Or the girls'? I couldn't tell. The storm was disorienting. But I wouldn't even allow the thought to enter my mind. It was the boys'. It *had* to have been the boys'. The children, all the sisters, had holed up together inside the girls' dormitory because it was newer. Stronger.

They were still safe inside.

Wesley's camera was still safe inside.

We could get to them. Get to it.

But just as I turned, prepared to motion to Matthew to row, a sickening crack, different from any noise the storm had thrown at us before, split through the charged air, ear-shattering even over the thump of the waves, the groan of the wind.

I started to scream before I even looked back. Because somehow, I already knew. Yet it didn't stop the horror from overtaking me as, through flashes of lightning, I saw the second dormitory collapse, its bricks splashing into the ocean below with an otherworldly splash.

As I watched, the remains of St. Mary's slipped beneath the sea, taking the pieces of my shattered heart along with it into the shadowy depths.

SEVENTEEN

APRIL 1900
CROTON-ON-HUDSON, NEW YORK

"Yet to all who did receive him, to those who believed in his name, he gave the right to become children of God—children born not of natural descent, nor of human decision or a husband's will, but born of God."

A murmured chorus of amens brought my mind back to the present. I had been trying to pay attention; I really had been. Something about adoption and identity and building our lives on Christ. But thinking about building made me think of the dam, and thinking about the dam made me think about Wesley, and soon the preacher's words were nothing but additional noise in my already too-crowded head.

It had been a week since our last meeting. I was supposed to meet Wesley later today, and I still wasn't quite sure what I was going to say to him.

I hadn't said anything to my father about the working conditions at the dam.

Even though I'd told Wesley I would, I hadn't "tried my best."

I hadn't tried at all.

Guilt swirled with apprehension inside my gut, intensifying my frayed nerves and muting everything else around me. The next thing I knew, the preacher was finished, everyone was standing, and I was blinking, trying hard to remember where I was and what I was supposed to be doing.

Not that it really mattered. No one was paying attention to me. Croton-on-Hudson's Methodist church may have been Pastor Larson's pulpit, but it was my father's stage. It was our pew around which bodies crowded after the message, eager for a handshake or a word with the only version of God in which most of these people truly believed.

I ran a hand over the messaline satin of my hat, letting my fingers brush each gray rosette before trailing them over the small pair of feathered wings adorning the flared brim. It was a beautiful hat. The latest fashion. Brought back from New York City a few days ago on one of my father's business trips. He'd unboxed it just as I was finally summoning the courage to speak to him about the dam.

And then he'd placed it on my head, and all the words had withered inside my throat.

It was beautiful. It made *me* feel beautiful. And the look in my father's eyes was so proud, so adoring, so apologetic for the last time he'd snapped at me, I didn't dare ruin the moment. I had felt so loved and appreciated, so much like his daughter again, I couldn't bear the thought of losing that warmth, not after weeks of the precariousness and tension that had taken up residence inside our home.

And, honestly, it was just such a lovely hat. The envy of Carolyn Gardner and the rest of them when they'd stopped by for tea and a stroll through the grounds.

There would be other chances to talk to him, I'd reasoned. To keep my word to Wesley.

But, even though there had been, I'd seized none of them.

Running my fingers over the soft, wispy feather, the images of the camp Wesley had captured on his camera flashed before me. The frozen beds, the waste buckets, the inedible slop. Though the pictures lingered in the recesses of my mind, how easy it had been to push them aside, safe inside my warm house with its indoor plumbing and abundance of food.

With this beautiful hat.

"Miss McDaniel?"

Swallowing a wave of guilt, I spun around, starched petticoat struggling in the narrow space between pews.

Theodore Walsh stood in the row behind me, dark three-piece suit nearly as stiff as his posture.

I tried to plaster a smile upon my face, but my anxiety tempered any attempt at manners. "What are you doing here?"

It was the wrong thing to say, the wrong tone. The slight twitch at the corner of his mouth confirmed it. But before I could backtrack, the look was gone, and Mr. Walsh was kissing my fingers with a slight bow of his head. "Everyone needs Jesus, Miss McDaniel."

I puffed out my cheeks, feeling them go hot. "Yes. Of course. How rude of me."

"Not rude. I understand your surprise. This is not my usual church." He glanced at my father, who was deep in conversation with three or four men I recognized vaguely as those who drifted in and out of our house at all hours of the day, and then back at me. "Would you allow me to escort you outside while we wait for your father?" He smiled, offering his arm.

I pretended not to notice the eyes on us as he led me from the sanctuary. The whispered titters and haughty gazes. Mr. Walsh was an upstanding, rich, eligible bachelor. And here he was, hand on *my* arm, rather than any of the other single daughters in our town. I should have been enjoying the victory.

So why did I have the sensation of spiders crawling down my spine?

He guided me out into the bright sunshine, down the wide concrete steps, and into the fragrant shade of the blooming cherry trees lining the edge of the boulevard. Pink, yellow, and purple tulips crowded their bases, spilling out onto the lush lawn of green grass that lay just beyond. Churchgoers mingled beside waiting carriages, ladies in all different hues beside gentlemen in browns and blues. There was the smell of hope in the air, of rebirth and the promise of life to come. I breathed it in, trying to draw in enough of the season's warmth to overcome my goosebumps.

"Kathleen."

Though it was spoken softly, my stomach clenched at the sound of my name. It was not proper for a man to use a lady's first name unless invited to do so or a certain amount of intimacy had been achieved.

I thought back to Wesley, to the sound of my name falling from his lips.

It had not bothered me then.

"I want to apologize for my absence over the past few weeks. I've been extremely busy in the city."

I managed a weak smile. Had he been missing? I hadn't even noticed.

"But that's no excuse for neglecting my commitment to you. I apologize."

"Oh, it's quite all right, Mr. Walsh. No need to—"

"Because I *am* committed to you. I . . . I hope I've made myself clear in that regard."

My corset suddenly felt too tight, the smell of flowers too overwhelming. I fiddled with the lace trim on my dress, trying to keep my head from swooning. This was it. This was the moment it was going to become official. I'd known it was coming, but now that it was here, it felt like a steam train, barreling toward me out of the night. I wasn't sure. I wasn't ready. I wasn't . . .

Wesley's face floated in front of me.

Those green eyes. Searching me.

Seeing me.

And then he was gone, and Mr. Walsh was standing before me again, brows raised hopefully, his eyes as empty as Wesley's were overflowing. Sweat began to bead along my hairline. Manners dictated that I respond, and that I respond in kind. I could practically feel Mademoiselle Dubois—and my father—screaming in my ear. But I could not force a single word from my lips.

Mr. Walsh cleared his throat. Shifted from one foot to the other. "Did you . . . uh . . . did you like the gift I sent along?"

Gift? What gift?

"The guinea pig?"

"Oh," I breathed, thankful for the explanation and, even more so, for the rapid shift in conversation. "Yes," I stammered. "She's darling."

A wide smile broke out across Mr. Walsh's face. The shadows cast by the tree branches highlighted deep wrinkles beneath his eyes I'd never noticed before. And had his beard always been that white? "I'm so glad you like her. Have you gotten her settled in the barn?"

"Oh, I keep her inside. Rupert set up a little cage for her with wood chips." My mouth was moving faster than my brain. But the longer I could keep Mr. Walsh talking about the guinea pig—and nothing else—the better. "I've named her Caramel, because of her coloring."

"What a sweet name. Perhaps you could have a whole candy shop full of guinea pigs once we—"

"Sometimes, late at night, I hear her squeaking," I said quickly, speaking over him. "I think it means she's hungry. I've been taking lettuce and carrots right from the garden. Father doesn't like it. But I don't care. He's—"

"There you are!"

My muscles liquified at the sound of a familiar voice. I spun around so quickly, I accidentally poked Mr. Walsh with one of the feathers on my hat. My relief was so intense, I couldn't even form words of apology. "Father!"

And, sure enough, there he was, striding across the sidewalk, Mr. Zimmerman at his heels. But there was no expression of the happiness he usually held when discovering Mr. Walsh and me together. Instead, there was only . . . anger?

I felt my shoulders rise, my whole body tensing as he reached us. But he barely seemed to register my presence, instead thrusting something at Mr. Walsh's chest. "Did you see this?"

Mr. Walsh started at the harshness of the gesture. Slowly, he unfurled the object, which soon revealed itself to be a newspaper.

"Mr. O'Donnell gave it to me. We were running late out the door this morning so I didn't get a chance to see it before church."

Mr. Walsh smoothed the wrinkles with one large hand. There, on the front page, in bold black letters were the words *Dam Construction Halted! Workers on Strike!*

And right below them were two of Wesley's work-camp pictures. For all the world to see.

Acid rose in the back of my throat.

"Those maggots didn't even have the decency to come talk to me. They went to the newspaper first!"

Mr. Walsh's eyes scanned the fine print. "It says they are striking against the twelve-hour, six-days-a-week shifts—"

"Yes, heaven forbid they actually *work* their *jobs*."

"—and low wages."

"I pay industry standard wages! Ask anyone around!"

"They also claim the conditions are unsafe and unsanitary, leading to worksite deaths and rampant diseases."

"It's their own poor physical condition that's caused it! What do they expect? To be put up in the Gilsey House on Broadway?" Redness crept up my father's neck, peeking out from his starched collar. "It's an absolute outrage!"

Mr. Walsh's eyes continued to rove over the page, though he read no more out loud. But I wouldn't have been able to hear him even if he had; blood thudded inside my ears. When he finally spoke again, it was as if through a long tube, distorted and far away.

"This is nothing." He folded the paper and calmly tucked it under his arm. "These strikes are just a fad. Railroad workers in Kentucky, mine workers in Pennsylvania—the lower classes get restless and believe they can get something for nothing by throwing a tantrum. But with so many people out of jobs, all it does is showcase their own ungratefulness." He waved a dismissive hand. "We have the tide of public opinion on our side. This will pass, just like all the rest of them."

"But these *pictures*." My father muttered an expletive I'd never heard in polite society. "These ridiculous pictures. Mr. O'Donnell said they're already causing some grumbling. They make it look like the strikers have a case. Like *I'm* the villain. Like . . ." He paused. "*We're* the villains."

Mr. Walsh's lips puckered, and I could see vestiges of worry crease his forehead. He had money tied up in this too. A stake. A name.

And so did I.

Without another word, the two of them strode toward the waiting carriage, heads together, hands moving rapidly in a conversation to which I was no longer privy. Mr. Zimmerman followed at a close distance. Without a backward glance, the men climbed inside and were gone. I watched until the last wheel disappeared out of sight before taking off in the opposite direction.

I had been forgotten. I should have been indignant.

But that was just the way I wanted it.

Let them have their words. I had a few of my own I needed to say.

To Mr. Wesley Odell.

"What were you thinking?"

I'd spent the entire walk through the woods trying to calm myself down, trying to remind myself of my name, my training, my class. Trying to summon the poise I needed to maintain a cool head. And the upper hand.

None of it mattered the moment I saw Wesley at our usual spot, black newsboy hat sitting cockeyed on his head. There was no usual flutter at the sight of him, no excitement tempered by trepidation.

This time, there was only anger.

"You printed those pictures in the newspaper? You went on strike?" I strode up to him, stopping only when my nose was level with his. He smelled of peppermint and tobacco, grease and sweat. "What happened to not doing anything rash?"

Though his lips twitched, he did not back away. "I told you I don't control those men."

"But you gave them the pictures."

He blinked, and something like contrition passed through his eyes. It was gone as quickly as it appeared. "Aye. I gave them the pictures."

"Why?"

"You know why. And I thought you understood."

Though his words were soft, I took a step back as if he'd shouted them, guilt slicing through my outrage like a sword.

"Did you talk to him?"

"It doesn't matter!" I threw up my hands, willing the rage to return. Anger was easier—more powerful—than shame. "He wouldn't listen to anything I have to say now anyway. You've made him angry by going on strike. I've lost any clout I may have held."

"But did you talk to him?"

"He's just going to replace you; you know that, right? All of you. He'll fire each and every one of you. Then you'll have *no* wages, which is far worse than little wages."

"Kathleen, did you talk to him?"

"And he'll never stop hunting for the source of the pictures. He'll destroy you when he finds out, Wesley. And maybe me, too, if he finds out I've been with you."

"He won't find out."

I barely registered his reassurance. I was pacing now, all the worst-case scenarios racing through my brain. "He'll throw you in jail. Or make it so you can never find work again. And who knows what he'll do to me?" I shivered.

"Kathleen—"

"You'll be on the streets, Wesley. Maybe even die of starvation. You'll—"

"Kathleen."

"What?" The word exploded from my mouth.

"Did you talk to him?"

"Would you stop asking me that? You ruined everything with those pictures! By going on strike! It doesn't matter anymore!"

"It matters to me."

His words doused the firestorm inside my belly. I froze in my pacing, shoulders instantly slumping. Though we were close to the damsite, I suddenly realized how quiet it was. No hammers, no explosions, no shouting men. Not even any sounds of nature. It was as if the tension between us had pushed everything else out. I felt his gaze on me, but I didn't dare meet it.

"You didn't, did you?"

There was no malice in his question. Instead, it was quiet. Pitiful, almost. I opened my mouth then closed it, opened and closed it again. I wanted to tell him I had tried, but I knew the time for falsehoods had passed. I had the sense Wesley would be able to see through them anyway; he already seemed to know me too well.

And, for some reason, that made me angrier than anything else he had done.

"It's not that easy, all right? You don't understand how things work! Yes, he's my father, but I can't just walk up to him and demand he start treating his workers better. That's not my place, Wesley!"

"Why is it not? What's stopping you?"

His words were so innocuous. So naive. So . . . piercing. I scoffed. "My father, of course. He would get angry."

"So?"

My vision tunneled as the edges of the world went red. I'd never spit in my entire life, and yet I had the sudden urge to expectorate in Wesley's direction. *So?* He had the nerve to ask *so?* Like my discomfort—my *life*—was nothing at all.

"So, my father is everything to me! All I have—everything I *am*—is because of that man. I owe him my respect. My love. And waltzing in, questioning the way he runs his business, is the exact opposite of that."

"Even if you know what he's doing is wrong?"

Again, his question was quiet. And yet, again, it echoed down to my very core. I collapsed onto a nearby log and put my hands over my face, trying to block a wave of unexpected tears. I was still angry. So very, very angry. But it was a different kind of anger now. Heavier and pointed inward rather than out.

Nothing is more loathsome than a truth you don't want to hear.

Yes, I knew the conditions in my father's work camp were wrong. Inhumane, even. And a big part of me—the part of me that had been nourished by my time away, by the words of the writers and poets deemed trash by high society, by my friendships with Louisa and Margarite and Hazel—knew I should speak up. Wanted to speak up.

But that part of me was weak. Easily overcome by fear.

And it wasn't just fear of making my father upset.

Seeing those pictures in the newspaper had brought it all into focus. For the first time, I began to worry that it could all come crashing down. Everything my father had built. Everything that defined my life. The name, the wealth, the possessions, the status. They could all be taken in an instant.

Yes, the reason I hadn't spoken to my father *was* fear. Fear of failing . . . and of succeeding.

Speaking up ran the risk of estrangement, of my father cutting me off not only from his love, but from his money. My father had reacted harshly when I'd—meekly—suggested time spent engaged in pursuits outside my station; I could only imagine his outrage at this egregious, meddling impropriety. This was the only life I had ever known. As a McDaniel. I had no employable skills, no clue how to even attempt life without the names and connections afforded to my privilege. Was I really willing to risk that?

But there was also the fear of what getting my father to change his business model would mean for us.

Would mean for *me*.

Our money situation was already precarious. And improving worker conditions would surely cost a lot. For all my high ideals and big dreams, was I ready to sacrifice my comfort, my lifestyle, all so the dam workers could have a bigger slice of bread and a softer blanket?

I hated that I was asking myself those questions.

I hated even more that I genuinely didn't know the answers.

Most of all, though, I hated myself.

"Kathleen..."

Though Wesley's voice was gentle, I couldn't bring myself to look up. I felt ashamed, ugly, and not just because of the tear tracks staining my face. He had risked everything, submitting those photos, joining the workers on strike. It was brave, not ungrateful. And he was only asking me to be brave too. For him. For all of them.

For basic human dignity.

And yet whatever it was I felt for him was not nearly as strong as my love for myself and my position.

I may have been higher class, but Wesley was the bigger person.

There was a crunch of leaves as he sat down next to me. A few moments of silence before he sighed. "All my life I've been surrounded by people who told me my identity was determined by where I was born, who my parents were, how much money I had in my pockets. But my *mam*... my *mam* used to tell me that wasn't true. She said it was God who defined us. God who was at the very foundation of who we were, who gave us worth. But *Mam* wasn't long for this earth. And, after she passed..." He paused. "Well, God's voice is quiet, while the world's is loud, isn't it? And, when you hear something loud and often enough, you start to assume it's true, not just for you but for everyone. So I lived most of my life believing those lies. And then... I met you."

The log beneath us creaked as my spine stiffened.

Wesley didn't seem to notice. When he continued, his voice was weary. "I wanted to hate you, you know? And I did at first. But I realized I was guilty of doing to you what I assumed you were doing to me. Judging me. Thinking you knew everything about me, just because of my job or my class. Most people of your station look past me. Through me. Not you. You saw *me*. My art. You made me feel like I had something to offer. Like there was a common beauty in the world, one both you and I, no matter our differences, could both see." He let out a small burst of air through his nose. "That day, taking those pictures . . . You threw me for a loop, Kathleen McDaniel. I didn't want to believe it, but you weren't your fancy clothes, your high-class manners, or your daddy's money any more than I was ripped trousers or day-old bread. And it made me think, maybe I was wrong. I mean, if you were more . . . then maybe I was too."

He slid his rough hand over mine, the calluses snagging on the delicate fabric of my gloves. They were the hands of a man twice his age, all scarred knuckles and jutting bones, skin paper thin with malnutrition.

It caused a fresh wave of tears to blur my vision. "But I'm not, Wesley. I know you think I am. But I'm not."

And then that unrefined hand was on my face, tilting my gaze toward his. "I know you can't see it," he said softly. "But I can. It's there, inside of you." He ran a thumb over my chin, so lightly it barely registered and yet heavy enough to sprout goosebumps down my spine. "My *mam* was right. But it took me meeting you to realize it. We have to decide whose voice we will listen to. Who is telling the truth. Because the answer to that determines who we really are . . . and who we can be."

And then, Wesley's lips were on mine.

My first-ever kiss.

It lasted for just a moment, for an eternity. Too much, and yet not enough.

"That's why we're striking, Kathleen," he murmured against my lips. "So people will finally see us. The way you saw me. And the way I see you."

My heart ached. My body ached. My *soul* ached. I reached out, needing to feel him again, but my fingers found nothing but empty air.

By the time I opened my eyes, Wesley Odell was gone.

"We have been absolutely unable
to hear a word from Galveston
since 4 p.m. yesterday . . ."

G.L. VAUGHAN, MANAGER, WESTERN UNION, HOUSTON
To Willis Moore, chief, US Weather Bureau, Washington, DC
Sunday, September 9, 1900

EIGHTEEN

SUNDAY, SEPTEMBER 9, 1900
GALVESTON, TEXAS

The wind was a monster, tearing at my clothes, ripping my hair, tugging at my skin, all while the water converged, seeking to drown me from above and below. Matthew was shouting—I could see him shouting—but whatever he was trying to communicate was snatched as soon as it left his lips. Blood still dripped into my eyes from the cut on my forehead. The entire world was noise and darkness and motion, an assault from all directions on every part of my body.

And yet I registered none of it.

After witnessing the collapse of St. Mary's, I became numb. It wasn't real. None of it was real. It couldn't possibly be. Mother Camillus, Sister Bernice, Sister Elizabeth. Billy, Josephine, Rebecca. All those nuns, all those *children*. They couldn't just be . . . *gone*. With the slam of a wave and the loosening of bricks.

It couldn't happen like that. It *shouldn't* happen like that.

Bile rose in my throat. All those souls dragged into the sea. Those innocent lives.

And the camera. The *camera*.

I'd never even gotten the pictures developed. I hadn't the money nor the stomach. What if they'd somehow been intercepted before they were returned to me? Stolen? Or, worse, what if they'd led my father to me? I couldn't risk it. Couldn't bear the thought of not having the camera with me, where I could see it, touch it.

I'd made a promise.

And now that promise lay at the bottom of the sea.

Along with so many others.

Matthew's hands landed roughly on my shoulders. Wood was shoved into my hands. It was an oar, I realized. He wanted me to row. He was already rowing. Ferociously, desperately. And he needed my help.

But what was the point now?

Still, I found my muscles dipping the oar into the water at the side of our skiff. There was resistance; the oar caught on something. I tugged at it, half-heartedly. It broke loose only to immediately be snagged again. Pressing one hand against my makeshift helmet, I peered over the side.

As another crack of lightning streaked across the sky, I was finally able to see. The dark water was barely visible under a rolling tangle of wood, metal, and wire. It was as if, rather than the ocean, we were attempting to row through a thick stew of civilization.

The wind was at our faces, the mess of debris scraping against the side with every impotent thrust of the oars. We were getting nowhere, going nowhere.

We would never make it back to the school.

To Emily.

To Maggie.

At my insistence, we'd come all the way out here for nothing. St. Mary's was gone. The camera was gone.

And soon, we would be too.

Because of me.

Matthew . . .

I don't know how long we rowed. My muscles gave out long before Matthew's. I was a shell of myself, watching outside my own body, through flashes of light and torrents of rain, as he heaved us forward, inch by inch, timber by timber, through one pile of wreckage and then another. At some point, my makeshift helmet was ripped from my head; I barely noticed its absence. Slowly but surely, open ocean once again became dotted with structures, black and slinking, night creatures on the prowl.

Slinking?

No. It was impossible. A trick of the light.

Only it wasn't.

The houses *were* moving. They were *floating*.

Entire buildings, four walls and a roof, shiny windows and decorative awnings, bobbing in the waves like a child's bath toys.

And, right in front of us, two of them were headed straight for each other.

There was no time to call out. No time to react. No time, even, to slam my eyes shut. Instead, I watched in horror as, with a boom that overpowered even the wind, the edifices slammed together, their timbers splintering with the force. At the breaks, the broken wood gleamed bright, a stark contrast to the darkly painted exteriors; for some reason, it turned my stomach, as if I were glimpsing blood or organs. But even the squeamishness soon passed, replaced by rapidly intensifying fear.

Not all the lumber had been pulled into the swirling ocean below. Several pieces, sharpened by their violent splitting, had instead been sucked upward by the wind and were now hurtling toward us with what seemed directed precision. I had just enough time to lock my gaze on a particular piece, its edge glinting like the tip of a knife, before Matthew's body landed on top of mine, knocking free what little air still remained in my lungs. My nose pressed into the body of the workman, still sprawled at the bottom of our skiff. I squeezed my eyes shut. If I could have stopped breathing, I would have. But, cursedly, my body still demanded breath; I took in the smell of oil and sweat on the man's shirt, remnants of his life that felt wrong to notice now, after his death. Above me, I felt Matthew jerk and squirm beneath additional weight, and I knew without being able to see that a flood of debris was raining down on us.

It was happening again. The crush of Matthew's body conjured scenes from my nightmares, from another night when a different body had covered mine, shielding me from death's relentless pursuit.

Unable to get to me, it had taken another victim instead.

The memory only added to my panic. I began to thrash. If I'd been able to scream—if there'd been enough oxygen between the horror both above and below me—I would have.

Suddenly, the weight was lifted. I felt a rush of air as Matthew rose. The scrape of wood, the rocking of the boat, as he tossed our inanimate assailants overboard. Fighting against the wind, I sprang up, away from the workman's body, and wrapped myself around Matthew's torso. After a few moments, I felt his arms grasp me back, his chest rising and falling rapidly in time to my own. Pulling back slightly, my fingers roved over his shoulders, his arms, his face. His shirt was torn, knuckles bloody, and there were several scratches across his brow.

But he was all right. He was *alive*. Tears streamed down my cheeks as my muscles fell slack with relief.

It was short-lived, however. His eyes met mine during a flash of lightning, briefly—too briefly—before we were thrust into darkness once more, and another mound of unremitting wreckage began its assault on our boat.

On us.

Still intent on protecting me, I found myself shoved once again into the keel as Matthew shielded me, all the while attempting to navigate through the rubble. I tried not to touch the workman's corpse. Tried not to look at it. But I did not raise myself up away from it either. I felt lightheaded. Sick. We had been given a short reprieve, but death was waiting both inside this vessel and out. It did not matter where I lay, where I looked. There would be no escaping it this time.

Curled wretchedly at the bottom of the boat, tears intermingling with the sea, I could only pray that when it did come, it would spare Matthew.

And take me instead.

The end did not come, however, but neither did the storm abate. Instead, time continued. Fast or slow, I had no idea. Wind and water, noise and movement, over and over and over again, like a bad dream from which you cannot awake. Danger came from every direction. Water and debris lashed at me from above and below, squeezing me, trapping me, drowning me, as the wind shrieked, angry for its piece of flesh. The cut on my forehead throbbed, my skin burned, my eardrums felt as if they would burst.

There was no escape, nowhere to go. Nothing but this storm, this *beast* that had devoured the island, killed my friends, stolen Wesley's camera.

And still was not satisfied.

But then, suddenly, there came Matthew's strong arms, lifting me from my seat. A press of air, suction, a bright light, and . . . silence.

No more water. No more wind. Just furniture. People.

I blinked, trying to see beyond the glow of a lantern being held near my face.

A living room.

A house.

"I'm fine," I heard a voice say. Matthew's. "But she got hit by something. A wire, I think."

A cushion at my back. The release of Matthew's hands. Then, a flurry of movement, a cloth against my brow, wet and stinging. I winced.

"Sorry," came another voice. Female. "I know that smarts."

The pain faded. As it did, my eyes slowly became accustomed to the light. A woman stood over me, her gentle hands tending my wound. Dark haired, soft featured. Short tendrils of curls framed a pale, sweat-beaded forehead creased with worry. "There now," she said, giving me a small smile. "That's better, isn't it?"

I blinked again, touching my finger lightly to the bandage on my forehead. "Where—" I stopped at the fire in my throat, raw from the salty air. I licked my cracked lips. "Where—" I tried again. This time, my question was halted by a familiar face swimming into view just beyond the woman.

"Mr. Cline!"

The corners of Isaac Cline's mouth turned upward, but the expression did not reach his eyes. "I must say, Annie, seeing you here, in my home, is quite a surprise. What are you doing here?" This last question was directed not at me, but at Matthew, who remained standing beside me.

"We were out. In the storm, I mean. And I saw a row of houses, still standing." He paused. "The only row."

There was a slight shuffle at his words, and I noticed the mass of people huddled behind Isaac, congregating in various groups throughout the sitting room. Dozens of faces, at least, maybe more. All of them bloodless. Agitated.

"There are no more street signs. No landmarks. It was only an act of providence that we found our way here." Matthew ran a hand through his hair, squeezing water droplets from the tips. "But it makes sense, Mr. Cline. Your house is one of the newest and strongest on the island. If any structure were to remain standing, it would be yours."

Normally, Matthew's posturing before his idol would make me roll my eyes. But now, it only made me sad. For I saw it for what it really was: a desperate plea for reassurance.

He didn't receive it. Instead, Isaac responded only with a question of his own, his tone clipped. "What were you doing out in the storm to begin with?"

Matthew opened his mouth to respond but was cut off by another voice from the back.

"What's it like out there?" Joseph Cline stepped out from behind an elderly couple. His face, like his brother's, was drawn, the area beneath his eyes dark and sunken.

All eyes turned to us. The room had been quiet before; now, it seemed downright soundless. In lieu of a spoken answer, the house let out a large creak, breaking the stillness, but also heightening the tension.

"It's . . . bad," Matthew said finally.

"All the more reason to praise God for this house." The woman to my right gave a tight, forced smile. "It's up on stilts and solid as a rock. My Isaac designed it himself." She glanced down at me and patted my hand. "You'll be safe here." Then, with a small squeeze of my fingers, "I'm Cora, by the way. Isaac's wife."

I attempted a smile in return. She was so kind, so sincere. I wanted to believe her. Especially after everything I'd already seen, endured, this day. And, by the look of it, so did everyone else inside that house. Despite the creaking of the walls, the thunder of the rain, postures relaxed, faces went slack. It was as if the entire room exhaled at once.

Perhaps I would have too . . . if I hadn't seen Isaac Cline's face.

He did not look proud at her words, assured, or confident.

Instead, though he tried to hide it, Isaac's lips twitched, and his expression twisted into an uneasy grimace.

Brushing off his fretful questions, I murmured reassurances to Matthew that I was fine, encouraging him to follow Isaac and Joseph as they slipped from the placated crowd. The three of them headed for the rear of the house, presumably to the back door through which Matthew and I had entered. I wondered if our boat was still there and, if so, if they would do something about the body of the workman, still lying inside it. I didn't want them to leave him there, nor did I want them to bring him inside or release him to the waves. None of those options seemed proper. And yet I knew one of them would have to be selected.

It was best I didn't know which.

Instead, I turned my head and allowed my eyes to wash over the other people who had come to seek shelter in the Clines' "indestructible" house. There were all ages and skin colors represented, from a baby, sleeping contentedly in its mother's arms, to an elderly African American couple, heads bent together in hushed conversation. I wondered how many knew Cline personally and how many had simply stumbled out of the storm, desperate for refuge in the first structure they'd encountered.

"What's your name?"

I started at the small voice behind me. Craning my neck over the back of the davenport, I saw a trio of dark-haired girls. I knew instantly they must be Cline's daughters. Though distinct in their own ways, each face beneath a mess of curls was the spitting image of Cora.

"I'm Annie," I managed.

"I like your hair," said the oldest, tilting her head. Her fingers twitched at her sides, as if she wanted to reach out and touch some of my red locks.

I ran a weak hand over them, suddenly aware once again of my appearance, which I was sure was frightful. Sure enough, I felt nothing but dampness and stubborn frizz. Still, I smiled at her, though it felt frail. "I like yours, too. What's your name?"

"I'm Allie May. That's Rosemary." She jerked her thumb at the girl next to her. "And Esther." The child at the end—the smallest—gave me a shy wave. "Do you know Mr. Richter?"

I felt heat rise in my cheeks at the mention of his name, ridiculous considering the circumstances. Placing a hand near my lips, I nodded. "I do. We're . . . friends."

That word felt even more ridiculous. And yet what else could I say?

"We're friends too," Allie May said excitedly. "He comes over for dinner a lot. And he always brings us popcorn."

Though the image she conjured was sweet, it stole the breath in my lungs. *Maggie.* Her toothless smile, chomping away on a bag of Matthew's popcorn.

Oh, Maggie, I'm so sorry. For leaving you, for not being able to save your friends. For the loss of your home.

For everything.

"Now, girls, let's leave Annie alone. She needs some rest." Cora appeared behind her daughters, shooing them away gently. She smiled down at me and, though I wasn't sure how I had any left, I quickly slapped away the tears that had sprung to my eyes.

Hoping to avoid questions, I gestured to the damask pattern beneath me, which had grown dark with the wetness from my clothes. "I'm sorry about your couch."

"Oh, pishposh. The state of my furniture is the last thing on my mind." She winked. "Thought you might need something to eat." Rounding the couch, she held out a slice of thick, buttered bread in one hand, a glass of water in the other. I started. It was the first time I'd gotten a full view of her. She chuckled when she noticed my gaze falling on her rounded belly. She patted it fondly. "This one's a doozy, she is. Taken it all out of me. Today, with the storm, it's been even worse." She handed me the food with a lighthearted shake of her head. "I'll have to give her a stern talking-to when she gets here in a few more weeks."

I managed a small smile before taking a sip of water. What hope this woman held. Even in the midst of all this destruction, hope for tomorrow. For the future. For her child.

I couldn't decide if it was admirable . . . or foolish.

"May I use your powder room?"

"Of course, dear. It's right through there."

I followed her gestures toward the back of the house. Light faded the farther I got from the living room; there had been no electricity for hours. Lanterns were kept in the living room where most of the crowd had gathered. I ran my hands over the wall, feeling my way down the hallway, letting out a small cry when the floor beneath me suddenly gave way. I yanked my stockinged foot back, heart pounding in my throat.

But there came no rumbles, no splintering. No signs of the house's imminent collapse.

After a few moments, I let out a shaky breath and crouched down. The floor was damp. And the opening I'd mistaken for a cave-in? It was a hole. A gap in the floorboards, frothy, dark water gurgling in its depths, the jagged edges showing its deliberate and intentional placement.

Just a hole. A hole put there by . . .

My initial relief soured as realization washed over me.

One of the men had chopped this hole. Isaac or Joseph most likely. Because they understood the rising waters needed somewhere to go. Because they feared if they didn't, the pressure from the water outside would grow high enough to wash the house right off its foundation.

Those miracle stilts Cora was talking about? They didn't matter anymore. Not when the water was this high.

And Isaac and Joseph knew it.

I rose to my feet on wobbly knees. And that's when I heard men's voices, just outside the back door.

"It's risen four feet in the past five minutes."

"That's impossible. Time it again."

"I've counted three times. It's not going to change the facts."

Recognizing the voices, I took a step closer but kept to the shadows. Sure enough, Matthew, Isaac, and Joseph stood on the top step of the porch, looking out over the expanse of ocean that had once been Isaac's backyard. Sheltered from the worst of the wind, their voices seemed to echo. Though I knew this had to be the entrance we'd come in, the boat that had carried Matthew and me here was nowhere to be seen.

"The last barometer reading I took at the Bureau was 28.48."

"That's impossible." Matthew shook his head. "Pressure doesn't go that low." He looked to Isaac for confirmation, but Mr. Cline's gaze remained focused on the waves now lapping at the men's feet. "You must have made a mistake."

"It wasn't a mistake!" Joseph grabbed the front of Matthew's shirt. "I saw what I saw. I also saw the wind-gauge reading . . . right before it ripped from its housing. Eighty-four miles per hour, with gusts over a hundred."

Matthew pushed Joseph away. His jaw clenched but, even from here, I could see fear rising above his willful disbelief.

"The water will be inside the house in a matter of minutes," Joseph was saying. "We have to evacuate."

"And go where?" Matthew interjected. "There's nowhere else to go. You yourself just said the wind—"

"I was wrong."

Isaac's voice was quiet, and yet it cut off Matthew's protestation as cleanly as a pruning shear. Both he and Joseph froze. An eerie quiet lingered in the air, space for a disbelieving intake of the words, during which the only sound was the groan of the timbers at my back, the whine of the wind around the corner.

"Mr. Cline?" Matthew said finally. "What do you—"

"I was wrong," Isaac repeated, more assuredly this time. "About all of it. The wind has rotated from the north to the east and now to the south. The gauges and instruments don't lie." He looked at his brother, holding his gaze for a moment before turning his attention to Matthew. "These aren't just waves. This is the sea itself." He raised his chin, peppered mustache trembling. "We cannot deny it any longer. This is a hurricane. And it is going to completely destroy this entire island . . . and everything on it."

From my spot in the shadows, I curled forward, wrapping my arms around my stomach. I felt detached, no longer pained by my raw skin or the stinging wound on my head.

A hurricane.

I'd known. Deep down, I'd known, even if I'd dared not speak the word aloud. This wasn't an average storm, not even just a strong one. I'd been out in it, felt its power, seen what it could do. And yet nothing had prepared me to hear Isaac Cline speak those words.

The impossible had become possible.

Matthew shook his head violently. "No. No, Mr. Cline. That cannot be true. You said hurricanes couldn't hit here. You said the geography of Galveston made it immune to such storms, immune to such destruction. You said—"

"I know what I said!" Isaac spun around, gripping Matthew's upper arms with white knuckles. "And I was *wrong*!"

Matthew's mouth continued to sputter, but all objections died on his lips, struck dead by Isaac's wild eyes and anguished expression. Beside him, Joseph hung his head, fingers curling into his hair and tugging with frustration.

"We need to get everyone to the top floor of the house, windward side."

"Why windward?" Matthew's question came out like a child's, lost and seeking reassurance.

Isaac turned to him. From my vantage point, I could no longer see his face. But I did not need to see him to recognize the seriousness in his words.

"Because there's a very high likelihood these walls are going to collapse. And when they do, we want to be in the best position possible to get on top of the wreckage. Or else this house could very well become our tomb."

NINETEEN

There was no air on the second story.

It was a bizarre sensation, knowing the magnitude and strength of the wind blowing just outside the creaking walls. Every crevice popped and groaned, every crack whistled. Yet here, on the top floor of Isaac Cline's home, there was nothing but stillness. Damp, suffocating stillness.

Cora had turned down the lanterns, a feeble attempt at reducing the heat exacerbated by too many bodies inside too small a space. Somehow, the darkness made the air thicker. The coughs and cries of our fellow inhabitants took up too much room. The constant drip of water from the leaky ceiling felt ominous, as if it would collapse at any moment. I was sweaty, smothered, the edges of my bandage beginning to curl away from my damp skin.

Trapped. By this house within, by this storm without.

This could not be happening. This could not be real.

And yet, somehow, it was.

"Annie?" Matthew's voice beside me in the dark. He hadn't spoken more than a cursory word since we'd climbed the narrow stairs and settled against a back wall in one of the Clines' bedrooms. But before Cora had turned down the lights, I'd noticed the tightness in his face, the gray pallor of his skin. "Are you all right?" he asked quietly.

No.

But I didn't have the energy to lie. So instead, I said nothing.

His hand found mine. The heat from it caused my body to itch, yet I did not push it away. In that moment, it felt like the only solid thing—the only real thing—in this world.

"I'm . . . I'm sorry."

I tilted my head. "Why are you sorry?"

"I don't know. I just . . . am."

I felt his body lift with a heavy sigh. And I understood. In the deepest, most wounded part of me, I understood. Matthew had built his entire life on Mr. Cline and his science; he'd told me as much. It was what he believed in, who he was, what he put his trust in. It had become his hope, his pride.

His arrogance.

And, tonight, it had been proved false, to the detriment of both himself and countless others.

Including me.

I should have been angry. Against all instincts, I had let my guard down around Matthew. I had trusted him. Trusted *his* trust in Mr. Cline. And now I was here. In this house with these people, the Gulf of Mexico steadily eating away at my final minutes on this earth. But I wasn't angry. Maybe it was because I knew it wasn't really Matthew's fault; he had not caused this storm any more than he had caused my presence within it. I had come to Galveston, chosen this as my hiding place. And, though I had feared many things during my time here, I'd never foreseen something like this happening. No one had. We were ignorant of the dangers.

But mostly, I held no anger toward Matthew because I knew exactly how he felt. The disappointment. The crushing blow of fundamental truth crumbling before your eyes, when everything you trusted, everything you thought you knew simply . . . disintegrated. My heart ached for him, for the pain and confusion with which I knew he wrestled.

So maybe that was the reason I did what I did. Or maybe it was because the wind continued to blow and the water continued to rise, and I understood there would be no escaping it; out in the storm, we'd been spared so many times already. It was a miracle, a kindness, that we'd even been afforded this moment. I could not bear the thought of wasting it.

Whatever the reason, though it wasn't proper or planned, I leaned over and pressed my lips against his.

It was my first kiss—my only kiss—since the one with Wesley, since that forbidden day in the forest near my home. I expected to feel guilty, and I did, momentarily. The sensation of kissing Matthew was so similar and yet so different. His head knocked back against the wall in surprise before he returned the kiss, softly at first, then more insistently. There was a hunger there but also sadness. A realization of what could have been but also never would be. Of hope and regret. Before I broke away, I felt a hot, salty tear drip onto our lips.

I didn't know whether it was mine or his.

"Annie . . ." Matthew's face was nothing but a shadow, but I could still read it. The hitch of his breath, the scratch of a dry swallow. The net of emotions squeezing his heart was also crushing mine.

I cared about Matthew, I realized. Deeply. I might even love him, something I didn't believe possible after that horrible, heartbreaking night so many months ago. And yet what else could explain this grief, this agony, but a love newly discovered, about to be extinguished, engulfed by wind and waves that cared nothing for human feelings?

My mind flashed back to Maggie. To Emily. I prayed they were safe. That somehow, against all logic, the storm had relented at the Rosenberg Free School, wind easing and the sea returning to its berth. I would cling to that hope, however foolish, for I had no other option. My fear for them was outweighed only by my remorse.

I would die without ever having told them the truth about myself. Without ever truly letting them in. They had loved me. Or, rather, tried to love me. But, if they survived to mourn, they would mourn only a stranger. A ghost.

A liar.

But that didn't mean Matthew had to.

"My name isn't Annie." The confession came out as a whisper. Yet it landed as heavy as an iron chain in the space between us. "It's Kathleen."

Beside me, Matthew's body didn't move, but there was a shift in the air. As if his heart, momentarily in tandem with mine, had pulled away. "What?"

"My name is Kathleen, not Annie. And I wasn't working at St. Mary's." My voice cracked at the name of the orphanage, visions of its facade crumbling into the sea nearly stealing my words. "I was hiding there."

I paused, waiting for Matthew to respond. To say something, anything. When he didn't, I felt both agonized and chided by his silence.

"I grew up in the village of Croton-on-Hudson in New York. My . . ." I paused, contemplating my next word. It felt wrong, distasteful in my mouth, yet I hadn't quite figured out another term. "My family was wealthy, high-class. My mother, Madelyn, passed away when I was eight, and I was worried my father would send me away. He was a businessman, always busy. But he didn't.

It was the opposite, actually. I became like his pet. He even called me Kitty Kat." A bittersweet laugh escaped my throat. "He spoiled me. Gave me everything I ever wanted. Nice house, fancy clothes, good school. He made sure I was everything a well-brought-up lady should be. I wanted for nothing . . . and, yet, as I got older, somehow . . . everything."

Matthew's hand was still in mine. I squeezed it, but he did not squeeze back. Instead, his fingers fell limp against my leg. Stifling a hurt I had no right to feel, I took several ragged breaths. In the space between them, I became aware of a steady *thump thump* just below us, vibrating the floorboards beneath my legs. Although I couldn't see the others in the room, I could feel their tension as they began to register the sound too. What could it be? There was no one left on the floor below. The wind? But the windows were still intact; we'd surely have heard if they'd shattered. Rats? Possible, but unlikely. The noise was much too loud for their small bodies.

Goosebumps sprouted over my arms as realization dawned.

The noise we were hearing was furniture, bobbing against the second-floor ceiling.

The waves had broken in.

And they were on the rise.

There wasn't much time.

"Things at home, they . . . they got out of hand," I managed through choked sobs. "And I was too stupid to see the truth. Too naive. Too selfish. Too *late*. And it cost me everything." Memories of that night rose before me, somehow overpowering and vivid even in the terror of my current situation. "I ran. Ran because I was scared. Because I had failed. Because everything I thought, everything I believed, everything I had relied on . . . was gone."

A large thump caused Matthew to flinch and several members of our party to cry out. There was a fresh roar of wind, muting a rumble of thunder. A flash of lightning cast an eerie light through the room, just long enough for me to see Matthew's downturned face.

"I'm sorry I lied to you. It was wrong. But I never meant to hurt you. I hope you believe that. I just . . . I'm lost, Matthew. I don't know what I'm supposed to do, where I'm supposed to go. I don't know where I belong. I don't even know who I am."

Sobs punctuated the end of my story. Matthew didn't speak. But, even if he had, it would not have been audible over the thud of debris. The earlier stillness in the room had fled; the hurricane was through being patient. Isaac's walls, our last vestige of defense, were weakening. Through blurry eyes, I watched them move in and out with each new gust. It was as if the house were alive.

Breathing.

Drowning.

A fresh scent of oil and a burst of light cast spots through my vision. Cora had relit the lamps, illuminating rows of pale, frightened faces.

I wasn't the only one crying.

A middle-aged man, face ashen, separated himself from the crowd. "What should we—"

"Train trestle!"

I barely had time to register the words before a violent crack erupted behind me. The remains of a train trestle, lit by lightning flashes outside the narrow window, had slammed into the house, sending cracks and vibrations through the wood that brought everyone to their knees.

"We need to prepare for collapse!" Joseph Cline emerged from the shadows. His eyes were bloodshot. "This building can't hold on much longer."

Chaos erupted. Stifled sobs became full-on wails and the stench of sweat filled the air as dozens of overheated bodies all began to move at once. There was no decorum, no order. Primal fear had taken hold; the storm outside was the most vicious and relentless of predators . . . and we were its prey.

Matthew rose quickly. I attempted to follow, but my clothes had dried stiff. They rubbed painfully against my already raw skin. I pulled at them, only to receive an inadvertent knee to my chin as someone moved past me. Pain exploded behind my eyes, lessened only when another person—or maybe the same one—stepped on my toes, still exposed from my missing shoes. Mouth full of saliva, I jerked upright just as the room went dark again. In the pandemonium, I wasn't sure if the light had been extinguished or simply moved to another room; there was too much movement, too much noise, too much fear. Arms and legs and torsos, bricks of bodies, all pushing against me, in every direction. I cried out as I was shoved one way, then another. But no one had time to listen.

Death was here.

Frantic, I stretched my arms out in front of me, blindly pushing through mounds of flesh and fabric until I felt something solid. A wall. My nails dug into the damp wood, clinging to it even as I knew it was slowly being turned to pulp, disintegrating from the salt and sea just on the other side.

Spinning around, I pressed my back against it, breathing hard. There was a window next to me. Outside, debris roamed like sea monsters, occasionally ramming the house with booms that made my skin grow taut. Inside, bodies scrambled over one another, a different kind of debris. A drop of water suddenly fell into my eye, blurring my vision. Confused, I looked up, only to immediately wish I hadn't.

Above my head, the ceiling had lifted from the wall, revealing a sliver of sky, even darker than the blackness around me, before coming back together again.

Like a mouth, licking its lips.

My lungs seized. Every intake of air was shallow, painful, not enough. My heart was thrashing in my ears, white spots floating up in front of me. I felt faint. Dizzy.

Just as I felt as if I was going to collapse, there came a warm hand on my back, a strong arm around my shoulders.

Matthew.

Another flash of lightning. His lips were moving; he was shouting at me. But I couldn't hear him, neither over the storm nor over the sound of my own thudding heart.

I pressed a hand to his cheek and shook my head, trying to convey my confusion.

He leaned forward. "We're going to jump!" Though his lips were right by my ear, still I struggled to hear. He gestured to the window.

I shook my head again, more violently this time. Jump? Outside? Into the storm? Was he crazy?

"We have to get away from these walls!" he shouted. "Hold on to me, as tight as you can. If we get separated, grab on to the first thing you see and don't let go." He gripped my chin, forcing my eyes to meet his for the first time since I'd given my confession. "Promise me you won't let go, Kathleen."

At the sound of my real name upon his lips, tears—fresh, cursed, inopportune tears—welled up in my eyes. This wasn't the time to cry. Wasn't the time to feel. And yet . . . what other time was left?

I opened my mouth to speak, but, before I could, Matthew's lips pressed roughly against mine. Then, before I could even register it, he was behind me, arms around my waist, and we were lunging backward through the glass window. I didn't even hear it break; all I felt was Matthew's chest pressed tightly into my spine before there was a sudden release, and we were falling.

No, not falling.

We were sucked right out of the house and into the raging sea. I didn't even have a chance to take a breath before the water pulled me under. The silence was immediate. It was dark, so very dark, and soon that darkness was inside me, filling my mouth, my nose, my lungs. I kicked and flailed but still my body continued to descend, the water full of invisible threads, tethering me to the bottom. Objects in the water bumped against me, knocking what little air I had from my chest; a fresh wave of grimy seawater invaded my mouth as those precious last bubbles escaped my lips. I tried to swim but my muscles soon went limp, drained and rendered inert by water as warm as a bath. I couldn't fight anymore. Couldn't . . .

And then, suddenly, there was air. My lungs sucked it in greedily without conscious thought. I sputtered and gasped. I had floated to the surface, but the ocean still tugged at me, trying to pull me back down, all while rain bore down on me from above. There was water everywhere, both inside me and out, pushing and pulling, ravenous and insistent, even as my numb body struggled to return to life piece by piece. The noise came first, bursting through my ears like a freight train. The rush of water, the shriek of the wind, the slam of debris, echoing in tandem with the constant thunder. Worst, however, were the screams. The cries. The wails that let me know that, though I could not see them, there were people all around me, fighting to survive. We were together in this and yet also completely alone.

Alone.

Matthew.

Feeling returned to my exhausted extremities. I spun in the water, kicking my legs, stretching my arms, grasping blindly. I felt wood and metal, timbers and poles, shingles and doors. But no people.

No Matthew.

"Matthew!" I choked on my own scream, salt and sand invading my throat. Coughing, I pushed myself to the surface once again. "Matthew!"

This time, the sound made it past my lips. But it didn't matter. The storm wouldn't let it go further.

"Matt—" The third cry was cut off by something large and hard slamming into my back. It slid over me, pushing me under. Both my eyes and my throat immediately burned, still not recovered from the first submersion. With what little strength remained, I thrust myself upward, taking in a fresh mouth of seawater when my forehead slammed into a piece of debris directly overhead. I felt along it blindly until I came to the end, using it to pull myself back to the surface just as my lungs threatened to give way. I only managed one breath before something else knocked into my ribs, pulling me under once more.

I had to get out of the water.

Using the last of my strength, I heaved myself upward, grabbing onto the largest piece of debris I could find. It was coarse under my fingertips. Shingled. A section of a roof.

Isaac's?

"Matthew!" I screamed again. My makeshift raft bucked savagely, bobbing on the rough swells, a swirl of constant motion exacerbated by the wind whipping my hair around my face, the beating of the rain. I felt as if I would be sick. And soon, I was. I expelled the sea violently from my body, but it did little to calm my stomach. The waves rose and fell, the lightning flashed and then went dark, each time revealing an impossible new landscape. Nothing was familiar. Nothing was *real*. Where were the other buildings? Where were the other people?

Where was *Matthew*?

A shimmer of white. A piece of fabric. A hand, an arm, rising out of the sea.

"Matthew!"

I reached over the side, trying desperately to grasp the fingers before the surf pushed me away. Somehow, I managed to get ahold of the hand. Heaving, I pulled it from the water, wrist, forearm, bicep. It was heavy, heavier than I ever could have imagined, but I could not stop. The top of the head crested the water.

"Matthew!" I screamed again.

But it wasn't Matthew.

It wasn't even alive.

Horrified, I dropped the hand, watching as the corpse immediately sank back into the depths. I wiped my fingers against my legs, sobbing, gagging. "Matthew."

This time, I didn't scream the word. I don't even know if I said it out loud. My raft rose and fell, bringing with it a fresh slam of debris that knocked me off my knees and onto my back. I grabbed a passing board from the water and pulled it over my body; thuds and dings from flying wreckage set my teeth on edge. My muscles ached from the exertion of trying to keep the wind from ripping it away, of keeping the raft underneath my body. All around me, screams carried on the storm, but their sources were faceless, hidden inside the relentless blackness. Soon, even those faded. I pressed my face into the damp wood. I no longer wanted to look. No longer *needed* to see.

There was no Galveston anymore, no island; there was only the sea. I closed my eyes, the faces of those I loved swirling in front of me. *Matthew. Maggie. Emily.*

Wesley.

Gone. All of them were gone.

As the wind tore at me from above, the water from below, I could do nothing but pray for it to stop. Or that, perhaps, in God's mercy, I would soon be gone, too.

TWENTY

APRIL 1900
CROTON-ON-HUDSON, NEW YORK

We have to decide whose voice we will listen to. Who is telling the truth. Because the answer to that determines who we really are . . . and who we can be.

I couldn't get Wesley's words out of my head; they lingered as potently as his unexpected kiss. It was as if he could see past everything else—the money, the clothes, the rules and regulations of my position and high society—to the real me underneath, where I existed after all other things had been stripped away. To the real me even I myself was still learning to identify.

He certainly had more faith in me than I did.

More faith than I deserved.

Because, three whole days after I'd seen him, I still hadn't worked up the courage to say anything to my father.

Granted, it wasn't as if I had exactly seen him. He and Mr. Walsh spent most of their time down at the damsite, while I was now confined to the house. I couldn't even go down to the barn, a rule I balked at—quite loudly—when I discovered it. But it was also a rule I could not break, as it was strictly enforced by the New York militia, who had shown up on our property less than a week after the strike began.

"Rumor has it your father fired all the workers," Stella hissed as she joined me at my bedroom window. Though her hands continued to work at the buttons on my pale-yellow dress, her eyes were directed at the manicured lawn below, where a handful of militiamen spread out like insects, some on the porch, others patrolling the tree line, their blue uniforms a jarring sight against the yellows, pinks, and greens of the spring bloom. She used one hand to move the lace curtain aside, peering through the thick pane with a worried expression on her lined face. "But the workers are refusing to leave. They've set up a blockade, and they're threatening violence if your father won't sit down and hear their demands. Mr. Roosevelt called in the militia as a favor to Mr. Walsh. To keep the peace . . . and to keep you safe."

The lump in my throat made it hard to swallow. "Where did you hear this?"

She gave a limp shrug. "We hear more than we're heard downstairs, Miss McDaniel."

There was no malice in her tone. Just a simple matter of fact. But still it made me feel guilty.

Something had shifted in me. And I knew it had everything to do with Wesley Odell. With his words and his touch. Because, although Stella had been a part of my life since I was a child, it was only now, in the weak sunlight filtering through my window, that I felt as if I was seeing her. Suddenly, she became more than just a name to me. More than just a face or set of hands, always present but invisible, in the background. It was as if I'd realized she existed outside of me. She was a human being—not just a cog in the machine, catering to my whims, but a real human with a life of her own, with needs and dreams and emotions.

Emotions like the fear I now registered in her dark eyes.

I grabbed at the arthritic hands faithfully securing my buttons. Her wrinkled skin was soft and papery, and her joints stiffened at my touch. I'd hugged Stella before, of course, usually because she was there and I needed an outlet for some childish, superficial glee, like a party invitation or a new pair of shoes. But this touch, this glance, was more intimate. More personal.

Meant for Stella herself, and not just what she represented.

"I'm sorry."

Stella's brow creased. Tenderness flickered through her eyes for a brief moment before fading, replaced once again with her usual steadfast professionalism. "Sorry for what, Miss McDaniel?"

It was a question that demanded no answer, as befitted both her position and mine. But, even if it had, what would I have said? There was no way to explain, at least not in a way Stella would have accepted.

Because I was the lady of the house . . . and she was my servant.

And, for the first time, I *cared*.

My lips parted, but I lacked both the courage and the words to force any sort of clarification past them, and after a few moments, Stella quietly excused herself downstairs to do the mending.

I spent the day by the window, my newfound awkwardness with Stella further knotting the coil of emotions inside me. Below me, the militiamen shifted in and out of their positions, patrolling the grounds and securing entrances, some looking bored, others excited. It was probably the first action any of their young eyes had seen, if action was what it could be called. Maybe even the first time any of them had been away from home. As I watched them, I stroked the guinea pig Mr. Walsh had given me, fiddling absentmindedly with the white spot on her crown; despite her origin and the innuendos it carried, I adored the creature, especially since the rest of our animals were now off-limits to me. I declined dinner, and as daylight began to fade, the rodent's unique purring sound was the only comfort from both the tension without and the turmoil within.

I knew I wasn't to blame for the strike. But I couldn't help thinking the situation might not have escalated so quickly—so precariously—if I'd just spoken up like Wesley had wanted. Father might have gotten angry with me, but would that really have been so bad? He was my *father*, after all. He loved me. Surely, in time, he would have forgiven me for speaking out of turn. And he might have ultimately seen my point, begun working to stitch the strained relations before they'd reached this point. If only I'd been braver, less selfish, more bold . . .

Been the person Wesley believed I was.

Believed I could be.

It was well past midnight when I finally made my decision. Seeing a pair of lanterns make their way up our long drive, I suddenly knew what I had to do. The flames inside them swayed and bumped in the familiar, unmistakable movement of a carriage.

Our carriage.

Father.

This time, I did not hesitate.

I might have missed my chance to avoid this mess. But I would not miss my chance to end it.

I gave Caramel one last squeeze, placed her inside her cage near my bed, and slipped from my bedroom into the darkened hallway. Every creak of the hardwood was a scream, an accusation, and yet I would not allow myself to stop. An orange glow seeped under the closed door of my father's study; he'd already entered the house and locked himself inside. I paused at the threshold, placing one hand to the thick wood, listening for the sound of voices from within. There were none. A small victory. It was going to be hard enough to face my father; I didn't know if I had the stomach to face both him and Mr. Walsh together.

I knocked softly and, when no answer came, louder. The wood pulled away from my knuckles, blinding me momentarily as light spilled out into the hallway.

"Kitty Kat?"

I blinked, hand still raised mid-knock, and waited for the spots to fade, revealing the tall, disheveled silhouette of my father.

"What are you doing here?"

"I . . ."

My words failed at my father's hand on my lower back, ushering me into his sanctuary. A fire burned low in the grate, casting shadows across the bookshelf-lined walls and plush leather reading chairs. Though I caught no sight of a lit pipe or cigar, the room swam with the smell of tobacco. A glass of amber liquid sat atop a pile of papers on my father's desk.

"What are you doing here?" he repeated. In the time it had taken me to consider our surroundings, he had straightened his tie, smoothed down his hair, and rebuttoned all but one of the buttons on his navy-blue vest.

"I was . . . checking on you," I finished lamely. "I hadn't seen you for a few days and—"

"And you were worried?"

I nodded. It wasn't technically a lie; I *was* worried. Just not about the things he assumed.

There was a weariness to him that even his smile couldn't touch. "Oh, Kitty Kat. I'm so sorry about all of this. It isn't fair to you. We should be preparing for your engagement, not fighting with a bunch of ungrateful immigrants." He ran a hand over his face. "I'm sorry I have to keep you locked inside the house at the start of the season. I know how much you must hate that."

I looked at the ground. New York society's season had been the *last* thing on my mind lately.

"I just can't take any chances. I even left Zimmerman down

at the dam with Walsh, though I'd rather he have come here with me. These savages . . ." He shook his head. "They're spreading lies about the wages and working conditions. Getting the whole doggone county stirred up."

I chewed the skin on my bottom lip. Now was my chance. *Say something, Kathleen.* Every nerve in my body tingled. My tongue twitched behind my teeth. And yet my stomach rolled. I feared if I opened my mouth, it was not words which would pour forth.

"Kitty?"

The internal chaos must have shown on my face, for my father stared at me with raised brows.

"Maybe you should talk to them?" The words fell at my feet, as heavy as lead.

"Excuse me?"

My mouth suddenly felt dry. Shadows crossed my father's face, turning his eyes liquid and his cheeks hollow, giving it an ominousness that I tried to reason away as a trick of the light. I licked my lips. "I think . . . I think the dam workers just want to be heard. They just want to talk. Man-to-man. Maybe if you do, this whole situation will go away."

"Man . . . to man?"

Though his tone was quiet, it still caused my chest to curl inward. "I . . . I believe all they want is fair wages. Better working conditions. Some adequate food and shelter." I swallowed. "They just want to be treated like people."

Though neither of us moved, the distance between us seemed to multiply then, my last words erecting a wall as real and as solid as the dam over which we disagreed. I saw the questions in his gaze, the hurt.

The betrayal.

My heart instantly panged. What had I done? This was my father. My *father*. My shield, my protector. My hero. The only family I had.

The man who had been everything to me, given everything to me—the only family *he* had.

My limbs twitched. I longed to climb into his lap as I had done when I was a girl. To beg him to forgive me. To tell him I was just a silly, naive child, ask him to forget the whole thing.

It was a sentiment that instantly evaporated when he spoke.

"You think you're so smart, don't you?" My father's eyes narrowed. This time, it was not a trick of the light. There was darkness in them, an anger I had never before witnessed. "Going off to Europe and coming back thinking you know better than me. As if that fancy school gave you any idea what the real world is like. What these types of men are like."

My breathing shallowed. I crossed my arms over my chest.

"Well, since you're so intent on giving me a lesson, let me give you one of my own." He sneered. "You want to know what men like that really want, Kitty Kat? They don't want better food or a nicer shelter. They don't even want better wages. What they want . . . is *this*." He spread his arms wide, gesturing around the room. "They want what we have. They want to take it from us. All the things we've worked so hard to gain, they want for themselves." He raised his chin. "And that includes you."

"M-m-me?" I put a hand to my throat.

"Don't play dumb with me, Kitty. Someone got to you. I don't know who, but someone from the dam got to you. Brillantmont put some absurd ideas in your head, but you would never have acted on them without outside influence. It's the only reason you're here now, saying these ridiculous things to me."

I pulled my elbows into my sides, hoping he didn't see the tremble in my limbs. *Wesley*.

"They smelled your innocence a mile away. Whoever it is, they're using you, Kitty. To get to me. They've gotten into your head. But they are not your friends. They don't want you on their side. They want you *gone* . . . after they've used you up first."

He was trying to maintain civility, not speaking the words. But I knew what he was implying. It made my cheeks flush.

Wesley would never do that. He would never hurt me.

Yet even as I tried to latch on to that reassuring thought, a memory floated before my vision. The other men at the damsite. The look in their eyes. The hate.

The violence.

I shivered.

It didn't escape my father's notice. He smiled, but there was no joy in it. "That's what you have to understand, Kitty. They don't just want what we have. They want to *be* us. Rather than working for this type of life, they want to *steal* it. And, if that doesn't succeed, then they want to tear it down, brick by brick, so no one else can have it."

"But . . . maybe if you talk to them . . ." My words sounded weak now, stupid, even to me.

"Oh, Kathleen," my father snapped. "Stop being so naive. There is no talking to these people. No negotiating. They only know one language, and that's brutality."

"What do you mean?" I barely had the energy, the courage, for a whisper.

"They're threatening to blow up the dam."

Ice dripped into my veins, my body understanding his words before my mind did. "What?"

He stared at the fire. Shadows of flames danced across his face. "If we don't back down, call off the militia, give them what they want, the dam workers are going to dynamite the whole thing. Release the water." There was a darkness in his gaze when he finally met my eyes. "And take down everything—and everyone—with it."

The night passed at a maddeningly slow pace. The next day, even more so.

I did not sleep. I could not eat. I could only replay my father's words over and over again in my mind.

Surely he was wrong. There was no way the workers would blow up the dam. Doing so would destroy thousands of homes and businesses downstream. More than that, it would destroy *people*. Innocent, upright people. There was no telling how many lives would be lost at the water's sudden release.

Wesley had said all their demands were humanitarian in nature. They were about making things better, not worse. The workers wouldn't kill people just to make a point. No matter how rough or angry, I didn't believe the other men were the savages my father claimed them to be. And I certainly didn't believe Wesley to be one.

Or, at least, I didn't think so.

Though I berated myself for it, I had to admit my father's words had caused enough of a rift inside my mind to make me doubt Wesley. Question his motivations, his character, his intent. After all, I knew my father . . . but how well did I really know Wesley? A couple of photographs, a shared admiration for a poet, and a fondness for nature explored over a few stolen afternoons did not intimacy make. Girlish infatuation had colored every encounter.

Could it have hidden his true nature as well?

But that kiss. That *kiss*. And those words. Words I wanted so badly to be true.

A version of *me* I wanted so badly to be true.

There was only one solution: I had to see Wesley.

To know for sure.

I thought the sun would never set. But sneaking out of the house in broad daylight with the militia positioned down below would be pointless. I had to wait until I would not be seen. I feigned a headache in hopes of keeping Stella from my room; for a number of reasons, I could not look her in the eye. Not now.

I was too fragile for that.

As darkness fell, I slipped into a braided navy-blue two-piece dress—the darkest thing I owned. While both the servants and the militia were distracted by their evening meal, I slipped from my room, tucking the last of the money I'd saved from my time abroad into my corset. My plan was to find out from Wesley just how much truth there was to rumors of a dam explosion and how deep his involvement went. From there, it would go one of two ways. Either I would convince Wesley to do everything in his power to call off the plan, using my money as a bribe, or else I'd have him come help me warn as many people downstream as possible, then give him the money to flee before he got himself killed.

Or, worse, got blood on his hands.

It was a feeble plan, and not a well-thought-out one. Money was never an easy subject to broach with Wesley. There was no guarantee he'd accept it either way, and there was a high likelihood he would be offended. Perhaps even angry. I would almost certainly be in danger, no matter what happened. But it was a risk I had to take.

And that included the risk to my own heart.

Sneaking from my house, down to the servants' entrance, and out the back door, was easier than I'd thought it was going to be. Too easy, in fact. I heard voices from the kitchen, from the portico, from the barn, and yet no one seemed to notice the girl-shaped shadow stalking along the edge of the property, disappearing into the rapidly setting sun. Only one person gave me pause: Mr.

Zimmerman. I hadn't even known he was in the house. But there he stood on the back patio, the orange tip of a cigarette illuminating his dark eyes.

Dark eyes that I swore locked onto mine as I paused, heart thudding, on the other side of the hedges.

I held my breath. He was looking at me. And yet he didn't speak, didn't move, didn't allow any form of recognition to cross his face. He simply stood there, cigarette slowly burning, watching me.

I don't know how long I stood, every nerve taut, waiting for him to call out to me, to come toward me, to do *something*. When he didn't, my nervousness slowly melted into impatience. If he was going to try to stop me, he needed to get on with it; I had more important matters at hand. Finally, after what felt like hours but could have only been minutes, I decided I'd had enough.

I took one step out from behind the hedges.

Mr. Zimmerman did not react.

I took another, bolder this time.

Still, he didn't move.

Letting out a shaky breath, I broke into a run. I didn't look over my shoulder until I reached the outskirts of the forest. Mr. Zimmerman still had not moved. From here, he was nothing but a shadow. A shadow and the orange tip of a cigarette, still glowing in the twilight from his spot on the porch.

I ran until my side began to cramp, until my legs ached and sweat began to pool under my corset. I wore no gloves, no hat, no powder. My father would have been horrified at my appearance. The absurdity of this thought nearly made me break out in nervous hysterics. Would have, if the damsite had not suddenly appeared, spreading below me like a scar on the valley below. In the purple twilight, the water being held by its massive stone facade looked like a living thing, black and monstrous, its gentle waves like the breath of a slumbering beast.

A sliver of cloud passed over the moon. Through the filtered light, I could just make out the tops of tents. Not the work-camp tents. These were newer, sharper. Militia tents. I shrank back into the shadows. I hadn't known they were here too. In the distance, farther down, were the work-camp tents, their gray peaks a stark contrast to the darkened, muddy land, even in the dim light.

Wesley.

I took a step. But then, a second, more ominous thought halted any further progress.

They want you gone . . . after they've used you up first. Even Wesley had warned me to stay away from the camp. The men had been angry before. There was no telling the mood among them now. There was a high likelihood they were looking for an opportunity to gain the upper hand. I couldn't afford to give them one.

But I also couldn't afford not to.

I managed two more steps before something else stopped me. Not a memory this time. Movement. There, on the top of the dam.

A shadow.

And a flame.

My stomach dropped to my knees. *Oh, God. Oh, God, please, no.* But I knew without knowing, saw without seeing.

I was too late.

The men were already there, preparing to blow up the dam.

Without thinking, I took off at a run. I had no idea what I was going to do once I got there; I only knew I had to try. I held no power, no answers, and yet I knew if I didn't get to the top of the dam, I would regret it every day for the rest of my life.

However long that might be.

I gave a passing thought to calling out to the men slumbering inside the militia tents. Only the realization that the man on top of the dam could be Wesley stopped me. It took much too long to find the crude, makeshift staircase leading to the top. The steps were narrow with only sporadic hand grips—in the form of crumbling bricks—every few feet. This was part of the old dam, and it was obvious it had been built with very little thought given to finesse or aesthetic.

Or safety.

My feet slipped several times on the slick concrete, and more than once I felt my body begin to plunge toward the thick mud below. But it was only a case of vertigo, of nerves and nausea, and somehow I managed to make it to the top in one piece. The smell of fish and damp earth was stronger up here, the water lapping at the side of the enclosure sounding very much like the snap of a dog's jaws, desperate to be let free. The only light left was the gentle silver of the moon, turning the world into a dance of shadows.

And one shadow in particular.

"Hey!" I didn't recognize the sound of my own voice. It was raw and guttural, hot and cracked, too sharp to have come from the lips of someone so practiced in elocution.

But it did the trick. The shadow started, causing the orange torchlight to waver. To wobble.

And to reveal the hand which held it.

"Kitty?"

It was not Wesley.

It was my father.

My mind seemed to move in slow motion. Though my eyes moved from his face to the dynamite to the silver glint of a pistol in the waist of his pants, I could not connect them. I could not make them all make sense.

Not even when my father let out a string of curses in my direction. "What are you doing here?"

"What . . ." But I couldn't say it. I didn't need to say it; the pieces had finally fallen into place. And the picture they created was so impossible, my tongue refused to give it voice. "You're . . ."

My father bared his teeth. "You weren't supposed to see this. You weren't supposed to know."

My mouth sputtered noiselessly. I had no words. No feeling. No breath.

"I have no other choice, Kitty. The workers, they . . . they actually gave me the idea. They've been threatening it for a week. And, naturally, I was horrified. But, precisely because I was so horrified, I knew others in the community would be too. So horrified they'd forget any nonsense they might have heard about unsafe working conditions or unlivable wages."

A metallic taste rose in my mouth. "But blowing up the dam . . . It would . . . it would kill people."

"But it would save *us*. It would show people the true danger of this labor movement. Put these greedy unions back in their place and remove the threat to us . . . permanently."

My head began to swim; I felt as if I was going to fall. I dropped to my knees, trying to maintain my balance. "You would kill people just to save your business?"

"I would kill people to save our *position*. Our name, our home, our reputation. Our *lives*." There was a startling note of desperation in his voice. "You have no idea how precarious all of this truly is!" He swung the torch around, leaving tiny sparks floating like stars in the night. "The world is changing. Power is shifting. We have to be willing to do anything to cling to it . . . or else be crushed under the rubble of our own making."

"And Mr. Walsh?" I don't know why his name came to my lips.

"He doesn't know anything about this. No one does." He lowered the torch until it was under his chin. Darkness encircled his head, and his eyes narrowed. "And it's going to stay that way, Kitty."

"No, it's not."

The voice came from behind me. Still on my knees, I turned my head to see a lantern flare to life, revealing the face of Wesley Odell.

Camera held to his chest.

It took my father several moments to realize what was happening. But I registered it right away. The snap of the viewfinder window, the click of the button. Though I wasn't sure how sharp the image would turn out in the low light, the glow from the lantern, the torch, and the moon had surely illuminated just enough.

Wesley now held photographic evidence of my father, dynamite in hand, standing on top of the dam.

Another expletive-laced thread wove through the air. My father made to move past me but stopped, finding the pathway both narrow and blocked. "Kathleen, get out of the way!" He pulled at my elbows, swearing, trying to move me, but it was useless—my muscles were rendered inert by grief. Frustrated, he slapped at my back. "If you're not going to move, then get the camera, you stupid girl! Grab it!"

In the chaos, Wesley managed to snap another picture.

My father took a step back and howled. "Get up, Kathleen! Get out of the way! Get the camera!"

I stumbled to my feet, feeling dizzy. There were too many words, too many instructions, too many competing emotions. I swayed slightly, both the water and the ground rushing up toward me.

My father lunged, trying to reach Wesley, who stood just beyond reach, but I grabbed him, as much for support as to stop him. With every bit of force I could muster, I pushed, causing him to stumble backward. He dropped the torch, which sizzled as it rolled into the blackened depths of the water. "What are you doing?" he shrieked, his anger matched only by his disbelief.

"Leave him alone."

"Excuse me?"

"I won't let you hurt him."

My father's jaw dropped. "You're going to take his side? *His?*" He sputtered for several seconds, then broke into an incredulous laugh. "Of course you are. *Of course*. It makes perfect sense, you being who you are."

I took a wobbly step back. "What do you mean?"

"Oh, come on, Kitty Kat. Are you really telling me you didn't suspect anything?" His lip curled. "You don't look a thing like me. Or Madelyn."

Behind me, Wesley drew in a sharp intake of breath. It was like he knew what was coming before I did.

"What are you—"

"You're adopted, Kathleen. We plucked you out of an orphanage when you were three years old. Both of your parents—some immigrant farmers, I can't even remember their names now—had succumbed to typhus. We couldn't have a baby of our own. Everyone told us to adopt a boy, but I knew a daughter would have its advantages. A son is an heir, but a daughter is leverage. They're how all solid partnerships are formed."

His words floated in the air between us, but I could not bring them inside my mind. Could not make them stick.

"So we chose you. Kathleen Anne. We kept the name your parents had bestowed upon you but swore that would be the only part of your past you would ever retain. From the day we brought you home, you were a McDaniel, through and through. Until, it seems, you decided that you weren't."

There was a challenge inside his last sentence, one I barely recognized; I was too busy trying to swim out of this wave of revelations. Adopted. All those emotions, those feelings, those visions . . . They weren't products of a homesick heart; they were memories. Memories of a different life, a different family.

A different me.

I wasn't Kathleen McDaniel.

I wasn't a McDaniel at all.

I was adopted.

But not out of love. Out of opportunity.

Out of greed.

My knees wobbled as another wave of dizziness overtook me. Falling. I was falling. I reached out a hand in desperation, for someone to catch me, to steady me, toward the father who wasn't my father, only to have it land on someone else instead.

Wesley.

"Kathleen . . ." My name was a hushed whisper as one of his strong arms gripped mine, pulling me back upright. The warm light of the lantern washed over me, but the world spun, blurring my vision. I could not see him. Could not read him.

But I could feel him.

"Grab the camera!"

My father's harsh yell broke through my fog. Swallowing a wave of nausea, I blinked, my gaze finally clearing enough to lock onto Wesley's green eyes. They were sharp, piercing, even in the dark. They were arresting. Always had been. But, in this moment, what I saw in them was more than their beauty.

I saw a reflection of myself.

Of a girl I no longer knew.

But a boy I did.

I reached up to touch his face, running my hands over the stubble just starting to poke through the delicate skin near his jawline. His breath hitched.

I dropped my hand to the strap around his neck. To the object dangling just below his chest. My fingers wrapped around the camera.

He let out a long, deep sigh. But he made no move to stop me.

"Grab it!"

I squeezed the soft leather coating.

And released it.

Wesley's lips curved into the faintest trace of a smile.

Behind us, there was another shout, another curse, another round of shuffling. I turned, putting my arms out in front of me, fully prepared to defend Wesley from my father's attack, only to find him still standing several feet away.

The silver pistol cocked in his outstretched hand.

"Is this how you repay me, Kitty? You may not be my blood, but I *chose* you. I brought you into my family, gave you everything you could have ever wanted." His voice was tinged with emotion, despite his cold stare. "I made you a McDaniel, Kitty Kat. Doesn't that mean something?"

My heart shattered. It *did*. It did mean something. But what? Did it mean fancy dresses and elaborate balls and classes that molded my behavior but not my mind? Did it mean that all those things, all that money, were what defined me? Were who I was? All I was ever allowed to be?

And did it mean becoming complicit in murder just to hold on to it all?

I never got a chance to answer those questions. Because at just that moment, my father's pistol fired.

I dropped to my knees, some primal instinct kicking in. But before I could even process that one bullet—the fact that it had come from my father's gun, that he had fired it at me or at Wesley or at both—the sound of a hundred others answered its call.

The militia camp, tensions high and believing my father's shot to be the start of an attack, had begun firing back.

Bullets began to rain down around me. Gunshots echoed in my ears, making them ring, even as small puffs of concrete spat up from the dam beneath me. I pressed my hands over my face, wrapping my elbows around my head and curling my knees to my chest. Suddenly, there was a weight at my back, pressing me harder into the damp ground.

Wesley was shielding me.

"Stay down!" he shouted, enveloping me in his arms and nuzzling his face into the back of my neck. His breath was hot, louder even than the barrage of gunfire that whistled and exploded all around us.

I felt tears spring to my eyes. The firing went on forever, until it seemed as if it was never going to end. As if there would only be this—bullets and noise and fear—until the world stopped. Until we died.

Until . . . silence.

My ears still rang with phantom bangs whizzing through air that was suddenly too thick.

Too *alive*.

Because I *was* alive. The gunfire had stopped, and I was still breathing.

And still wrapped in Wesley's arms.

"Wesley," I croaked. "Are you . . ."

And that's when I felt it. Wetness at my back. And not the wetness of the earth, of the Croton Reservoir, leaching through the stones. It was a warm wetness. A horrifying wetness.

Blood. Coming from Wesley's body.

"Wesley!"

I rolled over, out of his grasp, to find his eyes staring at me, no longer piercing, but wide and fearful. I grabbed the lantern, which had somehow miraculously survived both the gunfire and its drop onto the pavement, and held it up to Wesley's face. It was white and bloodless, his lips glistening with crimson.

"Wesley!" I screamed. I patted his body. It seemed as if everywhere I touched was damp; when I pulled my hands away, they were scarlet. "Wesley, no. Wesley—"

With a grimace, he pushed something hard into my hands. Something I hadn't realized had been wedged between us.

The camera.

"Take it," he rasped.

I shook my head. "It's yours. You need it. You—"

"Protect . . . the pictures." His eyelids fluttered. "Promise me."

My throat burned. I slapped at my tears, cursing them for obscuring my view of what I now understood to be the last few breaths of Wesley Odell's life. "I'm sorry," I murmured. "I am so sorry. I should have just done what you asked. I wish I had been braver." Tears threatened to choke me. "I wish I could be who you thought I was." The dam of grief finally broke. For Wesley. For myself. I clung to him, digging my nails into the crimson-stained fabric of his shirt. I needed his words of wisdom. His compassion. His reassurance.

But by the time I looked up, Wesley Odell was gone, the light extinguished from his eyes, leaving me with nothing but his camera.

And his still-warm blood on my hands.

I howled like a wild animal, my sobs carrying across the water. I would have lain there forever, desperately clinging to the last vestiges of his warmth, praying for a miracle, for an absolution that would never come, if it hadn't been for the voices. My skin felt frigid as I pulled myself from Wesley's body, sudden fear slicing my grief. But the spot where my father had stood was empty. I clambered to my feet, spinning. I had no idea where he was, if he'd fallen into the reservoir or fled. If he had even survived. The shouts weren't coming from him. They were coming from below.

The sounds of the militiamen, coming toward me.

Fear gripped me. I had no idea what they'd do when they reached me. What my father might do if he was still alive. I had no time to reason with myself, no time to think. I only knew I had to get away.

Not just for me. But for the pictures.

For Wesley.

I turned . . . only to be stopped by a pair of strong arms, grasping mine. I cried out, throat raspy with tears as Mr. Zimmerman's face came into view. I tried to wrench free, but what little strength I possessed had died with the man who still lay bleeding at my feet. Mr. Zimmerman's eyes traveled my body, taking in my tearstained face, Wesley's camera, my soiled dress. He let out a long breath of air. I barely registered the pain in my upper arms as he squeezed them.

What I did register, however, was their release.

Was Mr. Zimmerman closing his eyes and dipping his chin.

Mr. Zimmerman . . . letting me go.

I didn't have time to ask questions or process my confusion. There were more voices in the darkness. The militiamen were getting closer. Instead, I merely ran. Across the dam, into the forest, into the unknown of the wilderness beyond.

By the next morning, the entire countryside would believe that it was the dam workers who had fired the first shot at the militia. That their attempt to blow up the dam had been foiled by Lawrence McDaniel, who'd been there attempting a negotiation and who had miraculously survived the ensuing firefight. His daughter was missing, feared kidnapped by desperate workers; he'd vowed to never give up the search for her.

Within a month, the dam would be finished, a marvel of modern science, with Lawrence McDaniel its main beneficiary. Theodore Walsh, his money no longer needed due to all the sympathetic funds flowing in for the dam's completion, would move on; by July, he'd wed another naive young socialite, her father the president of a promising new textile mill.

But I wouldn't know any of this until later, from reading discarded snippets of newspapers and gossip rags. Because, by the next morning, I was already on my way to Galveston, using the money that was supposed to have been for Wesley, searching for salvation, for purpose, for myself, leaving behind both my name and the life that had never truly been mine.

"Galveston, Texas: Missing"

OFFICIAL US WEATHER BUREAU MAP
Sunday, September 9, 1900

TWENTY-ONE

SUNDAY, SEPTEMBER 9, 1900
GALVESTON, TEXAS

I'd come all this way just to die.

That was the only explanation for it. There was no noise. No roaring wind, no angry sea, no rumbles of thunder. And there was no motion. For the first time in what felt like ages, I was completely still, in both my body and my mind. How was that possible?

I could only be dead.

There was no way I could have made it through the night. I couldn't have simply passed out in the height of the storm, my body giving in to a deep exhaustion born of grief and exertion. It wasn't possible. No one could have survived that violence. And besides, savagery such as that which had descended upon Galveston . . . It didn't just *end*. The hours and hours of unmitigated cruelty I experienced, tossed about on my makeshift raft like a sadistic child's toy, proved that. It wouldn't have stopped until it had taken everything.

Including me.

And yet, as my consciousness stirred, I realized I was in pain. Every single part of my body ached. Slowly, torturously, I ran my hands over myself, eyes closed. I was still in one piece, but my muscles throbbed and my throat burned. Examining the pulsating sensation on my forehead, I discovered a soggy bandage, still half-attached, the wound beneath it hot to the touch. My skin felt shriveled and tight beneath my clothes, cured as if it were a piece of salted pork.

If I was dead, why was I still in so much pain?

Unless, of course, this wasn't heaven.

It was that thought that finally wrenched my eyelids apart. They were gummy, swollen, and I was blinded at first, my eyes too dry, the light too bright; it took several seconds for my vision to clear. When it finally did, two things became abundantly clear: I was not dead, and this most certainly was not heaven.

I also wasn't sure it was even still Galveston.

The first of the morning's rays were just breaking over the eastern horizon, kissing a clear blue sky. Already the air was hot, thick, and sticky. Not a single whisper of a breeze or hint of a cloud. After the violence of the night before, the stillness was so complete, so absolute, it felt eerie. As if the city sat inside a bubble.

The water had retreated. But now Galveston lay under a different kind of sea. An ocean of wreckage, twisted metal and broken timbers, lay scattered along washed-out streets, piled into mountains as tall as the buildings that once owned their pieces. What structures still stood were entirely new creations; nothing original remained. Beams, window frames, baths, bricks—the once-flat island was now a rolling hill of rubble. If not for the few trees—bare, but upright—still somehow rooted into the earth, I'd have sworn the very ground beneath me was gone and I was merely floating on a pile of wreckage in the middle of the Gulf.

It was in one of those remaining trees that I found myself. The fragment of roof on which I'd been afloat had somehow wedged itself between two branches, rendering it immobile and sheltering me from the worst of the flying debris after I'd given up fighting.

It was a miracle I had survived.

Or, given the state of things around me, a curse.

Matthew. Maggie. Emily.

Everyone.

Was I the only one left alive?

Gripping a branch, I attempted to climb down, a feat made trickier by the mountain of litter piled at the tree's base. I managed several feet before I slipped, scraping my legs on broken boards but landing on my bare feet on the soft ground. At some point during the storm, my stockings had disappeared. The pants Matthew had given me were now shredded from the knees down. I leaned forward to examine the pile. It was no wonder I'd slipped. Not only was the lumber wet, but it was also covered by a dark, slimy film.

No. *Everything around me* was covered by a dark, slimy film. The ground, my clothes.

Even the bloated, lifeless arm visible beneath the mound of splintered wood.

My blood ran cold. I backed away, only to bump into another pile. A child's doll, its face half-covered by seaweed, tumbled to my feet. Without thinking, I went to retrieve it, only to jump when what I believed to be a bit of hose began to slither and hiss.

A snake. *Two* snakes. Wriggling toward the dark safety of the wreckage.

Oh, God.

But my heart cried out in vain.

I didn't believe myself capable of any more tears. And yet the tears came, hot and despondent. Somehow, fighting for my life amidst the wind and waves paled in comparison to this, the precarious stillness that had come afterward. Perhaps it was because there had been other people. Distant, yes, but still bound by our collective hardship. Or perhaps it was because, even when suffering through what I could only describe as the very finger of God, I'd at least known His presence was there, however angry. Here, in this suffocating, dangerous wasteland, I could no longer sense Him.

I could no longer sense anyone.

I started to run then. I didn't know why. I had no energy, no sense of direction, no purpose. Just this overwhelming urge to escape. Which was ridiculous. I was on an island. Or, what used to be an island. Now, it was just a jumbled, confusing mess of devastation. I had no idea where I was. There were no landmarks. No street signs. No *streets*. There were only fractured poles, twisted train tracks, mangled machinery. Through blurry eyes, I saw a child's rocking horse crushed beneath a four-poster bed, a lone fork rammed through the remnants of a tin roof, and a streetcar, its wheels facing skyward like an upturned insect. There were piles of bedding, of tables, of chairs. Toys and clothing, books and photographs. Those objects and mementos, once cherished, that lay at the heart of everyday life, now lost. Sodden, slimy, and spoiled.

If anyone was even around to mourn their demise.

Because far worse than the stacks of household goods were the bodies. Bloated and battered, many of them nude, their clothing ripped off by the wind and the waves. Though I tried to avert my eyes, there was no escaping them. They were everywhere, some fully intact, some merely pieces. For every body I saw, I wondered how many more were hidden, crushed and twisted among the piles of lumber. The corpses were male and female, of every age, every color. The storm had no preference; it had devoured them all. And not just humans—horses and cows, chickens and cats, dogs and rats. A veritable landscape of death.

And me . . . somehow alive in the middle of it.

Why had God spared me? On that terrible night, there on the dam, I believed He had taken everything from me. My home, my family, my identity. Wesley. But that wasn't enough. Last night, He had taken the rest. This town, these people, any last strands of hope I might have held for a future, no matter how frayed—He had washed it all away along with the very ground beneath my feet.

And yet He had left *me*.

Here. Alone.

Last night, inside the fury of the storm, I believed I had experienced hell. But I was wrong.

This was hell.

Abandonment was a fate worse than wrath.

I felt disoriented, lightheaded, and nauseous, inexplicably thirsty despite the deluge of water I'd endured the previous night. I'd thought I'd never want to see water again. And now, suddenly, I craved it. But there was none to be found, save the grimy, oil-slicked puddles that littered the ground. Even they wouldn't last long. The sun was high in the sky now, almost obscene in its brightness and heat, making the ground sizzle and bringing with it a plethora of new smells to replace the aromas of salt and fish.

New smells I didn't want to think about, let alone name.

The devastation was absolute; the hurricane had left no structure untouched. How could mere wind and water cause such utter annihilation of stone and brick, these edifices that had, just yesterday, seemed immovable? A sudden thought rose from the recesses of my mind, squeezing my already constricted chest.

This wasn't so unlike the horror my father had been willing to unleash on the residents of the lower Hudson Valley. If he had succeeded in his plan to dynamite the dam, a torrent of water would have been released upon hundreds if not thousands of innocent men, women, and children, demolishing homes and extinguishing lives.

The memory of my near-drowning last night came back to me then in full force, the weight of the water, the burning inside my lungs. The vast, descending darkness.

My father had been willing to administer the same fate to countless others. Just so he could hold on to his power.

I stopped then, hands on my knees, and retched, an illness born from more than the horrendous smell. But the expulsion of bile and seawater did little to settle my growing nausea. Although I knew I would never be able to outrun the truth of my situation—the truth of the man I still, all these months later, thought of as my father—I took off running again.

I ran until I could run no farther, until the debris became too thick and a cramp stole my breath. My bare feet throbbed; they were slick and black, aflame from cuts on the soles I only became aware of after I stopped. I put my hands on my knees, heart thudding inside my ears. Sweat stung the wound on my forehead. With a breathless sob, I ripped the bandage off, though little relief was achieved by the stagnant air. Trying to ignore the stench, I took in several big gulps of air. My throat burned. But slowly, surely, my breathing and my pulse began to slow. My heart returned to its berth. And it was then that I finally began to register a sound, slicing its way through the stillness.

Shouting.

People.

Ignoring my screaming muscles, I took off running again, praying the noise wouldn't stop before I could locate its source. Piles of stones had mostly replaced the ones of timber. Here and there, ragged walls of concrete rose from the ground like ghoulish faces, gaping at me, the first solid structures I'd seen. Though my exact location was still a mystery, I surmised I had ventured closer to the north side of the island, perhaps the business district, where the more solid commercial buildings would have fared better against the storm than the rickety, timber-hewn beach houses.

Sure enough, when I rounded the bend, I came face-to-face with the largest building I'd seen still standing on the island so far.

Though the front was a fallen mess, I could make out the top of the back of the building, which looked to be mostly intact.

And it was from this area that the shouting emanated.

Giving little thought to what creatures—living or dead—might be hidden in the ruins, I began climbing over the rubble. Protruding nails snagged the threads of my pants, crumbled bricks scraping my tender feet. But I did not stop. Finally, I reached the apex. Directly below me were three walls and half a ceiling, forming a small alcove. And in those walls were two stained-glass windows, whole and unscathed, seemingly untouched by the brutality of the night before. Amid the panes of yellows and reds, glowing with the late morning sun, the crucified form of Jesus looked down from His rugged cross.

A church.

I'd found the remains of a church.

And, within it, digging through the debris near what remained of the altar, a group of weathered people. Not bodies. *People.* Alive, talking, breathing, all-in-one-piece people.

My muscles went limp. I struggled to remain upright. This close to salvation, and I worried I might melt right through that pile of rubble.

Because it was more than just exhaustion and relief tugging at my muscles.

Despite the carnage all around me and the despair inside my heart. Despite everything I'd seen, everything I'd experienced.

Of all the circumstances . . .

Of all the places . . .

My eyes welled with tears as I remembered Emily. Her words and her self-assured smile. *When we suffer, it reminds us that this life is short, and this world is not our home . . . Sometimes God has to tear down all the distractions, all the lies in our lives, in order for us to see the truth. To see that after everything else is gone, He's still there.*

Emily would have said that something—or, rather, *Someone*—had led me here. Would have said this was proof God wasn't gone after all. But I had little space inside me for the thought right now. Instead, I gave a large wave to the other survivors below me. They let out a shout and gestured with their arms for me to join them.

Maybe it was God. Maybe it was fate. Or maybe it was dumb luck. I could figure that out later.

All I knew for sure as I climbed down the rubble and into the embrace of strangers was that, against all odds, I had survived.

And I was no longer alone.

TWENTY-TWO

The Lopez family had sought refuge in St. Patrick's Church as soon as the water began to lap at their beachfront home. Mrs. Lopez had managed to grab only a handful of framed photographs and the family Bible before her husband had ushered both her and their three children—Ana, Manuel, and little Lucia—out into the wind and rapidly advancing seawater. They had spent a terrifying night with several other families within these stone walls, praying and crying as they listened to the storm intensify outside the sanctuary. Though water soon began to leak through cracks in the building's foundation, it was the wind they feared the most. Sure enough, sometime in the darkness—night or morning, it was impossible to tell—the roof of the building collapsed, bringing the front of the church down with it.

"We huddled under the altar for hours," Mrs. Lopez explained to me later, once I'd settled in with the other survivors, "praying for it all to stop. Surviving that night . . ." Her voice trailed off as she shuddered, kissing the dark hair of the babe in her lap to calm herself. "It was nothing short of a miracle."

The people around her murmured their assent but did not give voice to their own experiences. They didn't need to. I could see it in their eyes, just as I was sure they could see it in mine.

Everyone left on this island—if there were, in fact, more—now had a story to tell. But I wasn't sure how many of us would ever be ready to recount it.

Mr. Lopez had gone off with a couple of other men in search of help, though what help he expected to find I wasn't sure. I'd only been able to shake my head grimly when asked if I'd come across other survivors. And as for reports of the island itself? There was no way to describe the devastation; it was a horror each one would have to experience for him or herself. But, though I had little hope for the search team's mission, I tried to remain focused on the small victory I'd achieved in locating these new companions.

I tried to remember all their names. I really did. But my mind was too weary, my body too empty for specifics. There was an elderly couple—Mr. and Mrs. Ackerman? Alderman?—and a pudgy middle-aged man I believed was named Stephen. A quiet young couple sat together near a statue of an angel, but the only name that stuck with me was Lillian, their infant daughter, whose blonde curls lay matted against her forehead as she nursed fitfully. A dozen or so others milled about, restless. Waiting for someone to tell us what to do next.

For none of us knew. We'd all been so focused on surviving the storm, we'd given little thought to what to do when it was over.

When all that was left was nothing.

By the time Mr. Lopez and the others returned, the tension had grown thicker, more tangible even than the stifling humidity filling our open-air shelter. We needed to move, needed to stay; we needed to split up, needed to stay together. No one could agree; this band of strangers, once held together by the shared threat of the storm, was slowly becoming unraveled by hunger, thirst, and fear.

"They're setting up a shelter at City Hall," Mr. Lopez told the group after he'd kissed his wife and taken stock of his children. His dark mustache was beaded with sweat. "The building was not too badly damaged, but I do not know if there will be room for all."

"All?" came a voice from the back. "You mean there are more survivors?"

Mr. Lopez nodded. "*Sí*, there are others like us, still alive. But . . . not as many as I'd hoped."

His words hung heavy over the group, coughs and restless shuffles echoing off what remained of the high, vaulted ceiling. *Not as many as I'd hoped . . .*

The bodies. So many bodies. I dared not think of numbers, neither of the dead nor of the living.

Matthew. Maggie. Emily.

In which column were they tallied?

"But I do know there is food and water at City Hall. I saw it with my own eyes." Mr. Lopez's gaze locked onto his wife's face. "If we hope to get some, we should go. Now."

"But it's getting dark . . ."

The voice that came from the rear of the group was tinged with worry. Lillian's mother. Her blue eyes were snaked with red, and she clutched the back of her daughter's head with white knuckles.

The side of Mr. Lopez's mouth curved downward. "*Sí*," he assented after a few moments. "It is. Which means we need to hurry. I can find my way back to City Hall easy enough now, but it will be impossible to find anything after the sun goes down."

We didn't have to be told twice. The possibility of sustenance, of food, water, and bedding, was enough to cast off the pall of exhaustion and defeat. Within minutes, our group began to ascend the debris pile with renewed energy and unity, passing children and lending hands until every one of us was on the other side, the security of St. Patrick's released as quickly as it had been sought.

I kept my head down as we walked. Though I no longer felt the complete hopelessness I had when I walked these same ruins earlier, that didn't mean I wanted to see them again. I didn't want to relive the desolation by seeing it experienced on the faces of my fellow survivors. But the shocked cries and stifled wails were enough to cause my heart to grieve all the same. In my mind's eye, I saw what they were seeing; I understood what they were coming to realize.

Galveston as we knew her—as we had loved her—was gone.

And most of her people with her.

I kept my eyes on the ground, on the muddy-heeled boots of Mrs. Lopez, walking directly in front of me. The bottom of her blue dress was soon sullied with the same black slime that coated everything else on the island. Though we did not come across any more human survivors, plenty of animals emerged from the wreckage, dazed and frightened. Dogs. Cats. Horses. My mind wandered briefly to the poor creatures trapped at MacDoogal's Pet Shop—what had become of them?—before being tugged back to the present by the sight of a baby's bottle, half-filled with milk, lying just feet from a lump hidden beneath sodden bedclothes. I didn't want to think about what might have been inside. But I couldn't escape it. The smell I'd encountered earlier had grown more potent with the heat of the day, trapped by the debris and a blanket of unrelenting humidity. Before this day, I'd never experienced the odor, yet some part of me knew it immediately.

Death.

It made the muscles in my stomach clench, every nerve recoil. I had to fight the instinctual urge to run once more. I knew there was nowhere I could go on this island that the stench would not follow.

It was everywhere.

The cries of my companions grew quieter as we trekked along, dodging tree limbs and climbing piles of rubble, replaced by the steady scrape of shoes on wet pavement. It had the feeling of a funeral procession, somber yet determined, together in our quest but alone in our personal grief. Though the clear blue sky from earlier in the day had been replaced by bands of silver-gray clouds, the air around us remained eerily, remarkably still. Every cough, every sob, every footstep reverberated for miles. Or perhaps it merely seemed that way, trapped as we were inside an ever-changing canyon of wreckage.

"Oi!" came a shout.

Our party halted. At the front of the line, Mr. Lopez raised a hand to his brow like a visor.

I followed his gaze. In the glare of the sinking sun, a mass materialized, hazy at first but growing clearer as it made its way toward us from the east.

People. Another group of survivors.

The mood instantly lifted, dark countenances brightening. We'd known there were others—Mr. Lopez had told us as much—but to see them, in the flesh, alive. Walking. Talking. *Breathing*. There was a rush of movement as the two groups hurried to close the distance between us. Propriety forgotten, strangers hugged strangers, tearstained cheeks were kissed. One old man—easily forty years my senior—even lifted me off my feet and spun me around, laughing gaily.

Laughter. *Laughter*. In the midst of all this death and despair, I had never heard a more beautiful sound.

But as hands were shaken and stories were exchanged, my elation was soon tempered. They were survivors, people, and for that I was immensely grateful.

But, I soon realized, none of them were *my* people.

Matthew, Emily, and Maggie were not among them.

Though the smile remained on my face, inwardly my spirit stumbled. It plummeted completely when I caught a snippet of conversation between Mr. Lopez and a middle-aged blond-haired man on the edge of the crowd.

". . . came from Rosenberg School, 'bout four blocks down that way. Barely made it through . . ."

Rosenberg School.

I pushed forward, throat so thick I barely managed to squeak out apologies for the toes I crushed along the way. "Did you say Rosenberg School?" I asked, grabbing the man's elbow.

His shoulders jerked in surprise. "Yes," he said slowly, honey-colored eyebrows furrowing.

"Was there a girl there? Eight years old, dark eyes, blonde hair? She would have been with a nun. A novice nun, not in full habit but gray skirt, head covered."

The man shook his head. "I'm sorry, ma'am. I don't recall seeing anyone like that."

"Maybe they're with another group? Was there anyone left at the school? A second party? Venturing out—"

My words dissolved at the feel of his hand. He placed it over mine, which was still gripping his elbow. His touch was warm. Compassionate.

Regretful.

"I'm sorry, ma'am." His English accent was soft. "We were the only ones who made it through the night."

His words, though spoken kindly, burned like acid. I physically recoiled from him, eyes blurring with tears.

It wasn't true.

Maggie. Emily. They couldn't be . . .

I wouldn't allow myself to say it. Think it. As if somehow that would prevent it. Would undo everything this man was telling me.

This time, I did not fight my urge to run. Without thinking, without listening to the surprised and concerned shouts of the group, I took off. Four blocks down, the man said. But what was a block? In this sea of rubble, it was impossible to tell. A veritable dam of timber and iron had pushed across the island, razing everything in its path. There were no streets, let alone landmarks. Just mounds of wreckage, broken lives and broken bodies, all molding under the remnants of salt and sea.

There was no way I'd be able to find the school. No way I'd be able to find Maggie or Emily.

And yet I had to try.

I stumbled as something sharp stabbed the bottom of my left foot, but I did not stop.

"Maggie! Emily!" My voice cracked as I screamed, reminding me again of my overwhelming thirst, the cruel irony of being unable to remember my last drink of water after nearly drowning in a deluge of it. My tongue felt heavy, my mouth devoid of saliva. Every yell was torture. But still I continued to shriek. "Maggie! Emily!"

A dog began to howl in the distance, the only response to my query.

"Maggie! Emily!"

Tears streamed down my face, a response to pain both emotional and physical. They *had* to be here. They had to be. They weren't like the others. Not my Maggie. Not Emily. There was no way they were gone. No way they were a part of that smell, part of the debris. They couldn't—

"Ma'am?"

I spun around, heartbeat thudding in my ears. It was the blond-haired man, chest heaving, the corners of his dark eyes creased in concern. He had followed me.

"Are you all right?" His voice sounded far away.

"My friends," I managed to choke out. "My friends were in the school."

The man's mouth turned downward. "I'm so sorry."

"They're not dead." I shook my head violently, brushing off the hand he had laid on my arm. "They're here. Somewhere. We just have to find them. Maggie! Emily!" My voice splintered, fractured screams disintegrating in the air.

"Ma'am." The man tried to return his hand to me, but I twisted out of his touch.

"Maggie! Emily!"

"The school is right there." He raised his voice to be heard over mine. "I told you. There isn't anything—or anyone—left."

I turned to where he was gesturing, a strangled cry releasing from my throat. It was the Rosenberg Free School, though I wouldn't have known if he hadn't shown me. The entire right side of the building had collapsed. The first-floor entrance was covered by piles of bricks and stone; there was the plaque boasting the once-grand structure's name, now half-crumbled and stained black. Glancing up, I could see a third-story classroom hanging from the wall as if on a hinge, a pile of desks collecting precariously on the edge.

My stomach sank into the muck at my feet.

"I'm sorry, ma'am." He was once again quiet. "I don't know what happened to your friends. There were so many of us, it was impossible to keep count." He closed his eyes. "All I know is sometime, in the middle of the night, there was a loud crash, and someone started screaming that the upper stories were collapsing." He swallowed hard. "There was nowhere to go. The water wouldn't stop coming, and the wind wouldn't stop blowing. The first floor was flooding, but the top floor was falling. It was chaos as people rushed about, trying to make a decision—to drown or be crushed. And I don't . . ." He paused and tilted his chin skyward, taking several deep breaths. "I don't know how I survived, ma'am, let alone anyone else. I'm sorry."

Dampness soaked through my pants as I dropped to the wet ground, feeling as if I would retch once again. Maggie. Emily. How terrifying it must have been for them. How horrific. And

I had left them here to face it. I'd *left* them. I closed my burning eyes. Ghosts of my friends floated inside my vision, interspersed among the rubble. Emily's gentle smile, the twinkle in Maggie's mischievous eyes. My heart cleaved. They were gone. And yet, it was as if I could see them, touch them.

Could hear them.

"Annie?"

My eyes fluttered open. I was still on my knees, still in the street, the Rosenberg Free School still in ruins at my back. The visions of my friends were gone. But . . .

"Annie?"

That voice. I'd have known it anywhere.

It was impossible. It couldn't be. And yet it was. Climbing out of a window, blonde hair tangled, shirt and trousers darkened with grime. She was in my arms before I could process it, before I could say her name, before I could breathe.

Maggie. Alive.

Filthy, fragile, and frightened.

But alive.

I squeezed her, weeping, laughing, and shaking with both relief and incredulity. She had survived. Somehow, she had *survived*. I kissed her cheeks, tasting salt, and pressed her face into my chest. She smelled of the sea, and I was momentarily overcome by the image of her in the water, fighting for her life just as I had done the night before. The thought brought bile to my throat again. She was sobbing, her entire body trembling, and I held her as tightly as I could, trying to stem the shake.

"It's all right," I whispered in her ear through tears of my own. "I'm here. I'm here."

It was a long while before her cries quieted, before her quivers finally grew still in my lap. Before I dared to pull her face into my hands and ask the question whose answer I somehow already knew would put a damper on this joyous moment:

"Emily?"

Fresh moisture welled up in the corners of Maggie's eyes. She shook her head. "She brought me up to the third floor, away from the water. Said she was going to help some of the families with small children get upstairs too. But she . . . never came back."

Grief washed over me, as real as any wave. I pressed her head back into my chest as I struggled to take a breath. "Oh, Maggie. I'm so sorry. I'm so, so sorry."

I don't know how long we sat there holding each other, paralyzed by the tangle of our reprieve and our heartbreak. It felt unreal, the loss of Emily. As if I would lose Maggie too if I dared break the moment. I had never known joy and anguish could be so powerful, nor that they could coexist so painfully.

A small, uncertain cough finally brought me back to the present.

"Ma'am, um . . . we really should be going. It's getting dark."

I blinked. I'd almost forgotten that the blond-haired man was still there. And he was right. In the time it had taken Maggie and me to settle, the sky had changed from orange to pink, with streaks of purple starting to creep in from the east. The ruined buildings around us were now crawling with shadows, their desolation morphing to ominousness in the fading light. I lifted Maggie's chin until her red-rimmed eyes met mine. "This man's going to take us to safety, all right? Someplace there's food and water."

The man bent down at the waist, smiling at Maggie and offering his hand. "I'm Leonard."

I bit down on a guilty grimace. I hadn't even bothered to find out his name.

Maggie gave him a shy grin in return. "Maggie."

"Well, Miss Maggie," he said, straightening, "we best get going. But first—can I ask you a question?"

She nodded.

"We searched that building top to bottom. Called over and over for any survivors. Do you mind telling me why you didn't speak up? Why you didn't come forward and leave with the rest of us?"

Maggie glanced up at me, her expression questioning.

I smiled reassuringly. "I'm curious about that too. Why did you hide?"

"I was afraid if I left, you wouldn't be able to find me."

I tilted my head. "What do you mean?"

"I had to wait there because you promised you'd come back." She slipped her hand into mine and smiled. It was a gesture so familiar—one I'd thought I'd never experience again—that it caused my heart to ache. "And you did. Just like I knew you would."

"It is said that every wave of the sea has its tragedy, and it seems to be true here. In Galveston it has ceased to be anxiety for the dead, but concern for the living. The supreme disaster, with its overwhelming tale of death and destruction, has now abated to lively anxiety for the salvation of the living."

DALLAS NEWS
Wednesday, September 12, 1900

TWENTY-THREE

SATURDAY, SEPTEMBER 15, 1900
GALVESTON, TEXAS

After only a few days, it became apparent City Hall was not the salvation I believed it to be. There was food, yes, and more important, water, but not nearly enough to last. Maggie and I both received fresh clothes—I didn't dare to ask where they'd come from—and a doctor was there to clean and stitch the wound on my forehead. But there were no bathing facilities, no waste management, no linens, no beds. The stench from the living soon overpowered that of the dead. There wasn't even enough room for everyone to sleep inside the building's remains, away from the dampness and heat. Many—Maggie and I included—were forced to sleep outside, heads on the hard ground, surrounded by the sights and smells of a landscape we could not escape, awake or asleep.

But even worse than the physical condition of the survivors was their mental and emotional state. There was never a moment of silence. Crying, wailing, shouting, screaming—sounds of grief and anger always filled the air, leaving a tense bubble over the shelter that I felt would burst at any moment.

It was clear that Maggie and I needed to move on. The only question was where?

Many survivors, of which there were more than I'd previously believed, had already escaped the island now that ships had begun ferrying people over to the mainland. Those with friends and relatives in Texas City, Houston, Beaumont, or other parts of the country had fled the moment it had first become possible, both Leonard and the Lopezes included. While sad, I did not blame them. But their departure did settle a kind of melancholy over me and others who still remained.

We were the ones whose lives were truly shattered. For there was no other reason to stay in this ghoulish landscape unless, like Maggie and me, you had no money, no prospects.

Nowhere else to go.

Maggie grieved for days when I told her about St. Mary's. I hadn't wanted to, but when she begged to return there after the first night sleeping out in the open, waking in a panic when a stray dark cloud began dropping a smattering of rain on her face, I knew avoiding the truth would do no good. I found it unbelievable that either of us could conjure any more tears, but come they did, perhaps hotter and harder than ever before. I had seen the building's collapse; I'd already known what had befallen those inside. And yet sharing the news with Maggie, I experienced the tragedy all over again. Or, perhaps, for the first time, now that the grief was no longer tempered by thoughts of my immediate survival.

After her tears, Maggie grew quiet, withdrawing into a place I could not reach. Later that day, I caught her writing names into the mud beneath a partially collapsed pillar next door. It was one of the few areas not dried out by the relentless heat of a September sun that had not stopped shining since the storm's departure, as if it had been offended by the intrusion. *Rebecca. Sister Hannah. Mother Superior. Billy. Josephine.* Names of nuns and classmates, strangers who had become the closest thing to family Maggie had ever known. Even Angela, the ever-tormenting bully, made the list.

And, toward the bottom, another: *Emily.*

I didn't want to believe Emily was dead. I wanted to hold out hope that she'd survived somehow, perhaps floating on a piece of debris, just as I had done. But seeing her name on Maggie's small memorial made it feel real, final, in a way I couldn't articulate. Perhaps it was because, even in my absence, Maggie had somehow known to wait for me, had somehow known I was still alive. With Emily, there was no such confidence. So, even with no confirmation, it felt right to grieve her, there with the others. To remember her among the children and sisters to whom she had dedicated her life, in honor of the God she so loved.

All of the sisters of St. Mary's had lived this way. In their own ways, their own styles, but steeped in love, nonetheless. And, likewise, they had died in that pursuit—by loving those around them. By protecting them. Helping them. It was the same thing they had been trying to do for me.

It was too late now to thank them for it. To love them back, not just with words, but with actions. Because they were no longer here.

But Maggie was.

I vowed that from now on I was going to do everything in my power to let her know how much she was loved.

And here, in this place, that meant keeping her safe.

The gunshots had started the night after the hurricane. Rumors swirled that looters were pillaging the ruins, both killing and being killed in their search for food, water, and—in some cases—riches. Soon these sporadic bangs were accompanied by other, no-less-worrying night noises: the hoots of drunken survivors, wild with alcohol that could not drown their grief, as well as growls and rustles as ravenous dogs and disturbed snakes emerged to prey on the dead and the living both. Workers assigned with clearing debris wandered back to City Hall each evening with fresh stories of corpses decimated by animal and human alike. Even worse were whispers of another, even bigger impending storm on the horizon.

Not for the first time, my mind went to Matthew. If he were there, he would have been able to tell by the clouds, by the wind, if that last bit of gossip was true. Or would he? He had learned everything he knew from Isaac Cline. And Isaac had been spectacularly wrong about everything.

But it didn't stop me from missing Matthew all the same.

I had said my goodbyes to Emily. But even though every evidence pointed to his death, something inside me would not allow me to say goodbye to Matthew, even when Maggie asked to include him in her makeshift memorial.

Not yet, I'd told her, trying to ignore the questions in her eyes. Not. Yet.

I tried to keep hope alive for Maggie. Even more so, I tried to keep the tales of carnage and mayhem from her; she'd already seen and heard enough. But tittle-tattle seemed to permeate the very air we breathed, the macabre world outside pressing against our delicate illusion of safety. And when a woman in camp began to lash out one night, accusing another survivor of being the ghost of her deceased husband, and needed to be medically subdued by the camp physician before settling down, I knew it was time to go.

"Maggie. Maggie, wake up."

I hadn't slept the night before. Shadows had slithered just outside the glow of the firelight, though I hadn't been sure if they were human or animal. The gunshots had been closer too, the sounds of shouting and breaking glass lingering long after the bullets had been spent. But somehow we'd survived, unmolested, until the first rays of pink began to lighten the eastern sky.

I would not wait any longer.

"Maggie, wake up." I shook her gently, trying my best not to disturb the elderly woman snoozing beside her.

Maggie's eyes eased open a slit. A wave of putrid morning breath washed over me as she yawned, though I knew I had little room to judge. We were both in desperate need of basic hygiene.

"What time is it?" she mumbled.

"Early," I whispered. "But it's time to get up. We need to go."

Her eyes fluttered open, suddenly clear. "Go where?"

"Shhh," I hissed, glancing around nervously. Thankfully, no one appeared to stir. "We're heading for the beach. I heard a rumor the Red Cross is putting up some tents there. They have real beds. Blankets. Hot food." I peered over my shoulder at the still-dark ruins. "Soldiers."

Maggie understood my meaning without my having to explain further. She hopped up, brushing the dirt from her pants, and nodded at me.

Slipping my hand in hers, I smiled with what I hoped passed as reassurance. Leaving City Hall was a risk. I didn't even know if the gossip about the Red Cross camp was true. All I knew was we couldn't stay here.

Not one more day.

Not one more minute.

"Which way?" she whispered.

"East," I said. "We follow the sun."

My pockets thudded with what little supplies I allowed myself. I'd saved the can of salmon I'd been given for last night's dinner, along with a raw potato too hard to chew. The quality of food had steadily decreased during our few days at the shelter, though I never dared complain. I understood most of it was coming from what little could be salvaged from groceries and markets nearby. That same food, now a week post-storm, unprotected from the water and heat, was now quickly beginning to rot. Without fresh supplies from the mainland, hunger would soon overtake the island.

And the tension and violence would only get worse.

I had no idea where we were; I'd never been to City Hall before the storm. Perhaps the Strand? Maybe Market Street or Mechanic? What remained of the buildings around me told me nothing. As with everywhere else on the island, there was nothing but shells, half-collapsed walls and crumbling roofs, interspersed with piles of debris. Upturned carts, iceboxes already beginning to rust, a lamppost twisted around a half-destroyed porch swing. As the large pieces of rubble had begun to be cleared, smaller items were left in their wake: eyeglasses, handkerchiefs, shoes. But, even though navigating the island was a bit easier now, somehow these small pieces of humanity made it worse. The air felt ghoulish, empty of life while simultaneously too full.

The smoke only added to the morbid atmosphere.

There was no longer as great of a risk of stumbling upon a corpse, but you still couldn't escape death in Galveston. Burial on the island was impossible and attempted burial at sea had resulted in the gruesome discovery of corpses washing right back up onshore. With no other options, and with the stench of putrefaction becoming unbearable in the post-storm heat, the decision had been made to begin burning the island's dead. The fires burned day and night without stopping.

They had yet to run out of fuel.

Though I knew she had seen the fires, the story behind them was yet another thing I tried to keep from Maggie. I had a feeling, however, that she suspected the truth. The smoke lingering over what remained of the city was not normal; it did not smell of campfires or well-tended hearths. The ash that rained down caused people to scratch at their skin, to vomit, to wail. Maggie may have been young, but she was neither blind nor dumb.

Nor, after this hurricane, was she naive.

As we walked, I steered clear of the burn sites, though we could not escape the stench, an obscene, sickly-sweet smell I wondered if I'd ever be able to fully purge from my nostrils. At this hour, the island was mainly silent, the hooligans of the night retreating to the shadows with the morning sun, sleeping off their drink and their savagery. The few people we did see refused to meet our eyes. Here and there a stray dog nosed through the piles of rubble, but the viciousness I'd heard of back at City Hall must have also melted in daylight; all of them fled at our approach.

"Not too much longer." Maggie's feet had begun to drag; her small hand was sweaty in mine. Only a few hours had passed since we'd started, but already the heat was intense, the humidity stifling. We'd planned to go straight east, but avoidance of the pyres and the mountains of debris had made it impossible. It was slow going, and we'd taken more detours than I'd liked. "I can see a clearing up ahead."

It was true. Just on the other side of the next hill of waste, instead of another pile, I could see blue.

The beach.

We had made it.

"Just a little bit longer, Mags." I wrapped her arm around mine. "We're almost there."

"Miss McDaniel?"

Just as swiftly as my heart had begun to thrum in anticipation, it froze. My quickened pace skidded to a halt on the gritty pavement, the scrape of my boots as earsplitting as any scream. I pulled Maggie toward me, placing myself between her and the voice.

A voice I knew. A voice I *feared*.

I turned around slowly. Otto Zimmerman stood a dozen feet away, huge beefy arms flexed at his sides. Though his clothes were dirty and a faint scratch ran the length of his nose, he looked no worse for wear. With all the dead, all the dying, all the innocent lives lost . . . *he* had survived.

"Miss McDaniel," he said again.

"I'm not going back." I squared my shoulders even as my voice cracked.

He raised his chin, expression hard.

"Annie?" Maggie's frightened voice came from behind me.

I squeezed her arm, trying to give her a comfort I did not feel as I refused to take my eyes off my father's henchman. "Did you hear me? I said I'm not going back."

Mr. Zimmerman took a step toward me.

I moved back, tripping over Maggie in the process. I grabbed her arm, trying to pull us both up. "I won't! I swear I won't! I—"

"I'm not here for you."

His words snipped off my protestations, causing my muscles to tense. "What?"

"Mr. McDaniel didn't send me for you. He just wants the camera."

It took several moments for his sentence to land. I could blame it on the accent, thicker and more German than I remembered. But it wasn't that; I could understand him just fine. I just couldn't *believe* him. Disbelief—torturous, unbearable incredulity—formed a barrier between us, only faltering when my muscles gave way. I crumpled to my knees, the weight of a thousand emotions pushing me under, as heavy as the debris that had nearly trapped me beneath the waves.

All this time I'd spent running, hiding, and my father had never actually been chasing after *me*. He wasn't worried. He wasn't hurt. He wasn't even angry.

He didn't *care*.

Didn't care where I was, how I was doing, what I was feeling.

He cared only about what I was carrying. About Wesley's camera, and the possible damage the film inside could do. To himself, his name, and his reputation.

I should have known it. The shot he'd fired that night—even if he'd been aiming at Wesley, I had been so close to him in that moment that the risk of harming me would still have been immense. And when the militia's bullets began to fly, it wasn't like he had stuck around to make sure I was all right.

These were not the actions of a father who cared about the well-being of his daughter.

I should have known it. Perhaps, deep down, I already had.

And yet still an ache began to throb in my chest. I bowled over, clutching at it, eyes burning with tears. "I don't have it!" The words exploded from my throat, so violent I nearly choked. "I don't have the camera! It washed into the sea, along with everything else!"

Mr. Zimmerman tilted his head to one side, expression unreadable.

"Don't you understand? It's gone! Everything is gone!" I flung my hands into the air. Exasperated. Anguished. Broken. "Galveston! St. Mary's! All those sisters and orphans! Emily!" I faltered, barely able to speak her name. "Matthew." It was the first time I'd admitted it out loud. It was agony. And then, just as painful: "Wesley."

My cries collapsed then, wrapping me in the ghosts of my misery before being whisked away by the breeze, out to the waiting sea. The grief I'd tried to suppress all these months overtook me. Tears blurred my vision, and my cheeks burned. My entire body suddenly felt too heavy.

The hurricane had taken so much. But, in truth, it had only finished what had already started to collapse that night on the dam.

Gone. They were all gone.

Including my father.

Yes, I'd left that night. I'd been the one to run. But, despite everything, I'd never truly believed him gone until this very moment.

He was a flawed man. A bad man. But he was the only father I had ever known. I had needed him. Loved him. A small part of me still did.

But the bonds of family on which I'd built my life were gone, and would have been gone whether I'd chosen to flee or not. Because the moment I had chosen not to grab that camera, in his mind, I had ceased to be his daughter. Ceased to be of any value to him.

I was no longer worthy of the McDaniel name.

No longer worthy . . . of him.

I sobbed into the sunbaked ground. In the distance, the waves of the Gulf thudded against the sand. I hadn't heard the ocean since the hurricane. Gone was the anger, the hunger of that night. The sound of the swells was gentle now. Almost apologetic. It filled the debris canyon in which I lay as if trying to placate me.

But these wounds—this despair—cut even deeper than the storm had.

"And you?"

The question came softly. I jerked my head up. I could barely see Otto Zimmerman through my tears, but there was an unexpected softness in his tone. A slackening of his surly posture. I sniffed. "What?"

"Perhaps you are gone too, Miss Mc—Kathleen." He frowned, and I noticed a sadness deep within the recesses of his eyes.

I opened my mouth to speak but realized he was no longer looking at me. Instead, he stared at the wreckage around us.

"I rode out the storm at the Tremont hotel, along with about a thousand others. Every other building on that stretch of 23rd was demolished. And yet the Tremont—the hotel I'd picked at random in which to stay—survived with barely a scratch. That is . . . that is not a coincidence, Kathleen. It cannot be. We survived for a reason, you and I. So many died. So many . . ." He stopped. Pressed his lips together, burying them beneath the dark hairs of his beard. When he continued, his voice was gruff. "And yet . . . we are alive."

I blinked rapidly, trying to take in his words through the thousand other thoughts and emotions clouding my brain. But nothing penetrated until I felt something soft and warm slide into my palm. I looked up. It was Maggie's hand. Her eyes searched mine momentarily before she leaned into me, nuzzling her face into my neck. I placed a hand on her head, pulling her closer, breathing her in. The salt, the sweat, the sand.

Her.

When I glanced up, Otto Zimmerman was watching, forehead creased. It was several moments before he spoke. "Your father is not a good man, Kathleen," he said quietly. "And, contrary to his belief, he is not a great one. For he could not see the wealth that lay before him. Wealth that had nothing to do with that stupid dam." He smiled then. It was the first smile I'd ever seen cross his lips. It quickly faded, however, as he spoke his next words. "I should never have accepted his job offer. But I was blinded by the opportunity, so blind I nearly allowed his money and his power to corrupt me as well. To influence morals I once believed were immovable." He shook his head. "I am not thankful for this storm; the nightmare of it will remain with me always. But I am thankful for the clarity it has provided. It is time for me to make a change. I will return to Germany, perhaps. Or maybe somewhere out west, far from the sea." He paused. "But first . . . first I will return to your father. I will tell him what happened here. About the storm. I will tell him the camera is gone. And, if he cares to know . . . so are you."

I drew in a sharp breath, the impact of his words like the clipping of a heavy chain, falling from my soul.

If my father believed the camera to be gone, believed *I* was gone, he would no longer search for me. I would no longer be hunted, no longer be pursued. He could go about his life . . . and I could go about finding mine.

Otto Zimmerman was handing me my freedom.

His gaze locked onto mine. "Our survival was not an accident, Kathleen. God has given us this chance to make a fresh start. To rebuild. Stronger. Wiser."

He extended a hand. After a moment's hesitation, I took it. He pulled me to my feet. Maggie remained pressed into my side, staring up at him through several strands of loose, dirty hair.

He smiled at her, then returned his attention to me. "Goodbye, Kathleen. Or whoever it is you wish to be."

And then Otto Zimmerman walked away, the remnants of sea salt crushing beneath his boots and seagulls, recently returned, squawking overhead. The noonday sun beat down on my skin as I watched him. Watched until he disappeared, until the remains of Galveston swallowed him, leaving nothing but his ghost.

And a beautiful eight-year-old girl clinging to my hand.

She smiled up at me, her face filthy, hair tangled, front teeth missing. And, in that moment, I realized he was right.

I was no longer Kathleen McDaniel. Perhaps I never really had been. But it wasn't because of blood; blood is not the only, or the most important, thing that defines a family.

Love is.

Love based not on what you can give, but on who you are. Love like the kind I'd shared with Wesley. Like what had been offered to me by Matthew, Emily, and so many of the sisters and orphans inside St. Mary's.

Love like the kind Maggie felt for me, and I for her.

And, most important, love like what God had shown me. Emily had been right; God had taken everything away and, in doing so, He had shown me something so much more. Lawrence McDaniel was not the only father I had ever known. I'd had another one once, however fleeting that time had been. The memories of him were not a curse, as I'd originally believed. They were a gift. A gift to make me realize how much I had already been loved and cherished in my short life. Just because his death had parted us, it did not mean that love was not still a part of who I was.

But I also had another Father. A bigger one. A *perfect* one. One who had opened my eyes and my heart in ways I'd never believed possible. One who had spared me from the storm.

Who had given me a second chance to love—truly *love*—and be loved in return.

And it was this love—not money, not status, and not a name—that I would build my life on. Build my *future* on.

Kathleen McDaniel had died in the Galveston hurricane.

But, by God's mercy, she had also been reborn.

Epilogue

SUNDAY, SEPTEMBER 23, 1900
GALVESTON, TEXAS

"Finally, brothers, rejoice. Aim for restoration, comfort one another, agree with one another, live in peace; and the God of love and peace will be with you."

The group gathered under the white tent all murmured amen after the preacher's benediction. It was the second Sunday after the hurricane, the second time this congregation from across Galveston had met inside this Red Cross shelter to mourn and rejoice, to worship and pray. The second time this preacher had left us with this exhortation of restoration and comfort from Paul's letter to the Corinthians.

It was a small assembly. Most of those gathered on the beach couldn't be bothered with God. Even on the faces of some who'd stepped into the shade of the flapping canvas, I saw flickers of doubt and reticence. They might have been here but that didn't mean they weren't angry with Him.

Maybe I should have been too. After all I'd seen, all I'd lost, it would have been the most natural thing in the world. I still had nightmares about the water. Still woke, more often than not, in a cold sweat, sure the waves pounding on the beach just beyond the city of tents were coming to devour me. Though we were assigned cots side by side, most nights Maggie made her way into mine; she had the dreams too.

So, yes, perhaps I should have been angry. The pain and the suffering were far from over. My future was uncertain, my past full of regrets. I still wept far more than I rejoiced. But I had not lost everything. Unlike so many others, I had *survived*.

And I had found myself . . . and God . . . in the process.

I saw Him in Maggie, in her resiliency and quiet strength. I saw Him here on this beach, where people had poured in from near and far with food, clothing, and medicine, seeking to help people they'd never met in any way they could. I saw Him in the rebuilding that was already starting to take place on parts of the island. I saw Him in the miraculous stories of survival that circulated throughout the camp, life beating out death against impossible odds.

I even saw Him in the grief, the heartache and sorrow over those we had lost.

For there is no grief without love.

"Are you ready?" I stood and stuffed my wild red hair back beneath my straw hat. One of the Red Cross volunteers had given it to me to keep the sun off the still-raw wound on my forehead. "I heard the mess tent got a shipment of sausages in."

Maggie's eyes widened. "Really, Kathleen?"

It felt good to hear her call me by my real name, though it had taken some time and I wasn't sure she truly understood why I'd been using the name Annie in the first place, even after I tried to explain. "That's what I heard."

"Please let it be true! I can't eat any more potatoes. Or lentils."

I laughed. "We can't be picky. Food is food." At her chastened expression, I lowered my voice and gave her a wink. "But I really hope it's true too."

Side by side, we exited the tent, squinting against the bright midmorning sun. The ocean breeze brought in the familiar scents of salt and fish, smells that still prickled my nerves, even after all our days on this beach. Perhaps they always would. In the distance, white-sailed ships and freighters amassed in the sparkling waters, carrying food, supplies, and people both to and from the island, the traffic as thick as it was prestorm, though the purposes of the voyages were much changed.

"Hold on, Mags," I said as we passed the medical tent. "There's something I need to check."

Normally, Maggie would have whined about her hunger. But, from the expression on her face, I also knew she understood what I needed to do. It was a daily occurrence, a routine that held little hope but one I couldn't give up, nonetheless.

Stepping into the tent, I blinked several times to adjust to the dim light. Rows of cots were lined up on the sand, though the number filled was less than half, a stark improvement over the early days after the storm. The most severely injured had either succumbed or else been transferred to the mainland, where they could receive proper medical care. Those that remained suffered from lesser ailments—sunburn and sand fleas, dehydration and diarrhea. Nuisances really, compared to what had come before. But still the Red Cross workers remained, treating every malady with compassion and care.

As it did every time I entered the tent, my mind flitted to Hazel. Last I'd known, she was volunteering for the International Red Cross. I smiled, imagining it was her preparing bandages, applying salve, taking temperatures. I wondered if she knew about the hurricane; what a shock it would be for her to know her old friend was at the receiving end of a mission she held so dear.

I wondered if she would even recognize me now. Switzerland felt like a lifetime ago. Those idealistic afternoons with her, Louisa, and Margarite were the closest I'd come to being the person I wanted to be.

Until now.

Perhaps, when everything had settled down, I would write to them. I certainly had a more interesting story to tell than needlepoint and tea now.

A tall black-haired woman waved at me from across the tent, where she was listening through a stethoscope to the heartbeat of a freckled lad whose face was a concerning shade of green. She rose, removing the earpieces and smiling at me. "I thought I told you to take some time off."

Miss Clara Barton, the head of the American Red Cross, had shown up less than two days after the storm—and hadn't stopped working since. She was a warm, calming presence inside the camp, the stories about her from the Civil War not even coming close to the kindly, courageous woman she was in real life. She made it a point to know each and every refugee by name.

And she most assuredly knew mine.

As I'd taken to visiting the tent every day anyway, Miss Barton soon began asking me for assistance. Securing clean towels one day, cutting bandages the next. Soon, she and other nurses began giving me lessons on checking vitals, tending wounds, and reducing fevers, and I found I enjoyed the feeling of being useful, of easing another's pain. I still had a long way to go in terms of knowledge and practice, but the ever-patient Miss Barton had told me I had a gift, one I could surely hone if I stuck with it.

I waved back. "I am! I'm just . . ." I pointed to the post at the far corner of the tent.

Her face softened, and she nodded, understanding.

The Galveston newspapers had begun printing again less than a week after the hurricane, something I'd believed to be superfluous until I realized what it was they were printing: daily lists of the confirmed *dead* and *not dead*. Miss Barton posted these records inside the medical tent every morning, and every morning I was not alone in my perusal of either the faces of the wounded or these registers, hoping both to see and not see familiar names.

Emily had made the list of the dead. It was a day that had both relieved and devastated me, the finality of seeing her name in black-and-white giving bittersweet closure. She was gone, but she had been found. She could rest.

Both Isaac and Joseph Cline were on a list, too, along with Allie May, Rosemary, and Esther. All had survived. Cora, on the other hand, as well as the new babe inside her for whom she already held so much love, had not. Though I'd known her only a short time, the news saddened me. I wondered how Mr. Cline was faring. Though it would have been easy to, I did not blame him for what had happened, as so many others did; I grieved for him. He, too, had put his faith in the wrong thing. And he was not immune to the disaster of his folly. Like the island he believed invincible, his life—and perhaps his reputation—had been shattered. I genuinely hoped something good and perhaps a bit more humble would arise from the ashes.

There was no word on the sisters or orphans at St. Mary's.

It didn't surprise me. I knew they were gone, of course. I'd seen the collapse, witnessed the ravages of the sea. And for every identified body on Galveston, there were ten more mangled beyond recognition, and perhaps a hundred more washed out to sea, never to be recovered. I knew thousands would likely never be accounted for.

I wished better for them. But lack of names on paper would not keep me from mourning them.

Or making sure they weren't forgotten.

I probably should have stopped checking. But I ran my finger down the fine print anyway, holding my breath. One name. There was still one name I hadn't seen. And maybe I never would. But, though the lists were growing shorter by the day, I would not stop reading them. As long as there were records, I would look. I would hope. I would pray.

Today, just like every other day, the name of Matthew Richter was not listed.

Shoulders slumped, I gave one last wave to Miss Barton, who returned it with a sad smile, before rejoining Maggie outside the tent. She met my eyes momentarily and then looked away. The same question, the same answer. Giving her hand a stoic squeeze, I led her toward the mess tent where—to our instant delight—the smell of cooking sausages did indeed fill the air.

A small group was gathered outside, talking animatedly. As we passed, I noticed a few scribbling in notebooks, their pencils moving furiously over the lined paper. I sighed.

Reporters. More reporters.

Galveston had rebounded quickly over the past few weeks. Telegraph lines had already been restored, trolleys were running again—albeit on limited routes due to the mountains of debris still clogging most of the tracks—and parts of the island hummed with restored electricity. This was due in no small part to the resourcefulness and tenacity of its citizens, but it was also a feat that could not have been accomplished without the funds from people such as Joseph Pulitzer and William Randolph Hearst. Although laymen, small churches, and various charity groups also contributed, these titans of journalism had both the position and the means to secure the millions of dollars Galveston would need to rebuild.

But with their money came their reporters. The world had an appetite for the macabre that the hurricane and its survivors were all too ready to feed.

I gave Maggie a gentle nudge toward the tent. I'd already been approached for my story several times; I was in no mood to refuse again. And Maggie certainly didn't need to relive that night all over again, especially not for another's entertainment. "Come on," I whispered. "Let's go ea—"

Eat. I'd meant to say *eat*. But an object on a nearby table caught my eye before I could finish. My breath caught in my throat. It was small. Brown. Square.

Completely and utterly ordinary.

And yet it was the only thing in the world that could have negated my hunger, now that fresh, smoking meat was mere yards away.

I took a step toward it, absentmindedly dropping Maggie's hand. "Hold on just a minute," I murmured to her. My fingers hovered over the object for several seconds before, gingerly, I began trailing them over the leather casing.

It wasn't Wesley's. That was impossible. This one was newer, cleaner; it had certainly never seen the inside of a storm. And yet, when I touched that Kodak Brownie camera, I felt him all the same. Dozens of memories raced through my mind, both grieving and comforting me. His smile. His laugh. His eyes. His kiss.

"Do you know how to work one of those things?"

I pulled my hand back and spun around. A reporter—I could tell by the notebook in her hand—had separated herself from the group and taken a step toward me. And, yes, it was a woman, no matter how much her clothing tried to convey otherwise. Dark trousers held up by suspenders and a green button-down could not disguise the curly red hair—hair very much like my own—falling from its pins beneath a faded fedora. Nor could it mask the distinctly feminine smile radiating from the woman's face.

"Do you?" she repeated kindly.

I felt my cheeks go red, but I gave her a slight nod. "A little. Someone taught me the basics. He . . . he said there was an art to it."

"That's true. Light and angles make all the difference." She picked the camera up off the table and held it out to me. "Changes the way you see things."

You saw me.

I stared at her outstretched hand, Wesley's words echoing through my soul.

She winked. "Go on. Show me."

Fighting tears that were somehow both happy and sad, I took it from her slowly. I raised the viewfinder to my eye, moving the camera around the beach until the perfect subject came into frame: Maggie Sherwood, her face scrunched in barely contained annoyance as she stared wistfully at the mess tent, small tongue poking out of the corner of her mouth. The late-morning sun shadowed her face while creating a halo around her head. In that moment, she looked beautiful.

She looked . . . like Maggie.

It felt as if Wesley's hands were guiding my own as I pressed down on the shutter lever. Maggie turned at the sound, her expression both curious and pleading. I suppressed a laugh and, with a full heart, handed the camera back to the reporter.

She raised her eyebrows at me, nodding. "Not bad. Not bad at all. Of course, I'll have to see the picture to know for sure, but it certainly seems as if you know what you're doing, Miss . . ."

"Kathleen," I finished for her. "Just Kathleen."

The woman raised her chin. A sly grin spread over her lips. "Well, Kathleen, my name's Winifred Black. I'm a reporter with the *New York Journal*." She stuck out one delicate hand, which I shook. It was surprisingly cool, despite the rapidly warming temperatures. "Your teacher taught you well. Have you ever thought of putting those skills to use? There's a high demand for photos in journalism now, but it's rare to find someone who knows how to get a shot worth getting."

I smiled and shook my head, fighting the urge to laugh. *Oh, Wesley. If only you were here now . . .*

And yet, I had a sense he was.

And that he, too, was smiling.

After promising Miss Winifred Black I'd give her offer some thought, I ushered a grateful Maggie out of the sun and into the mess tent. We filled our plates with as much as the rations would allow, rolls of sausages, a slice of crusty bread, and half of a crisp red apple, then settled ourselves at one of the corner tables. Aside from Maggie's quick blessing, neither of us spoke for several minutes. The pop and spice of the sausage felt like a dream on our tongues, a memory or—perhaps—a sign of better days to come.

"You know," I said eventually, using the last of my bread to soak up the grease on my plate. "Miss Barton believes we'll all have real houses before Christmas. What do you think about that?"

Maggie chewed thoughtfully. Her lips glistened with the remains of sausage. "How?"

I shrugged. "People all over the country have been putting money into a fund for survivors. They want to parcel it out so that everyone has enough to rebuild."

"That's nice." She swallowed. "I'd like to have a house."

"Here?"

Her chin dipped to her chest. "I don't know."

I pressed my lips into a line, heart panging with tenderness. Rebuilding the island would take time, yes. But rebuilding our lives? That would take even longer. For every blessing, every step forward, the horrors of that night still lingered. The hurricane would always be a part of us; I understood her reluctance to remain on this island, haunted by its ghosts.

"I don't know either," I said softly. "But . . ." I paused, willing myself to give voice to an idea I'd been mulling for days. "What about a house with me?"

She raised her eyes, meeting mine.

"Maybe here. Maybe somewhere else, far away. But . . . together."

A thousand emotions flashed across Maggie Sherwood's face.

Questions to which I didn't know the answers quite yet. Any record of Maggie's birth, her previous life, had been washed away in the storm. Legally, financially, I didn't know how to even start to make this dream a reality. All I knew was that this felt right, her and me. That somehow, as He always did, God would make clear our pathway forward. And as I watched her eyes fill with joy, I knew Maggie understood this too.

"What do you say?" I said, voice growing thick. "You and me? The two of us?"

"How about three?"

A deep male voice behind my back caused my muscles to stiffen. I felt all the blood drain from my face. Maggie, however, had the opposite reaction. She released an elated scream and, within seconds, was out of her chair, disappearing behind my back where a joyful *"oof"* told me she had thrust herself into the arms of the speaker.

I found myself unable to turn around.

That voice. I knew it. I'd searched for it every day, heard it in my dreams. But it was impossible to be hearing it here, now. *Impossible.* I'd all but resigned him to the sea, to the pyre. And I couldn't bear turning around, for fear that small flicker of hope might be extinguished completely. I couldn't handle the disappointment. The agony of fresh grief.

But I also couldn't wait a second longer. Not when a warm hand found its way to my shoulder and I heard the sound of my name, so strange and yet so familiar: "Kathleen."

Matthew.

I had barely risen to my feet before I collapsed in his arms, overtaken by sobs. He was here. He was alive. And he was hugging me, kissing me, propriety and rules now pieces of debris, washed out with the storm.

"I found you," he whispered against my ear, his tears as hot as my own. "Not Nun or Annie or Kathleen or whatever your name is. I found you." His fingers knotted in my hair, tugging it gently as if to prove it was real. "And you," he said with a laugh, one arm scooping up Maggie, who had been smooshed between us. "I found you too."

"But how?" I managed. "How . . ." *did you find us,* I started to ask. But a bigger question floated up, one I was unable to speak, even now, with Matthew safely in my arms.

How are you alive?

"I floated on a piece of wreckage all the way up to Texas City," he said, reading my mind. "Severely dehydrated from the saltwater and covered with cuts and bruises but somehow, miraculously, unharmed." He licked his lips, and I could see the memory of that night, of his own horrific voyage, swimming in his hazel eyes. "And I have spent every day since then trying to get back." He held my gaze. "To you."

"What took you so long?" Maggie demanded, her brow furrowing.

Matthew laughed, the most beautiful sound I'd heard in days. "It wasn't exactly easy to get passage *to* Galveston, little lady. Not unless you were an aid worker. The bridges to the mainland are gone. Boats are the only option. I booked the first ticket I could."

"And now you're here," I whispered.

He looked down at me. When he smiled, it was one of both anguish and relief. "And now I'm here."

"I love you." The words fell out before I could stop them. But I don't believe I would have, even if I could. Because, while I didn't know a lot of things, I knew now that life was too precious not to.

Not to feel it. Not to say it. Not to have it.

He pressed his forehead to mine. "I love you too."

Later that day, as the three of us sat on the beach, sharing news and stories, heartbreaks and triumphs, I looked from where Matthew's fingers lay intertwined with mine out to the rolling waves, white-laced and calm, glowing pink in the advancing twilight.

Many here couldn't stand to look at the sea, lest it inflame fresh nightmares or—worse—dredge familiar faces onto the shore. But I wasn't one of them. The sights, the sounds, the smells of the beach were forever changed for me; it was no longer a place of frivolity or escape. I had experienced the sea's awesome power, and many beloved people and places now lay within its depths. I felt bound to look at it. To ponder it.

To remember.

I didn't know what the future held. Maybe I'd become a photographer, as Winifred Black had suggested. Let Wesley's dream live on through me. Or become a nurse, like Miss Barton believed I could. Or perhaps a teacher or a librarian. Maybe even a clerk at MacDoogal's, where I could spend my time caring for animals and making sure they all found loving homes. I wasn't sure. I didn't know where I'd end up living, how I'd make money, or what my life would be like tomorrow, let alone in a year or two's time.

But it didn't matter. Because I finally knew who I was. I was more than a name. More than what I had or what I did, more than money, status, or possessions. All those things—both good and bad—could be gone in an instant, washed away. But who I truly was, my worth and value, lay deeper, inside my inmost being, where my Creator had lovingly stitched me together.

And no matter what, when new storms came—as they most surely would again, whether we remained on Galveston or not—this foundation, my *true* foundation, would still hold.

In the meantime, in the here and now, I had air in my lungs, sand at my feet. The man I loved beside me, back from the dead, and the girl I cherished like my own flesh curled up between us.

And the God who adored me, with His hand in it all.

Discover more great historical fiction by Jennifer L. Wright

"Jennifer L. Wright is a storyteller with the distinct gift of bringing history to life in full color."

Susie Finkbeiner, author of *The Nature of Small Birds* and *Stories That Bind Us*, on *Come Down Somewhere*

IN STORES AND ONLINE NOW

JOIN THE CONVERSATION AT crazy4fiction.com

Author's Note

The Galveston hurricane of 1900 remains one of the deadliest and most costly disasters in United States history. Estimates put the number of dead from the storm at roughly 10,000 people, though exact numbers are impossible, and the damage at $20 million (over $700 million today). While it's easy to attribute the tragedy to a lack of modern forecasting and building standards, the true failures behind the storm are much more complex.

Distrust, racism, and political wrangling played a huge role in the hurricane's destruction. As early as Sunday, September 3—nearly a full week before the storm made landfall in Texas—meteorologists in Cuba were tracking the cyclone. Having already unleashed heavy rain and damaging winds on Antigua and Jamaica, the tempest had only intensified as it made its way through the Caribbean. Father Lorenzo Gangoite, a Jesuit priest and head of the Belen Meteorological and Magnetic Observatory in Havana, recognized the storm for what it was: a hurricane. At the time, Cuban meteorologists were at the helm of some of the most cutting-edge storm-prediction science; through the years, they had learned to accurately predict both the timing and track of hurricanes based on cloud formation. However, Cuba was also a land of political unrest and upheaval. The Cuban fight for independence had spilled American blood when the USS

Maine, sent by President McKinley to protect Americans living in the city, exploded and sank in Havana Harbor in 1898. Soon afterward, the United States declared war and blockaded Havana. It was a conflict still very much heated in September 1900, when Father Gangoite first observed the hurricane and deduced its tracks north and west . . . right toward the coast of Texas. However, the US War Department had severed all telegraph lines between Havana and weather offices within the United States; Father Gangoite's only option was to send his forecast directly to Washington, DC.

Where it was promptly ignored.

Forecasters in Washington, including head of the US Weather Bureau Willis Moore, believed the Cubans to be inferior in their reporting, primitive and given to flights of hysterical panic. So, instead, Washington's forecast to Galveston that week, though mentioning the storm (but still refusing to call it a hurricane), maintained it would fall victim to the law of "recurve," which prevented storms from the Caribbean from heading northwest. It would instead head northeast, toward Florida and the Atlantic states, weakening as it went. Storm warnings went up along the east coast . . . but not in Galveston.

But the failure of the day's leading scientists wasn't limited to Washington.

As mentioned in the novel, Isaac Cline was a Galveston celebrity. He wasn't just the town's chief meteorologist and head of the Texas section of the US Weather Bureau. He was one of the country's leading authorities on storms. His absolute trust in the still-burgeoning science of meteorology—and his own powers of making predictions based on that science—had saved many lives. But, in the case of the 1900 hurricane, it also cost thousands.

Given his expertise and level of respect within the community, it's no surprise that civic leaders approached him with questions about Galveston's vulnerability to hurricanes. The island had already been hit by a number of storms, though, fortunately, damage had been minimal. Other Gulf-shore cities hadn't fared so well. To stem growing anxiety (and ensure that local businesses continued to invest), a group known as the Deep Water Committee was formed. It proposed building a breakwater out in the Gulf to hinder the roughest of waves. It also expressed interest in building a seawall on the beach to keep storm surges at bay. But the cost of such projects would be astronomical so, before undertaking them, the men decided to consult an expert.

Isaac Cline assured the men, in no uncertain terms, that if a storm ever pushed the Gulf onto the island, it would merely flow over the city, into the bay, and onto mainland Texas. The coastline was too shallow, he said. It would fragment any incoming surf. "It would be impossible," he wrote, "for any cyclone to create a storm wave which could materially injure the city." And besides, he wrote, hurricanes didn't strike Texas. He called anyone who believed otherwise "delusional."

No seawall was built.

Unfortunately, Cline was wrong on both accounts. Not only did a hurricane strike Galveston in September of 1900, but the bay did not act as a kind of "release valve" for the rising Gulf. Instead, it had the opposite effect; both bodies of water rose simultaneously, trapping Galveston in the middle. The highest point on the island was only 8.7 feet above sea level; meteorologists estimate the storm surge at 15.7. Coupled with rotating winds that reached 140 mph, the city—and its inhabitants—never stood a chance.

Remarkably, however, despite the devastation, the island rebuilt quickly. With the assistance of many of the United States's wealthiest tycoons, and aided by the American Red Cross, Galvestonians began the arduous task of disposing of the dead while restoring the island for the living. Though some citizens fled, never to return, over half the population remained . . . and became steadfast in their determination to prevent another such tragedy. The previously "unnecessary" seawall was built, rising seventeen feet above the beach, to protect the city from future storm surges. In addition, the people took on the astounding task of raising the elevation of the island itself by painstakingly, block-by-block, lifting every single building, street, and utility pipe up on jacks, filling the ground beneath with sand, and then returning the structures to their places on the now higher ground. Most of current-day Galveston Island now sits at least seven feet above sea level, compared to zero in 1900.

But what about the people?

Although many characters in this novel are fictional, several are based on real people. Isaac Cline, of course, really was the chief meteorologist in Galveston. After the hurricane, he continued his career with the US Weather Bureau, eventually moving to New Orleans, where he headed a large district that included the entire Gulf Coast and much of the Southwest. He successfully predicted the Gulf Coast flooding of 1912 and 1915 as well as the great Mississippi flood of 1927. His true feelings about his failures on Galveston Island are unknown; for the rest of his life, he maintained he did the best he could over the course of those fateful days and never publicly expressed any kind of remorse for the role he played in the tragedy.

After losing his wife and unborn child to the storm, however, he never remarried.

Joseph Cline was another historical figure I decided to include in this novel. After the hurricane, he transferred to Puerto Rico and set up a meteorological station in the remote mountains there. Later, he served the US Weather Bureau in both the Midwest and in Dallas. Though he, too, never publicly acknowledged any kind of role in the disaster, what is known is that the two brothers later became estranged. Only they knew if the catastrophe of that night—and the resulting aftermath—played a role in this.

Whatever the case, both brothers remain well-regarded figures in the history of meteorology.

The story of St. Mary's is, heartbreakingly, also taken from the pages of history. Although I have embellished some of the names held within the walls of the orphanage, a few of them were real, including Mother Camillus Tracy, who perished along with nearly a hundred others when the dormitories were swept into the sea. Only three people from St. Mary's were known to have survived that night: Albert Campbell, Will Murney, and Francis Bolenick, who outlasted the storm by grabbing onto a tree that became lodged in the mast of a wrecked ship.

The storm itself moved onto mainland Texas after Galveston, flooding parts of Houston. From there, it brought heavy downpours and high winds to parts of Oklahoma and the Midwest before turning east and sweeping all the way into New York City, where it blew down signs and snapped light poles, killing one person. It even brought down a bathing house near Coney Island. Finally, after nearly a solid week of destruction, it made its way back out to sea near Novia Scotia, leaving several swamped fishing fleets in its wake.

On the other side of this story is the Croton Dam strike, which was also based on a real-life event in the spring of 1900. Strikes were becoming more common at the turn of the century, as more and more workers fought back against unfair wages and dangerous working conditions. This was true of workers at the Croton Dam, who laid down their tools and demanded higher pay and cut hours. Most were immigrants, working ten-hour days for only $1.35 an hour, far less than the standard $1.50 an hour guaranteed to New York State employees. While the walkout had been largely peaceful, after thirteen days, rumors began circulating that strikers were preparing to blow up the dam and flood the valley below. Local deputies swarmed the area, often becoming violent in their attempt to keep the peace, which only further incensed the striking men. Governor Theodore Roosevelt then called in the militia, heightening the tension. On April 16, at approximately 8:15 p.m., one of these militiamen, Robert Douglass, suddenly cried out and fell to the ground, dead of a bullet wound. No one remembered hearing a shot. Some believed it was the strikers; others believed it was a fellow militiaman, desperate to paint the workers as villains and give the troops permission to end the standoff. In real life, cooler heads prevailed, and the impasse was eventually resolved peacefully, though the striking workers' demands were never met. The scene on the dam in this book (as well as Lawrence McDaniel, Wesley Odell, and Theodore Walsh) arose purely from my own imagination.

If you are interested in learning more about the Galveston hurricane, I highly recommend *The Storm of the Century* by Al Roker (yes, that Al Roker), *Isaac's Storm* by Erik Larson, and *Story of the 1900 Galveston Hurricane*, which is a collection of newspaper articles and survivor testimonies as well as historical information compiled by Nathan C. Green. I also encourage you to check out galvestonhistory.org and rosenberg-library.org for their invaluable collection of photographs and information about pre- and post-storm Galveston.

Acknowledgments

The journey to this book was full of detours, but I was never alone on my expedition. First and foremost, I give thanks to God, who saw me through the storm and guided my words when I felt I had none left. I would be nowhere without His grace. To Him always and forever is the glory.

In addition, copious thanks are due to the team at Tyndale, including Jan Stob, who calmed many a tear, as well as Elizabeth Jackson and Sarah Rische, who were always ready with a kind, supportive word. I would also be remiss if I didn't thank my agent, Adria Goetz, who was the first to encourage me to pursue this story and without whom this book would have taken nearly twice as long to write.

To my church family, especially my weekly small group as well as my LDG and Bible Study ladies: Thank you for continuously pouring into me. I have been both motivated and challenged simply by being a part of these organizations; they are a breath of fresh air when the world starts to feel a little bit too stuffy. Thank you all so much for loving me and giving me space to grow.

To Amanda Cox, Jamie Ogle, and the other members of our author refresh group: Thank you for showing up, listening, and offering a hopeful word. We were together for only a short time, but that short time coincided with the most intensive writing on this book, and I know that wasn't just a coincidence. Thank you for your friendship.

To all the authors who provided endorsement, publicity, or in any other way expressed excitement and support for this book: Thank you. From the bottom of my heart, thank you. I am so very blessed to be a part of the Christian fiction community, if nothing else but to have connected with women like you.

To my book-club peeps, Brooke, Lauren, Jenny, and Elise: Thank you for giving me a place to talk about books that aren't my own. With you all, books can just be fun again. Our gatherings are my favorite night of the month. Thanks for hanging out with me. (And Brooke, many more thanks are needed for you for a myriad of reasons, all of which can be summed up in one simple phrase: "This is why we're friends.")

To my family, Jonathan, Matthew, and Meredith: Thank you for keeping me tethered to reality and forever showing me what matters most. Without you, this book would have been written much sooner, but it also would not mean nearly as much. It's always and forever for you three. I love you all, so very much.

And, last but certainly not least, to the readers: Your cheers and enthusiasm are what keep me writing, even when I want to quit. Trust me when I say that every email, every message, every comment—they matter to me. *You* matter to me. As long as you keep reading, I promise to keep writing. I pray God blesses each and every one of you as much as you have blessed me.

Discussion Questions

1. Early in the story, Kathleen faces the choice to stay at St. Mary's and become a nun or leave and make her own way in the world. What would you have counseled her to do?

2. Why do you think young Maggie Sherwood bonds with Kathleen, when she has struggled to connect to anyone else at St. Mary's? What draws Kathleen to Maggie?

3. Kathleen returned from boarding school looking for purpose, for a life of substance and meaning. How does this longing develop as the story unfolds? What does she ultimately conclude about her purpose?

4. Matthew respects and even idolizes Isaac Cline for his work in weather prediction but then must grapple with Isaac's failure to anticipate the Galveston hurricane. How does he process this disappointment? Was there a time when you had to face the failings of someone you'd put on a pedestal? How did you respond?

5. Both in New York and in Galveston, Kathleen encounters instances of human arrogance or prejudice that have dire consequences. How do these attitudes shape the events she witnesses? What parallels do you see in the world today?

6. What draws Kathleen and Wesley to each other? Why do you think the camera becomes so significant to Kathleen? What do you imagine she would've done with it, if not for the storm?

7. Throughout her life, Kathleen has struggled to truly feel at home anywhere. What made her feel out of place in New York and in Galveston? Where does she ultimately find a sense of belonging? How would you define what *home* means to you?

8. When sharing her own story, Emily tells Kathleen, "Sometimes God has to tear down all the distractions, all the lies in our lives, in order for us to see the truth. To see that after everything else is gone, He's still there." How does Kathleen come to see this as true? Have you gone through a time when it felt as though everything was being stripped away? How did it affect your view of God?

About the Author

JENNIFER L. WRIGHT grew up wanting to work for *Dateline* and become the next Jane Pauley, but it took only a few short months of working as a reporter in both print and radio journalism for her to abandon those aspirations for the greener pasture of fiction writing. She loves to reimagine and explore forgotten eras in history, showcasing God's light amidst humanity's darkest days. Her books, which include *If It Rains*, *Come Down Somewhere*, and *The Girl from the Papers*, have been nominated for both a Carol Award and a Golden Scroll Award.

She currently lives in New Mexico with her husband, two children, and an ever-growing collection of pets. While she enjoys writing, her true dream is to one day own and operate a guinea pig farm. If you want to connect with her (and can handle a barrage of pictures of her animals), you can find her on Facebook at @JenniferWrightLit, on Instagram at @jennwright82, or by visiting her website, jenniferlwright.com.

crazy4fiction.com

TYNDALE HOUSE PUBLISHERS IS CRAZY4FICTION!

Become part of the Crazy4Fiction community and find fiction that entertains and inspires. Get exclusive content, free resources, and more!

JOIN IN ON THE FUN!

- crazy4fiction.com
- Crazy4Fiction
- crazy4fiction
- tyndale_crazy4fiction
- Sign up for our newsletter

FOR GREAT DEALS ON TYNDALE PRODUCTS, GO TO TYNDALE.COM/FICTION